Thornapple Girl

James A. Brakken

Thornapple Girl

Copyright ©2020 James A. Brakken

All rights reserved.

ISBN-13: 978-0-9976249-5-3

Badger Valley Publishing
45255 East Cable Lake Road
Cable, Wisconsin 54821
BadgerValley.com   715-798-3163
treasureofnamakagon@gmail.com

James Brakken's books are available at select outlets and at his website, **BadgerValley.com** where you'll find discounts and secure, online credit card ordering. Badger Valley Publishing offers *free shipping* to all USA and APO addresses and pays your Wisconsin sales tax.

Badger Valley can publish *your* book, too! Reasonable rates. Fast processing. Inquiries welcome. More at **BadgerValley.com** where you'll see images and excerpts from all of our 13 titles.

As with all Badger Valley books, *Thornapple Girl* is written for adults but suitable for young readers.

Thornapple Girl is the story of Myra Dietz, a young woman caught in the midst of a violent land dispute between her steadfast father and the world's largest lumber syndicate.

This novel is set near the Thornapple River in Winter, Wisconsin, in the early 1900s, a time when Myra and her brothers stood by their father, John Dietz, when he demanded his back wages from the Chippewa Lumber Company. But rather than settle, Frederick Weyerhaeuser, the wealthiest-ever of all lumber barons, chose to use his influence over the county, state, and federal government to push Dietz aside. Warrants were issued. Posses were formed. Myra and her brother, Clarence, nearly died after they were shot by Sawyer County lawmen. Headlines *exploded* coast-to-coast after nearly 100 deputized thugs fired a thousand rounds into the log home housing a family that became regarded nationwide as heroes of the working class. The assault on the Dietz family shocked a nation into realizing the abuse of power by companies that monopolized the USA back then was beyond control.

Thornapple Girl is a disturbing glimpse into the past and the wrongs wielded upon American workers over 100 years ago. The story is based on press clippings, court records, and Myra Dietz's personal recollections, featured in her previously unpublished 1929 memoir, now in print as a companion piece to *Thornapple Girl*. See more at http://badgervalley.com/

James Brakken

Books make wonderful gifts. Excerpts from this and James Brakken's other books can be found at **BadgerValley.com** where you'll find special discounts and free shipping to all USA and APO addresses.

In Appreciation ...

Thanks are due to **Jim Ferguson,** president of the Sawyer County Historical Society and the volunteers who work tirelessly to keep our Northwest Wisconsin history alive. Authors, educators, and history buffs appreciate all you do for our community and our culture.

Special thanks to **Karen Duffy** for hours spent researching the lives of Myra Dietz and her siblings. We know a lot more about them because of Karen's expertise in genealogical research.

Thank you, **Wisconsin Historical Society, Chippewa Valley Museum,** and the **Public Libraries** of **Winter, Hayward, Cable** and **Rice Lake, Wisconsin.**

My hat is off to the **Yarnspinners** writers group, **Sybil Brakken**, and Scrabble champ, **Nola Hembrook**. All generously helped improve *Thornapple Girl* by applying their proofreading and editing skills.

And thank you, **Priscilla Dietz Anderson** for offering clues that helped round out my research into the lives of your Aunt Myra, and your grandfather, John F. Dietz, the stalwart defender of Cameron Dam. Thanks, too, to **Dan Mercer**, great-grandson of John Dietz.

Thanks also to the many **independent bookstores** willing to offer self-published authors your shelf space. Your service to readers and writers does not go unnoticed.

Finally, thank you, readers. *I sincerely hope you enjoy this novel as much as I've enjoyed bringing it to you.*

James

"An invitation from indie" Author, James Brakken

Unlike writers who rely upon "brick and mortar" publishers, we independent authors depend on our readers to spread the word about our books. If you enjoy this novel, please encourage others to visit **BadgerValley.com**. Every purchase helps inspire more stories.

Copies ordered from **BadgerValley.com** are signed and shipped free to any USA address, including to men and women in service overseas.

Give your favorite James Brakken book a five-star review on Amazon. Google *James Brakken Books*, then choose the Amazon link.

Facebook users can "like" the Brakkens' 13 books at **www.facebook.com/jim.brakken** where you'll see the latest news about our "up north" novels and short story collections.

Thanks for your help!

Table of Contents

For Myra

Thornapple Girl

Foreword
by Myra Dietz
Precise wording excerpted from her 1929 memoir,
The Life Story of Myra Dietz of Cameron Dam.

"Here at last is a reliable and truthful story of the John F. Dietz family, of Cameron Dam, in Northern Wisconsin.

"Although the events narrated in this book took place many years ago, I have found that our melodramatic story is still fresh in the memories of thousands of people. Everywhere I go, I am asked to relate our experiences as they actually happened. And always I find that the hearer has retained a memory of 'an outlaw family of squatters' instead of realizing the truth. Our name and our fame will go down through the years in Wisconsin history and I feel that a true account of our wrongs and sufferings, together with an explanation of our ideals and our principles for which we stood so firmly, should be preserved for posterity.

"My father died five years ago, leaving no record in writing. My brothers, who stood so valiantly by my father in his fight, are now too busy to write the story of our lives. I am left to tell the story of things as they actually happened at Cameron Dam.

"Thousands of newspapers which carried stories of our feud hailed me as '"THE HEROINE OF CAMERON DAM' because, like my brothers, I was always near my father in every encounter. Perhaps it was for that reason that I was so cruelly shot down in ambush in 1910 when three of our father's enemies, with blackened faces, shot at my brothers and myself as we drove our team to town for the weekly mail, singing lustily from sheer youthful gayety as we trotted along in the October sunshine.

"And because I was a 'Dietz,' the District Attorney of Sawyer County refused to serve a warrant on the sheriff and his posse who had shot us.

"I have suffered with and for my father. Therefore I feel that I am logically the one to give our family story to the world.

"Laden with my family scrapbooks, which my mother carried from our home after the house and all its furnishings had been riddled with bullets, I went to the home of my friend, Peggy Kemp Lyon, where we turned my reminiscences into a readable story. I have not exaggerated. I have not omitted anything. My method of putting the story together consisted in going over the story of our lives month by month, year by year, and writing it down. I've made no attempt to arrange a climax or follow any technique, so unique is our family's story that it formed its own high spots and left us with the 'living happily ever after' ending.

"It is not unusual to find melodrama in the North Woods. What is unusual is to find a man willing to pit his feeble strength against a great lumber company over the possession of a small dam on a babbling little creek and forcing that lumber company to spend a good portion of a million dollars to overcome him.

"Actual expenses of the company ran close to two hundred thousand dollars, and nobody knows, unless it is the corporation heads, how many more thousands were expended in bribes and payments to grafting county officials.

"My father lost, in the sense that he was imprisoned in a travesty of justice for trumped-up charges, but three years before his death he was pardoned by the Governor of Wisconsin, with the full restoration of his citizenship. This, in Wisconsin, means that my father was finally exonerated of all the charges, indicating the Governor knew them to be false. And in the years that followed, not one of the many warrants which led to the final battle at our log home was ever served. What became of them, nobody knows.

"The memory of my father's steadfast adherence to his rights will always be bright. We suffered much because of them, but we honor and revere him for his firm stand.

"I will let the reader determine whether my father was right or wrong. I hope the story will prove entertaining."

MYRA DIETZ
February, 1929

See page 229 for more information on Myra Dietz's 204-page memoir.

The Dietz Family
Left to Right: Helen, John, Leslie, Myra, Stanley, Clarence, Hattie, & Johnny.

Prologue

Thornapple Farm
October 1, 1910

A young newspaperman for the *Minneapolis Tribune* stood on a footbridge stretching across Northwest Wisconsin's narrow Thornapple River. He wore a high button, single-breasted jacket with narrow lapels paired with blue, pinstripe trousers. In his left hand, he carried a leather satchel. In his right, he held a straw skimmer that he waved overhead, hoping to get the attention of those on the farmstead across the river. Behind stretched a ten-mile walk to the small lumber town of Winter, now crowded with other reporters. Like him, each one hoped to get a new angle on a story six years in the making—the story of a farmer standing in defiance of America's most powerful lumber syndicate and its creator, Frederick Weyerhaeuser.

"Hello?" the reporter shouted. "Mr. Dietz? Are you there?"

He listened for a reply. Instead, he heard a young woman singing.

"East Side, West Side, all around the town. The tots sang, 'ring-around-rosie, London Bridge is falling down.'"

Her clear, angelic voice carried across the meadow.

"Boys and girls together, me and Mamie O'Rourke."

The reporter leaned forward.

"Tripped the light fantastic on the sidewalks of New York."

There, ahead, he saw the dark-haired young woman with the sweet voice. She carried two pails of water toward the cabin.

"Can I help you with those?" he asked.

She turned with a jerk, splashing water onto her white apron and button shoes. "Father!" she shrieked. "Father, someone's here! Father!" She turned back to the young man. "Who the blazes are you?"

"Floyd Gibbons," he replied. "From the *Minneapolis Trib*. You must be Miss Dietz. I've read your columns."

"Yes. I am." She nodded toward the cabin. "And *he* is my father!"

The screen door sprang open. In two bounds, a lean, mustached man carrying a rifle jumped off the porch. As he rushed toward them, a second man, younger and also armed, stepped out. Then a third, scanning the river bottom with binoculars.

"And those must be your brothers, Clarence and Leslie," said Gibbons.

John raised his rifle. "Myra! Get away from him! Get back!"

"I mean no harm, Mr. Dietz," said Gibbons, raising his hands. "I'm Floyd Gibbons. From the *Trib*. I'm here to get your side of the story."

"How do I know you're not some spy sent here by the lumber syndicate?"

Myra set her pails on the ground. "He is who he says, Father. I recognize him from his photo in the newspaper. Mr. Gibbons's articles have been quite sympathetic all along."

John stared at Gibbons and then lowered the rifle. "What's in that grip you're holding?"

"Only pencils and paper, sir. And an apple for my dinner."

"Save your apple for another day," said John.

"Sir?"

"Our guests sit at the same dinner table as we do. If my daughter says you're on the level, that's good enough for me. Now come meet the rest of the family."

Gibbons handed his satchel to Myra and picked up the water pails. "I'm terribly sorry I startled you."

Myra looked down at her water-soaked shoes. "Oh, no real harm done, Mr. Gibbons."

"Please," he said with a smile, "call me Floyd. All my friends do."

Within minutes, Gibbons was scribbling notes while listening to the man beside him on the porch. John, still within reach of his Winchester, rocked slowly to his daughters' songs, coming from inside the cabin.

"It surely is a beautiful spot, Mr. Dietz. Paid for with money you received from the Chippewa Lumber and Boom Company?"

"Bah! Those tightfisted misers refuse to pay me my rightful comeuppance."

"Mr. Dietz, if you're owed money, why not go to court?"

"Oh, I dassn't go before a judge."

"Why, sir?"

"Because, Gibbons, around here the syndicate controls everything." They own most of the land, the lumber camps, the railroads, the county board, the sheriff, *and* the judge. Heck, they run the whole shebang. I wouldn't stand a ghost of a chance in court."

"I see. So in order to force the company to pay up, you stopped their men from using your dam to drive the logs downstream? Is that it?"

"By golly, you're pretty smart for a city feller."

Gibbons smiled. "Can you do that? Hold his property ransom?"

"Ransom, Mr. Gibbons? I am merely asking that I be paid what's owed me. You see, the Wisconsin Charter of 1874 gives owners of dams that were built for log drives the right to assess ten cents per each one thousand board feet of timber that passes through. A pittance compared to the seven-dollars-a-thousand those logs will bring once milled into lumber. I'm merely asking for a few crumbs left on the table after the cake's been wolfed down by the lumber barons."

"And how many board feet are we talking about?"

"Oh, I figure twenty million. At a dime-a-thousand, that comes to two-thousand dollars. That's what they owe me for *this* year."

"My word, sir. A small fortune!"

"Oh, that's not the half of it. The company ran other drives since we bought the place nine years ago. That means they owe me the same tariff for every log that passed over my dam during those drives."

"And how many board feet would you estimate?" asked Gibbons, jotting down notes.

"Eighty million or thereabouts."

"That means he owes you ..."

"Eight thousand, give or take."

"Gracious sakes! Eight thousand dollars?"

"Oh, they can afford it. Keep in mind, Gibbons, that Frederick Weyerhaeuser has an interest in most of the lumber mills from here to St. Louis. It's what made him rich. Some folks say he might be wealthier than John Rockefeller. So, Mr. Gibbons, you can see how easy it would have been for the company to simply pay my rightful comeuppance in the first place. They chose not to. But now, it's all different. You see, *I* own the dam, Mr. Gibbons. And I'll not let one of their logs cross over until I've been paid what's rightfully mine. Tell your readers that. The company has but two choices. Pay up or let all of that pine rot in the woods. Tell your readers it's my *right* to claim what's owed to me, and *right* always wins out over *might*."

"Pa," came a shout from the barn. "Are we still heading into town?"

John turned back to his guest. "Saturday is when we go to town for groceries and our mail." He shouted to his eldest son. "Clarence, we have a guest, here. You and your brother will have to go without me."

"Can Myra come along?"

"That's up to your ma."

Clarence rushed inside to find Myra giving a haircut to seven-year-old Johnny, youngest of the five Dietz children. "Myra, Pa says you can go to town with us." Clarence turned to his mother. "Uh, if it's all right with you, Ma."

"Oh, dear," said Myra. "Clare, I'd love to go. But I've so many chores to tend to today."

"Nonsense," said Hattie. "It's not often you get a chance to go. It's the first of October and a beautiful fall day. A perfect time for a ride through the woods. I'll finish up here."

"No, I'd better not, Mother. There's still sewing to be done and I know you wanted me to …"

"All that will wait, dear. This fine fall sunshine won't. Go get ready. You've earned an afternoon of fun. Clarence, I've a list of items for you to purchase at the dry goods store. Take three dollars from the egg money jar in the cupboard. Spend the change on ice creams for the three of you."

"Gee, thanks, Ma!"

Minutes later, Myra's younger brother Leslie walked two colts from the barn. He hitched them to the buckboard. Clarence climbed on, taking the reins. Leslie hopped up, then reached to help twenty-one-year-old Myra climb on board. Dressed in a snug black brilliantine suit and white blouse, she took her place on the springboard seat between her brothers.

John called to his children. "Now don't go talking to folks about family matters. Should anybody ask about the goings on between me and Weyerhaeuser, you tell 'em I said it's nobody's business. Just get the mail, pick up your ma's goods and get on back home."

Myra turned back. "Yes, Father. Bye, Mr. Gibbons … er … Floyd."

"See to it you're home by suppertime," said John. "Mr. Gibbons will be sharing our table and staying the night."

"Okay, Pa," said Leslie. "We'll be back before sundown."

Myra waved as Clarence snapped the reins, shouting, "Giddy up!"

Gibbons watched as the horses trotted away. "That daughter of yours is quite a looker."

"And smart as a whip-snap, Mr. Gibbons."

"You're letting them go alone?" he asked. "After all the threats made by the county?"

"Folks 'round these parts have come to understand what I'd do to them if they tried something. Nobody would *dare* touch my children."

"Not even in light of that thousand-dollar reward on your head?"

"Like I said, Gibbons, nobody would dare. *Nobody.*"

The afternoon ramble down the winding, ten-mile country road to the tiny village of Winter was delightful. The leaves had turned brilliant reds and golds. The air felt crisp and clean. As they rode, Myra, Leslie, and Clarence sang every song they knew at the tops of their lungs, a Dietz tradition while traveling. Around a bend, a family of raccoons skittered off the trail. A half-mile later, a covey of partridge flushed in front of the team, causing the buckskins to rear up. Every turn in the road seemed to bring more surprises and laughter. Until …

A gunshot from the woods shattered the air. Then another. Myra jerked back as the bullet tore through her midriff.

Clarence reeled when a slug smashed through his arm.

Then another blast. And another. Then, a volley of gunshots, each bullet sending splinters flying from the wagon.

Writhing with pain, Myra collapsed, slipping below the buckboard's seat.

Clarence, bleeding, held fast to the reins. Leslie sprang from the wagon onto the road and dashed into the woods.

Seven more gunshots sent bullets screaming past him. Crawling on hands and knees, he hid behind a windfall, waiting to see what would happen next and listening to his sister's cries for help.

1
Camp Four
Ten Years Earlier

Sixty miles north of his home in Rice Lake, Wisconsin, a mustached man with a ruddy complexion opened the door of a lumber camp cook shanty. He shook the snow off his shoulders and stepped in. The tall, muscular woodsman wore a wool coat, canvas overalls, and laced, calf-length boots, common attire for a man trying to eke out a living in Northwest Wisconsin. A cold north wind slammed the door behind him.

"I'm looking for the foreman," he said.

A big man with a heavy beard and shoulders nearly as wide as the door stepped forward. "Who are you?"

"My name is Dietz. John F. Dietz."

"I'm Red Mulligan, the foreman of Camp Four. State your business, Mr. Dietz."

"I'm looking for work."

"What kind of work?"

"Any work that will help me feed my wife and five children."

"Where you from?"

"Barron County. My brother's the sheriff down there."

"I ain't interested in your brother. You're the one who's askin' for a job. What can you do?"

"Whatever needs being done," said John, lighting his pipe. "Unlike most of your men, I can read, write, and cypher."

"That's why I should hire you? Because you can cypher?"

"No. You should hire me because I give a full day's work for a day's wage. And I always say what I mean and mean what I say."

The Camp Four boss stood silent, considering these words. Then, "Dietz, we're due to commence driving our pine downstream soon. I could use a dam tender over on the Brunet River. Two dollars a day. There's a shack and a horse barn there. We don't use 'em no more. If you take the job, you're welcome to them both."

"Two dollars?" John drew from his pipe.

"That's what we pay most of our crew nowadays. Whether they be sawyers, skidders, or swampers, it's the same. Two dollars a day, cash on the barrelhead."

"Those other men, those sawyers, skidders, and swampers you cite, they get three squares a day. Should I not get equal recompense?"

"Is not a roof over the heads of your wife and children compensation enough? Don't fiddle with me, Dietz. The offer is two dollars. Take it or leave it."

"Very well," said John, extending his hand. "I will tend your dam commencing at first light tomorrow."

The shanty at the Price Dam on the Brunet River barely provided more than basic shelter for John, his wife, Hattie, and their five children. A lack of chinking between the shanty's logs allowed in the winter wind. High above, missing cedar shakes resulted in snow on the floor after every storm. Early each morning, John built a fire in the pot-bellied stove to warm the room his family shared.

With no cook stove, Hattie's meals were prepared on the same pot-bellied stove. Bed sheets draped over hemp ropes separated the sleeping quarters for John and Hattie, their daughters, Helen and Myra, and the boys, Clarence, Leslie, and Stanley.

A washtub doubled for scrubbing clothes and for the family's weekly bathing. Water, carried from below the dam in metal buckets and placed on the hearth, provided hot water. John built a table and benches from lumber he'd stripped from a shed behind the barn. Horse blankets spread on the wood plank floor provided makeshift rugs for the younger children's play.

Evenings, Leslie and Clarence busied themselves by playing chess using pieces they'd whittled from basswood and a chessboard they'd painted atop a discarded nail keg.

Fourteen-year-old Myra preferred reading her father's books out loud to the family. Occasionally, they all sang along while John played a violin he'd fashioned himself. All the Dietz family's evening activities took place under the light cast from a single kerosene lantern suspended from a rafter.

Tending the dam required little effort and even less time. On his first day at work, John closed the gates to allow a head of water to build. Within days, a large flowage had developed, expanding above the dam. Two weeks later, water backed up for miles. At month's end, with the log drive about to commence, he got word from Mulligan, the camp foreman, to open the gates. The resulting surge of water rushing downstream carried thousands upon thousands of enormous pine logs from the Brunet to the Chippewa River, and eventually to the sawmills in Chippewa Falls. The gates remained open through the end of the drive when orders came to close them part-way. Weeks later, a pond had formed, perfect for fishing and swimming.

Red Mulligan, the Camp Four boss, stopped by to pay John seventy-two dollars for his first thirty-six days of labor. Although the log drive had ended, John kept watch over the dam, feeling his duty was to serve as watchman and see to it no one tampered with the gates or the water level. He often delegated this job to Myra, giving him and his sons time to make repairs on their borrowed home.

They also took time to explore the surrounding forests and streams. Not long after Leslie and his father returned from one of their woodland treks, John shared some news at the supper table.

"Mother," he began, "today, when Leslie and I were scouting the timber country east of here, we met someone."

"Who, Papa?" asked Helen.

"A woman by the name of Jennie Cameron. She owns a farm over there. You ought to see it. One-hundred-sixty acres in all, much of it already cleared. There's a big log cabin with glass windows and screens to keep out the mosquitos. There's a barn, woodsheds, and even a two-hole privy. All in all, she's got herself a nice spot to call home."

"And there's a stream nearby," added Leslie. "The Thornapple River. And a dam. Just like here!"

"It's known as the Cameron Dam," said John. "So called after Jennie and her late husband."

"Oh, it's a sight to behold," said Leslie. "Why, the Thornapple River wraps right around the farm just like a moat around a castle in those Robin Hood stories Myra reads to us."

"Oh, but that poor, poor woman," said Hattie. "This is no country for a widow to make her way in alone."

"Well, that's just it, Mother," said John. "Jennie told us the place has come to be too much for her to cope with, what with the crops, two cows, the horses, and the chickens."

"And her sheep, Pa," said Leslie.

"Yes. Sheep, too," John replied. "Mother, Jennie Cameron has family in Eau Claire. She wants to move there. Problem is the poor soul doesn't have the money. She's tried, but can't seem to find a buyer and doesn't want to just abandon the place."

With a twinge of dread in her voice, Hattie asked, "What's all that got to do with us, John?"

"Hattie, children," John took a long sip of coffee. "Jennie Cameron wants *us* to take over her place."

Hattie glared at her husband. "Honestly, John, how could *we* ever afford a farm?"

"Not we, dear. You."

"Me?"

"Jennie said she will sell us the whole lot of it for two hundred eighty dollars. What's more, she'd take a hundred now, enough to allow her to move back to Eau Claire and let us pay off the rest over time."

"We don't *have* a hundred dollars dear."

"I can spare forty from what I got paid by the lumber company, Mother. You can borrow the rest from your pa."

"John!" Hattie blurted. "I'm surprised you'd even suggest such a thing. You know quite well that my father won't go along with something like this. Not the way you two barnyard roosters get along. For heaven's sake, *why* would he do such a thing?"

"Because loaning you money I don't have is sure to pluck the banjo strings of that crotchety old father of yours. He'll help you out, if for no other reason than to spite me."

"Oh, I don't know, John. We lost our first farm. Then that real estate sales business of yours went up in smoke. What makes you think this would be different?"

"Now, see here, Hattie. You know well that the sparse bounty we harvested at the Barron County farm didn't cover the monthly rent. And the passing of our dear, little Leanna was the final straw. We had no choice but to leave. As for the other, 'twas my brother, not me, who soured the Rice Lake land deal I had going. You dassn't blame me for what no man could foretell."

"I worry that you're asking for trouble again, John. Like that land deal, perhaps this will become more trouble than you could know."

"I'll be the judge of that, Mother," said her husband. "It's a fine farm for the Dietz family and surely worth a look-see.

"Ma," said Leslie, "you could at least visit the Cameron place. It's got everything we need. Much of the land is already cleared. A bunch more is cutover. Clarence and I can pull the stumps in no time. Then we'll put in crops, Ma. Potatoes. Rutabagas. Corn, too. There's grazing room galore for our livestock. And plenty of marsh hay that we can cut and stack in the hayloft for winter. It's a perfect place for us, Ma."

"Hattie," said John, "the soil's rich, there's a freshwater spring, and inside the cabin, there sits a huge Monarch kitchen range just a-waitin' for you to put your first fire in it."

"And bedrooms, Ma," Leslie said, "with curtains! And a copper bathtub. Just think of it!"

"A copper bathtub?" asked Hattie. "Oh, how elegant!"

John finished his coffee. "Mother, from the kitchen window you'll see majestic sunrises every morning and from the back porch, beautiful sunsets over the Thornapple River. I know we can make a go of it there. Make a *home* of it. Our own home. A place for the lot of us—the entire Dietz family."

"Oh please, Mother," said Myra, "let's do go have a look at the Widow Cameron's farm. I'll pack a picnic lunch. We'll make a day of it. It will be so fun."

"Can we, Mama?" begged Helen. "Please?"

"Oh, all right," said Hattie. "Next time you head that way, I'll go along." She turned to her husband. "But, John Dietz, don't you *dare* try to sweet-talk me into something that could set us to ruin."

"Set us to ruin, my dear? Why, if my hunch is right, investing in this place, moving into our own Thornapple River farm, will once and for all give me a chance to make my mark in this world. What's more, it will put our family in the limelight. By God, everyone 'round these parts will soon know the name John F. Dietz. *Everyone!*"

Hayward

Early one August morning, Leslie hooked up the horses and the entire Dietz family climbed onto the buckboard. They were headed for the county seat, a bustling, timber industry boomtown, named for a man who a decade earlier was regarded as the wealthiest lumberman in Wisconsin, Anthony Judson Hayward. But now, this company town was under the thumb of two other moguls, Edward H. Hines of the Hines Lumber Company and his partner, Frederick Weyerhaeuser.

With Clarence at the reins of the buckboard, the family rode through the dusty streets of the City of Hayward. Halfway down Iowa Avenue, John pointed toward a large brick building. "Look, children," he said. "That's one of Frederick Weyerhaeuser's banks."

"Who is Mr. Warehouse?" asked Helen.

"Well," said her father, "in a way he's my boss. You see, I get paid to tend to the Price Dam. And it's owned by Camp Four. And Camp Four is owned by the Chippewa Lumber and Boom Company which, in turn, is owned by Frederick Weyerhaeuser. See, Helen?"

"Sorta," she answered. "Golly. Mr. Warehouse must be really rich."

"Rich?" said Myra. "Oh my, yes, Helen, I'd venture to guess that he's quite well-off."

"Can't say as I agree," said John. "A man may have more money than any one soul has a right to, but all the money in the world can't make him truly well-off. You see, some men work from daylight to dark in one office or another and rarely see their wives and children. Now, as for me, I get to spend nearly every hour of every day with my family. In my mind, that's what makes a man well-off. In fact, I believe I am *far* better off than even the richest of all the lumber barons."

"Gosh, Pa," said Clarence, "how the devil did Mr. Weyerhaeuser get so much money?"

"Years ago, when the lumber mills along the Mississippi were bickering over whose timber they could mill and whose they could not, he devised a plan. He called them all together for a meeting in Chicago. Somehow Weyerhaeuser got them all to agree to work as a team instead of against one another. He gathered them into what he called the Mississippi River Logging Company. Once the mills started cooperating, they made more money than ever. Of course, Weyerhaeuser saw to it that he got a slice of every pie. Then he used his profits to buy up lumber camps, sawmills, and every scrap of land he could, as long as it had trees to cut. Pretty soon he had enough to open his own banks. And along with banks come lawyers and politicians."

"I bet he can do anything he wants and get away with it," said Leslie.

"The bigger they are, the harder they fall," said John.

"What, Pa?"

"Think about this, Leslie," said his father. "A short stack of firewood isn't likely to tumble. A tall one might. But if you stack your firewood as high as the sky, the slightest breeze could bring it down. Now, Weyerhaeuser might be a big shot, but being big also means he has many threats to endure, more eyes watching his every move, more politicians with their hand out, more businessmen waiting for the chance to chisel off a piece of his fortune for their own gain. Being the biggest doesn't always mean being the strongest, Son. In fact, often it's the smallest man who brings the big shot to his knees. Keep in mind, one man who knows how to swing an ax can bring down the tallest tree in the woods."

"Like David and Goliath, Pa?" Helen asked.

"Precisely, Helen," said Myra. "Pa's right. The bigger they are, the harder they fall."

Ascending a gentle hill in their buckboard, their father pointed to another large building.

"That's the courthouse, children," said their father, "where the county board meets and where the sheriff works."

"Is that where the jail is, too, Pa?" asked Leslie.

"I believe so."

"Papa, are there bad people in the jail?" asked Stanley.

"Might be," replied his father. "But sometimes a person might end up in jail of no accord. That's why there's a courtroom there and a judge to decide who deserves jail and who doesn't. See?"

"Yes, Papa."

As Clarence drove the team past the courthouse, a mansion overlooking a small pond came into view. "My heavens, Mother," gasped Myra. "Look at that magnificent home."

"It's owned by Robert McCormick," said her father. "Another lumber baron. The big bosses get the big houses while their workers sleep in shanties and tents."

Myra stared at the mansion as they passed by. "Father, I'd feel like a princess if I slept in a house that grand."

John looked at his daughter. "You and Helen are my princesses, Myra. And a princess is *always* a princess, no matter where she sleeps."

"Clarence," said Hattie, "we passed by a dry goods store a bit ago. Take me there so I might buy some fabric, thread, and such. You boys and your father could use new overalls. And you girls need new smocks."

"And you deserve a new Sunday dress, Mother," added Myra.

"From there, we need to find the feed mill," said John. "Then we'd best be on our way home. We've stock to tend and supper to prepare before sundown ushers us indoors. But Clarence, before we leave town, I want you to find a confectionery. A trek to the city mustn't end without a bag of licorice whips for the journey home."

The Courthouse Gang Riot

The Dietz family's weekly mail brought two newspapers to them at their temporary home on the Brunet River. One, *The Hayward Enterprise,* was a progressive weekly. But *The Hayward Republican,* was published by a close relative of the conservative county board chairman, Harry B. Shue. *The Hayward Republican* received all of the county's press business and regularly touted the interests of Chippewa Lumber and Boom Company and Shue's administration. Chairman Shue's daughter had married the county judge who, in turn, appointed her as clerk of court. An associate of Shue's helped guarantee election success to keep the corrupt officials in place. He did this by trading dry goods and liquor for votes to the nearby Lac Courte Oreilles tribe. He also hired buckboards to haul them to and from town on Election Day. Another Shue confederate, a pudgy hotelkeeper named William Giblin, wore the sheriff's star and did as Harry Shue ordered.

Known throughout the region as "the Courthouse Gang," these six officials ruled the county, often drawing allegations of malfeasance and deceit and lining their own pockets through outright graft. In truth, as strong as they'd become, the Courthouse Gang answered to the lumber barons who controlled the company store, the bank, and Hayward's immense sawmill.

The other newspaper, *The Hayward Enterprise,* began publishing in 1901 in response to demands from those citizens who'd become tired of the lumber company and the Courthouse Gang calling the shots and rigging the elections so they could continue their shady dealings. Now the outlying farmers finally felt their vote might make a difference. And in the spring election of 1902, many, including John Dietz, made the long trip to the county seat to vote. Within minutes of riding into the city, John cast his vote and left for the feed mill and hardware store.

His supper at the Clark House was interrupted by a boy sent around town to spread news of the election result. To everyone's surprise, Chairman Harry Shue lost. The vote wasn't close. Two out of three voters wanted Shue and his cronies booted out.

John returned to the courthouse to find a cheering crowd and joined in the merriment. But the revelry soon turned to angry shouts and threats. Shue and his collaborators had locked themselves in the courthouse and refused to recognize the election. From a third floor window, Shue announced that the Courthouse Gang would not vacate their offices.

Within minutes, enraged citizens broke through the courthouse doors, intent on wrestling the now-invalid bureaucrats from their offices. But a revolver held by a nervous Sheriff Giblin stopped their advance. Cooler heads soon marshaled the Courthouse Gang and the horde of rioting voters into the main courtroom to debate the matter. With Shue and his cronies secure behind the judge's bench, William Schei, editor of the *Hayward Enterprise,* spoke.

"Gentlemen," began Schei, "we know that today's vote was conducted on the fair and square. There's no justification for Harry Shue and the other ousted officials to declare this election illegitimate."

"You're wrong," shouted Shue. "The vote was rigged. Therefore it is my sworn duty to declare the Election of 1902 null and void."

"You say that only because you lost, Harry," said the *Enterprise* editor. "Today's election was conducted on the up and up and you dang-well know it."

"Harry, we've had enough," came a shout from the crowd. "It's time you pack your bags and leave."

"And take your shady band of boodlers with you!" another angry voter shouted.

Shue ignored the demands. "Now see here," he bellowed. "I've declared this an invalid vote. I will not allow my county clerk to sign the certificates of election. And that's that! Now go home, all of youse!"

A handful of men rushed the bench. They stopped when Sheriff Giblin drew his revolver again. "Any man comes forward with violence on his mind does so at his own peril," shouted Giblin. "I'm not opposed to defending these public servants. And I have empty jail cells in the cellar for those I only happen to wound."

"Now everybody just hold your horses," shouted Dietz. "Nobody need suffer injury or arrest if we can calm down and talk this through. Now Sheriff, holster your pistol and let's see if we can't come to some sort of agreement, here."

"And who might you be?" asked Shue.

"The name is Dietz," he replied. "John F. Dietz. I keep watch over the Price Dam for the Chippewa Lumber and Boom Company. My family and I plan to move to the Cameron farm next spring. It's over on the Thornapple River, if you know where that is."

"Of course I know where it is," Shue blurted. "I'm the county board chairman. So, Dietz, what makes you think you have any say in this?"

John stroked his chin. "Because, Mr. Shue, I am as much a citizen of this county as are you. By my backwoods logic, that gives me the same right to speak as you."

"Nonsense!"

"Let Mr. Dietz say his piece," said the newspaperman.

John stepped to the front of the room near the sheriff, close enough to smell the whiskey on Giblin's breath. "Like most of you here," he began, "I labor long and hard to keep the wolf away from the door. I plow and plant in the spring, put up hay in the summer, harvest in the fall. I hunt, trap, fish, and pick berries when they're ripe. My wife sells hen's eggs, milk, and butter to the men at Camp Four. My children help with the livestock and tend to other chores. And, like most of you, I do this hoping to pay my taxes and store food in the root cellar and keep shoes on my children's feet in the wintertime.

"But what separates me from some folks in this room is that I don't mind paying the state and county taxes I'm faced with each year. However, it riles me to no end when I learn that some of the tax revenue I contribute to the county ends up in the pockets of county officials and their friends rather than being used to benefit our people. But I don't point my finger at individuals, not even these local politicians. For it is *not* the little fellow who's at the root of the problem. No, gentlemen, it is the lumber companies that are at fault. They're the ones that jerk on the strings, making all of us dance like marionettes in some five-cent circus sideshow."

"Precisely where are you headed with this, Dietz?" asked Shue.

"Harry, from what I read in both of the Hayward newspapers, I believe the lumber tycoons are pulling the wool over our eyes, including those of the men on our county board. There they sit down in Chippewa Falls, Eau Claire, and Menomonie, and all we see in the papers is that they can't seem to make ends meet due to high operating expenses and exorbitant taxes. I ask you, should we be taken aback when we learn of favors they do for some of our county officials in order to get their taxes lowered? Should we be surprised to hear they receive special concessions? Well, I should say not! So, before you go condemning these good public servants, look at it from their side."

"Just what is it you're getting at, Mr. Dietz?" asked the newspaperman.

"Instead of assailing our public servants with anger and spite, I think we should thank them—acknowledge them for their service—heck, throw a gol-dang, full-blown jamboree in their honor. They aren't the problem here, the lumber syndicate is!"

John turned to Chairman Shue, now smiling at him. "Harry, in your defense, have you ever been asked for favors by representatives of any of the lumber companies? The North Wisconsin Lumber Company? The St. Croix Boom Company? The Chippewa Lumber and Boom Company? The Mississippi Lumber Company? Any of them?"

"Well, I … I suppose I have," replied Shue, quickly adding, "but I always had the county's best interest at heart."

"I'm sure you did," replied John. "Now tell us, were you ever paid for these favors? Either in cash or goods or other properties?"

"Well, not exactly."

"Can you tell us how you were rewarded for helping them?"

"They made sure their employees at the sawmills and in the lumber camps voted for me. For us. Oh, yes, and for the good of the county, you understand."

"Anything else?"

"Well, they saw to it that my family and friends got good jobs. That, and some cheaper prices at the company store," he said in a softer voice.

"There!" shouted John, turning to the crowd again. "How on Earth can we condemn a man for doing what he thought best for himself, his family, his friends, *especially* when the problems within our county were caused by the lumber syndicate?"

"That don't matter," shouted a man in the crowd. "These scoundrels have illegally taken control of the election. They need to be tarred, feathered, and rode out of town on a rail." Red faced, he rushed forward, his eyes brimming with rage.

Giblin drew his revolver again. Instantly, John seized the sheriff's arm, gave a twist, and yanked the revolver from Giblin's fleshy hand.

With a hard left, he sent the sheriff to the floor. The approaching assailant stopped short. Giblin looked up at John who opened the pistol's cylinder, dropping all six cartridges on the floor.

"Giblin," John said, "you are no longer Sheriff of Sawyer County. I'm going to hold onto this pistol so you don't find yourself in one of the cells you mentioned." He turned to Shue again.

"Harry," he said, "you have a reputation for being a hard-headed, stubborn-as-a-mule, set-in-his-ways man. Although that might be the case, I want you to know that you may have met your match in me. I know this because my wife reminds me every day that, on God's green Earth, *I* am the most hard-headed, stubborn-as-a-mule, set-in-his-ways man she's ever encountered."

Dietz's words drew a laugh from the crowd.

"And I know you and your associates want to continue your service to our county. But gol-dang it, right is right. And unless you wish to be lumped into that horde of unscrupulous men President Theodore Roosevelt is working hard to rein in, those robber barons like Rockefeller, Carnegie, Vanderbilt, and Morgan, you and your minions had better let life go on as it should. If today's newly elected officials don't satisfy the public, you can always run for office again. Meanwhile, if you relinquish your offices tonight, you'll be looked on as heroes rather than scalawags. What say you, Harry?"

Shue considered Dietz's words a moment. Then, "Mr. Dietz, for a poor dirt farmer from back in the boondocks, you certainly do have a silver tongue. All right. I will accept your advice. And, like you say, if these new officials don't live up to their promises, you will all see my name on the next ballot."

A cheer roared from the third floor windows of the Sawyer County Courthouse that night. John Dietz, this back woods farmer, had won the day. And that night, he slept soundly, a guest of Robert L. McCormick in the mansion he'd built overlooking Harry Shue's Pond. John slept well, having but one regret. He wished that he'd asked his daughter, Myra, to come to town with him that day. She too could have slept in McCormick's magnificent home if only for one night, so that she might feel like the princess John knew she was.

4

John Dietz's Second Claim

A severe 1903 winter resulted in a sixty-two inch snow depth and a forty-seven below zero temperature in mid-February. Myra had read and re-read the books on the family bookshelf. With so much time spent indoors on dark, snowy days, the kerosene supply required rationing to two hours each evening. Strings on John's violin broke from long hours of use. He had no replacements but continued to play on three, and then two strings, as the family sang along to pass the time. Their temporary home at the Price Dam made them eager to move to their own farm on the Thornapple River. The trek from the cabin to the root cellar, barn, and privy often had to be made on snowshoes. With the Brunet River frozen down to the riverbed, the children hauled in snow that their mother melted for water. Weekly treks to put up firewood wore out John, Leslie, and Clarence as well as their workhorses, Meggie and Paul, whose increased appetite shrunk the stockpile of hay in the loft.

John worried that a late spring could mean added hardship for the struggling household. "We'll overcome this test, children," he would say. "We are the Dietz family. We can weather any storm, beat down any peril, no matter when it comes or where from. Stay together, stay strong, and we shall survive."

"Mama, I'm cold." Helen often complained.

"Then stand closer to the fire, child," counseled Hattie. "Or climb under the covers with little Johnny and think of how nice it will be to soon play outside in the summer sunshine at our Thornapple farm."

Outside, Clarence and Leslie stood their snowshoes in a drift near the door. They spent the next half-hour toting in armloads of firewood.

"Wind's from the east, Pa," said Clarence. "And the clouds look to be full of snow. I think we're in for it again."

"Think we'll survive, Clare?" asked his father.

"Yes, Pa. We're the Dietz family. We can weather any storm, beat down any peril."

And the Dietz family *did* survive. An early spring renewed their spirit. The snow vanished and the family tapped maples and boiled down sap for syrup and maple sugar candy. Soon, longer days and bright sunshine brought buds to the aspens and turned the hayfield green once more.

In the woods, skunk cabbage bloomed, followed by cowslips, trillium, and delicate pink lady slippers.

On one of their trips to their Thornapple River property, John and his sons found that the gates on the Cameron Dam had been closed.

"Looks like Camp Four is readying for their spring log drive," said Clarence. "The river's backed up plenty."

"They'll open the gates any day now," said his father. "But in the meantime, just look at the flood they've sent onto our fields. It'll take a month or more for that hay crop to recover. It'll cost us at least one cutting this summer. Maybe five or six ton of feed for our stock by my reckoning. They've no right to do that."

"But there's nothing we can do about it, is there, Pa?" asked Leslie. "There's no going back. What's done is done."

John stroked his chin. "I'm not so sure about that. The lumber company might control the dam, but your mother owns the land. We might be small potatoes in their eyes, but we have rights. And the Chippewa Lumber and Boom Company has infringed upon them."

"What you planning to do about it, Pa?" Clarence asked.

"I don't rightly know as yet. Maybe something. Maybe nothing. We'll see."

That evening, at their temporary home near the Price Dam, John dipped his pen into the inkwell.

> Mr. H. G. Chichester, Secretary
> Mississippi River Logging Company
> St. Paul, Minn.
>
> Dear Mr. Chichester,
> A visit to my property on the Thornapple River today revealed that your Camp Four men have closed the gates on the Cameron Dam in preparation for the spring drive. However, in doing so, they have flooded thirty acres of my land, including hayfields important to keep my livestock fed through next winter. I estimate that I will lose 8 ton of good hay at $4 per ton or $32. I'm certain that your company does not want to take responsibility for livestock lost to starvation. Therefore, I require compensation of $32 for the lost crop of hay. In addition, I've owned the property for 3 years so I expect to be paid a total of $96 for lost crops. The money should be delivered to me in cash by Red Mulligan, foreman of your Camp Four.
>> John F. Dietz
>> Winter, Wisc.

John waited patiently but received no reply from the Mississippi River Logging Company or its subsidiary, the Chippewa Lumber and Boom Company. He sent a second letter.

Mr. Horace G. Chichester, Secretary
Mississippi River Logging Company
St. Paul, Minn.

Dear Mr. Chichester,
    Receiving no reply from you regarding my request for compensation, I now wish to amend my earlier request for compensation as follows:
    On April 3, 1901, your Camp Four boss approached me with a request to oversee the Price Dam on the Brunet River until I received other orders from your Company. I was promised compensation of $2 a day for my work. Since then, I have received $72 for 36 days. I now require payment for the remaining 845 days. With meager interest, the amount you owe is $1,717. When combined with the $96 owed to me for crop damage, the total comes to $1,813. Therefore, please prepare a draught for that amount at once and have it delivered to me by courier or the U. S. Postal Service.
                                    John F. Dietz
                                    Winter, Wisc.

Again John waited. And again he received no reply from the company. His patience exhausted, he sent a third letter. This one added another fifty dollars in interest.

The next morning, Clarence hooked up the sleigh. He and Leslie accompanied their father to Winter to mail the letter and pick up a few supplies. Then, on another trip to town two weeks later, John received a reply from Horace Chichester, secretary of the Mississippi River Logging Company. He read the letter to himself and then stuffed it into his coat pocket.

"Clarence, turn the team," he ordered. "We're going home."

Clarence obeyed, saying not a word.

A quarter mile down the road, Leslie asked, "Is the company going to pay up, Pa?"

His father remained silent.

"What'd they say, Pa?" asked Clarence.

"Never mind. It's my business." Another quarter mile passed. "All right. I'll tell you. Horace Chichester wrote back that I should have known better than to buy land that any fool could see would be flooded each spring."

"He said that?" Clarence asked.

"Not in so many words, but he might as well have."

"What of your second claim, Pa?" asked Leslie. "Your back pay?"

"Chichester said I am to take that matter to Red Mulligan, the foreman at Camp Four. Chichester said it was him who hired me so it's him who must send in a voucher for my back pay."

"You think Mr. Mulligan will do that?"

"He'd better. There'll be trouble if he won't stand behind me on this."

"Golly, I'm sorry it's working out this way, Pa," said Clarence. "I hoped they'd stick to their bargain and pay up."

"Boys, rich folks don't get rich by spending their money. I've heard tell that Frederick Weyerhaeuser looks over every expense endured by his companies, right down to the last pennies spent on pencils by his many clerks. But mark my words. One way or another, they *will* pay."

The horses trotted down Winter Road. Without prompting, they turned onto the tote road leading to the Price Dam and their suppertime feeding.

Crossing the bridge near home, John said, "Boys?"

"Yes, Pa?"

"Don't mention this to your ma. It will only serve to upset her."

"You can count on us, Pa," Clarence replied. "Mum's the word."

5
Red Mulligan

Late one frigid February afternoon in 1904, John tramped through the snow to Camp Four. He stood his snowshoes in a snowdrift and entered the cook shanty. Seventy-three lumberjacks turned as he walked past the mess tables and up to Red Mulligan.

"What brings you out in weather like this?" asked the foreman.

"Just stopped by to visit," replied John. "A man needs to get clear of the house from time to time."

"Coffee?"

"I'd like that."

Mulligan turned to a boy clearing tables. "Say, Herman, bring over a cup of coffee for our guest."

"Thanks," said John. He pulled an envelope from his pocket.

"Something on your mind, Dietz?"

"Red, I got this letter from Horace Chichester not long ago."

"Chichester? What's he writin' to you for?"

"It's about the back pay I'm owed for watching over the Price Dam."

"You've got no back pay coming. What the devil you talking about?"

"Red, You hired me as your watchman in 1901. Third of April, to be precise. You told me to tend the dam, to not allow anyone to raise or lower the gates without word from you. You also told me to stay on the job until I heard otherwise from the Chippewa Lumber and Boom Company. Red, I've been the company watchman for the Price Dam ever since and not once heard a peep from the company. That means I'm owed for eight hundred forty-five days. With interest, that comes to seventeen hundred and seventeen dollars."

Mulligan laughed. "You don't say!"

"Read it yourself," John said as he slid the envelope across the table. "Chichester gives you sole authority to see to it I get what's owed me. Help me out and I'll drop my original ninety-six dollar claim for crop damage and we can both go about our business."

Mulligan stared at John, then slid the envelope back. "Three years ago you came here with your hand out. You needed work. What's more, you needed a roof over the heads of your children. I felt sorry for you, Dietz. For you and for them. So, even though I had no plan to hire nobody to watch the Price Dam, I put you on the payroll. But I did so only for the duration of the spring drive, see? Thirty-six days. Seventy-two dollars. And that's what I paid you. I figured that would get you through until the spring thaw and not raise an eyebrow in the office. You and me have been friendly ever since, at least by my reckoning. Now you come here and try to talk me into taking part in this ... this swindle? By God, Dietz, you have more dang gumption than any Chicago politician."

"I was hired on but never let go of, Red. As an employee, the company owes me ..."

"Nothing!" shouted Mulligan. "The company owes you not one red cent! You've been squatting on Chippewa Lumber and Boom Company land for three years. Why, instead of trying to hoodwink Chichester, you should be sending him a thank you letter. You've no right to lay claim against us for wages. Or anything else, for that matter."

"Mulligan, I didn't take you for a company man. I thought you had some backbone."

"And I never would have let you through that door in the first place if I'd seen this side of you."

"I have seventeen hundred dollars coming. Read the letter. Chichester spells it out. All you need to do is sign a dang pay voucher."

"I don't care what Chichester says in his letter." Mulligan stood, his wide, brawny torso overshadowing his guest. "That's it, John Dietz. You and me is done with. Get out before I throw you out."

John sprang to his feet. "Strong words from a yellow-bellied company man."

Men at nearby tables grabbed their cups and plates and stood back. John turned to them. "Is this how it must be?" he shouted. "The company wrings every last bit of sweat and blood from the workers and then casts them to the wind? For Pete's sake, boys. Stand up for yourselves!"

"That's enough," shouted Mulligan. "One more word and I'll break your jaw."

John ignored the warning. "How long are you men bound to put up with this? Are you going to let the company walk all over you? Isn't it time you got your fair share?"

Mulligan drew his clenched fist back, grabbed John by the shoulder, and spun him around.

John ducked. Mulligan's blow glanced off his head, knocking his hat to the floor. John countered with a sharp jab to Mulligan's ribs.

The foreman exhaled sharply, then took two more blows, one striking his gut, the next his chin. He shook it off and wound up for another swing at his opponent. But before he could deliver, John's hammer-like right fist slammed into the side of the foreman's head while his left smashed into ribs. Mulligan wobbled, stumbled, and fell to the wood plank floor.

Another man grabbed a stick of firewood from the pile and charged at John who sidestepped, dodging the blow of the club. John's extended boot tripped the lumberjack, sending him head-first into the log wall, knocking him cold.

John spun around, fists clenched and up. "Who's next?" he shouted.

"Some of us are with you, John," answered one of the lumberjacks.

Mulligan stirred, then sat half-way up. "You'll never beat the company, Dietz. It's too big. Too powerful. It will eat you alive."

"You're a fool, Mulligan," said John, reaching down to pick up his hat. "It's the company's policy to ask workers to risk life and limb, then sends them off with a few pennies in their pockets. It is downright wrong. They expect workers to slave away for a pittance, essentially giving away the value of their labor to the bosses. And while the families of the lumberjacks struggle to get by, those tycoons bank thousands upon thousands every day. Don't you see, Red? It can't last. Society won't allow it. Sooner or later, workers will stand up for themselves and put a stop to it! *Right* is stronger than *might!*"

"You're wrong," said Mulligan, still trying to catch his breath. "As long as there's money to be made, there will be some tycoon there to take the lead and siphon off the lion's share. And when he steps aside, there will be another. You'll never win, Dietz. Now, get out."

Outside, John strapped on his snowshoes for the long, dark trek home to the Price Dam on the Brunet River. Red Mulligan's words resounded as he plodded down the winding trail in the moonlight. "You'll never win, Dietz. You'll never win," echoed with every step. Before arriving home, he'd made a decision. "Hattie, children, get a good night's sleep. Tomorrow we pack up all we own and move out of this fallen down company shack to our new home."

"Tomorrow, Papa?" said Helen. "But it's Valentine's Day."

Her father laughed. "Well now, I believe you're right, princess, but just think of it. *This* Valentine's Day you will eat breakfast in your old home and eat supper in your new one on the Thornapple River. What could be more fun?"

"And what brought this on?" asked Hattie.

"If we should have an early spring, the trail might turn into mud.

Days are getting longer, Mother. We need to move now, while we still have snow for our sleigh. If we give it our best, we should be able to be moved in within a week, lock, stock, and barrel. Free and clear from the Chippewa Lumber and Boom Company for good."

"Oh, my!" said Myra. "This is so exciting. I'll not sleep a wink tonight. Not a wink!"

6

At Your Own Peril

The Dietz family settled quickly into their new home. Conveniences such as the wood-fired, Monarch kitchen range with a built-in water heater and a copper bathtub in the washroom pleased Hattie. And the hand-cranked washing machine would surely make washday a pleasure.

Jennie Cameron also left behind a large, braided wool rug that stretched out before the fireplace. No longer would the children play on horse blankets each evening.

Myra arranged the family's collection of books on the mantel. It included three of her father's favorites, Upton Sinclair's *The Jungle,* Jacob Riis's *How the Other Half Lives,* and Mark Twain's *The Gilded Age.* Books of poems by Dickenson and Tennyson were sandwiched between Twain's *Tom Sawyer, Huckleberry Finn,* and *Roughing It.* Nearby, Poe, Longfellow, Hawthorne, and Harriet Beecher Stowe volumes leaned against two dozen others.

"My word!" shouted Hattie from the kitchen. "Jennie Cameron never came back for her icebox."

"She left it for you," said John. "She thought we'd make better use of it than her."

"John, we will need ice."

"It's already put up, Mother. The boys and I stacked more than enough behind the barn to get us through until fall. We'll make more come January."

"There's another surprise waiting for you in the pantry," shouted Clarence from the front porch.

Hattie looked behind the pantry curtain. "Oh, my stars!" Hattie squealed. She joined the others in the living room, carrying a wooden ice cream machine. "Goodness sakes. 'Twas so thoughtful of Jennie to leave this for us." She set it on the dinner table and turned to hug her husband. "Oh, thank you for all of this, John. I feel in my heart that this is our first, true home. And I'll do all I can to make it our family palace—our Thornapple Farm."

An early spring had the family spending more time outdoors. Clarence, Leslie, and John plowed for days and then used dynamite to blast stumps from the cutover, creating more fields. They planted long rows of rutabagas, potatoes, and corn while Hattie, Myra, and the little ones planted a small flower garden. The men built a half mile of rail fence for the livestock and made repairs to the barn roof and root cellar. The Dietz property soon took on the look of a modern, 1904 farm—a pleasant, safe place for John and Hattie to raise their children, now numbering six with the birth of little Johnny.

But the words of Red Mulligan kept returning to John. He felt torn inside. On one hand, he wanted to be rid of the Chippewa Lumber and Boom Company for good. On the other, he resented the fact that they'd refused his request for crop damage compensation. Had they paid as they should have, he'd never have demanded back pay as a watchman. But now he felt he'd been taken for a fool. He'd been attacked by Mulligan. And he'd been ignored by Frederick Weyerhaeuser's managers. He wanted to get even—to show them all that John F. Dietz was king of this small mountain his family called home.

"But how?" he wondered as he stared north from the front porch. Then, like a bolt of lightning, he saw the answer. "The Cameron Dam!"

"Boys!" he called.

"Yes, Pa?" answered Leslie.

"Fetch a rope. A long rope. And find your older brother. We've something to tend to."

Minutes later, Clarence and Leslie stretched a long rope across the yard. John counted as he paced it off.

"Two-hundred feet," he said. "About twelve rods. All right, boys. Come with me."

"Where to, Pa?" Clarence asked.

"The dam. If my hunch is right, part of it might be on our land. I need to know."

Within an hour, John and his sons had measured twice. It appeared that a small portion of the dam was on their side of the property line.

"What good is it?" Leslie asked. "We don't use the pond upstream except for some fishing and maybe a swim on a hot summer day."

"What good is it?" John repeated. "Without that dam, Mulligan's men can't drive their logs. If we own even part of that dam, we have a say in that drive. Just you wait until Red Mulligan hears about this. Maybe then he'll see fit to get me my rightful comeuppance. Boys, this might just be a red-letter day for the Dietz family. Yessirree!"

The next day Clarence and Leslie crossed the walkway above the dam and turned north. Following his father's instructions, Clarence handed an envelope to the first lumberjack they encountered. "Give this to your boss, Mr. Mulligan," said Clarence.

"Ya, okay, den," said the big Swede, taking the envelope.

The boys made a beeline back to the dam. They crossed on the walkway and sprinted to the cabin for breakfast.

Four days after sending word to Camp Four, the Dietz family had a visitor. He carried a wooden case and a tripod.

"Mr. Dietz?" came a shout from beyond the Thornapple. "Hello?"

John stepped onto the porch "If you're looking for Camp Four, it's that-away." John pointed south. "Downstream and across the dam."

"I'm not looking for Camp Four," the stranger replied. "I'm looking for Mr. John Dietz."

"Well, friend, you found him. C'mon in and have a cup of coffee."

The man crossed the river on the footbridge. He set his cargo on the porch and followed John inside.

"Hattie, Myra, children, we have a visitor," said John, turning to the young man.

"My name is Thomas Sargent. I'm a surveyor for the Chippewa Lumber and Boom Company. My boss, Mr. Irvine, sent me here to verify the boundaries of the company's property. It seems there's some confusion about where the quarter line lies."

John smiled. "Mr. Sargent, I have no faith in your company or those who run it. I want you to promise me right here and right now that your findings will be honest and accurate. Can you do that?"

"I certainly can, sir. My job is only to find the borderlines, mark them, and record them. I'm licensed by the state and not beholding to the company or anyone in it. The fact is, sir, any surveyor who deliberately falsifies records or knowingly offers incorrect information is subject to fines and loss of license and his job. The lumber company pays me, tells me when and where to survey, but that's where it stops. You see, sir, my boss, Mr. Irvine, merely wants to know where the company stands. After I report my findings, he will contact you to work things out."

"Irvine?" asked John. "William Irvine?"

"Yes, sir. You've heard of him?"

"Heard of him? Why, we're brothers!"

"Sir?"

"Fellow Masons, Mr. Sargent. We've met on occasion in Rice Lake. You must let him know that John F. Dietz offers his kindest regards."

"I'll do that, sir. Now, if I may, I'd like to conduct my survey."

"Very well, Mr. Sargent. Meanwhile, I will fetch the deed and abstract so you can see that Hattie's land is ours free and clear."

"That won't be necessary, Mr. Dietz. I'm only interested in the actual boundaries. I will do my utmost to find the true corners of your property, as well as the company's."

"You'll let me know what you find?"

"Yes, sir. Of course. Today, sir."

John stroked his chin. "Well, Mr. Sargent, have at it!"

While Clarence and his father seeded the rutabaga field, Leslie assisted the surveyor. Three hours later, they returned to find John in the barn.

"Pa," said Leslie, "Mr. Sargent is all done. He found the corners and we drove a post at each one."

Shoeing one of the workhorses, John looked up.

"I have news, sir," said Sargent. "I found your measurements to be wrong."

"I thought you'd say as much. You're just another company man."

"No, Pa," said Leslie. "It's not what you think. Hear Mr. Sargent out."

John turned to the surveyor again. "Well?"

"Like your son said, we drove posts on the corners and shot a line between each one. Mr. Dietz, not only does your land intersect the Cameron Dam, it goes beyond your estimate. By my calculations, your line cuts just clear of the center gate. You own more of that dam than does the Chippewa Lumber and Boom Company."

John silently measured Sargent's words. Then, "*Beyond* the middle?"

Sargent nodded. "A full eighteen inches beyond."

John fell quiet again.

"It's good news, Mr. Dietz," said Sargent

"Good news, Pa," echoed Leslie.

"By golly, Son. I think you're right."

"Mr. Dietz," said Sargent, "I'm no lawyer, but if I'm not mistaken, you control the Cameron Dam. And that letter you sent the company? Well, by my thinking, you have every right to your claim."

John extended his hand. "Thank you, Thomas. Thank you for coming. And for being forthright."

By dawn the next day, signs had been posted on both sides of the Cameron Dam.

Two days later, Myra set down her water pails and ran from the cistern to the root cellar where her father and Leslie were installing shelves for jars of canned goods. "Father!" she yelled. "Father, there are men up at the dam."

John rushed from the cool, dark interior into the bright April, sunshine. Leslie followed. Squinting at the dam, they saw movement.

"I think there are two of them," Myra said. "Or maybe three. I couldn't tell. They're so far off."

"What do you suppose they're up to?" her father asked.

"I don't know. I noticed them a moment ago while I was fetching water. I came straight here. I thought you'd want to know."

John stared at the dam. Then, "Leslie?"

"Yes, Pa?" his son said from the door of the root cellar.

"Fetch my rifle. It's time the company learned a lesson about trespassing on Dietz property."

Leslie took off for the cabin. He returned seconds later with a Winchester .30-30. "Can I tag along?"

"You sure can. You too, Myra. This is your home as much as mine."

"I better not," she replied. "I need to give the baby his daily bath."

Leslie and his father sprinted the five-hundred yards from the barnyard to the dam. Standing on the bank of the Thornapple River, John counted three men below. One held a pipe wrench and a hammer; another, a crowbar.

"Hold up, there!" John shouted.

The three workers looked up.

"What do you think you're doing?"

The men looked at each other and then at Dietz, his son, and the deer rifle. One worker, a man wearing a red, wool shirt, answered. "We got sent here by the boss to straighten out gate three, Mr. Dietz. It's a little catawampus from last winter's ice."

"Didn't you see my sign?"

"Yeah, we saw it. But our orders are to fix this gate. We don't mean no harm."

"That gate is fine just as it is. Now get your tails up out of there and off my land."

"Soon as we're done, Mr. Dietz. We won't be but a minute." Two of the workers returned to their task. The man in the red shirt watched as John raised his carbine. The worker's eyes widened. He stumbled back, tripped, and fell into the stream as John squinted at his sights, took careful aim, and fired.

The others jumped as the bullet smacked dead center into the middle gate, four feet from them. Dropping their tools, they scrambled up the side of the dam, cresting the top. The third man slogged out of the river, clambered up the bank, and then slipped near the top and slid back down, shouting, "Don't shoot! Please, Mister Dietz! Don't shoot! I'm going! I'm going!"

John and Leslie laughed as the first two ran upstream, ignoring the drenched man in the red shirt. "You tell Mulligan that John Dietz will not tolerate trespassers until I get what's owed me. And tell him not one log will cross this dam until I am paid. Next man who sets foot on my property won't be shown such mercy as you've been afforded!"

Laughing at the sight of three men scattering like frightened mice, John and Leslie turned back toward the farmyard.

"Think they'll be back, Pa?"

"Not them. Those three have had a bellyful. No, someone else will come. If I know Red Mulligan, he will seek out his boldest man to finish the work when we're not paying attention. Mulligan might even send a sharpshooter to watch over him."

"What then, Pa? You planning to shoot one of 'em?"

"Shoot one? Leslie, those men are no more than worker bees sent out to make honey for the company bosses. Now, should Mulligan show up, I might be tempted. But not his men. No, they're only pawns on the Chippewa Lumber and Boom Company chessboard." John broke into a sprint. "C'mon, boy. We've got to finish up in the root cellar before your ma puts dinner on the table."

On that April morning, a father and son raced the quarter-mile through the pasture between huge pine stumps, unaware that they'd set the stage for the bloody showdowns ahead.

7

The Third Letter

Late that night, Hattie closed the bedroom door. The cabin was quiet now, the children in their rooms fast asleep. She doused the lamp and slipped into bed. Her husband, half-asleep, stopped snoring long enough to turn over. Hattie reached out, placing her hand on his shoulder.

"You've made us a fine home here in the woods," she whispered.

He stirred.

"There's not a woman across this land who wouldn't desire such a comfortable, safe place to raise her children, in spite of being set off so deep in the woods—so far away."

"Not that far," said John. "Just far enough that others can't interfere. No one can touch us here, Hattie. Thornapple Farm can be likened to a gleaming castle on a mount, much as in Myra's book about Robin Hood."

"Yes. Our own castle. And you're my king, John." Hattie wrapped her arms around him and pulled the covers over them to keep the world away.

The next morning, Hattie arose to find her husband at the dinner table writing another letter.

> Mr. Horace G. Chichester, Secretary
> Mississippi River Logging Company
> St. Paul, Minn.
>
> It recently came to my attention that the Cameron Dam on the Thornapple River is on my wife's land. Since we purchased our property in 1900, your company has conducted three log drives, sluicing 80,000,000 board feet of logs across our dam. The State Charter of 1874 declares that the owner of any dam used to sluice timber has legal right to claim ten cents per thousand board feet. Thus, regarding my previous demand for rightful compensation, I now must amend as follows:
>
> In addition to my claim for $1,717 back pay and the $96 crop damage owed me, I now assess the Chippewa Lumber and Boom Company 10¢ per 1,000 board feet which comes to $8,000 even. Therefore, the total amount owed to me by your company is $9,813.00.
>
> Until I receive payment in full, NOT ONE LOG shall pass through my gates. And if I see any of your men tampering with my dam, I'll blow it and them sky-high. Your remaining 6 or 8 million feet of pine now waiting

upstream for the spring drive will be stranded in the woods.
Mr. Chichester, if I don't get what's due me, those dag-
blasted logs can lay and rot for all I care, and you will have
to answer to your boss to explain.

John F. Dietz
Winter, Wisc.

Hattie read the letter over her husband's shoulder.

"John," she said, "do you think you might be asking too much?"

"They could have gotten by for less had they met my earlier claims. Now I'm going to make them squirm."

"But nearly ten-thousand dollars?"

"I'm claiming only what's rightfully due us. Not one penny more. We'll soon see how badly they want that pine."

"I worry that you're stirring up a hornets' nest. By your own account, Frederick Weyerhaeuser has enough wealth to do anything he wants."

"This is a man's business, Hattie."

"But you mustn't put our family at risk over this. Please, John!"

"Don't fret, Mother. The company will pay up. I've a plan that will force their hand. We'll have what's due us and this whole affair will be behind us soon. You'll see."

Hattie stared at her husband with concern. "I hope you're right, John. Oh, I *so* hope you're right."

John Dietz's demand coupled with his decision to fire a warning shot near the Chippewa Lumber and Boom Company workers created a stir within the company. The wheels had been set in motion. But neither John nor Hattie could foresee the trouble ahead. Several days later, the children, playing in the yard, heard a familiar voice from the far side of the dam.

"Papa! Papa!" shouted Stanley. "There's a man by the river calling for you."

John grabbed his Winchester and field glasses and ran outside. "Mister Sargent?" he shouted. "Is that you?"

"Yes. I've come with news from the company, Mr. Dietz. Very good news, sir."

"Well, don't just stand there. Those signs aren't meant for you. C'mon up!"

Thomas Sargent trotted across the footbridge and through the pasture, meeting John halfway.

"You're back soon, Mr. Sargent."

"Mr. Dietz, we parted as friends and I return as a friend. Please, sir, call me Thomas."

"Very well, Thomas. And you can call me John." The middle-aged farmer and young surveyor shook hands. "What news have you, Thomas?"

"I've been sent to make an offer on behalf of the Chippewa Lumber and Boom Company. They'd like to see this matter promptly put to an end."

"Yes, I imagine they would."

"I can offer you a fair sum in order to resolve this conundrum."

"It's about time. They know I'm holding all the cards now. Why, they should be bent over backwards trying to appease me. So, what's their offer?"

Sargent unbuttoned his shirt pocket and pulled out a roll of twenty-dollar bills bound with a rubber band. "Five-hundred dollars, John. Cash on the barrelhead."

John laughed. "Thomas, you know I've got no quarrel with you. But hear this. I'm no fool. And I'm not about to let the lumber company buy their way out from under a nine-thousand-eight-hundred-dollar debt for a piddling five-hundred bucks. No, sir! Thomas, you scurry back to Chippewa Falls and tell your superiors that John F. Dietz expects payment in full. In greenbacks. Either that, or they'll not see one solitary stick of pine float down the Thornapple ever again. Tell them, Tom. And don't lower your eyes when you do. For they're not half as worthy of respect as are you, a man making a living, trained with a useful skill, rather than those penny-pinching weasels getting rich off the backs of their workers."

"John, are you sure about this?"

"Goodbye, Thomas Sargent. Godspeed."

On April 27, 1904, two weeks after Thomas Sargent's offer, another caller arrived—Sheriff Charles Peterson—a friend ever since John rescued the election from the Courthouse Gang two years earlier.

"Hello, John," the sheriff shouted from across the river. "I brought your mail."

"By all means come across, Charlie." John shouted. "I'll have Hattie brew us up some coffee."

Soon the men sat in the living room, the sheriff at the table and John in his wooden rocker with his feet up on a nail keg stool, looking through his mail.

"John," said the sheriff, "You'll see among your mail a blue envelope. It's from the clerk of courts. That's an injunction demanding you not interfere with the Chippewa Lumber and Boom Company log drive."

John looked at the sheriff before pawing through the half-dozen letters on his lap. He studied the blue envelope. "Odd," he said.

"Odd?"

"I see *my* name on the envelope."

Sheriff Peterson looked puzzled.

"Charlie, they are barking up the wrong tree. I'm not the owner of this farm. Hattie is. The whole shebang is in her name. She owns it. Thus, whatever's inside this envelope isn't worth a hill of beans."

The sheriff laughed. "Judge Parish wrote that up after hearing from the Chippewa Lumber and Boom Company."

"You tell Parish that I said he should keep his nose out of this matter. My claim has nothing to do with Sawyer County. It's between me and the company." John leaned forward and flipped the envelope into the fireplace.

Watching it burn, Sheriff Peterson nodded his approval. "It's just as well, John. It was only a bluff, anyway. I wouldn't pay it no mind."

"I don't intend to, Charlie. More coffee?"

Right to Left: John, Hattie, Myra, Clarence, Leslie, Johnny, Helen, & Stanley

My Home is My Castle

Under a silky silver moon, Clarence, Leslie, and John Dietz shared the narrow walkway above the Cameron Dam. Next to them stood the capstans, large, iron wheels that controlled the gates. Each brother had a crowbar. Their father held a stout chain, a padlock, and his loaded Winchester.

"All right, boys, first, we open gates one and two."

Leslie placed his crowbar in the capstan above the gate. Clarence followed his lead.

"Ready, Pa?" Leslie asked.

"Let her go!"

As the boys pulled, the capstan turned and the gates lifted, allowing water to rush out from underneath.

"Higher," said John. "Right to the top."

Soon the roar of rushing water thundered down the river channel, almost cresting its banks. Several logs floated toward the gates. But with no lumberjack there to sluice them through, they lodged crosswise. More logs soon jammed in behind. Both gates reached the top, held wide open by the capstans.

"Good," said John. "Now for the third. Open her up."

With all three gates open, Leslie secured the capstans with the chain. Clarence snapped the padlock shut.

"That's fine, boys. Now we'll stand watch for a while. The roar coming up from the dam is bound to bring someone from downstream to nose around. And I don't want those gates tampered with by some Camp Four do-gooder."

"I don't get it, Pa," said Leslie. "If we strand all their timber upstream, what makes you think the company's gonna pay you a penny?"

"Because what's done can be undone," answered his father. "As soon as I get what's due me, we will remove the chain and lower the gates. Then, once the pond fills up again, Mulligan's men can run their drive and do whatever they want with those logs."

In the moonlight, John and his sons watched the far side of the pond. More logs floated down and jammed in above the gates, the force of the water piling them atop each other. The roar from below the dam intensified.

"Look," Clarence said, pointing across the pond. "Two men. See 'em?"

"Hold up there!" yelled John.

The men kept coming.

"Stop where you are!" John screamed.

"They can't hear you over all the noise, Pa," said Leslie.

"Let's see if they hear this." John raised his rifle, aimed high, and fired above the men who immediately stopped.

John fired another round, the bright flash from his rifle showing his location. "Stay off my dam!" he ordered.

Both men turned and ran back downstream into the darkness.

"You think they'll be back, Pa?" Clarence asked.

"There's no telling what Mulligan might do now that we've shown our colors. Go back and get some sleep, boys. I'll be along in time. I want to stand watch for a bit. Make sure nobody tampers with those gates. By daybreak, there won't be enough water upstream to float a gol-dang duck."

"We're staying, Pa," said Clarence.

"What?"

"In case something goes wrong."

John shook his head. "Nonsense. You boys need your sleep. Chores to do tomorrow. Plowing, too. Now, git!"

Leslie plopped down next to a birch tree. "I'm staying as long as you, Pa. And, by gosh, that's that."

"Goes for me, too," added Clarence, sitting against the same birch.

"You boys must've inherited your stubborn streaks from you mother," their father said with a grin. "All right. Stay if you want. But there'll still be chores to do tomorrow, tired or not."

John jostled his sons at dawn's first light. "Wake up, boys. It's time we headed home."

Clarence stirred, then stood and stretched. The river no longer roared. He looked upstream to see thousands of huge, pine logs mired in the mud on the exposed riverbed. The timber stretched far up the sides of the now-drained holding pond where the logs had floated hours before.

"It worked, Pa," he said. "Just like you said it would. There'll be no driving those logs for a month or more." He nudged his brother. "Get up, lazybones. You gotta see this."

"Gosh," said Leslie, rising to his feet. "Just look at all that pine stuck in the muck with no place to go. Wait till Mulligan sees that! He's bound to be hoppin' mad, Pa."

"That's not our concern, boys. By golly, we've sent a loud message to the lumber trust that the Dietz family means business. If they thought for one minute we were bluffing, this should convince them otherwise."

"Somebody's coming," said Leslie, pointing downstream.

John raised his field glasses. "It's Mulligan."

"You gonna shoot him?" asked Clarence.

"He's not carrying a gun that I can see. I won't shoot an unarmed man. Not even a no-good mud-sucking lumber company foreman."

Nearing the dam, Mulligan stopped and raised both arms. "I'm not armed, Dietz." His voice boomed through the early morning mist. "I don't mean no trouble."

"Turn back, Red. I'd rather not shoot you but will if I must."

"I only want to talk."

"You can come as far as my dam, Red," answered John. "But not one step more. If you or any Camp Four man sets one foot on my dam, I swear I'll shoot his toes clear off."

Mulligan stood at the far side of the dam, forty yards from John and his sons. "You sure went and done it this time, Dietz. Only a fool like you would dare to twist a wildcat's tail."

"The company's been given my terms. Yet they sits down there in Chippewa Falls and disregard me. Well, Red, once they learn that they stand to lose about to lose six-million board feet, they're bound to take notice."

"That timber don't mean nothin' to a fella like Weyerhaeuser. He's got so many camps strewn across the land that it's no more than a drop in the bucket."

"Who are you trying to fool, Mulligan? At seven-dollars-a-thousand, that pine stranded in the mud upstream is worth over a hundred thousand dollars. Don't tell me that he isn't twitching every time he thinks of it and itching to get it to the mill. Why, I bet it's the first thing he thinks of when he rises each morning and the last thing before he turns in."

"Dietz, do you really think he'll meet your demands? I mean … almost ten-thousand dollars? You may think you've got the upper hand. But mark my words. The company will find some way to get you off their back."

John laughed at the camp boss. "You listen and listen good, Mulligan. Go tell your bosses that John F. Dietz will shoot on sight anyone who trespasses. The law says a man's home is his castle and affords that man the right to protect it. And, by God, that's just what I intend to do until I receive my rightful comeuppance. Now git!"

Red Mulligan took three steps toward the camp then turned back. "You ain't heard the last from me, John Dietz!" he shouted. He turned again and headed back toward Camp Four.

"Boys," said John, "grab your crowbars. We can go now."

"What do you think the company will do next, Pa?" asked Leslie.

"My guess is that they will send someone here to dicker with me, offer a pittance to get control of their pine again. But I won't have it. And that's when they'll finally understand that John F. Dietz means business."

9

Uncle Will

John and his sons looked back at the logs stranded upstream from the dam.

"Boys, I could go for a hot cup of coffee and a stack of buttermilk flapjacks before we do the morning chores. How about you?"

"With butter and maple syrup," added Clarence.

"And sausage?" asked Leslie.

"Why not?" said their father. "We've got the upper hand and that's cause for celebration. This calls for a feast."

Suddenly, Clarence bolted homeward. "Last one there's a rotten egg," he yelled.

Their father watched his boys race ahead, satisfied he'd done what was best for his family. But Leslie's question prompted him to wonder what the Chippewa Lumber and Boom Company might do next. If they make a fair offer, should he compromise? Accept less than the nearly ten thousand he'd demanded? A month earlier, he would have settled for eighteen hundred dollars for back wages and crop damage. But the company ignored his request so he increased his claim, demanding more. Now they'd laughed at him. "By God, they won't laugh now," he said to himself. "Never again will anyone laugh at John F. Dietz. *Never*."

April turned into May and the thornapple trees along the river blossomed bright white, contrasting with the lush greens of the balsams lining the hills across the river. Flock after flock of northbound geese let slip news of another coming summer. Myra watched them from the front porch, wishing she, too, could spread her wings for some unknown destination. As she followed them with her envious eyes, she noticed the man across the river, heavily burdened with two cloth satchels.

"Uncle Will?" she yelled. "Uncle Will!"

Her shout brought barks from Abe, their shepherd, and a wave from her uncle, William W. Dietz. He straightened his hat before coming forward with his load, the straps of the bags over his shoulders. She watched him struggle across the footbridge and plod into the yard.

"Myra," he called. "Come help me with this luggage."

Myra ran across the yard. William set down the bags and hugged his niece. She picked up the smaller of the two satchels.

"Gracious sakes, this is heavy." she cried. "What the dickens?"

"Too heavy for you?" asked Will, offering the larger bag. "Here. I'll trade."

"Too heavy?" she scoffed. "Heavens, no. I carry a dozen buckets of water up to the barn each day. I hardly think hauling your carpet bag from here to the porch could be a burden."

Myra hefted the satchel, threw the strap across her shoulder, and walked with her uncle to the cabin. Hattie greeted them at the door.

"Morning, Hattie," said Will.

"Well, William! What brings you to Thornapple Farm?"

"I'm on my way to Ashland on business. I wanted to stop by and say hello." He stepped inside and shrugged the strap from his shoulder. "Besides, your daughter has a birthday coming up, does she not?" He turned to her. "I brought something for you Myra."

"For me?"

"Yes. A girl shouldn't be denied modern day pleasures no matter where she lives, even out here in the hinterland. Especially a girl going on sixteen. Now, Myra, would you like to chance a guess as to what I have here?"

Myra hefted her bag again and set it on the table. "I know what this is, Uncle Will. You've been saving up magazines for me. Oh, thank you so much! I read every newspaper and magazine that father brings from town cover to cover. I pour over them until the words are nearly worn from the page. Oh, this is wonderful! I don't know how to thank …"

"No, Myra. Not magazines," he said with a grin. "Something far better."

"Books?"

"No."

"New shoes? A dress? The latest from Chippewa Falls? Oh, but your luggage is far too heavy for clothing."

"No, not clothing, either," he said. "Think *music,* Myra."

"Oh, Mother! Uncle Will has brought us sheet music we can use with the pump organ." Turning to William, "Oh, thank you, Uncle!"

"Myra," he said, "It's high time you opened the satchel to see for yourself. Go ahead. Unbuckle the straps. See what awaits you."

Myra pulled the first strap back to release the buckle. She smiled at her uncle and her mother, and then unfastened the strap. Her sister, brothers, mother, and uncle watched her tug on the second strap.

"What's this?" said her father, stepping in from outside. "Well, William! What a surprise!"

"Not now, Papa," said Stanley. "Myra's about to open her birthday gift."

"What gift?" he asked.

"Tsk, tsk, Papa!" scolded Helen. "You mustn't interrupt."

Everyone watched as Myra opened the satchel. She removed a heavy package wrapped in white butcher paper tied with string. She pulled the ends of the string. The paper opened revealing a stack of phonograph records. She picked up the top one and read the label. "'Bill Bailey?'" she wondered aloud. "But …?"

"And twenty-two others," said William.

She pulled another from the stack. "'In My Merry Oldsmobile.' But, Uncle Will, …"

"You're not finished, Myra. Keep looking."

She opened the satchel wider. "Oh, my stars!" She turned to her uncle. "Is this a …?"

Will unbuckled the second satchel and pulled out a large, metal, cone-shaped object. "This goes with it, Myra," he said as he placed the horn on the table. "Now go ahead. Take out what's in your bag and show the family."

Myra lifted the body of a record player from the satchel and set it on the table. William attached the horn, inserted a crank in the side of the box, and turned it a dozen times. With the children fidgeting with excitement, he removed a record from its paper sleeve and set it on the turntable. Will lowered the needle and flipped a switch. Suddenly, John Phillip Sousa's "Stars and Stripes Forever" flowed from the sound horn and filled the room to the delight of everyone there.

Tears filled Myra's eyes. "Uncle Will, I don't know what to say. This is by far more than I deserve."

"Nonsense!" he said. "Modern music is something every young woman across the country wants today. And you deserve it as much as anyone I've ever come to know."

"Oh, thank you, Uncle. I'll cherish every moment we spend playing this … this …"

"*Gramophone*, Myra. It's the latest model Victrola, fresh from downtown Rice Lake."

Her father shook his head. "I'm not so sure I approve, William. Such infernal contraptions are meant only to poison the minds of our youth, purloin their virtue, and pinch the last remaining pennies from the working man's pocket."

"Nonsense, brother. The gramophone is no more evil that that organ you bought last winter. The only difference is that the music flows out by itself. No need to pull stops, press keys, or pump foot pedals."

"Oh, Father, please let me keep it." Myra begged. "Consider the cheer and merriment it would add to our evenings."

"Take it back, William," John ordered. "It's merely one more method for the robber barons to beguile our nation's young people— snake their way into our children's heads— manipulate them. That machine and other such contrivances are unholy insults to God!"

William reeled, and then dug through the stack of records. He stopped abruptly in the middle, pulled the paper sleeve from a disk, and placed it on the turntable. "John," he said, "I beg you to listen to this and then tell me if the gramophone insults our Lord in Heaven."

Myra cranked the crank and flipped the switch and the gramophone played "Nearer My God to Thee."

Hattie faced her husband, but spoke to his brother. "William, thank you for doing this for Myra. I know she will cherish it. We *all* will."

Myra hugged her uncle, and then her father, whose shoulders slumped when she embraced him. "Oh, all right," he grumbled. "For Pete's sake. I know when I've been bested."

"Thank you for letting us keep it, Father." She turned. "And thank *you*, Uncle Will. This is the best day of my life!"

On May 3, 1904, less than a week after the Cameron Dam gates had been raised and thousands of dollars' worth of timber lay stranded upstream, the new county sheriff, Fred Clark, paid a visit. John invited him in.

"John," the sheriff began, "we've been friends for a time."

"Yessir. Goin' on two years, I'd venture."

"Yes. Two years. And I want you to know that I've come today not as the county sheriff, but as your friend."

"Well, that's good to hear, Fred."

"I want you to know there's been some talk around town. In fact, a good deal of talk."

John leaned back in his chair, struck a match, and lit his pipe. "What kind of talk?"

"You've gained many supporters over this Chippewa Lumber and Boom Company ballyhoo."

"As I should. Anybody in my shoes would want what's rightfully coming to him. What's right is right. It's about time the lumber syndicate shared some of the wealth. Why, it's no wonder folks are getting riled up over this."

"*The Hayward Enterprise* has your story plastered all over the front page this week," said the sheriff, handing John a copy. "And I hear that the *Gates County Journal* in Ladysmith is behind you full tilt."

John skimmed over the *Enterprise*. "Says here on the bottom of the front page that President Roosevelt plans to take on the railroad trust. I wonder if he knows what's going on with the lumber trust."

"John, it's true that you've garnered some support, but you should know there are others against you."

"Is that so?"

"Do you recall the night of the riot after the '02 election?"

"Like it happened yesterday."

"The county board you helped to oust that night is back in power."

John puffed on his pipe considering the sheriff's words.

"I want you to know that I'm behind you on this. But, at the same time, I've sworn to uphold the law. John, there's been a warrant issued for your arrest."

"A warrant? I've committed no crime."

"Red Mulligan filed an assault complaint against you. Said you busted into the Camp Four cook shanty and attacked him."

John laughed. "Busted in?"

"That's what he told me."

John puffed on his pipe. "He's a bald-faced liar, Fred. I was invited in. Did Mulligan mention that he offered me coffee and Johnnycake?"

"Coffee? Well … no."

"Of course he didn't. Why would he? Fred, I went there to ask to be paid what the Chippewa Lumber and Boom Company owes me and my family. And I went there on the suggestion from one of Mulligan's superiors, Horace Chichester."

"Are you saying you didn't attack him?"

"I defended myself after that big oaf came at me with both fists, hell-bent on beating the tar outa me. Oh, you should've seen it, Fred. I laid him out flat. Red Mulligan, that muscle-bound Irish bulldog who brags that no man ever once knocked him down was lying in a heap on the cook shanty floor when I left."

"So, *he* started this brawl?"

"And I ended it. With a right and a left and another right. That's when this other fella came at me with a stick of firewood. Let me tell you, he won't ever try that again. No sir."

"So, you'll swear in court that you didn't start the fight?"

"You go ask any man there, if you can find one who won't lie to save his job. Heck, Fred, half the camp stood by and watched. And I gave them a good show. They saw me give their boss a good shellacking. It was Red Mulligan who threw the first blow. But I threw the last."

"Nevertheless, it's my duty to serve the warrant. Come to town with me. We can sort this whole matter out in front of Judge Parish."

"Parish?" John laughed again. "John Parish is in the pocket of the gol-dang lumber syndicate sure as hell is hot. I don't stand a chance to get fair consideration from him and you know it." John drew on his pipe again. "Go back and tell Parish that you did your best to serve the warrant for my arrest as ordered, but I refused to accept it."

"I can't do that. I'm sworn to uphold the law and that includes serving warrants and bringing in those served."

"Look, I regret putting you in an awkward position, Fred, but I have a farm to run. Mulligan's lies don't change that one iota. And neither does a piece of worthless paper from some crook of a judge. No, I'm not going with you as your prisoner. And although you're always welcome to stop by for a visit, I don't want any more lawmen coming out here with warrants and writs and injunctions and such folderol. Tell our county chairman that. Go tell Harry Shue that I said this place is my home. My *castle*. And I have every right to defend it from the lumber syndicate and any weekend lawmen send to invade it. And tell them I keep my rifles loaded and that I said John F. Dietz won't be taken alive. See how that sits with them, Fred."

"All right. I will deliver your message. That will put it on them to figure out what happens next. Meanwhile, I think you should be prepared. When Judge Parish and Chairman Shue hear I didn't bring you in, they'll surely send others."

"Let them come."

"Bill Giblin would be thrilled to bring you back in chains."

"Giblin? The portly souse I disarmed in the courthouse that night?"

"Now he's Deputy Giblin. Sheriff Peterson swore him in before leaving office."

"Well, let him come. I'll box Giblin's ears good this time. Much the same as I did Red Mulligan's."

"He won't come alone."

"Like I said, let Giblin come, Fred. If he or anyone else from the county sets foot on my land, I'll send him back with his rump heavy with birdshot. And I'm not the only one in the family who can wield a firearm."

Sheriff Clark shook his head. "John, you don't understand what you're up against. The company has ways of getting what they want. There's even talk about bringing in the state militia."

"State militia?" John drew from his pipe again. Then he pointed the stem at the sheriff. "Fred, if the county board wants the blood of our soldiers on their hands, that's up to them, not me. Sure, the militia might get me, but not before I sting some of them."

"You'd do that? Shoot at our soldiers only doing their duty?"

"Duty? I will defend my home and family. That's *my* duty. And my God-given right. As for you, I think you'd be better off tending to your hotel business than getting mired up in this lumber trust turmoil."

Sheriff Clark put on his coat. "My friend, it would be far easier for you to come along with me," he pleaded. "Face this minor charge and get back to your farm, back to your family."

"And give Mulligan time to drive his pine downstream? I won't do that, Fred. You probably knew that before you came."

"Yes, I suppose I did." Fred Clark reached his right hand out for a shake. "So long, John. We'll see each other soon, I'm sure."

10

Valentine

On the 10th of May, 1904, one week after Sheriff Clark's visit, Clarence and Leslie heard shooting far to the west as they forked the last of the winter hay from the back of the loft.

"Hear that gunfire, Clare?" Leslie asked.

"Better go tell Pa. It's probably nothing, but he should know just in case."

An hour later, as Clarence and his father laid fresh straw in the stalls, Leslie shouted from the hayloft. "Pa, there's a man on horseback coming down the tote road. He's carrying a white flag."

"Can you tell who it is?"

"No, Pa. Too far."

John set down his pitchfork and reached for his field glasses. Peering from the dark interior of the barn, he focused the binoculars. "Why, it's Valentine Weisenbach," he said. "What the dickens is he doing here this time of day?"

"And why's he carrying a white flag?" asked Clarence.

John stepped out into the sunlight. "Leslie, run to the cabin and let your mother know we have company." Then he cupped his hands around his mouth and bellowed, "Come on in, neighbor."

Valentine lowered his flag and rode forward at a trot.

Leslie slid down the rope from the hayloft and sprinted across the yard to the cabin.

John reached for his rifle, then handed it to Clarence. "Here, Son. Keep watch from inside the barn. Mind you, stay in the shadows."

"Pa," said Clarence, "Mr. Weisenbach is a friend. Why …?"

"Clarence, right now I can't afford to trust anyone other than family. Two sheriffs have failed to serve papers on me. I figure by now the county board chairman is just itching to bring me in. Might even have a reward posted. There's no telling who might try to hog-tie me and haul me off to jail for some whiskey money."

Valentine rode up to the barn. "Whoa, girl," he said, tugging back on the reins.

"Morning," said John. "Sort of early in the day for a visit, isn't it?"

Valentine, out of breath, slipped off his mare. "John, there's men comin'."

"What?"

"Comin' for you."

"Who?"

"Lawmen. Three of them. By wagon. From Hayward. With rifles."

"How do you know?"

"I seen 'em up close. All three wore badges. John! They shot at me!"

"What?"

"Scared me half to death."

"Where?"

"On the road. Up a spell from my cabin."

"They took a shot at you?"

"Three shots."

"Why?"

"I think they thought I was you."

"Me?"

"I heard this wagon comin' down the road, see? So I dove into the brush and hid behind this big oak to watch them pass by. That's when I seen 'em. Three men ridin' along slow. They's passing around a whiskey bottle, laughin' and carryin' on. I'm pretty sure one was Red Mulligan. 'Bout that time, one of them sees me and hollers out, 'There's Dietz! Shoot him! Shoot the SOB!' That's when him and this fat fella start blastin' away at me."

"My God, Valentine! Are you all right?"

"Both of them missed me clean. Another fella sprung off the far side of the wagon and run like a scared rabbit into the woods."

"But they missed you, Valentine. Fate was on your side."

"Fate? It probably had more to do with them being half drunk."

"What did you do?"

"What the heck could I do? I put up my hands and hollered out, 'I ain't Dietz! I ain't Dietz!' Once they saw that I didn't have a gun, the fat one asked me about you. I told him I ain't seen you for a 'coon's age."

"Do you think they're coming here?"

"I don't know. But I thought it best to ride over here by the back trail and forewarn you."

"I'm glad you did. You're a good friend. You've always been a good friend."

In the barn, Clarence rested his father's Winchester against the wall. He stepped out into the sunlight and nodded hello to their neighbor.

"How do, Clarence?" Valentine said. He turned back to John. "I've been watchin' the papers. Like most folks 'round here, I figure you got to stand your ground. You're entitled. The company makes a fortune off the pine. They can afford to pay you what you have comin'. Instead they get the sheriff's men after you. By golly, it ain't right."

"I'm ready for them," said John. "If those men who shot at you have no more sense than to show up here, they'll wish to Heaven they hadn't. I'll send 'em back down the road with their tails between their legs."

"There's no tellin' what them fools might do, John. I'm headin' back to my place. If you need me, send over one of your boys and I'll be here in a wink." Valentine mounted his horse.

"Mr. Weisenbach!" said Leslie from the porch. He crossed the yard carrying a flour sack. "It's a loaf of Myra's bread, fresh from the oven."

"Leslie, you tell your sis I said thanks a heap."

John waved his hat as their neighbor turned his horse. "Come back any Tuesday and we'll have another loaf for you, my friend."

Valentine rode off. "Pa," said Clarence, "what should we do?"

His father stroked his chin. "First we finish up in the barn and then we get to weeding the rutabaga patch."

"But what about those men who shot at Mr. Weisenbach?"

"Three drunken lawmen? Nothing much to do. By now they're shaking in their boots, wondering if I know about the shooting and if I'm coming after them. No, we'll not see hide or hair of them today. Best thing for us to do is to carry on. Do our chores as usual."

"You sure, Pa?"

"I'm sure. But there's something we are bound to do first."

Perplexed, Leslie looked up at his father.

"Let's go get us a slice of Myra's bread—while it's still warm."

Sheriff Charles Peterson

Sheriff Fred L. Clark

Sheriff William Giblin

11

Subterfuge

Bill Elliott, the Sawyer County Deputy who had jumped from the wagon and run into the woods, wandered for hours. Lost in the vast forests surrounding Winter, Elliott spent the night in the rain. At daybreak, shivering from cold, he began wandering again.

Bill Giblin and Red Mulligan, the men who'd fired at Valentine Weisenbach, searched for Deputy Elliott all day. That evening, as darkness settled throughout the forest, they made their way to the Hotel Winter, booking a room for the night. They ordered a supper of boiled potatoes and salt pork, then spent the rest of the night in the hotel bar.

"You figure Bill's dead by now?" asked Giblin.

"Nah," grunted Red. "A man can live for days out there if he uses his wits. Long as he doesn't do something foolish like drown in some river or fall through a bog."

"What about wolves?"

"Aw, they don't bother anybody. Not unless there's some weakness. Or the smell of blood. No, wolves are no problem. The cold might get to him but not the wolves."

"That's good. I'd just as soon not have to tell Sheriff Clark that one of his deputies is dead."

"Well now, think about that."

"Huh?"

"If word should happen to get out that Bill Elliott was shot by John Dietz and suffered and died out in the woods, it sure would turn folks against Dietz. Nobody would trust him ever again. Get my gist?"

"Yeah, I get it, Red. I could let the newspapers know that Dietz and his pal, Weisenbach, jumped us. Then Dietz shot Elliott as he ran off into the woods. The papers would eat it up. Dietz would be ruined."

"He'd never be able to show his face in public again."

"But what happens if Elliott walks out of the woods?"

"I thought about that. I know people in St. Paul who can deal with such things. Private detectives that work for the company. Men who could keep Elliot under wraps while folks chew on this for a time. Once people get it in their heads that Dietz is a coldblooded villain, he'll be done for. Then Elliott makes a miraculous return from the deep forest. By that time, nobody will trust John Dietz."

"I'll do it," said Giblin. "You send word to your boss first thing tomorrow. Let him know our plan. If he approves, I'll contact the newspapers." Mulligan motioned to the bartender for another round. "There's something else we can do, Red."

"What?"

"Tomorrow morning, John Dietz is going to fire a couple of rounds at Camp Four."

The bartender brought two more bottles.

"Giblin, you don't need another beer."

"No, no. Listen, Red. Tomorrow you and me head out to your camp just about the time your work crews are showing up for their breakfast. You go inside and go about things as usual. I'll stay back in the woods a ways and fire at the cook shanty. Everybody will think it was Dietz. That ought to put the frosting on the cake."

Mulligan grinned. "Giblin, you're not half as dumb as people say."

Rain fell across the forests, swamps, lakes, and streams of Sawyer County throughout the night. Around ten the next morning, Deputy Elliott, tired, wet, and hungry, stumbled onto a trail that led to a tote road leading to Camp Four. Utterly exhausted, he staggered through the cook shanty doorway and collapsed, unconscious.

"Who the heck is that?" asked the camp cook looking between the rows of tables and benches.

"One more mouth for you to feed, Mr. Rice," joked one of the men.

"That's exactly how my uncle looks after he's been on a three-day drunk," said another.

"Is he one of ours?"

A lumberjack sitting nearby lifted Elliot's head and then dropped it to the floor with a thud. "He ain't nobody I ever seen before. Maybe he got lost and wandered away from some other camp."

"Could be that he's some trout fisherman from down south," came another guess. "Milwaukee or Chicago, perhaps."

"Splash some water in his face," said the cook. "If he don't come to, then lay him down on an empty bunk until Mulligan gets back. He's the boss. Let him figure out what to do with the drunken stumblebum."

Mulligan and Giblin reached the cutover surrounding Camp Four later that morning. Mulligan pointed at a knoll overlooking the Dietz farm and, two-hundred yards northeast, the Camp Four cook shanty.

"Bill," he said, "that rise over there is a good place to hide. Keep to the brush and behind a stump. You'll have a clear shot at the cook shanty from there. It's the long building with two chimneys on one end."

"I see it, Red." He checked the action of his rifle, confirming it was loaded. "I'll aim for that small window on the right and fire two shots. Then I'll head back to the hotel. Meet me there later."

"No, Bill. I need to stay here. It's fine that you deputized me and all. I want John Dietz out of the picture as much as you do. But I'm paid by Chippewa Lumber and Boom. I better stay here. You head back to Hayward and start spreading the news about Dietz killing Bill Elliott. You might start by suggesting that Sheriff Clark contact Elliott's pa."

"His pa? What's he got to do with it?"

"Bill Elliot's pa is the sheriff down in Chippewa County. If this news don't stir up the hornets' nest, nothing will."

"We still have to find Elliot. We should mount search parties."

"I'll take care of that. I can send my men out to search. If he turns up, fine. If not, better yet." Mulligan pulled out his pocket watch. "No time to lose. You'd better get set. I'll head for camp."

"Mulligan," said Giblin, "stay clear of the windows."

The Camp Four boss waved without turning around. Minutes later, he entered the cook shanty. "What's for dinner, Mr. Rice?"

"Burnt beans and tater-bug stew," laughed one of the men.

"Say, now!" shouted the cook. "If you don't like my cooking, go fill your belly someplace else."

"There *is* no place else," came a reply. "We're ten miles from Winter and a dang long hike to Hayward."

"Then don't complain," said the cook. "Look at all the shoe leather you're saving!"

"Saving us shoe leather is one thing. Making us chew it is another," one man joked.

The laughter and jeers ended when Mr. Rice said, "Boss, some tramp stumbled into camp today. He barely made it through the door before he passed out cold."

"Drunk?" asked Mulligan.

"I figured so. I had him laid out on one of the empty bunks to dry out. When he does, should I send him on his way?"

"Let me have a look," said Mulligan. "But *after* I get some food in me, burnt or not."

Mulligan left for the sleep shack after his meal. There, on the third of eighty-eight bunks, he saw Deputy Bill Elliott. Mulligan looked behind to be sure nobody heard him. He shook Elliot's shoulder. "Wake up, Bill. Wake up."

Elliott stirred.

"It's Red."

Elliott looked up. "Who?"

"Red. Red Mulligan." He shook him again. "Bill, listen. It's important you don't tell anybody your name. Tell them you forgot it. Hear me? Bill? Bill?"

"Why?"

"Orders from Giblin," said Mulligan. "You are not to tell anyone who you are. It will help us get Dietz. Understand? Do you understand, Bill? Do-you-un-der-stand?"

Elliot sat up. "Sure. No name. I'm hungry. You have any food?"

"Stay here. I'll bring you something from the cook shanty. Remember, Bill, you gotta keep this under your hat."

"Okay, okay. Under my hat."

As Mulligan crossed from the sleep shack to the cook shanty, he looked toward the knoll, wondering why Giblin hadn't fired yet. Mulligan avoided the window, and then passed through the doorway just as Giblin pulled the trigger.

The bullet fired from the knoll shattered the cook shanty window. A split-second later, the report of Giblin's rifle startled everyone.

"Get down!" shouted Mulligan. "It's Dietz. He's gone mad!"

A second bullet tore through the window frame, grazing the arm of one of the lumberjacks. The rifle's report echoed down the river.

Everyone but Mulligan waited for a third shot. He walked confidently to the broken window and peered out. "There he is!" he bellowed. "There's Dietz! I seen that yellow-bellied coward hightail it over that knoll beyond the river."

"Where?" asked another man looking over his shoulder.

"Running back to his farm," Mulligan said. "Didn't you see him?"

"Maybe so. I saw something out there," replied the lumberjack.

"It was Dietz, all right," said Mulligan. "I seen him plain as day, running across the cutover with his rifle in hand."

"Johnny Tracy took a bullet in the arm," said the cook. "I'd better get a bandage on it."

"Aw, I'll be fine," said Tracy. "Barely a scratch."

"Nonsense!" Mulligan shouted. "As soon as we get you bandaged up, you'll be off to Chippewa Falls to get that nasty wound of yours tended to by a doctor."

"Nah," Tracy said. "I'll be fine."

"You could get an infection," said his boss. "Gangrene. You don't want to lose your arm, do you, Johnny?"

"Well, no. But …"

"Fine. We're agreed then. The company will cover the doctor bills and your pay for as long as it takes. What's more, the newspapers will make you a hero. Folks will soon know you as Johnny Tracy, the hardworking lumberjack who got shot by the mad outlaw, John Dietz!"

In the sleep shack, Deputy Bill Elliott slept soundly in another man's bunk. He'd neither heard the gunfire nor knew of the plan to tell the newspapers he was dead. A quarter mile south, John and Clarence prepared the seeds they planned to sow the next morning. They counted on the rutabagas from those seeds to feed the family over the next winter, a winter that seemed so far away on this sunny spring day in 1904.

12
Myra's Sharp Tongue

Three days later, John Dietz strode across the freshly tilled north field as a pale sun crested the eastern treeline. Around his neck hung a bag of seed oats that fed into a hopper strapped around his waist. As he turned a crank on the right side, the oats sprayed out before him.

Suddenly, a bullet tore into the ground twenty feet in front of him. John flinched at the sound of the shot. He looked up to see a puff of smoke four hundred yards away, near the Camp Four ox barn. More smoke. Another bullet screamed by, smacking a stump. As the echo from the second shot ebbed, John cupped both hands around his mouth.

"You there!" he bellowed. "Fire once more and I'll come over there and beat you bloody with your own rifle." A moment later, a man carrying a Winchester scrambled from the barn and ran toward the cook shanty. Laughing, John shouted, "Tell Mulligan no more shenanigans!"

John resumed his up and down stroll across the tilled field, turning the crank on his seeder before returning to the cabin to find his children seated at the table for a breakfast of eggs from their own chickens, bacon from a hog Clarence butchered, and rye bread baked fresh that morning.

"John," Hattie said, "were those gunshots I heard?"

"Hmm?"

Myra sensed he wanted to avoid the conversation. "Shots, Father. First one, and then another, mere seconds apart."

"Oh, that?" John scoffed. "It was nothing. Just some fool across the river whistling bullets overhead."

"My word, Father! Was he shooting at you?"

"Don't fret, Myra. I was so far beyond range that he could have shot all day without hitting me."

Shocked, Hattie turned to him. "What if one of those bullets was to hit its mark? What then?"

"Bah. Not to worry, Mother."

"John, what would I do if one of those bullets laid you up? You know I can't run this farm myself."

"We'd run it for you, Ma," said Clarence, pouring more coffee.

Leslie nodded. "Maybe not as good as Pa, but we could do it."

"That's far from the subject at hand, Clarence," declared Myra. "My gosh, we are talking about losing Father. Maybe forever. It's a far greater concern than who can and who cannot manage a farm."

"Lose Papa?" asked Helen.

Hattie returned to the cook stove. "John Dietz, you've no right to put this family at risk."

"Nor yourself," said Myra. "Heaven forbid you'd fall to one of the company's riflemen."

"Papa? Are you going away?" Helen cried.

"No, Princess. Never." John shook his head, perturbed by the tone of the conversation. "Aw, you all fuss over nothing. Don't worry. The Almighty looks over us." Quick to change the subject, he added, "Tomorrow's Saturday. I intend to take the wagon into Winter for store goods and our mail. Leslie, Clare, you'll both be coming along."

"Can I come with?" asked Helen.

Stanley looked up from his breakfast. "I want to go, too."

"Not this time, children," said their father. "Your brothers and I will have our hands full. I need seed corn and onion sets for planting, salt licks for the sheep, and chicken feed. *Bushels* of chicken feed."

"I'll prepare a list of dry goods I'm short of," said Hattie.

"Say, Pa," said Clarence. "Molly went and stepped on her milk pail this morning. Dumb old cow."

"Busted, is it?"

"Leaks bad."

"I'll add a bucket to my list," said Hattie.

"Boys," said their father, "on our way to town, we're stopping off at Emil Hanson's farm. He's got a cultivator up for sale. I need to strike while the iron is hot."

Hattie, at the stove, took notice. "Dear Lord," she said over her shoulder, "how much will *that* cost us?"

"Mother," he replied, "modern farms need modern machines. If it helps us turn this ground into the successful farm we fancy, it'll be well worth the money."

"How much, John?"

"Don't you go worrying about it, Mother. I'll figure a way to pay for it. And I won't dip into your egg money."

"Pa's right," said Clarence. "I hear some outfits now use tractors with gasoline engines instead of horses to work the fields."

"Bah!" said his father. "They tried that with steam engines. They were so dag-blasted heavy that they spent more time stuck in the fields than plowing them. Machines powered by gasoline won't be any different. They are merely one more underhanded ploy by the factories back east to pilfer money from hard-working farmers."

"Well, I don't agree, Father," said Myra. "I read in *Harper's Bazar* that the modern gasoline engine will change life forever. In fact, *Harper's* says that one day more folks will travel by automobile than by horse-drawn carriages or wagons. And *Harper's* says …"

"*Harper's, Harper's, Harper's!*" barked her father. "Child, you'd be better off reading my books than those loathsome periodicals. They'll twist your mind if you're not wary about what they print."

"Father, modern magazines tell us what's changing day by day."

"Your sister, May, should not be saving those magazines for you. Myra, I'll not have you bringing those amoral, unprincipled journals into my home!"

"Fine! I'll read them in the barn."

"Myra!" snapped her mother. "You mind your sharp tongue. You're not talking to one of your brothers!"

Myra lowered her head. "I'm sorry. But I so enjoy *Harper's*."

"John," said Hattie, "Myra needs to see such magazines from time to time. How else can a young woman this far out in the pinery know what's fashionable?"

"Fashionable, Mother?" he replied. "Mackinaw coats and Oshkosh overalls, *that's* what's fashionable. And vulcanized rubber barn boots. And manure forks made by Sears and Roebuck."

"And Winchesters," added Clarence. "Don't forget Winchesters."

Myra glowered at her brother. Her father rose from the table, crossed the room, and entered the bedroom. Seconds later, he returned.

"Here," he said, flopping a Sears and Roebuck catalog on the table. "You'll learn more about fashion from this book than any of those magazines." He glared at Myra. "Young lady, never let me catch you bringing that big city bunkum into my home again. Never!"

The children, afraid to make eye contact with their father, stared in silence at the thick book. Finally, Stanley reached for the catalog. "See that?" said his father. "Little Stanley is a boy who minds his pa. Once he's done with the book, you others can take turns with it. But *after* your chores. Now finish up your breakfast and get to it."

The Dietz children finished eating without a word. One by one, they excused themselves. When Myra left, her mother noticed tears welling in her eyes.

"John," she said quietly, "I wonder if you're being a little too harsh."

"With Myra? Bah! She's strong. She's a Dietz, isn't she?"

"But Myra needs more than we can offer her out here in the woods," Hattie reasoned. "I worry that without proper tutoring she'll never grow to become a wise, broad-minded woman. She needs a teacher."

"You taught school children before we were married, Mother. You still can."

"Perhaps the little ones, John. But Myra needs to learn from others.

She's a bright girl. We need to allow her to expand her knowledge, to develop into a modern-day woman. She needs a different teacher, John, someone from outside of our family, someone from beyond Thornapple Farm."

"Send my daughter to some faraway schoolhouse?"

"It is precisely what our children need."

"Children? You mean to say …"

"Clarence and Leslie need schooling as much as Myra and Helen. And soon, so will Stanley."

"I won't hear of it. The closest schoolhouse is in Winter, ten miles away. Two hours' morning ride, then two hours each night. What's more, they'd be traveling in the dark from fall till spring. And I'd have no one here to help with chores. No, Hattie. I won't hear of it."

"Then we must tell the town board to build a schoolhouse someplace near. One way or another, the children must have their education. It's their right by law!"

"Mother! Once you get an idea stuck in your corset you don't leave as much as a hair's breadth worth of room to wheedle you otherwise."

"For once, John Dietz, think not of yourself, but of the children."

John glared at his wife, then softened. "I'll look into it, Hattie."

"That's all I expect of you, my dear. Thank you."

The curtains draped before the door to the girls' room parted. "Thank you, Father," said Myra pushing it aside. "I so want to be the best I can be for you and Mother. And if I … if *we* can learn more about the world outside, I know I will be."

"You were eavesdropping?"

"I tried not to. Really I did. Oh, don't be cross, Father." Myra tilted her head like a puppy pleading for a morsel from the table. "Please?" As always, her gentle, beguiling tone of voice dissolved his anger. "And trust that if schooling is provided, I'll do my best, not just to learn my lessons, but to help Helen and Stanley and our neighbors learn theirs."

Disarmed by his daughter once again, John turned to his wife. "Mother, you're right. All children have a right to an education. The Village of Winter shall make no exception. By God, I'll see to it they provide an education for our children, come hell or high water."

Excitement flashed across Myra's face. "Father? Do you mean we might …"

"Child, I'm going to get you and the others proper schooling."

"Really?"

"Princess, you can count on it."

13
All Lies!

The next morning, when the boys came in from chores, they found Myra at the table reading a copy of the *Chippewa Weekly Herald.*

"Where the heck did you get that?" asked Clarence.

"Clarence Dietz!" shouted Hattie. "You want your mouth washed out with soap again?"

"I'm sorry, Ma. Wasn't my fault. It sort of slipped out."

Myra shook her head. "Helen and Stanley were playing outside after breakfast. They found the paper stuck in the woodpile."

"You mean someone came into our yard last night?" asked Leslie. "Who in the world …?"

"Stanley," said Hattie. "Fetch Father from the barn. He needs to know about this."

Minutes later, Stanley followed his father into the kitchen.

"What's so dag-blasted important that I can't tend to my work?" asked John.

"Pa," Leslie said, "Somebody hid a newspaper in the woodpile last night."

"I heard no shepherd's bark," he replied.

"It must have come from a friend," said Myra. "A person the dogs trust."

"Brought by the light of the moon?" said Clarence.

"More likely brought while we were at chores," said Leslie.

"Father," said Myra, focused on the paper, "I think I know why someone brought us this newspaper."

The others turned to her.

"*Deputy sheriff is murdered!*" she exclaimed.

"Murdered?" shouted John. "A lawman? Where 'bouts?"

"Not far from here. Listen, Father." Myra read from the newspaper. "*Desperado resisting court order slays deputy. Escapes to the woods on Winter Road. Posse in pursuit. Desperate fight is looked for.*"

"My heavens," said Hattie. "How could such a thing happen?"

Myra continued. "*Sheriff's Deputy, William Elliott, fatally shot along the Winter Road by John Dietz, who …*"

"Me?" asked John. "They accuse me?"

"*… Who, with his family, has been holding up the Chippewa Lumber and Boom Company's drive at the Cameron Dam*"

Her father interrupted again. "Hogwash! It's all nonsense. What other lies did they print?"

Myra continued. "*Dietz has been holed up on the Thornapple River with rifles for the past two weeks. An injunction was issued, but he paid it no attention.*"

"The company is trying to turn the public against me," he said. "Making me look like some animal. Go on, Princess. Read on."

"Dietz told the sheriff he did not care if President Roosevelt himself issued the injunction."

"There's the first thing said that's right," he said. "Go on."

"Sawyer County Judge John K. Parrish ordered Dietz arrested Wednesday. The sheriff was driven away by Dietz. The Judge then ordered the sheriff to capture the desperado with a posse. Deputies Giblin, Mulligan, and Elliott left for Dietz's home, believing they could affect the arrest without a posse. When the dam was reached, Dietz rushed from ambush, ordered them to hold up their hands, and fired, fatally wounding Elliott. Dietz then hurried into the woods and has not been located. The posse is now scouring the woods. It is believed that Dietz will not be taken alive."

"Will not be taken alive?" Hattie shouted.

"The sheriff ordered his deputies to get the drop on Dietz and kill him if necessary. Dietz is a desperate character. For ten years he has lived in abandoned lumber camps, hunting, fishing and trapping."

"All lies!" shouted John. "Ten years, indeed! They make us sound like squatters. And for them to announce to the world that I murdered some deputy? What nonsense!"

"We know better, Pa," said Leslie. "It's all claptrap to make you look like an desperado."

"Go on, Myra," said Hattie.

"Dietz was sheriff of Barron County at one time," read Myra.

"Another lie," said Clarence. "That's Uncle William who was sheriff there. Who writes such gobbledygook?"

Myra continued. *"The dam in dispute was built in 1877. The Chippewa Lumber and Boom Company owns land on the north side and claims that it has owned it for four years. Two weeks ago the company sent their surveyor Thomas Sargent to interview Dietz. Sargent found him desperate. Deitz demanded ten cents per thousand board feet for logs that had passed through the dam in the past four years. He wanted from $15,000 to $20,000. He refuses less and continues guarding the dam with Winchesters."*

John huffed. "Well now. Sounds to me like they've raised the stakes. I asked only for nine thousand. They say fifteen? Twenty? Perhaps it is time I raised my demand. What else does it say, Myra?"

She read on. *"The logs are held at another dam above the Cameron Dam and cannot be brought to this city. Dietz frequently fired at men who attempted to get logs over the disputed dam."*

"More lies," he said. "I fired only three times and not once near enough to any company man to do harm. And I sure as heck didn't murder any sheriff's deputy."

Myra read on. *"Elliott resided at Eau Claire, the son of Chief of Police Chub Elliott. He was thirty-eight years old and once undersheriff of Eau Claire County."*

"Mother," said John, "It's time I wrote to the papers and told them the truth. There must be a few editors out there that ain't in the pockets of the lumber syndicate. It would take but a few good newspapermen on my side who are willing to print the truth to remedy this."

"Helen," Hattie said, "be a dear and fetch your father pen and ink."

"And paper, Mama?" Helen asked.

"Yes, Princess," replied Hattie. "Paper would be nice, too."

"Perhaps Father is right," said Myra. "Maybe the newspapers can help us clear the air."

Helen placed the paper, pen, and ink on the table before her father, her small hands dwarfed by his.

"I'll write to several of the papers not obligated to the trust," he said. "I know of a smattering. Osceola, comes to mind. And the *Hayward Enterprise*, of course."

"The *Minneapolis Tribune* should be included," Hattie added.

"And the *Star*," he said. "And the *Milwaukee Journal*. I'll post my letters Saturday when we go to town."

"Do you really think it will help, Pa?" asked Leslie.

"Son, few people realize the power of persuasion our newspapers have with the public. And when it comes to the lumber syndicate, folks have been woolgathering far too long. It's time someone stirred them from their slumber. It could be that I am best suited for the task. Perhaps, now, it's up to me to wake up the people."

14

Harper's Bazar

Late Saturday evening, Myra paged through the family's Sears and Roebuck catalog by the light of a single kerosene lamp. Their calico cat purred, sleeping near the hearth. The children played with their wooden toys on the braided rug before the fire. Suddenly, Helen looked up. "It's Papa!" she shouted. "Papa's home! I hear him singing!"

The children raced to the door, Myra and Hattie close behind. Standing on the porch, they watched the wagon and team appear out of the darkness with Clarence, Leslie, and their father, singing "Oh, Susannah!" at the tops of their lungs. They pulled a rattling, clattering cultivator behind the wagon. As the horses came closer, Myra and the others joined in the singing. *"Oh, don't you cry for me. For I come from Alabama with my banjo on my knee."*

After tending to the horses, the Dietz men entered the cabin. The calico cat raced to the door to greet them. Leslie stooped to pet it.

"I'm so hungry, I could eat a horse," said Clarence, hanging his barn coat on a nail.

"Then you'll have to butcher old Meggie," said Hattie. "But if you'd rather not, I have venison and baked beans in the oven. Your favorite. But I hope it's not burnt. I've had it in since before sundown, thank you very much."

"We didn't dilly dally, Ma," said Leslie. "Not one iota."

"Sit down, the three of you. Myra will dish up your supper."

"I've news from town, Mother," said John.

"And plenty of it!" blurted Leslie. "Myra! Wait until you hear!"

"That's enough, Son," said his father. "I'll explain."

Hattie sat back in her rocker, her knitting in her lap and a basket on the floor beside her. The cat sat near, eyeing the colorful balls of yarn in the basket.

"First off, I bought the cultivator from the Hansons."

"Are we now broke?" Hattie asked.

"No, Mother. We are not broke." John sipped his coffee. "Emil said I could pay it off on time. He wanted fifteen dollars now and five dollars-a-year for the next three years."

"Thirty? Thirty dollars?" replied Hattie. She rocked faster. "Well! I'd never figured you for a man who'd go into debt, John Dietz." The calico's tail twitched to and fro as Hattie pulled a strand from a ball of yarn.

"Tell her, Pa," said Leslie.

"I offered Emil five dollars cash and a bull calf next spring. He said that was fine. We now own a cultivator."

"And a dandy one, too," said Clarence. "It's even got a seat to ride on and everything!"

"My stars," said Myra, placing plates before her father and brothers. "No more walking behind the horses to work the field? How modern!"

"Imagine," said Leslie, "having clean boots after working a field."

"That's good news," said Hattie, rocking slowly now. The cat batted a ball of yarn out of the basket and ran after it.

"There's reason for Emil's generosity," John said.

Hattie stopped rocking. "And what is that?" The cat returned, taking cover under her chair.

"Emil's been reading the papers. He told me face-to-face we've been cheated by the company. And he's not the only one who thinks so. Others know of our plight. Many others."

Hattie rocked again, focused on her knitting. The cat batted another ball of yarn from under her rocker.

"Ma," said Clarence, watching the cat, "I had four men shake my hand in town. Can you imagine? Four men! And I didn't know a-one of 'em."

John sipped his coffee again. "Seems as though the whole town is on our side. Even Charlie O'Hare. Although he was hesitant to admit it outright."

Myra's eyes widened. "You spoke with Mr. O'Hare, Father? Mr. O'Hare of the school board?"

"I did."

"About sending us to school?"

"Yes. But I'm afraid you won't be going off to school each day come September, Myra."

Myra's shoulders slumped. "Well then, our home lessons simply will have to do, I suppose."

John laughed. "No, Princess. They won't. And that's what I told Charlie O'Hare."

"In no uncertain words," said Clarence. "Right, Pa?"

"Right, Son. And thanks to there being a crowd gathered to pat us Dietzes on the back, Charlie *reluctantly* succumbed."

"Succumbed?" asked Helen. "What's that mean?"

Curiosity flushed across Myra's face. "Yes, Father. What *does* that mean?"

"Just you wait till Pa tells you," said Leslie, grinning.

"Children, I finagled us our very own school. The county is going to pay for it and, come September, they will provide you with your own teacher."

"Really, Father?" Myra exclaimed. "Our own private teacher?"

"Nonsense," said Hattie, rocking faster again. "Where will this woman sleep, John? And who's going to feed her?"

"Oh, that's the best of it, Mother. Not only will the county pay the teacher to live here, it will also send books and a chalkboard and slates and even money for the teacher's room and board. Not much mind you, but if we're prudent, it should prove to be adequate."

"I'm not keen on this," said Hattie, rocking rapidly. "A stranger in our home? Another mouth to feed? Who is this person? Does she have any of the skills that make a good teacher? Or is she some wayward woman that the county wants out of its jail? Oh, John. What *have* you done?"

The children looked at their father for an answer. He finished the last of his beans, drank the rest of his coffee, and said, "Hattie Dietz, you were a teacher before we wed. You will know if the person they send is up to the task. If she's not, I'll haul her straight back to the school board and tell them to find someone better."

"And what makes you think the board would listen to you, a backwoods farmer?"

John stared at his wife coldly. "Hattie, do you think the county would dare send us someone inexperienced? Some … ne'er-do-well? My word, Mother! After all the guff that's been given us? Why, *The Examiner* would have a field day with such a story. *All* the papers would! And with so many folks now in sympathy, we'd have a new teacher out here in a wink."

Hattie didn't reply.

"Oh, please, Mother?" begged Myra, "This is the chance of a lifetime."

"Pa says we'll have to add on a schoolroom," said Leslie. "Right, Pa?"

"Yes. It'll have to be finished by the beginning of the school term."

"My stars," said Myra. "It's a dream come true. Father, will there be other children coming here?"

Hattie cringed, rocking fast again. "Heavens, John. Other children? What have you gotten me into?"

"Not to worry, dear. There'll be no other children. At least not this year. For the first school term, the students will all be Dietz family children."

"Mother?" said Myra, "I swear I will do all I can to help make our little Thornapple School the finest in the county."

"I'm sure you will," said Hattie, nodding. Her rocking slowed again. "I will, too, in spite of it all."

Myra turned to her brother. "Leslie, are you ready for a second helping?"

"You bet I am."

"Likewise," blurted Clarence.

She took their plates to the stove.

"Myra?"

"Oh, I'm sorry, Father. Are you ready, too?"

"I brought you … something."

"Oh, wait till you see, Myra!" said Leslie.

John pulled a rolled up magazine from his pocket. "Here. This is for you, child. It's the latest *Harper's Bazar*."

Hattie stopped rocking. The cat peeked out from under her chair as Myra took the magazine from her father's rough, calloused hand.

"But … Father, you said …"

"Never mind what I said. Your mother was right. You *do* need to see what lies beyond the forests of Winter, Wisconsin. But Princess, although you're sure to become a woman of the world someday, I want you to know that you will always be my Thornapple girl."

With tears welling, a speechless Myra hugged her father.

"I will finish up here, Myra," Hattie said. "Go now. Read your *Harper's.*" She placed her knitting in the basket and rocked forward to stand.

"*Yowl*" screamed the cat, its tail pinched by the rocker. It raced from under her chair, across the braided rug, and into the boys' bedroom.

"Dag-blasted cat!" said Leslie. "You'd think it would learn."

15

Master J. C. Gates

Clutching her magazine, Myra vanished behind the girls' bedroom curtain. By candlelight, she poured over her *Harper's Bazar* page by page, absorbing every word. Her sister and brothers turned in. Myra blew out her candle and closed her eyes but remained awake. From the other room, she heard her mother.

"Thank you, John," said Hattie.

"Shh. You'll wake the children," he whispered.

"Thank you for everything," she replied quietly. "But especially for trying to understand Myra. She's changing, you know. From a girl to a young woman. She needs … understanding. Now more than ever."

"I'm doing my best."

"I know you are. But it will take more than magazines. She needs to spend time with others."

"Others?"

"Of her age."

"How might that be done?"

"John, we should invite our neighbors to come visit on Sundays. The Olsons up the road, perhaps. They have a daughter her age. As do the Klinghoffers."

"Klinghoffers? Invite Gus and Mable here, Mother? Would they even come?"

"I believe they'd enjoy being asked."

"I hear Oscar Lukenbachen is fixing to hold a barn raising next month. Every man, woman, and child will turn out for three days. And his place is only a half hour walk west of here. Myra could meet all the young people in town. And there's sure to be a Saturday night dance once the barn's put up."

"What about all the lawmen prowling these woods, John?"

"I'll get word to them. Maybe they'll come help."

Hattie laughed. "Goodness, John."

"Speaking of lawmen, there's other news from town, Mother."

"Yes?"

"Valentine's been arrested."

"Mr. Weisenbach? Our neighbor?"

"Seems Giblin and two other deputies surprised him one morning. Nabbed the poor fellow in his own privy. Charged him right there on the spot and hauled him off to the county jail."

"Lord's sake. What's this country coming to?"

"He's charged with the attempted murder of Bill Elliot, that deputy who ran for the woods and got lost."

"But … that was last year. And they found Elliot safe and unharmed."

"It matters not to the county board. It's their way of getting to me."

"But, how is Valentine's arrest going to affect you?"

"Oh, I imagine they'll want me to testify at his trial. They figure they'll get me to go there to speak on his behalf. Then they'll arrest me for the warrants they have against me and Lord knows what else."

"But, John, the papers said Elliot turned up fit as a fiddle in Chippewa Falls."

"I know. This is Bill Giblin's dirty work. I'm sure of it."

"Oh, dear. Poor Valentine, sitting in the county jail. Going stir-crazy, I imagine."

"He's not in jail, Mother. The sheriff didn't keep him."

"No?"

"Somehow our neighbor found enough money for bail."

Hattie turned, her brow furrowed. "Valentine? Where in the world would he get any money?"

"That's the question, is it not? It surely came from the Chippewa Lumber and Boom Company. Mother, they got to him. Valentine is working for them now."

Hattie and her husband sat in silence. Then she spoke. "The marshals want you. The sheriff wants you. This is far from over. They'll come for you again."

"Let them come. I've done nothing. I'll not let them take me. Not alive."

"Don't say that, John. Please. You mustn't."

"I'll defend our family to the gates of Heaven."

"There must be another way. You, me, our children have done nothing more than stand up for our rights."

"Yes. And now we know that folks around here are on our side."

"We'll show them, John. God willing, we will deny them of their hollow victory and live out our lives in good health and prosperity here on Thornapple Farm."

"Oh, but … it rips my heart to say it, Mother."

"Yes?"

"I've lost a dear friend. Valentine can no longer be trusted. The company found a way to get to him. He's now one of their spies. He'll be along tomorrow. I'm sure of it. It's Tuesday. Baking day."

Hattie sighed. "Oh, dear, I'm so sorry. I'll tell Myra. No more bread for Valentine."

But Hattie didn't have to tell her daughter. Lying in the dark in the next room, she'd heard every word.

The next day, as Helen and her mother finished washing the mid-day dishes, they heard a shout from Stanley, playing in the front yard.

"Mama! Come see!"

"What is it?" Hattie yelled through the kitchen window.

"Men, Mama!"

Hattie stepped outside. Stanley pointed beyond the dam. "Over there! See?"

Hattie stretched, staring beyond the pine stumps and summer haze. Two figures stood on the far side of the Cameron Dam's catwalk. "Stanley, where's Papa?" she asked.

He pointed in the opposite direction. "That way."

She turned, peering far across the pasture to see John, Clarence, and Leslie repairing the north fence. Both dogs accompanied them, hundreds of yards away. Hattie turned back to the strangers, and then rushed inside for the field glasses. Helen followed her outside, carrying little Johnny. Myra came next, loading a Winchester.

Hattie fumbled with the binoculars and raised them, turning the focus ring back and forth.

"Who is it, Mama?" asked Helen.

"I can't tell." She adjusted the binoculars and then looked through them again. "Oh, these darn spyglasses!"

"Trade!" said Myra, handing her the rifle. Then, "Oh, my stars!" she exclaimed. "Can it be?"

"Who is it?" Helen asked again.

"I think that's … Uncle William. Yes! What in the dickens?"

Hattie waved her arm vigorously to invite John's brother across.

Hattie turned north again. "John," she yelled across the pasture. "John!"

Realizing her call went unheard, Hattie pointed the rifle skyward and pulled the trigger. The crack of the rifle shattered the still afternoon air. Little Johnny bawled. Near the dam, William Dietz and the man behind him dove to the ground. To the north, the men stopped their fence work to look. Both dogs streaked toward the cabin, barking.

"Mother!" cried Myra. "What were you thinking? You scared the wits out of the lot of us!"

"Oh, dear," Hattie replied. "But, look." She pointed north. "Here comes your father."

John and his sons spanned the pasture on the run, reaching the front porch only moments after the dogs. "What is it?" said John. "Why did you shoot?"

Hattie pointed toward the dam. "We think we saw William."

"Uncle Will?" asked Clarence. "You shot at Uncle Will, Ma?"

"What? Oh, my, no!" replied Hattie. "I shot merely to summon your father."

"Well, Mother," said Myra, "I dare say it worked."

"But … where *is* Uncle Will?" asked Clarence.

Facing the dam, Hattie bellowed, "William! All is safe, now."

The family watched as, two hundred yards away, John's brother slowly emerged from the waist-high marsh grass along the river. He looked side to side and behind as he brushed off his coat and trousers. The second man stood, clutching a carpet bag in each hand.

Clarence waved. "Hello, Uncle Will!"

John cupped his hands around his mouth. "It's all right, William," he shouted. "You fellows won't be ducking any more of Hattie's bullets."

The callers crossed the yard and stepped onto the porch. Hattie smiled sheepishly, noticing the stern look on William's face and grass stuck in his collar. "Oh, dear me," she sighed.

"John," he said. "I spent six years as sheriff of Barron County and only once had the bejesus scared outa me by gunfire. Your better half just doubled that score."

Hattie handed the rifle to Clarence. "Oh, my. I'm so sorry, William."

"Aw, no harm done, Hattie. But next time ring the gol-dang dinner bell. It's less likely to give a body the fits."

John extended his hand. "It's rare for you to visit our Thornapple Farm, Will," he said. "What brings you?"

"This gent," he replied, latching onto the arm of his companion. "Meet your teacher, Master. J. C. Gates. Your county sheriff hired me to escort him here safe and sound so you could make his acquaintance. Master Gates will return in September for your children's schooling."

The skinny, bespectacled, Jeremiah Gates tipped a slightly rumpled derby hat. He stood not as tall as Clarence, Leslie, or Myra. His double-breasted, twill coat seemed out of place here in the woods. His thin moustache was noticeably crooked, as was his smile. J. C. Gates fit the image of a young man eager to be respected as a schoolmaster in order to compensate for his shortcomings. Nevertheless, he'd accepted the position and the Dietz children had their schoolmaster.

The field glasses now suspended from her neck, Myra, came forward. But her father stepped in front of her, hand extended. "Mr. Gates, welcome to Thornapple Farm."

"Er, um, thank you, sir," he replied. "And you, Madam, er, Mrs. Dietz," he stammered, tipping his hat again. "I'm pleased to be of service."

"Pleased and paid well," said William. "Right Jeremiah?"

"Er, well, I shan't complain about my salary, if that's what you're driving at."

William laughed. "The county saw fit to offer extra pay in order to persuade a teacher to come here. Apparently word's gotten out that this might not be the safest place to practice the trade. It encouraged Jeremiah to step forward when no other teacher would."

Myra squeezed out from behind, her hand extended. "We're quite pleased you did, sir. We've long awaited our return to formal schooling."

"This, Mr. Gates, is Almyra," said John, "perhaps your most promising pupil."

"Father, please." She shook Gate's hand vigorously. "Sir, you may call me Myra. When do we begin?"

Gates smiled his crooked smile. "The first Monday of September, Myra. As with the other schools."

"Teacher, we built a schoolhouse," exclaimed Stanley. "Just for you!"

Gates looked left and right.

"Actually, sir," said Myra, "it's little more than a room we've added to our home."

"Hmm," said Gates. "A room? Built for schooling? Why, Stanley, that would make it a *schoolroom*. And schoolroom is merely a hop, skip, and a jump away from schoolhouse, isn't it?"

William laughed. "Now, that's a died-in-the-wool teacher for you. Not a minute has passed and already he has the children working on vocabulary." He turned to Clarence and Leslie. "Boys, on the far side of the dam you'll find in my wagon, a slate chalkboard, another grip, and several boxes for the school. Fetch those so prior to our leaving Mr. Gates can put his *schoolroom* in order for the fall term."

"Yes, sir, Uncle Will," said Leslie.

John pulled the Luger from his belt. "Here, Son," he said, "take this along in case of snakes in the grass."

Gates backed up a half-step.

"A euphemism, Mr. Gates," said Myra, now peering at the wagon through the field glasses. "My father refers to a more devious reptile than you might imagine."

Leslie grinned, slipping the pistol into his barn coat. "Pa, if I see one, should I wing him? Or just shoot to scare him off?"

"Now, hang on, Leslie," said William. "Don't do anything foolish. I can't get tangled up in this tug of war you folks have with the lumber company."

"You aren't on our side, Uncle Will?" Leslie asked.

"Oh, I'm on your side. But I work for Rusk County, now. And even though it's a different county, it's the same syndicate that calls the shots there, just as it does here."

John stroked his chin. "So, Mr. Gates, do you know of our … situation, here on Thornapple Farm?"

"Mr. Dietz," Gates replied, "you'd be hard pressed to find *anyone* in the Midwest who's unaware of your struggle."

"And where do you stand?"

"Me? Oh, my, with *you*, sir. Along with nearly every other citizen in these parts, all but the very wealthy and the politicians the lumber syndicate keeps in their pocket."

"Father is a good man wronged," said Myra. "If not for the greed of the lumber barons and the graft within our county, we'd not be in the fix we are today. I hasten to say that our nation's founding fathers did not have this in mind when they wrote the United States Constitution."

William laughed. "John, when it comes time for you to embark upon the tent show lecture tours, it sounds as though this child may be your best carnival barker."

"Child?" Myra scoffed. "I'll have you know I am no child. I'm soon to be sixteen years, Uncle Will. And like my father, I mean what I say."

"And you say it quite well," said Gates. "Young lady, it will be my pleasure to help you broaden your speaking skills that you may one day share word of your family's quest for fair treatment—if that's what you mean to do, of course."

Myra beamed. "Oh, I'd like that, sir. And as Mother can tell you, I've pledged to work my hardest for you."

"Me, too, sir," Helen blurted.

"Me, too, sir," Stanley repeated.

"You'll find Helen and Stanley eager for schooling," said Hattie. "Leslie? Well, not so much. And as for Clarence ... well ..."

Myra interrupted. "Clare says he won't attend class. He is the eldest and inclined to be rather obstinate."

William chuckled. "A Dietz family trait, eh John?"

"And what's that supposed to mean?" huffed his brother.

"Isn't that what got you into this Chippewa Lumber and Boom Company pickle? Your bullheadedness?"

"No, brother. As Myra said, it was the graft of the county and the greed of the company."

"Whatever the cause, I can't risk my job by getting involved. However, I must mention that on our way here we met several lawmen."

"Lawmen?" John asked. "Where?"

"In the woods across the river. Just beyond the ridge. They've pitched tents. I imagine they're waiting for you to make a mistake, get caught unaware so they can nab you and haul you in."

"And run their dag-blasted log drive," added John. "That's the county's real interest, you know. Those indictments and warrants for my arrest mean nothing. I'm sure they'd be dropped if I'd concede and let them run their drive. Well, I won't allow it!"

"But shots have been fired! And could be again. If so, who might be wounded next? Who might *die* because you and the company can't come to terms? John, for the sake of your family, you must resolve this stalemate and get on with life as it should be."

"Amen to that," said Hattie. She turned to Gates. "I'm sorry, sir. We seem to have forgotten our manners."

"Oh, here come the boys," said Myra.

Hattie took Myra's hand. "Come. Help me set the table. John, I have mutton in the stewpot and potatoes in the oven. We must provide Mr. Gates and William with a proper meal before sending them off."

Helen and Stanley showed Mr. Gates to the schoolroom. Hattie and the others went inside, leaving William and John on the porch.

"You know the company won't yield," said William. "You must settle up when the first opportunity presents itself."

"So, that's your advice? Settle? Sell out? Give up my lawful rights? My *family's* rights?"

"Perhaps you're looking at this all wrong, John. Before all this happened you had nothing. Now you seem to want everything. You and I both know you won't get it. So why not find a place to alight? Compromise. Doing so will make you far wealthier than any of your neighbors. And it will offer something more important than your pride— peace of mind."

"Come and get it!" Myra shouted from the kitchen.

As they walked inside, John turned to his brother. "William, there's no peace of mind to be had as long as the injustices of the robber barons run roughshod over our nation, over the people."

"One man can't change the tide, brother."

"That's what they tried to tell John Brown," John snapped. "Yet he proved them wrong—took on the government— showed them that one man *can* turn the tide. Perhaps *I* am now that man."

"John Brown was a fool."

"But, William, never forget that, because of his heroism, there is no slavery in our nation today."

"There's no John Brown, either. Never forget, they *hanged* John Brown."

Chippewa
Lumber &
Boom Co.

Chippewa Falls,
Wis.
1903

F. WEYERHAEUSER, President
O. H. INGRAM, Vice President
Wm. IRVINE, Manager

16

William Irvine of Chippewa Falls

Helen and Stanley steadied the ewe while Myra squeezed the clippers. A large pile of wool lay beside them. "Thank the Lord this is the last to shear today," said Myra. "My aching hands need a rest."

"What about the others?" asked Stanley.

"Tomorrow is another day."

"Papa said this wool should bring in a few dollars," said Helen.

"Quite a few, I imagine," Myra added. "The market is high this year. After that terrible winter we had, folks are clamoring to buy wool. And we have such a nice flock. So many lambs," she said, motioning toward the sheep pen.

"But must we shear Blackie?" asked Stanley. "She's so beautiful."

"And will be again come fall," said Myra. "But tomorrow she needs to be clipped. Just think of how you'd feel wearing a thick wool coat all summer long."

Myra cleaned and oiled the shears, then bundled the shorn wool into a tight bale. She tied it with twine before stacking it on the other bales. "There!" she said. "Another day's work done. Now who wants to go for a swim?" Both children screamed with delight. "All right," said Myra. "Let's fetch our bathing suits!"

Stanley and Helen both bolted for the cabin, abandoning all thoughts other than the late afternoon swim ahead. Then …

"Brother Dietz!" The shout came from across the river, sending the Dietz dogs into a frenzy.

Clarence and his father cautiously stepped out of the barn. Leslie followed, carrying his father's rifle and the field glasses. Myra, Helen, and Stanley looked on from the porch, quieting the dogs.

"Brother Dietz!" the man shouted again.

"Myra!" bellowed her father. "Get those children inside and keep them there until I say."

"Come, children," ordered Myra. She shuffled them inside.

"Halloo, Brother Dietz!"

"Is that Uncle William?" asked Clarence.

John peered through the binoculars.

"Who is it, Pa?" asked Leslie.

"Danged if I know. But he's dressed like he's bound for a funeral. And he's not alone."

"Why's he calling you brother?"

The answer immediately followed. "I am looking for a fellow Freemason. Brother John Dietz."

"I'm Dietz. Who are you?"

"Brother William Irvine. From down in Chippewa Falls. We met at the Rice Lake Masonic Temple some years back."

"What's he talking about, Pa," asked Leslie.

"I became a Freemason when I sold real estate in Barron County. If I'm not mistaken, that man over there is the Secretary of the Mississippi Lumber Company and overseer of the Chippewa Lumber and Boom Company. A died-in-the-wool lumber tycoon."

"The enemy, Pa?"

"We'll soon see." John turned back toward the river. "Brother Irvine. State your business."

"I've come to settle this minor dispute between us. May I come across?"

"Are you armed?"

"No. Never."

"You may cross. Alone."

John and his sons watched the visitor cross the dam and approach. The tall, thin lumber company executive wore pressed trousers, a gentleman's coat, and a tan top hat. One of his gloved hands held a black walking stick. The other carried a leather briefcase. He crossed the pasture between the large stumps, meeting John who stood on the porch, rifle in hand. Clarence and Leslie stood nearby, each leaning on a pitchfork.

"Brother Dietz," said Irvine, "it's good to see you once again. I've come to help resolve our differences in an amicable fashion."

"Then you've brought my back pay? Money for my damaged crops? Good! And what's owed me for sluicing logs over my dam? Did you also bring that?"

Irvine laughed. "Better yet, Brother, I carry with me news of an offer that's sure to satisfy both parties, relieve you of all court complaints, and give both of us the quietude we deserve."

"I'm listening," said John.

"Certainly you'll agree that, even though you and I represent two completely different sides of this predicament, it is best for two Freemasons to work things out, to find the best solution to whatever conundrum we may face. Don't you agree, Brother Dietz?"

"I'll give you that much."

"And we owe it to the other Freemasons in our brotherhood to find an mutually satisfying solution. No?"

"Yes, I suppose we do."

"Well, here is my offer, Brother Dietz. I will *personally* guarantee full payment of your claim for $9,813 directly from the treasury of the Chippewa Lumber and Boom Company, provided we both enter into arbitration."

"Arbitration?" John turned to his boys and wrinkled his nose as if he smelled a foul odor. He turned back. "And who would you choose to arbitrate? Perhaps … Red Mulligan? Or Bill Giblin? Or maybe that old coot Frederic Weyerhaeuser, himself?"

Irvine laughed. "I enjoy a man with a sense of humor, Brother Dietz. No, I would insist on this being a fair process for both sides. Our primary arbitrator would be none other than the Honorable David H. Wright, Grand Master of the Illinois Freemasons. He would appoint four more former grand masters from Wisconsin and Minnesota to assist. We would then meet in St. Paul where you and I lay before them our claims, counter claims, and arguments. Naturally, my company would shoulder all expenses. After they deliberate, we abide by their final decision. Of course, I would see to it that all charges against you would be dropped. So you see, Brother Dietz, this would be eminently fair to both parties and would allow my company and your family to tend to far more pleasant business. What say you?"

John contemplated the offer a moment and then asked, "Are you saying that your company is in position to have all charges, all warrants, all injunctions against me dropped?"

"Precisely."

"And these charges would not surface later, perhaps in some different manner?"

"I would see to it, personally."

John paused in thought again.

"Brother Dietz, this is a good way for both of us to free ourselves from this tangle. The best way out."

"Do you read the newspapers?"

"Newspapers? Yes. Of course."

"Then you saw the headline in *The Chippewa Weekly Herald* that your superior, Frederick Weyerhaeuser, might one day be wealthier than even John D. Rockefeller?"

"Yes. I did see that."

"And when asked by a reporter how much money he had, Weyerhaeuser answered by saying not even his accountants can tally the total sum. Did you read that?"

"Well, yes. I saw that in the *Herald,* too. But, what has that to do with …?"

"It causes me to wonder, Brother Irvine. Having that much money— that much power—well … might he be able to cast wide influence?"

"Sir?"

"Can he not manipulate anyone on God's green Earth? Anyone?"

"Are you suggesting all five grand masters could be swayed, Brother Dietz?"

"Oh, I'm not suggesting any impropriety. I'm merely asking a question, wondering aloud if the lumber syndicate might already know the future result of such arbitration—might have already known the future outcome even before you left Chippewa Falls."

"Now see here, Dietz."

"Dietz, you say? Hmm. Not ... *Brother* Dietz?"

William Irvine rose from his chair and stood in silence staring at the wary woodsman before him. "I came here in good faith," he said. "I want to help find an equitable solution. This arbitration idea is a worthy opportunity, a chance for you and your kin to return to normal life. Will you help your wife and children, John? Will you agree to arbitration?"

John paused, considering his response. "At first your company offered nothing. Later, your surveyor, Thomas Sargent, offered five hundred dollars. Now you show up with this arbitration ruse."

Irvine huffed. "Ruse, sir?"

"It's now quite clear that the company will offer more. But how much more? Perhaps when they realize they stand to lose millions of board feet, they will come to terms."

"I assure you, sir, we *are* trying to come to terms."

"If that were true, you'd have come with a cash offer in hand. Have you the cash?"

"I do not."

"Precisely! Therefore, it is obvious to me that my best option is to wait and see what comes next rather than frog leap into your dubious arbitration scheme."

"Be sensible, Dietz. Arbitration is the best way out."

"No, Brother Irvine," said John, pointing toward the dam. "*That* is the best way out. I suggest you make haste. It's a long buggy ride back to Chippewa Falls."

17

US Marshal William Pugh

Myra, her brothers, and their father shared the task of watching over the dam through the summer and into the fall. Winter's freeze up came early, ensuring the timber above the dam would stay put. Snow soon masked the logs from view. For the next five months, the Thornapple bottomland looked like any other north country river landscape.

Following every winter storm, Clarence and Leslie shoveled paths between the cabin and the root cellar, privy, and barn. They watched over the livestock, cleared the rooftops, and broke the ice covering the cistern that provided water for the family and the livestock, all in addition to their daily farm chores.

In the cabin, Helen, Myra, and their mother kept the fireplace and the cook stove burning. When not in the kitchen preparing the next meal, they were sewing the clothing the family would need for next summer's farm work, knitting new socks, or darning the holes in old ones.

Washday meant heating ice-cold water, washing and wringing out the clothes, and either hanging them outside on the clothesline where they'd freeze stiff in the wind or hanging them inside where they'd clutter their rooms until dry.

Though it was true that winter brought many changes to their daily routine, two things remained constant—the unity and love that kept the Dietz family strong, and the plotting by the lumber syndicate to overpower them, take over the dam, and drive the timber come spring.

And yet, day by day, the children completed lessons in reading, penmanship, arithmetic, and grammar. Each night, the children sang songs or listened to stories read aloud by Myra. The little ones played before the fireplace while the older boys whittled. Sunday evening saw the family engaged in Bible readings, worship, and song.

Unbeknownst to the Dietz family, their case had found its way to the Chicago Federal Building. Ownership of the Chippewa Lumber and Boom Company had been transferred to the multi-state Mississippi Lumber Company, Frederick Weyerhaeuser's syndicate of sawmills and distributors. This allowed the company to seek recourse before a federal judge and enforcement by federal marshals. An injunction, a subpoena, and orders to capture and bring John F. Dietz to justice followed.

On the rainy morning of March 11, 1905, all seemed right in the Dietz cabin. On the floor before the fireplace, baby Johnny played with wooden toys carved by his brothers. Hattie busied herself sewing flour sack curtains for the cabin windows. In the schoolroom, Myra, Leslie, Helen, and Stanley concentrated on their studies under the tutelage of their schoolmaster. On the front porch slept the family's dogs, Abe a shepherd-wolf mix, and Quincy, a water spaniel. High above, Clarence repaired cedar shakes loosened by winter's ice.

Suddenly, Abe and Quincy barked.

"Pa!" Clarence shouted from the rooftop. "Somebody's here!"

John ran from the root cellar to the cabin for his rifle. He stepped onto the porch to find a lone man curbed by the dogs in the yard.

Fear in his eyes, the cowering intruder held both hands high. "Call them off! Please!" he screamed.

"Who are you?" shouted John.

"Deputy United States Marshal William Pugh, sir. Please! The dogs, Mr. Dietz ... sir."

"What do you want?"

"I'm unarmed, Mr. Dietz. And on the fair and square."

"Answer my question, Marshal. What do you want?"

The marshal tried backing away from the dogs. "I've ... I've come from the state capital."

"What on Earth for?"

"It's the Cameron Dam, sir. I wish to speak with you about ..."

"Save your breath, Marshal. You might as well turn back right now. Ordering me to kowtow to the Chippewa Lumber and Boom Company won't do either one of us a lick of good."

"Please Mr. Dietz," yelled Pugh. "I've traveled two days by train and buckboard. A few moments of your time is all I ask. I assure you, sir, I am unarmed. I swear."

John stared at the trembling young man standing in the drizzle. He then scanned the woods beyond the cutover and across the river. Seeing no conspirators, he shouted, "All right. But keep your hands up where I can see 'em."

The rest of the Dietz family and Mr. Gates stepped onto the porch. Clarence seized the dogs. He ushered Abe and Quincy into the cabin and returned.

John turned to the children. "Get back to your studies. Myra, take little Johnny to the schoolroom for a time while your mother and I visit with this young fellow. We won't be long."

"Yes, Father," replied Myra, scooping up Johnny from the porch floor.

"Marshal," said John, "This is my wife, Hattie."

The marshal nodded hello. "It's a pleasure, ma'am."

"Come in," she said, "I'll fetch some coffee."

"Have a seat," said John, flopping back into his reading chair.

Marshal Pugh hung his hat on a nail near the door and draped his rain slicker onto the back of a chair before sitting. He looked around the living room. A small pump organ stood next to the fireplace. Books lined the top of the mantel. Next to them sat two Luger automatic pistols and a box of cartridges. Above the books hung two Winchesters. To the left, a double-barrel shotgun stood near the door. Near the window, another Winchester. Pugh looked down at a handsome, braided wool rug. There, both dogs lay staring up at him. Neither blinked.

"State your business, Marshal," said John.

"It's a mighty long way one must travel to find you, Mr. Dietz."

"Yep."

"You've no train nearby?"

"Marshal, you knew that before you left Madison."

"Yes, I suppose I did." He glanced at the dogs again. "Um, your farm is ... isolated."

"Isolated?" replied John, his patience waning. "Oh, I hadn't notice that. Why, thank you."

"Far from town, I mean," continued the marshal. "Rather ... remote."

"Remote?" said John. "We like to consider it *secluded*."

"Ah, yes, secluded," said the marshal staring at the dogs staring at him. "A good word, secluded. And remote."

"Marshal Pugh," said John, "precisely what brought you way out here to the *remote* edge of the frontier, rife with dangerous wildlife and snarling desperados?"

"Well, to find you, sir."

Hattie brought each a cup of coffee, before taking a seat at the table with hers.

"Mother," said John, "this man came all the way from the capital just to find me. Can you imagine that?"

"Alone?" asked Hattie.

"Mrs. Dietz?"

"Let me try again, Marshal," she said. "Did. You. Come. Alone?"

"Well, um, no, ma'am. I'm here with others."

"Marshals?" asked John.

"Yes, sir. Other marshals."

"How many?"

Pugh glanced at the dogs and then the rifles and the Lugers over the mantel. "Five. Five other federal marshals, sir."

"And just where are these five other federal marshals?"

"Well, they ... they elected to wait."

"Wait?"

"On the far side of the river, sir."

John sipped from his cup. "Six of you, eh?"

"Yes, sir. Six."

"And how is it that *you* are the one chosen to enter the lion's den?"

"Lion's den, sir?"

"Come now. Surely you'd not travel all this way without hearing of my reputation as a bloodthirsty outlaw. Tell me, William, did you draw the short straw?"

"Straw? Well, no. We are federal marshals. We do not draw straws."

"Then, why you, sir?"

"Because I am the leader of my team."

"You are the leader of your team, and yet, *you* crossed the dam. *You!* What raw courage! But why in the dickens, Marshal, would you do such a foolhardy thing? Why not send one of your underlings? Why, Marshal, you could be set upon by outlaws or wolves or swarms of mosquitoes and disappear into the swamps never to be found! Why risk your life?"

"Sir?"

"Have you no good sense?"

"Well, you see, Mr. Dietz, it was my duty."

"Ah, yes." John turned to his wife. "Hattie, did you hear that? *Duty!*"

"I heard it, dear."

John stared at Pugh. "*Duty* to every American, eh Marshal? Or perhaps *duty* to the timber tycoons and their crooked pals in government, to the men who tinker with the nation's purse strings. *Duty* to the wealthy few who keep us all in rags, surviving on rutabagas and boiled potatoes while they dine on roast leg of lamb, lobster salad, and strawberry tarts a la crème served on saucers imported from China. All while sipping imported wine. No, Marshal! Admit it. You aren't serving the good people of the United States. You are serving the robber barons."

"Mr. Dietz, may I explain?"

"Marshal!" bellowed John. "What in God's name happened to your constitutional duty to protect the average citizen from those black-hearted scalawags who would steal from the common man all that he might ever possess?"

Marshal Pugh didn't answer.

John sipped his coffee again. "As I said before, Marshal, state your business."

"Hmm? Oh, yes." Pugh glanced at the dogs again. "Well, uh, I have news from Madison, sir."

"Did you hear that, Mother? Marshal Pugh says he has news from Madison. Came all the way up here to share it with us."

"What news?" asked Hattie. "Did Governor La Follette intercede on our behalf as my husband requested?"

"Governor? Why, no, ma'am. I mean ..." He looked at the dogs again. "Well, that's not why I'm here."

"Hattie, dear," said John, "our governor is a busy man. Isn't that so, Marshal Pugh?"

"Well, I wouldn't know. You see, I'm not with the state. I am a *federal* marshal."

John ignored him, turning instead to his wife. "Hattie, it's not been long since we wrote to the governor. Or spoke with Bob McCormick."

"United States Senator McCormick?" asked the marshal.

"We're old friends."

"John and Senator McCormick go back quite a ways," agreed Hattie.

"I see. But ...." The marshal glanced at the dogs again, noticing their eyes trained only on his. "Well, I'm not here on behalf of Senator McCormick or the governor, Mr. and Mrs. Dietz."

John leaned back, finished his coffee and leaned forward again. "Then, Marshal Pugh, just why did you come all this way? Over three-hundred miles. Two days by train and buckboard. What the devil do you want?" Louder, now, "What is so dag-blasted important that you and five others came way the heck up here in the dreary month of March?"

Pugh locked eyes with the dogs again, and then slowly reached into an inside pocket, pulling out an envelope. A growl from the shepherd sent the envelope back. "S-sir, I've come to serve an injunction."

John bellowed with laughter.

"And a subpoena."

John laughed louder.

"William," said Hattie with a smile, "you'll have to excuse my husband. You see, we've already refused enough injunctions and subpoenas and claptrap and prattle and gabble and twaddle to keep our fires burning until summer. What makes you think we'd accept yours?"

"Well, I ..."

Hattie continued. "I think you should go now, William."

"Mrs. Dietz, I came to serve these papers." He reached into his coat and then glanced at the dogs again and withdrew his empty hand.

John slowly rose from his chair and set his coffee cup on the table. "Is there anything else, Marshal?"

Pugh stood, bringing another growl from Abe. "Mr. Dietz, I hereby place you under federal arrest."

John laughed again. "Marshal," he replied. "I have work to do. Three hogs to castrate this morning. I suggest you be on your way."

Nervously, Pugh asked, "You'll not submit to arrest, sir?"

"Of course not. Not to those who came before and not to you now."

"I must inform you that resisting arrest will go on your record, sir."

"Look, Marshal Pugh. I am not resisting arrest. I am *refusing* arrest. Put *that* on my record."

"William?" said Hattie, "is there anything else?"

Pugh looked again at the dogs and the guns on the mantel. "No," he replied, "I suppose not."

John put his arm around the marshal's shoulder. "Well then, Marshal William Pugh, it has been a pleasure visiting with you. Isn't that right, Mother?"

"Leave your cup on the table," she said, opening the door.

"Yes, ma'am." The marshal carefully placed his cup on the table. Stepping onto the porch, he pulled on his slicker, then left.

"Stop right there!" ordered John.

The marshal gasped. Eyes wide, he turned, trepidation pasted across his face. "Sir?"

John tossed him his hat. "You'll need this. And watch your step crossing the dam. It'll be a mite slippery in this dag-blasted drizzle."

The Cameron Dam

18

Mary Almyra Dietz

Hattie returned to the kitchen. Myra joined her father on the porch. Together, they watched Marshal Pugh cross the yard. As he passed by next winter's firewood, he turned back to see John and Myra watching him. He laid the blue envelope on the woodpile before hurrying off. Like the lawmen who'd come to Thornapple Farm before him, he left empty handed.

"An odd sort of fellow," said Myra.

"Odd, indeed."

"Father, what do you plan to do with that envelope?"

"Oh, burn it like the rest. Or let the river take it. To me it's nothing."

"He spoke of other marshals. Need we worry?"

"We must keep our guard up and our eyes peeled. Warn the others to stay clear of the river bank and the woods. Should these marshals seize one of my children, I'd be forced to surrender and face the courts."

"Yes, Father."

"Meanwhile, the Dietz home is a fortress. Our castle on the mount. The walls are thick. The windows are few. No one can approach within thirty rods without being seen. And they know that if I sense someone is about to invade our home, I'll not hesitate to shoot."

"But shoot only to scare them, Father. Am I not right?"

John didn't reply.

"Father?"

"I've no intention of taking another man's life. But Princess, this is our home. Should anyone approach, intent on harming us—any one of us—I will do all within my power to stop them."

"So many people are now on your side, Father. That will end if you kill someone. Certainly, you know that."

"What I know is that my family and this farm take precedence over all. Nothing else in life matters to me, Princess. Nothing."

Across the river from the farm and beyond the first ridge, stood five large military tents. A ring of stumps encircled a fire pit between them. Nine men, three in militia uniforms, conversed, warming their boots by the fire. Two other men cleaned their rifles. One whittled. Another scratched out a melody on a poorly tuned fiddle while the fellow next to him wrote in a journal.

A short fellow wearing a blood-stained apron, stepped from one of the tents. He hung a copper pot from a hook suspended inches over the hot coals before returning to the tent. A moment later, he returned with a large chunk of raw meat that he dropped into the pot. Next, he added a bucket of water and a handful of salt. Looking around, he studied each man. "Where's that fifth?" he boomed, startling the others.

"Here," said the whittler. He put the whiskey bottle to his lips before handing it over. "Say, Mr. Rice, you're not fixing to pour good, store-bought liquor into your pork belly soup, are you?"

"Bite your tongue," Rice replied. He raised the bottle and guzzled his fill. "Wake me up in a couple hours," he said, handing the fifth to the nearest man.

"Will do, Mr. Rice," replied the lawman, tipping the bottle up. He finished off the little whiskey left, slapped in the cork, and pitched the bottle over his shoulder into the brush behind.

From the woods to the west emerged three uniformed men carrying rifles. "Our watch is up," said one. "Next crew better get a move on."

"What's the rush?" asked the fiddler. "You figure Dietz is about to mount an attack? Like Teddy Roosevelt charging up San Juan Hill?"

"Orders are orders," replied Marshal Pugh. "And whether you're one of my men or one of the private detectives hired by the lumber company, you *will* follow my orders. Singleton. Jeffries. Brady. Get your tails to the lookout posts on the double."

"Remind me what we're watching for, Marshal," said Jeffries.

"Comings and goings. Anything unusual. And don't forget to make a written note of what you see. That's what your log book is for."

"How 'bout that little missy?" asked one of the men by the fire. "Did you see her struttin' around this morning?"

"I seen her, Jake," answered a thin, uniformed man. He leaned his rifle against a tree. "She was out there hanging her bloomers on the clothesline. Mercy, me! Now there's a sight to turn a fella's head."

"Did you log it in your book?" asked the fiddler. "That's bound to be the most interesting entry of the day—the sight of a girl hanging up her bloomers far out in the woods."

Quiet laughs spluttered from all but Marshal Pugh.

"Now you sidewalk detectives listen good," Pugh said. "You might draw your seven-dollar-a-day wage from the lumber company, but it is the federal government that's running *this* campaign. You will do as ordered or you will pack your rucksack and start walkin' home. And that's *without* pay. Any questions?"

The only sound came from the boiling of the soup in the copper pot.

"Now, get to your posts on the double," said Pugh. "And, for Pete's sake, try to stay awake."

"Myra?" John called from his rocking chair. "Myra!"

"I'm in the schoolroom, Father."

"Fetch me pen and ink."

"Right away, Father." Myra came in carrying an ink bottle and paper. She set them on the dinner table along with two thin, black pen holders and two pen tips. "Anything else?"

"Yes," he replied. "Fashion several envelopes."

Myra began folding sheets of paper into envelopes. "How many?"

"Three," he replied. "I've been reading these damnable newspapers. *The Herald,* from Chippewa Falls, the *Hayward Republican,* and the *Milwaukee Journal.* Every one of them is out to sell more papers by keeping my name in the news. Yet they don't bother to get the dag-blasted story right. Well, I've had enough. If they won't come to me for the truth, then I must write it myself and send it to them."

"Will they print what you write?" Myra asked. "I thought the newspapers were beholden to the lumber trust."

"Beholden, yes, but that means little when it comes to selling a nickel newspaper. Well, by gosh, I'll give them something to spark their readers. I'll tell them about Harry Shue's crooked courthouse gang. And how the lumber company has twisted the law against us. That they pay their henchmen to foil us, yet have failed in every attempt."

"Yes, Father. I imagine that would sell newspapers, all right."

"You could do the same, Princess."

"Me? Who wants to hear from a girl who lives out in the forest?"

"I would," said Hattie from the kitchen. "Mothers read, too. I'm sure they'd be interested in hearing your thoughts."

"The view of a sixteen-year-old?"

"Editors might see your words as a way to sell papers," said John.

"All right," Myra agreed. "I'll try. I'll be honest and forthright in my writing and send my article along with yours, Father. We'll see if anyone takes note."

Myra pulled up a chair, dipped her pen in the ink bottle, and began.

My name is Mary Almyra Dietz. My father is John F. Dietz, defender of the Cameron Dam. We live on the Thornapple Farm, deep in Wisconsin's north woods. I am sixteen years of age and this is my story.

By suppertime, not three, but eight envelopes sat on the sideboard waiting to be mailed. The following Saturday, Clarence, Leslie, and their father climbed aboard the wagon. Myra handed the letters to her father. He stuffed them into an inside coat pocket. Below his coat, the butt of his Luger pistol protruded from its holster.

"Hurry back," said Myra. "Mother and I'll have chicken and dumplings waiting for you."

"Molasses cookies, too?" Clarence asked.

"Clare," replied Myra, "just for that sweet tooth of yours, I'll bake up a batch."

"In that case, we'll be back in the wink of an eye." Clarence snapped the reins. "Giddy up!"

Myra watched her father and brothers ride out of sight. "Mother, do you think any of those newspapers might post my letter?"

Hattie thought for a moment. "It's a good message, Myra. It spells out the wrongs that our family has had to endure since coming here. *I* believe it belongs on every front page. Were it from a young man, it would be printed, I'm sure. But, like you, I fear newspaper editors won't place much value on the words of a young woman."

"I dare say I can compete with any boy when it comes to composing such a statement," Myra countered.

"Oh, I don't doubt it for a moment," said Hattie. "Like your father, you are well read. Your vocabulary is mature. Your ability to convey the heart of an issue is sure to sway the reader. If you can find an editor willing to overlook your gender and age, your missive is certain to see light of day."

"Perhaps I should have signed my name as Clarence. Or Leslie."

Hattie turned to her daughter. "Perhaps. But wouldn't that make you a hypocrite?"

"Hypocrite?"

"Your letter offers the truth. It makes folks aware that we've been wronged and they've been duped by newspapermen who are either rewarded for disparaging us or too lazy to seek out the facts behind a story. Myra, should you masquerade as a man in order to explain your feelings? Or express the feelings of a young *woman* caught up in this quandary?"

"You're right, Mother," said Myra. "I will use my own name. I must! Let those editors with genuine interest in *truth* print my letter. As far as I'm concerned, the others can go to blazes."

"Mind your tongue," warned her mother. "There's no room for such coarseness under our roof. You'll do well to remember that we are a family of God's creation."

"Sorry. Forgive me, Mother?"

"Go dress two hens for supper. Well-plucked, mind you. And be prompt about it."

"Right away, Mother. I'm sorry."

19

His Chosen Path

The Dietz men returned to Thornapple Farm at dusk. Clarence and his father unloaded the wagon. Leslie walked the team to the barn. Minutes later, they joined the family at the supper table.

"More potatoes, Papa?" asked Helen.

"No thank you, Princess. I've had my fill."

"I'll have some," said Clarence, reaching across the table.

"Mind your manners, boy," said his father. "They'll come around soon enough."

"Ma, you should see the goings on in Winter," said Leslie. "The whole town is over the moon about it."

"About what?" Myra asked, helping herself to the carrots.

"Railroad's coming in."

Myra looked up. "Really, Leslie? Coming to Winter?"

"It's about time," said her father. "Just think. No more long, bumpy buckboard trips to Hayward. We'll soon be able to make the trip in less than half the time and in the comfort of a passenger car."

Clarence piled potatoes onto his plate. "Word has it they plan to run tracks clear from Park Falls to Winter, then onto Raddison and Hayward, then on down to Ladysmith."

"We'll be able to hear the whistle from here," said Leslie. "That's how close they'll come."

"Gracious sakes!" said Hattie. "These *are* modern times."

"Ma," said Leslie. "Clare and I visited the new mercantile store in town. You'd love it. That store has everything you can imagine. Everything! Even a toaster that runs on electricity."

"Not much good out here," Hattie replied. "We'll have to content ourselves toasting our bread in the fireplace like normal folks."

"Father, do you think we'll ever have electricity at Thornapple Farm?" Myra asked.

"Never," he replied. "It's one thing to have electric streetlights in cities where people live all piled atop one another. That's where the electric company shareholders make their millions. But it would cost a pretty penny to run copper wire through miles and miles of forest. I don't imagine folks who live beyond city limits will ever enjoy such luxury."

"No matter," said Clarence. "We've got daylight from dawn to dusk and enough kerosene to keep our lamps lit. Right Pa?"

"And lightning bugs, too, Papa," shouted Stanley. "I saw two last night."

"Mama," said Helen, "can Stanley and I have a pickle jar to catch some lightning bugs tonight?"

"Why, I think that's a wonderful idea," Hattie replied. "Leslie will go with you to the root cellar and find a jar for each of you. But take care not to drop them. Mind you I want those jars returned in one piece."

Helen and Stanley excused themselves and rushed for the door. "C'mon, Leslie!" shouted Helen.

"Slow down, you two," said Leslie, finishing his supper. "The fireflies will wait."

John pushed his chair away from the table and stretched. "Dear me, that buckboard is hard on a body." He reached behind him, pulling a stack of papers from the sideboard. "Oh, Myra, I brought you your magazine."

His daughter's eyes lit up. "*Harper's?*"

He sorted through the stack. "Here it is, child."

"Oh, thank you, Father." Myra clasped the magazine close to her bosom.

"And more newspapers. Mrs. Phelan at the hotel saves them for us now. I told her of your letters."

"Mary Phelan is doing that?" asked Hattie. "For us?"

"Oh, goodness," gasped Myra. "You shouldn't have mentioned my letters to her."

"Mary is a such nice woman," said Hattie.

"Father, what if no newspaper is willing to post my letters? I'll be so embarrassed! I'll never set foot in town again."

"Young lady," said her mother, "I'd wager there's not one person in the whole of Winter who either has the knack or the notion to write a letter to any newspaper. Once word gets out that you've written to many papers, they will envy you whether your letter gets printed or not."

Her father looked up from his reading. "Remember, Princess, merely because some lamebrain editor turns down your writing doesn't mean it's not excellent. Like others in his profession, it might be that he lacks even the slightest idea of what people really wish to read."

Myra laughed. "I suppose in a way you're right." She opened her magazine. "Oh, wouldn't it be grand to have a magazine like *Harper's* publish something I wrote?"

John looked up from his paper, smiled, and turned to Hattie. "Mrs. Phalen says we're the talk of the town, Mother."

"Yes, I imagine we are. I believe Winter, as small as it is, has been besieged by Sheriff's deputies, marshals, detectives, and possemen, ever since you first took control of the dam. The Winter Hotel must be doing a fine business."

"Yes. And the town's saloons are crowded day and night," he replied.

"All because of that squabble you're having with the company."

Myra lowered her magazine. "Father, do you think I should send my letter to *Harper's?* I know it's a silly thought, but ..."

Hattie continued. "Most towns have little to natter about. But here in Winter, it seems you and that Winchester of yours have settled that problem."

John laughed. "Mother, I don't know if I should take that as a commendation or a condemnation. You know very well that my stand against the syndicate is just. My actions have been both appropriate and honorable."

"Do you think I should, Father?" asked Myra.

"Hmm?"

"Send my letter to Harpers?"

"John," said Hattie, "I know that your intentions are proper. Yet sometimes I wonder if your stubbornness doesn't dominate your decision-making."

"You sound like my brother, Hattie. Stubbornness, indeed."

"You and that old timber tycoon—two headstrong Germans—neither willing to bend."

"Oh, think of it," said Myra, oblivious to her parents' exchange. "I'd be thrilled to see my letter in *Harper's.*"

John bristled. "Headstrong, Mother? Unwilling to bend? Don't you see I am merely standing up for our family? Demanding nothing but fair recompense for the *injustice* that the lumber syndicate has set upon us?"

Myra stared out the window into the darkness beyond. "Can you imagine? A letter from Myra Dietz in *Harper's Bazar!*"

"John, of course I know that," replied Hattie. "But I sometimes wonder where this is going. Will is right. A compromise could resolve all of it. The injunctions. The warrants. The detectives camped in the woods across the river. Not to mention my apprehension of one of our little ones getting shot at when they go out to play."

"Nonsense! The company's toadies would never risk harming any child of ours. They know what fury it would bring forth."

"John, all I am suggesting is that you be willing to accept a compromise if offered. We've little to lose and so much to gain. Consider the joys of returning to normal life."

"*Harper's Bazar,*" said Myra. " "Just think of it."

"Hattie, don't you see? Kowtowing to the lumber trust now would be tantamount to throwing away our rights. The robber barons of our nation have had their day. It's time for the common man to make a stand. To show them we won't settle for this treatment anymore. To take up arms if need be!"

"And jeopardize all we have? Risk injury? Imprisonment? Harm to our children? Maybe even death?"

John came to his feet, startling Myra. He threw his newspapers onto the floor. "So, now you're taking *their* side? Against your own family?"

"I hardly think Mother meant it that way," said Myra.

His anger turned to his daughter. "What I do now, what I have done, what I *will* do for the sake of this family, I do in the name of what is just, what ought be done, what every red-blooded worker in this nation must do if we hope to throw off the chains of slavery put upon us by the corporations. Yes, I am only one man, one insignificant stone in the construction of the enormous castles those tycoons are building on the backs of the working man. But, because the Cameron Dam lies on our Thornapple Farm, I have a voice. And, by God, I will shout until I'm heard. And when others hear me, they will shout. And more will shout. Soon the politicians will see that they must choose between standing tall for the working man or seeking *honest* employment."

He turned to Hattie. "No, Mother. I will *not* compromise. I will see this to the end." He stomped outside, slamming the door.

The sudden silence jarred Myra. "I've never seen Father so upset."

"I have," Hattie replied. "Once when your little sister, Leanna, died from that spider bite. Your father felt he was responsible. It wasn't so, of course. How could he have known? Again when we lost our farm south of Rice Lake. And, again, not his fault. Many farms failed that year. And I'll never forget when his business partnership with his brother fell apart. Your father learned that he'd lost every penny we had on a single real estate speculation made by Henry."

"I never knew," said Myra.

"Your father and I have sheltered you children from such troubles," Hattie replied. "Your older sister knew. Thank the Lord May found a good man to wed and remained in Rice Lake rather than coming to this God-forsaken place."

"Oh, but I can't imagine not living on Thornapple Farm. The beauty of the forest, the river, our animal friends. Mother, living in Rice Lake was special, but I've never seen Clare or Leslie as happy as they are here on the farm. And as for me, I doubt I could ever be content elsewhere."

Hattie placed her hand over Myra's. "With your optimism, your outlook on life, you'll be happy wherever you alight. I only hope that ..."

A gunshot shattered their moment. Another shot rang out, followed by another. Myra cautiously peeked through the small kitchen window. "It's all right, Mother. It's only Father target shooting."

"Oh, it's more than target shooting," said Hattie. "This is his way of telling me that he plans to take this to the finish. Your father's pride has blinded him."

"But gunfire? That's Father's answer? Is there no other way?"

Three more rapid shots echoed down the river bottom.

"Not for your father," Hattie replied. "I fear it's his chosen path."

20

Detectives

Hoping to catch a mess of trout before breakfast, Clarence slipped out early the next morning. Carrying a split bamboo fly rod, net, and creel, he hiked through the pasture and then descended the bank to fish the deep pool below the dam. But in the first light of morning, something looked wrong. The pool seemed too small. Shallow. Nearly dried up.

Clarence scrambled up the bank and crossed on the catwalk to find all three gates closed and the water upstream rising. He raced back home to alert his father.

"Pa!" he shouted from the yard. "Pa! Come quick!" He bounded up onto the porch. "Pa!"

John rushed outside, rifle in hand. "Clare! What's the matter? Why are you up?"

"The gates are shut, Pa. Water's on the rise."

"What?"

"Somebody must've tampered with the gates while we slept. Shut them all the way. Tight. Water's rising. Fast!"

"Wake your brother. We best get those gates open."

"That's just it, Pa. Whoever did this removed the capstans. There's no way to open those gates."

"This is the company's dirty work. Red Mulligan must have something up his sleeve. Must plan to get enough head upstream to wash his timber clear over the top of the dam. If Mulligan thinks he's going to deny me my rightful comeuppance, he'd better think again. Clare, we've got to find a way to stop this. Go wake your brother."

Minutes later, John and his sons stood atop the catwalk, inspecting the dam.

"You're right, Clarence," said John. "There's nothing we can do without those capstans except let the water rise. And rise it will in this warm April weather. The snow's melting fast. Our hayfield will be flooded in no time. Lord knows when we'll be able to seed the rutabaga field or plant our potatoes."

"Looks like Mulligan might get his log drive after all, huh, Pa?" asked Leslie.

"I don't see how. Even with water flowing over the top, only a few logs will go downstream. As long as we guard the dam, *our* dam, the company can't sluice their logs through. And no company man would *dare* step onto this catwalk much less stand atop my dam sluicing timber. Every last lumberjack of theirs knows what might befall him."

"But they've got marshals to protect them," said Clarence. "Don't they?"

"One crack from my Winchester and they'd all turn tail."

The three Dietz men watched the water level slowly rise. "Boys," John said, "After chores we're going to hitch the horses to the plow and bank the cabin with soil in case this dam should back water up that far. We'll need a good berm all around the building to insure we don't get flooded out."

"Flooded, Pa?" said Leslie. "What about our animals?"

"Nothing we can do but get them to high ground. Especially the sheep. They won't do well against rising water. And we better drag the rowboat up to the cabin in case we need it to get to solid ground."

"Gee, Pa, you really think we might get flooded out?"

"Always better to be prepared, Clare. And prepared we shall be. Meanwhile, let's go have us breakfast. Plenty of work to do today."

The next morning, as the sun crept above the treetops, a thick fog blanketed the remaining snow cloaking the river bottom. Soon, a warm, southern breeze drifted across Thornapple Farm. By the time John and his sons finished their chores, the fog had lifted. Clarence was first to notice two men walking near the dam on the far side of the river. Abe and Quincy saw them next, barking their displeasure.

"Pa! Two men!" shouted Clarence, pointing across the river.

"Are they armed?" asked John.

"Don't think so."

"Go warn them against trespassing on our land. And don't mollycoddle, Clarence."

John's eldest boy ran toward the dam, Abe and Quincy by his side. But the men were gone. He stood there, watching, waiting for some movement. Abe suddenly barked. Clarence saw one of the two rush from behind one tree to a larger one.

"Say, there! You behind the willow! You are trespassing onto Dietz land at your own peril. Be assured that my father's Winchester is trained on you at this very moment. Best you leave or else." Clarence waited for a reply. "I said get!" he bellowed.

"We mean no harm!" came a shout from the woods.

"What's your business?"

"Landlookers."

"What?"

"We work for Ezra Cornell. He's wanting to buy up a few sections in these parts."

"Thornapple Farm ain't for sale. Get out!"

"Son, we'd like to talk to your pa about land in these parts. Can we come over?"

"How do I know you're not lawmen, come here to spy on us?"

"Lawmen? I should say not. Like I said, we're landlookers. We work for Cornell. Can we talk to your pa?"

"I'll have to ask him. You stay put. I'll be back." Clarence turned to the dogs. "Abe. Quincy. Stay! Keep them from crossing till I get back. Hear me? Stay!"

Clarence returned to the cabin. "Pa, those two men out there want to ask some questions about buying timber land around here. They say they work for Ezra Cornell."

"Landlookers?"

"Yes, sir."

"Are they armed?"

"No, Pa. Not that I could see."

"Let them come over, then. But you and your brother stay close. Keep an eye open until they leave." John turned. "Leslie, lean a couple of rifles behind the door, just in case."

"Sure, Pa."

Clarence returned to the dam. Both dogs sat guarding the catwalk. "Pa says it's safe to cross," he shouted. "But come unarmed, mind you. My pa's not one to be tested."

As the pair crossed, Abe growled.

"It's all right, boy," said Clarence. "They're lumbermen, not lawmen."

Leslie watched from the porch as Clarence ushered the landlookers to the cabin. "I'm Leslie Dietz," he said. "I see you've met my brother."

"And your watchdogs," replied one, stepping onto the porch.

Abe's growling continued. Both lumbermen turned to take in the landscape. The first greens of spring poked through shrinking snow drifts. A muddy path led from the cabin to the barn, another to the privy. Chickens dotted the yard. Four horses stood behind a rail fence near the barn, and beyond a herd of cows. Both men noticed the heavy berm protecting the cabin walls.

"What's the reason for all the dirt around the cabin?" asked one of the men.

"Protection," said Leslie.

"From gunfire?"

"Gunfire? Why, no. From rising water. Why would you think ..."

Clarence interrupted. "It's there to keep our cabin safe."

"Looks more like a fort than a home," said the other man.

"Pa's inside having his coffee."

"Come!" shouted John, listening from the living room.

The men entered and inhaled deeply, greeted by the aroma of freshly baked bread. Clarence and Leslie followed, leaving the door open.

John looked up from his coffee and newspaper. "Have a seat," he said. "I imagine you'd accept coffee and a slice of fresh bread with jam?"

"Oh, my. Yes, Mr. Dietz! Coffee and fresh bread would be a delight," said one of the two.

"We've suffered only campfire-cooked vittles for the last two weeks," added the other. They sat across the table from John. Leslie and Clarence watched from the doorway. Abe and Quincy sat on the porch staring through the open door.

"I see your britches are wet," John said. "Is the water over the dam already that high?"

"It's a torrent, Mr. Dietz," said one of the men. "Nearly washed me off the gol-dang catwalk."

"We don't talk like that here!" snapped Myra. Both men turned. Her stare warned of her tenacity. She placed a plate of bread and a jar of jam on the table. "Holler if you need more, Pa," she said, returning to the kitchen.

As she did, Hattie brought coffee. She sat next to her husband and scrutinized the two visitors. "How are things at the sawmill?" she asked.

One of them looked at her, and then turned back to John. "Mr. Dietz, my name is Jonas, Herman Jonas. This is my partner, Charlie Callaghan."

"Tell me, how are things at the mill in Chippewa?" Hattie repeated.

Again, Jonas ignored her. "Mr. Dietz, we were sent to these parts by Ezra Cornell in order to scout timberland. Mr. Cornell's looking to buy up several sections east of here. We were wondering if you, being one who hunts and traps in these woods, might advise us."

"You're too late," said John. "The Chippewa Lumber and Boom Company has everything sewn up from here to Fifield."

Hattie leaned forward. "Say, how's Ezra's wife doing with her charity work, these days?"

Jonas looked at her. "Fine, ma'am." He turned back to John. "You're right about the land, sir. Chippewa Lumber and Boom has acquired much of the land in these parts. But not all of it. And what they passed up, Mr. Cornell has been able to purchase for pennies on the dollar."

"Is Ezra's mill working around the clock, these days?" Hattie asked.

"Yes, ma'am," said Callaghan. "They're milling hemlock."

"Hemlock?" asked John. "You're sure about that?"

"Seems there's plenty of hemlock to be had in these parts."

"Hemlock?" repeated Hattie. "Ezra Cornell should know there's no market for hemlock."

"I'm sorry, ma'am," said Jonas. "Did Charlie say hemlock? I'm sure he meant … uh … birch."

Hattie scoffed. "John, these aren't landlookers. Not by a long shot."

"Yes, Mother. I've known that since the moment they walked in." He turned back to his guests. "Friends, your outfits are far too tidy for men out tenting for two weeks. Why, look at those boots of yours. Tell me they don't have the sheen of leather fresh off the cobbler's workbench."

"And hemlock, gentlemen, is cut only for its bark," said Hattie.

"Bark, Mrs. Dietz?"

"For tanning hides," said her husband.

"Er," grunted Callaghan. "I meant … birch, Mr. ...."

Hattie interrupted him. "Ezra Cornell, bless his heart, is a widower."

"He is?"

Myra, overhearing, came from the kitchen, a wooden spoon in her hand. "Shame on you!" she scolded. "You came here masquerading as honest, working men. Clearly, you are neither."

"Why are you here, Jonas?" asked John.

Silence hung in the air for a moment. Abe, watching through the open door, growled again as Jonas reached into his coat pocket.

"I have a letter for you, Mr. Dietz." He held up a thick, blue envelope. "From Ezra Cornell himself."

Hattie shoved the table toward the visitors, preventing Jonas from handing the envelope across. Abe barked. "Don't touch it, John!" she shouted. "These men are detectives!"

Both Dietz and Jonas jumped to their feet.

Leslie slammed the door closed and snatched a rifle.

Clarence grabbed the other.

John reached out, grabbing Jonas by the collar, and slammed his right fist into the agent's jaw, sending him to the floor.

Hattie pushed Callaghan's chair over before he could stand.

John pulled his Luger from a drawer on the bureau.

"John!" Hattie yelled. "Not in the house! Think of all the blood!"

As Jonas came to his feet, John bashed him with the butt of the pistol, sending him down again.

Callaghan lay on the floor. Myra stood above him, ready to strike with her spoon. He cowered, hiding his face in his hands.

Hattie threw the envelope into the fireplace. It burst into flames upon striking the glowing coals.

"Get out!" she screamed.

"Get out before my father blows your fool heads off!" shouted Myra.

"I'd give a month's pay not to be here right now," said Callaghan, helping Jonas to his feet. Both men raised their hands high, now staring at two Winchesters aimed at them.

"On your way, *detectives,*" said John. "Tell your pals back in the woods that I will shoot any man trespassing on my land or my dam, including you. You can swim back across the pond."

"You won't let us cross on the dam?"

Clarence jabbed the rifle's muzzle into Jonas's ribs. "You heard my pa. Now, get!"

21

Something's Amiss

Stillness engulfed the Thornapple Farm that afternoon. The air felt heavy. The cows huddled in the stand of spruce trees near the river. Myra opened the barn door for the sheep as Nannie led the flock inside. Hattie, Helen, and Stanley rushed to take in the still-damp wash they'd hung on the clotheslines that morning. The sky darkened as Clarence, Leslie, and their father finished chores. Shortly before supper, lightning danced above the treetops to the west and the rumble of distant thunder rolled down the Thornapple River valley.

"Wash up, children," said Hattie. "Supper's on."

Myra placed baby Johnny next to her in his highchair. "Here you are, precious," she said, handing him a buttered bun.

"Horses in their stalls?" John asked, looking out the front window.

"Yes, Pa," Clarence replied. "And edgy as can be. They must know a storm's coming."

"Odd how they can tell," said Myra, setting a platter of roast venison on the table.

"Oh, not so odd," said Hattie. "If I can feel it in my bones, I imagine they can, too."

"How come I can't feel it in *my* bones, Mama?" asked Stanley.

"Just wait, child. You will," she replied. "And don't speak with your mouth full."

"Nannie lured her whole flock into the barn," said Myra. "It's something how all the other sheep follow her wherever she goes."

"Some creatures are born to follow," John replied. "Others to lead."

"Lead like you, huh, Papa?" asked Helen. Her father patted her on the head. "Maybe, Princess."

"Golly," said Clarence, stabbing a baked potato with his fork. "With all the sheep in the barn, it must be as crowded as a Saturday night ball in the village opera house."

"How would you know?" Leslie asked. "We've never been in town on a Saturday night."

"Our sheep don't seem to mind congregating," said Myra. "As long as Nannie's nearby, they're content squeezing together."

"What if lightning hits the barn?" asked Helen. "Will the sheep …"

"Not to worry," said Myra. "That's what the lightning rods are for."

The wind picked up as the storm swept in. Lighting flashed. Thunder rattled the dishes in the kitchen cupboard. Hattie lit two kerosene lamps as the room darkened. Heavy rain followed.

"I imagine this will be the bitter end of the snow," said Myra.

"And good riddance," blurted Clarence.

"Yes. Let it melt," added Leslie. "Seems like I shoveled enough this past winter to last me a lifetime."

"I like the snow!" said Stanley.

"Wait till you have to shovel it, squirt."

"Don't call names," ordered Hattie.

John pushed his chair back and walked to the front window. "Our fields will be flooded after this rain."

"Think so, Pa?" asked Clarence.

"The frost is still in the ground. This rain and the melting snow have no place to go. And with the gates closed on that dag-blasted dam, our fields will suffer."

"Oh, but not for long," said Hattie. "Once the weather turns, the flood will subside and our fields will be ready to plant. It happens every spring."

"What's for dessert?" asked Stanley.

"Not until you finish those carrots," Hattie replied.

"Aw, Mama."

"Chocolate cake, Stanley," said Myra, feeding baby Johnny with a spoon.

"Oh, all right," he sighed. "I'll eat my carrots."

John returned to the table. The storm passed as quickly as it had come and all grew quiet until a final, exceptionally loud thunder clap shook the building. Helen shrieked. Baby John squealed and then cried. Myra scooped him up in her arms. John rushed to the window again.

"Golly! That sounded close," said Leslie.

Myra wiped Johnny's tears with her apron. "It's okay, dearest," she whispered. "Don't be frightened." She carried him to the door. Opening it she said, "Look. That bad old storm has passed, see? Soon it will be far away. Like all life's storms. Far, far away."

"That strike sounded loud enough to scare the bark off an oak tree!" said Clarence, stabbing another baked potato.

"No flash?" wondered John aloud.

"I saw none," Leslie added. "Kind of odd, don't you think?"

"Lightning can fool a body," offered Hattie, scraping the last of the carrots onto her plate.

"Oh, how pleasant an evening!" said Myra, from the doorway. Stepping onto the front porch with the baby, she pointed east. "Oh, look, Johnny. It's the first rainbow of spring!" She called to the others. "Come see!"

One by one, the Dietz family stepped onto the porch to take in the beauty of a double rainbow burning bright against ebony clouds beyond. Each absorbed the tranquility and calm left by the April thunderstorm and inhaled the pure springtime air cleansed by the rain.

"My stars," Myra said, "just listen to that wind." She pulled Johnny closer to her breast.

The family listened to the eerie roar.

"Something's amiss," said Hattie. "Look. The balsams. They're … still."

Myra turned to her. "But we can hear it."

"That's not wind, Princess," said her father.

The others looked to him for more.

"It's the river." The roar grew louder.

"The river, Pa?" Clarence asked.

Beyond the yard, a surge of water raced down the channel. Then the first logs charged by, pushed by a mountain of mud-stained water. More and more thousand-pound white pine logs rushed by. The horde of timber tore down the channel, tumbling like toothpicks, end over end, bashing into each other as if battling for first place in a race to reincarnation at the sawmill.

"Red Mulligan," said John.

"What?" asked Leslie?

"That wasn't a lightning strike we heard. It was dynamite. Probably a whole case of dynamite. Mulligan blew up our dam."

"You mean he is running the drive? Without men?" asked Myra. "No river pigs to move the logs along? How foolish!"

"If so, they'll lose half-a- million board feet of lumber," Clarence said. "Right, Pa?"

"Probably more."

"Why would the company do this?" Myra asked. "I mean, why waste all that good pine?"

John stroked his chin. "I suppose they figured it would be better to lose one million board feet than to sacrifice six."

"Or perhaps they did this to get back at you," said Hattie. "If so, by the looks of things, they just wasted more money than all your claims put together."

"Lord knows they can afford it," said Myra.

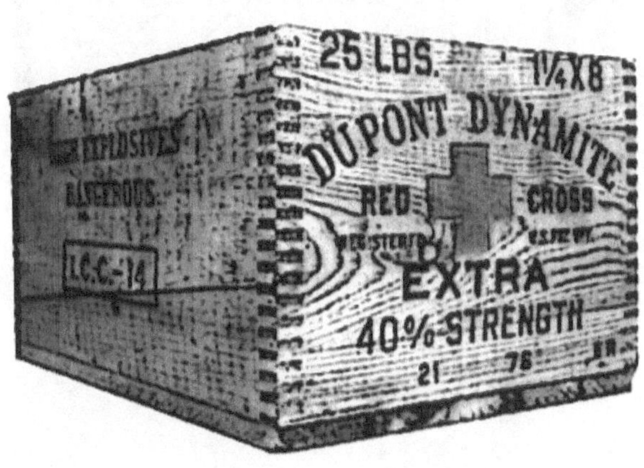

"Leslie," said John, "fetch my rifle. I need to take a look at our dam before dark sets in."

Leslie bolted inside, returning with a Winchester.

"C'mon, boys," said John, jumping off the porch. "Make haste!"

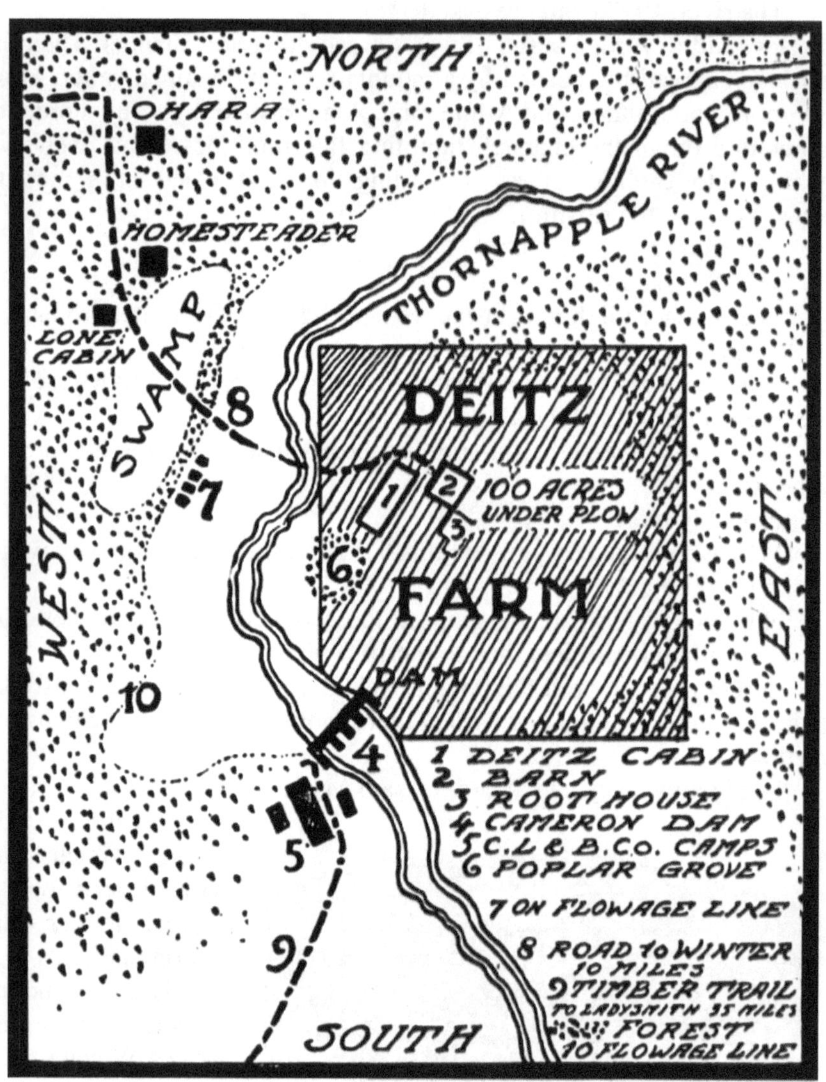

NORTH
O'HARA
HOMESTEADER
LONE CABIN
WEST SWAMP
EAST
THORNAPPLE RIVER
DEITZ
100 ACRES UNDER PLOW
FARM
DAM
8
7
6
10
1
2
3
4
5
9
SOUTH
1 DEITZ CABIN
2 BARN
3 ROOT HOUSE
4 CAMERON DAM
5 C.L.&B.Co. CAMPS
6 POPLAR GROVE
7 ON FLOWAGE LINE
8 ROAD TO WINTER 10 MILES
9 TIMBER TRAIL TO LADYSMITH 35 MILES
10 FOREST TO FLOWAGE LINE

22

The Flood

Within minutes, the three Dietz men stood above the river watching thousands of massive pine logs descend. The Dietz side of the dam remained intact. But the far side, the side nearest Camp Four, was gone. The explosion had not only removed half the dam, but also the entire abutment beyond, creating a wide, deep pool that now surged with timber—tumbling, thrashing, and crashing—dominated by the force wrought by raging, roaring water.

"Boys," said John, "take a good look. For you will never again see a sight like this. No doubt Mulligan has opened the gates on both of the dams upstream in order to push all his pine down in one fell swoop." He shook his head in disgust. "'Twas a foolish, foolish thing to do."

"What now, Pa?" asked Clarence.

"Not a thing. The Cameron Dam is gone. Gone for good. Blown out by dynamite and a flood of water."

John and his sons stood atop the remains of the catwalk watching the logs blast through the channel only yards before them. "Boys, take a good, long look. For this day marks the last ever Thornapple River log drive. What's done is done."

Suddenly, the third gate blew out, taking tons of soil with it. John dropped his rifle and grabbed his boys by their arms, yanking them to safety. Clarence regained his balance, then dove forward to rescue the Winchester. Waist deep in muddy water, he handed the rifle up to his father. "Here, Pa," he said with a grin. "You dropped this!"

"That was a foolish thing you just did, Clarence," scolded his father. "No rifle is worth a man's life." The three now watched from shore as the force from upstream heaved hundreds more logs past.

"Pa, look!" said Leslie, pointing below. "The river is swirling back our way. Cutting into our bank. Our land!"

The force of the water blasting through the rift on the far side of the dam created a large eddy, a swirling, muddy pool aside the river channel. The raging water carried logs by that bashed into the river bank, digging out tons of soil. As it washed downstream, the pool before them widened and widened, stranding logs on the Dietz side of the stream.

"Step back, boys. With all of that water, all of that *might* stockpiled upstream, there's no telling what this river's bound to do."

"Pa," said Clarence. "With no drivers, what's to stop the pine from jamming up downstream and causing more pools like this?"

"Not one dag-blasted thing, Clare. And each pool made will capture more logs. Maybe hundreds more. Why, if old Weyerhaeuser had half an inkling of what's going on here tonight, he'd not sleep a wink."

"What about you, Pa?" asked Leslie. "I mean, doesn't this mean you won't get your comeuppance?"

"Me? Why, I'm going to sleep like Rip Van Winkle," he chuckled. "Oh, but don't forget to wake me. We still have our chores, you know."

By the time John and his sons returned home, water had washed over the riverbank west of the barn and swept into the yard. In the twilight, the barn and root cellar reflected in the great pool before their cabin. The three men stepped inside to find Hattie, Myra, and Helen stacking furniture.

"What in the world …?" said Leslie.

Hattie interrupted. "Don't just stand there. Help us!" she demanded.

"The water's not likely to rise this high, Mother," said John.

Hattie ignored him. "You boys put some firewood under the pump organ to hold it off the floor. Myra, you set the gramophone atop the table. Your basket of recordings, too."

"I'll get them," said Stanley.

"Be careful with my records!" snapped Myra, taking the basket.

"But I want to help, too."

"Then pick up your toys, child," Myra ordered, "lest we trip on them. Mother, I hung your sewing and knitting baskets on the drying hooks in the kitchen."

John opened the door. "I repeat, Mother, we needn't fret over this."

Hattie turned, "John, I'm not about to take chances with my good furnishings. Now, give a hand or get out of the dang way!"

"Mother!" shouted Leslie, Helen, and Myra at the same time.

"God will forgive me, children. But he won't replace my goods."

"What about our ice cream machine?" asked Helen.

"Well, now," said John, lifting Helen by the waist. "Isn't that just like my little princess? Wanting ice cream when Mothere thinks we should be building Noah's Ark!"

Myra hung two shotguns over the mantel. "Clare," she said, "lay the other guns on your bed. And get your shoes out from under."

"And anything else you have hiding there," Hattie added. "Other than your commode. Don't you dare put it on the bed. It's fine where it is."

"What about our dogs?" asked Stanley, petting Abe, their shepherd.

John laughed. "Son, if the water comes in, they'll just have to sleep in your bed."

"Really?" shouted Stanley. "Oh, boy!"

John arose before dawn. He pulled on his shirt, overalls, boots, and hat, and then stepped outside. The entire yard was flooded, the cabin now an island resting upon a quiet lake in the crisp April air. He stepped back inside and lit the kerosene lamp in the kitchen. Finding the floor dry, he carried the lamp into the living room where he added an armload of wood to the still-glowing embers in the fireplace. Returning to the kitchen, he made a fire in the cook stove and filled the coffee pot.

Hattie, rising to the fresh aroma of brewing coffee, pulled on her robe and slippers, pushed the curtain aside and stepped into the kitchen. "How bad is it?" she asked.

"The worst is over. I figure we'll have our yard back by evening."

Hattie stepped outside and then returned to start breakfast. "The water's lapping at our home," she said.

"Yes, but the berms will keep us dry. The flood's bound to recede soon. We'll be fine." John turned toward his sons' room. "Clarence! Leslie!" he shouted. "Morning chores to get to. Get up."

"Yes, Pa," came a muffled reply.

"Myra," shouted Hattie. "Help the children get dressed for inside play. No point in putting on boots. They're not going outside today."

After breakfast, Clarence, Leslie, Myra, and their father used the rowboat to cross the yard to the barn where a parade of cows waited, most standing in a foot of muddy water. Myra opened the barn door and called to Nanny, who led the sheep out to higher ground. Myra then climbed up into the hayloft. Using a pitchfork, she threw fresh hay to the horses in stalls below. When done, she walked the length of the barn, swung open the loft door, and gazed at the scene before her.

The rising sun cast bright reflections from the river and the pond that now flooded this corner of Thornapple Farm. The beauty of the high water masked the mud and debris that would later appear. The snow had vanished. Grass and clover would soon flourish and the flooded yard would bear the greens of spring long before the surrounding landscape. Myra watched as a log drifted slowly downstream past the farm. It stopped abruptly, piling onto others across the river. Curious, she stared at the log jam. Then she shouted.

"Father, I see men!"

"How's that?" yelled Clarence from his milking stool.

"Men. Five or six. Across the river."

"They carrying rifles?" asked her father.

"No. Pike poles. And Peaveys, I think. Or cant hooks. I can never tell them apart."

"Peavey's have a spike at the business end," said Clarence. "Everybody knows that."

Her father climbed the steps to the loft two steps at a time. He stared out the hayloft door. "Well, now, that solves the mystery of all this high water, Princess. They must have one heck of a log jam down on the bend. Big enough to back water up all the way to here."

Clarence and Leslie stared over their father's shoulder. "Aren't they trespassing, Pa?" asked Clarence.

"That they are. But I'm not about to raise a fuss over it. The sooner they bust open that jam, the sooner this pond recedes."

"Look!" said Leslie. "Upstream! Two men with rifles, Pa!"

John watched them a moment. "Marshals, I suspect. Most likely come to assure the safety of the Camp Four men working on that jam."

"Why on Earth would they send marshals?" asked Myra. "Surely by now they know you would never shoot at men for just doing their job. Heavens, Father! They must think you to be the devil incarnate."

"Mulligan must've sent them. I imagine he's worried about what I might do should I catch *him* on our land. I'm sure the others know full well that I won't cause them any harm as long as they mind their business. Meanwhile, let's finish our chores and get back to the cabin. Your mother will be pleased to know her lovely Thornapple Farm will soon emerge from this flood intact and unscathed."

"Father, now that the dam's been breached, you have no bargaining power. Does that mean it's over? Will the sheriff and the marshals finally leave us in peace?"

"Well now, that's a good question. You're right that with the logs gone, I don't have a hold over the company. Now, if they come after me, it's only triggered by revenge for the embarrassment I've caused them."

"What about the reward they put up for your capture?" asked Leslie.

"Well, there is that," said John. "Perhaps Will can influence the county board to drop the charges and save that five-hundred dollars."

"You think he can do that?" asked Clarence.

"If anyone can, William can," replied his father. "He's been both Sheriff and Justice of the Peace of Barron County. He'll know what to say. Whether Harry Shue and his cronies pay heed is another matter."

After their midday dinner, the boys hiked to the dam to inspect the damage in daylight. Twenty minutes later, they returned out of breath.

"Pa!" Clarence yelled, "You know that bay we saw last night? The one that formed on our side of the river?"

"Yes? What about it?"

"Well, you won't believe it!"

"Never in a hundred years," said Leslie.

"Well, are you gonna tell me? Or must I go look for myself?"

"It's plumb filled with timber," said Clarence.

"*Plumb* filled, Pa!" added Leslie.

"White pine logs stacked in there like … like …"

"Like what, Clare?"

"Well, stacked in like cordwood, Pa. Big ol' logs laying all helter-skelter, one atop the other in the muddy water like … like …"

"What, Clare? Like what?"

"Like, um … nobody's business!"

"Hundreds and hundreds," explained Leslie. "Must be a million board feet of pine. Boy, oh boy! When old Weyerhaeuser hears about this, he's bound to have himself a hissy fit. He'll be mad as heck!"

"Don't let your mother hear you talk like that."

"Sorry."

John considered his sons' remarks and then stepped inside. "Mother," he said, "Fate may have finally sided with the Dietz family."

"How's that?"

"The boys say the good Lord saw fit to deposit a trainload of prime timber on Thornapple Farm last evening. I'm off to see it for myself."

"I'm coming, too," said Helen.

"Me, too," Stanley shouted.

"No, you're not," said Hattie. "I won't have the lot of you stomping around in the mud outside and then tracking up my clean rugs."

"Aw, Mama," whined Stanley, "you spoil all the fun."

"Spoilt fun is a small price to pay for clean rugs to play upon," said Myra. "Come now. Sit with me and I'll read you more from our story."

Clarence, Leslie, and their father pulled on their overcoats and hats and left for the dam, each with a loaded rifle in hand. The three youngest Dietz children gathered on the braided rug in front of the fireplace while Myra continued a tale by O. Henry she'd found in a New York newspaper. "All right, children. Listen.

"And then, for an hour I had to try to explain to him why there was nothin' in holes," she read, *"How a road can run both ways and what makes the grass green. I tell you, Sam, a human can only stand so much."*

"Myra?" said Stanley. "How *can* a road run both ways at once?"

Under a bright, early April sun, the three Dietz men stood on shore near the half-destroyed Cameron Dam. The torrent of Thornapple River water that blasted down the riverbed the night before had now receded. Thousands of huge, white pine logs had been washed downstream overnight, beginning and ending the final log drive down this small, yet important stream.

But many logs never made it downstream. The rush of water through the dynamited east side of the dam had caused an eddy below on the west side—the Dietz side—of the river. And that eddy captured upwards of a thousand logs. There they lay, heaped helter-skelter, stranded in the mud.

Leslie said it first. "Pa, those logs. They're on our property. Does that mean they belong to us?"

John thought for a long moment. "By golly, Son, you might have something there. If my mind recalls correctly, there's also a law that says any logs abandoned on another man's property can be sold off to the highest bidder and carted off."

"You really think that pine might be ours?" asked Clarence.

"I'll check with your Uncle Will. Boys, those logs you see below might be ours. If so, they could be the makings of a fine house we could build for your mother. The Thornapple Manor."

"Leslie," whispered Clarence, "what the heck's a manor?"

23

Deputy Sheriff Waite Ackley

On the first Monday in September, the schoolmaster adjusted his coat and tie and left his sleeping quarters in the Dietz home. Jeremiah C. Gates fastened a flag to a rope and hoisted it up the twenty-foot tamarack flagpole erected days before. With no breeze, the flag hung limp against the hazy blue sky. But it was there, the Stars and Stripes, suspended above Thornapple Farm on the first day of school, 1905.

"How now, Mr. Gates!" John shouted as he waved from the barn loft door. "Let the enlightenment begin!"

Minutes later, Gates joined the family at the breakfast table. Myra served soft-boiled eggs, sourdough pancakes, and fried pork sausage. "Eat your fill, children," she said to her younger brother and sister. "I read in *Harper's* that a hearty breakfast leads to a better report card."

"Oh, there's little doubt about that, Myra," said Gates. "Learning takes energy and energy comes from fuel. Every culture that has succeeded throughout history has done so because of well-fed citizens with full larders."

"My stars!" said Myra. "If there's a connection between the amount of food a boy eats and how smart he is, then little Johnny is destined to be a genius. Just look at him devour those flapjacks."

"But he can't say his A B Cs, teacher," said Helen. "But *I* can!"

"And how old is Johnny, Helen?" asked Gates.

"Um, two," she replied, ushering in a round of laughter. "And a-half."

"Let's not be in a rush," said his father. "Johnny will learn soon enough."

"How about you, Clarence?" Gates asked. "Will you be joining us today?"

"Me? What for? I know everything I need to know about running Thornapple Farm."

"The world doesn't end at the boundaries of our land," said Myra.

"Look, Sis," Clarence snapped, "you can spend your time with your nose stuck between pages of a book if you want. As for me, I can't afford to fritter away daylight in some schoolchild's desk. I got chores waiting."

"Clarence," said Hattie, "some chores can wait. You need to learn ciphering and improve your reading skills. Farming might not be your life's work, you know."

"And history, Son," said John. "You must learn about the past. A body can't choose where to go in life if he doesn't know where we've been."

"Aw, Pa. Don't make me sit in there with the tots."

"I beg your pardon?" chided Myra. "Tots, Clarence?"

"I may have a solution," said Gates. "Clarence, how about you tend to your chores while Myra and I get the youngsters started on their studies. Then you join us around ten o'clock. I'll introduce you to a good book I brought along. It's about Abraham Lincoln. I'm certain you'll enjoy it. And there's no need for you to read it in the schoolroom. Stretch out on a haystack if you prefer, or sit down by the river. Set your own pace. Read a chapter or two. Then you and I can discuss what you read over supper. How's that sound?"

Clarence looked at his father for support but found himself met with silence. "Oh, all right. I know when I'm licked."

"Atta boy," said John.

"If I must, I must. But I'd sure rather be walking behind a plow."

Clarence dove into the Lincoln book head first, then asked for another. Within six weeks he'd read every book Mr. Gates brought to Thornapple School. Then, one October evening after supper, they listened while Myra read the latest news posted in the *Ladysmith News-Budget*.

"Father, listen to this," said Myra. *"Sheriff could not subpoena Dietz,"* she read. *"William W. Dietz of Rice Lake, brother of John F. Dietz, famous owner of Thornapple Dam, is here in relation to the case of the State vs. Valentine Weisenbach, which comes on at Chippewa Falls, in circuit court next week. Sheriff Ackley of Chippewa County, who went to the Thornapple region with a subpoena for John F. Dietz, as a witness in this case, was unable to find him as he was out fishing at the time. He does not expect Dietz will be in court inasmuch as no subpoena was served on him. If he appears, other papers may be served as well."*

"Just as I thought," said John. "They think they can hornswoggle me? Get me into a courtroom so they can slap the handcuffs on me? Exercise those worthless warrants? Set me before a judge? Well, I guess I showed them once again that I'm no fool. As much as I'd like to help out Valentine, I'll not let them subpoena me. Not John F. Dietz."

"Papa," said Helen, "What does *subpoena* mean?"

John laughed. "It's nothing but another scrap of paper the sheriff wants to use to rope me in. That fool says I was out fishing, but I was right here when he arrived and still here when he left. Clarence and I were in the barn, greasing the hubs on the buckboard. I watched Ackley come and go, empty handed like all the rest. The marshal's camp across the river has a dozen lawmen, all waiting for their chance to hogtie me and haul me away. But they'll never get ol' John Dietz. No siree, Bob!"

24

The First Pitched Battle

The Dietz family spent the morning of July 25, 1906, putting up hay. The rope above Clarence stretched tight from the pulley above the hayloft door to the hay grapple suspended below. Hattie guided the the rope to keep it from tangling. A dozen cows supervised from beyond the cedar rail fence as Clarence swung the grapple into the haystack and gave Myra a nod.

"Giddy up, Meggie," Myra said softly. "Easy now." She walked the aging mare forward, tightening the rope and lifting the two-hundred-pound load. It climbed high and then snapped into the track that routed it into the loft. Leslie caught the grapple, pulled it inside, and released the hay, dropping it on the loft floor. Using a pitchfork, his father spread the hay into the corners of the loft. He then stepped it down, making room for more. Meanwhile, Leslie pulled the grapple back to the loft doors. He whistled. Myra walked Meggie backward, lowering the grapple for the next load.

Nearby, Helen, Stanley, and Johnny played in the shade of the barn. A faint roll of thunder, unnoticed by the others, made Helen look up. "Storm's coming," she yelled.

Clarence, Myra, and Hattie looked to the sky. Seeing only blue sky and a few scattered clouds, they turned back to their work.

"Hurry up down there," shouted John. "Plenty of hay to put up before supper. No time to dillydally."

Clarence tried to ignore the comment. He leaned toward Myra. "After all the dang work we've done in the past week to get this hay cut, dried and stacked, you'd think Pa would stop cracking the dag-blasted whip."

"What's that, Clare?" shouted his father.

"Oh, nothing, Pa. Nothing."

Hattie shook the rope to untangle it. "Don't go blaming your pa," she said, guiding the rope. "He doesn't want to end up borrowing hay from the neighbors like last year. My! That pained him something awful."

Clarence swung the grapple into the haystack. "But that doesn't mean he should work us like he does old Meggie. It ain't right to make us suffer."

"Meggie is *not* overworked," said Myra. "Neither is old Paul. Why, those horses live for every chance they get to pull a plow or a hay wagon or feel the tug of a rein."

"Well, they might, but I don't," said Clarence, giving Myra another nod. "Soon as the haying is done, I'm going for a good, long swim so I can wash off some of this dag-blasted barn smell."

"What's that Clare?" shouted his father, leaning out of the loft doors again.

"Nothing, Pa. 'Nother load coming up."

Myra prodded Meggie ahead. Hattie leaned back on the rope, removing the slack. As she did, she noticed something odd about one of the cows. Unlike the others, Molly held her head high. Ears perked, she watched the riverbank, a hundred yards away.

"Ma!" shouted Clarence. "*Ma!* Stop your mind from gallivanting and pay heed to that rope."

Hattie jerked the slack out from it, and then looked back to the cow. "Helen," she shouted. "Do you see how Molly Brown's acting?"

"What, Mama?"

"Molly. She's acting peculiar. Like she sees a fox or a skunk down by the river's edge. See what I mean?"

"Yes, Mama."

"Run down there, sweetie. See what it is that's got her so upset."

Helen jumped up, delighted to be asked to help. She climbed through the fence rails and ran toward the river.

"Don't get too close now," shouted Hattie. "It might be a wildcat."

"Mother!" Clarence shouted. "For Pete's sake. Pay attention to the dag-blasted rope!"

Hattie gave the line slack as the hay grapple came down. "Clarence Dietz, you watch your foul tongue!" She looked back to the river.

"Mama!" screamed Helen, running for the barn. "Mama! Mama!"

Helen's disturbing cries made everyone stop.

"Soldiers, Mama! Men with guns!"

"Dammit!" said John. "You might know! And at a time like this." He leaned out of the hayloft doors. "Gol-dang you trespassers! Don't think for a moment that I don't see you out there. Now get off my land!"

From the hayloft, Leslie and his father could see the marsh grass move near the river as several men crawled through. To the left, more movement deep within the stand of popple trees.

"There's a bunch of them," John shouted. "Hattie, you best get the children inside. Myra, go fetch me three deer rifles."

"Right, Father," she replied, running ahead of the others.

"Clare?"

"Yes, Pa?"

"Can you see anyone from atop the wagon?"

"No sir. I can't."

"Walk down there a ways. See if you can get a look at who's trespassing *this* time."

John heard thunder to the west. He turned to see dark clouds far away. "Blast the luck!"

Clare jumped the fence and trotted to the knoll overlooking the river. Seconds later, he turned toward the barn. "Military, Pa," he shouted. "Down by the rutabaga field. Five soldiers."

"Think they're militia men, Pa?" asked Leslie. "Sent by the governor?"

"It's bound to be, Son. I imagine that dag-blasted lumber company convinced Davidson to send up the militia. Do they think I won't take a pot shot at a man because he's in uniform? The fools."

Leslie and his father slid down the hayloft rope just as Myra came running from the cabin with three Winchesters across her arms. "Here, Father. All loaded."

Leslie took one rifle. His father, the next.

Myra," he said, "hang onto that other rifle till Clarence gets back here. And stand tall so you can be seen. I want them all to see that our whole family endures this together. Ready to protect our home."

"Here," she said. "An extra box of cartridges. Though I hope you won't need them."

"Clarence," he shouted. "Can you see anybody?"

"No."

"Then come back for now."

Just as Clarence turned, the crack of a rifle split the air. The bullet struck Clarence in the forehead. He fell, tried to stand, stumbled a few feet toward the barn, and fell again.

"Clare!" shrieked Myra, dropping her rifle. She climbed through the fence and ran toward him.

John and Leslie jumped over the fence behind her and raced to Clarence. He rolled onto his back, clutching his head with both hands.

Myra reached him first. The bullet had cut the flesh and split his skull. Blood flowed from the gash and ran down the side of his face. Leslie knelt next to him. A second later, their father joined them.

Myra pressed her kerchief against Clarence's head, trying to slow the bleeding. "We're here, Clare," she cried. His eyes opened, but failed to focus on her. "We'll get you fixed up, Clare. You'll be all right." Tears streamed down her face. "Oh, Clare!"

John turned toward the river. "Look! There! The assassin who's killed my son!" He raised his rifle.

"Father!" Myra shouted. "Clare is *not* going to die!"

John fired five fast rounds into the cloud of white gun smoke still hanging in the stand of popple trees.

Leslie pulled Clarence to his feet. "Can you walk, Clare?"

"Get him, Pa," he breathed, taking two steps toward the cabin. "Shoot him. For me."

Myra rushed forward and wrapped Clarence's arm around her neck to help shoulder his weight. "I'll get him home, Father," she cried. "Leslie, you stay with Father. And, please! Don't let him kill anyone."

Myra and Clarence stumbled and staggered through the pasture. "I'll fix you up, Clarence" she sobbed. "Good as new. You'll see." They clumsily climbed over the fence and struggled toward the cabin.

Leslie knelt next to his father, peering into the popple stand.

"See that gun smoke, Son?"

"Yes, sir."

"If you see *anything*, move down there, you open fire."

"On a state military man, Pa?"

"Oh, he's no military man."

"What makes you think …?"

"Because no honorable soldier would ever shoot an unarmed working man. No, Son, he's no soldier. He's an assassin!"

"Assassin, Pa?"

"Hired to kill us off. One-by-one. Ten-to-one odds he's a high-paid henchman for the lumber syndicate. All dressed up in a military uniform. Wouldn't you agree?"

"Me? Uh, well … yes, Pa. I suppose."

"Keep that rifle at the ready. If you see him, shoot." John turned to see Clarence and Myra nearing the porch. Hattie pulled them both inside and slammed the dooreyond . Beyond the cabin, the sky darkened. John looked back to the marsh grass near the river. Then to the popple trees again.

"There!" whispered Leslie, raising his rifle.

The first crack from his boy's Winchester startled John. The second did not. Nor the third. Or fourth. Or fifth. Or sixth. John raised his rifle, unsure of where Leslie aimed.

"He's behind that rotted out birch stump, Pa."

"Shoot through it. You'll hit him for sure."

With one eye on the popple trees below and the other on his son, John watched Leslie take careful aim. His finger trembling on the trigger, Leslie held and held … then squeezed.

Click.

"Dang it all!" Leslie screamed. "I thought Myra said the rifles were loaded full!"

John cupped his hands to his mouth. "You there!" he bellowed. "Behind the stump! Surrender now and you won't be shot."

"There!" Leslie shouted, watching the gunman run from the stump to a fallen log. He slipped another round into the rifle.

"Hold your fire, Son. He's hit. Looks like you clipped him in the neck. That's enough burden for him to bear. I expect it's also enough to scare the others away."

Leslie and his father each reloaded their Winchesters.

"Let's go check on your brother."

As they turned, a volley of rifle fire came from the marsh grass near the river. Slugs whizzing by, they dropped to the ground. Bullets screamed overhead, striking the barn behind. John came up—rifle first. Round by round, he emptied his Winchester toward the cloud of gun smoke hanging above the thick marsh grass. Seconds later, he and Leslie watched five men in olive drab khaki uniforms scramble down the riverbank and into the stream.

John stood, holding his Winchester overhead. "Cowards!" he thundered. "You dishonor those uniforms!" He helped Leslie up. They watched the marauders swim across the river, some without their rifles.

"Now I'm certain they're not Wisconsin militiamen," said John. "Soldiers don't abandon their arms. C'mon, let's get back to the cabin."

"Pa," said Leslie, "I hope Clare … I hope he doesn't ..."

"You'll have to take his place, you know."

"He's going to be all right, won't he, Pa? Won't he?"

"Hmm?"

"Is Clare going to *die*?"

"Die? Not Clarence. He's tough. He's a Dietz."

"Then …"

"What I meant, Son, is that you'll have to take his place on the hay wagon. Take over his job." He pointed to the western sky. "There's a storm coming. We've got to get that hay stowed away before it pours."

"But, what about Clare, Pa? And what about the man I shot? He could be suffering. Shouldn't we ...?"

"We'll soon know how Clarence is faring. As for the assassin, he's not our concern. This was his doing. It's up to his accomplices to find him and get him to a doctor if that wound on his neck warrants."

"But, Pa, *I* am the person who's responsible for injuring him. Maybe even … killing …"

"No, Leslie. You are the young hero who defended his home and his family from some bloodthirsty brigands—assassins who descended upon us to inflict the worst kind of harm. You are a *champion*, Leslie Dietz. A champion to every working stiff who carries good in his heart whilst the dag-blasted robber barons pilfer the last dang pennies from his pocketbook. Leslie, you are a *hero*. Don't you *ever* forget that."

Doctor Henry Burns

Hattie, Helen, and Stanley held Clarence down on the bed while Myra gently washed his wound with warm, soapy water and a dishrag. He struggled momentarily, falling in and out of consciousness.

Hattie wept. "Oh, Clarence, don't you dare die on me. First Harry at twelve years, then Leanna, a child of merely seven. And now, you. All because of your stubborn father and that pigheaded lumber tycoon down in Chippewa Falls. Two stubborn Germans—neither willing to give an inch."

"Don't blame father," said Myra, sopping up blood. "He's merely standing his ground as he should. The company tried to shortchange him and now he has the upper hand."

Hattie wetted a second rag. "Upper hand? A man who has marshals encamped nearby, waiting for the chance to arrest him? Shoot him? Shoot his sons? No, Myra, a man whose son lies bleeding after being shot by hooligans hired by the lumber company does *not* have the upper hand!"

Clarence moaned and then tried to sit up. Hattie gently guided him down again.

"Helen," said Hattie, "fetch the turpentine. Stanley, there's a cotton sheet on the clothesline. Go get it. I'll need it for bandages."

"Yes, Mama." Stanley left by the kitchen door as Helen returned with the turpentine. Myra poured some into a bowl. Its pungent scent filled the room. Stanley returned with the sheet. Hattie tore it into long ribbons. Handing one to Helen, another to Stanley, she said, "We need these rolled up. All of them."

Both children began rolling the bandages as told. Next, their mother tore one of the strips into small rags. Myra used one to wipe blood on Clarence's head and neck. She dipped another into the turpentine. "Clare," she said, "this is bound to sting. Be strong."

Clarence didn't reply.

Myra gently wiped the five-inch slice through his scalp with the turpentine-soaked rag.

Clarence didn't wince.

Myra's rag caught on something. She lifted out chips of her brother's skull, dropping each into the bowl of turpentine. "Clare, are you doing all right?" she asked.

Clarence didn't respond.

"Clare?" said Hattie. "Clare?" she repeated, louder.

"I don't think he can hear," said Myra . "Nor does he feel the turpentine's bite."

"Clare!" Hattie said, loud enough to startle the children.

No response.

Tears returned to Myra's eyes. She reached for a clean rag, dried her tears, and finished cleaning the wound. Hattie folded two rags lengthwise before applying them to the wound. She placed her arm around Clarence's neck and lifted him a few inches. Myra quickly wrapped one of the bandage rolls around her brother's skull. By the time she'd finished, blood had already soaked through.

"Tighter," Hattie ordered. "Tight enough to stop the bleeding."

Myra used a second roll to cover the first tighter than before. Hattie raised Clarence again. "His bleeding will slow if we keep him upright."

"Listen!" said Helen, hearing the thudding of boots on the porch.

The door swung open. "Good to see you're already sitting up, Son," said his father.

Hattie glared at him. "He can't hear you. He's gone deaf."

"But he's alive," Myra added. "But Mother's right. It seems his hearing is gone. And his skull's broken. The bleeding keeps on. He needs a doctor."

"Clare can't hear nothing?" asked Leslie.

"Nor feel any pain," said Myra. "That's the only good in this."

"John," sobbed Hattie, "how could you …? Why did you send him out there? Why?"

John ignored her. "Has he lost much blood?"

"Some," Myra said. "But the bandage seems to have slowed the bleeding. He needs Doctor Burns."

"You've wiped the wound down with turpentine?"

"Of course, Father. But he needs a doctor."

"I'll go," said Leslie.

"No," said John. "There's a storm coming and hay to put up. If Clarence doesn't improve by nightfall, I'll fetch Doc Burns myself. Have him here by first light."

"You've no right to risk our son's life," snapped Hattie. "This isn't about some lame horse or ailing sheep. This is your eldest son!"

"Yes. *My* eldest son," snapped John. "*I* am the head of this family. As such, I say we get the rest of the hay put up before the storm. Now, as much as I'd like to stand around and jabber, that storm isn't waiting. Hattie, you and Johnny stay here and tend to Clarence. I need the rest of you out by the barn. The quicker we get to it, the quicker we finish up. Let's get on with it."

Beneath a darkening sky, John took Clarence's place on the wagon. Stanley guided the rope. Helen led Meggie as she'd seen her sister do, and Myra brought the hay into the loft, stomping it down as fast as she could. The crew stowed the last wagonload minutes before the storm hit. They ran to the cabin as rain began to fall.

Inside, Clarence moaned. Blood oozed through his bandage and dripped onto his bed.

"John, it's time you went for the doctor," said Hattie.

John looked at his son, bleeding, unable to hear. "All right," he said. "I'll saddle up Bullet."

"No, Pa," said Leslie. "I'll go. There might be someone waiting to capture you. Somebody who saw Clare fall and figures you'll ride in to fetch the doctor."

"Too dangerous, Leslie," warned Myra. "Let me go. Nobody will stop a girl trying to help her injured brother."

"All right," said her father. "But strap on my holster, just in case."

"Take your pistol? You know I would never ..."

"Just keep it in sight and you won't need to," he said. "As many times as I've worn that gun to town, I've not once felt the need to draw it. The mere sight of it keeps the peace."

The storm passed quickly. In the evening twilight, the buckskin colt navigated the back trail from the farm to Winter. A kerosene lamp hung from a sign reading *Dr. H. J. Burns.* Soon the doctor rode alongside Myra on his own horse.

"Who did you say fired on Clarence?" asked Burns.

"All we know is that they were dressed in khaki uniforms. Like militiamen."

"Soldiers?" said Burns. "They may have looked the part, but they weren't sent by the governor."

"How do you know?"

"I heard that seven uniformed men stayed overnight at the hotel. Before the night was over, the whiskey had their tongues wagging in the barroom. Word has it they came up from Milwaukee on the train."

"For what purpose?"

"To capture your father. All were recruited by Sheriff Gylland."

"Paid for by the county?"

"I asked the same question, Myra. It seems that Gylland himself acquired the uniforms from a Milwaukee theatrical supply store and paid for them with money he received from the Chippewa Lumber and Boom Company. The rifles, the train fare their wages, the whole shebang."

"My heavens. There's no limit as to what ends the company will go to in order to deny my father his rightful claims. It seems they are willing to cut down the apple tree rather than part with one apple."

"Yes. It does seem that way."

"So, the lumber syndicate has its own soldiers, now? Why were we not warned?"

"I suppose nobody thought much of it. You've had marshals and detectives camped across the river from your cabin two summers, now. They come and go like bouts of rheumatism. Most are there because they're on the dole and glad to have the work. I doubt anyone figured these men were any different."

"Well, my brother sure does," replied Myra. "His skull is cracked and he can't hear, not to mention the scar he'll carry for the rest of his life—if he lives. Oh, Dr. Burns, tell me he will. Please!"

"I'll do everything I can, Myra."

"Oh, my poor, poor brother. And he's such a kind, gentle person."

"And you say these men in uniform crept toward your home undetected?"

"Slithered like snakes through the marsh grass along the river's edge. Firing first on Clarence and then at Leslie and Father. Though I must add that, after seeing Clare fall to an assassin's bullet, my father's rage compelled him to shoot back at the intruders."

"I'm not surprised. What man would not fire back at intruders firing upon a family member? You're father showed amazing self-restraint in not hunting down the lot of them and snuffing them out one by one."

"Lord knows he could have," she said. "But he's not like that. True, my father will defend our home and family. But he's not out to hurt anyone just to draw blood. Not him. He's a good-hearted, God-fearing Christian, not a killer."

They rode in silence a ways. "Myra," said Burns, "I've a friend in Milwaukee, Clive Rowland. He's the managing editor of the *Milwaukee Journal*. I'm certain he'd delight in hearing of this attack on your brother and this dastardly treatment of your father. Do you suppose …?"

"That's a question for my father, not me," Myra replied. "But I think he will approve. Father is always pleased when the newspapers tell his side of the story. Most editors simply kowtow to the lumber trust."

"Then, if your father approves, I'll write Mr. Rowland upon my return to town. We shall see what the county board has to say when news gets out of lawmen shooting down an unarmed boy on his own property!"

ONE FAMILY DEFIES EVEN THE U. S. IN DEFENSE OF CLAIM TO PROPERTY

(Special to The Press.)

MILWAUKEE, Aug. 12.—Backed by his rifle, his wife and his family of six children, John Dietz for two years has defied officers of the county, state and national governments at his cabin on the Thornapple river in the heart of the northern Wisconsin forest. Several men have been shot in battles waged in the woods with the Dietz family.

Thornapple river constitutes a dead line which Dietz boasts will be maintained until he is carried from the palce feet first, his family dead and his rifle empty.

Dietz's position is based upon his claims to Cameron dam, over which the Chippewa Lumber & Boom Co., drives its logs. He demands a tollage of 10 cents a thousand feet for all logs schuted over the dam and for wages for 445 days in which he was in the employ of the company. In two years he has jammed 20,000,000 feet of logs in the Cameron dam

is inaccessible, although in the winter narrow sledges have been taken over the uncertain trail through the hardwood forest. The lonely family subsists on deer and other game shot along Thornapple river and the produce from the

114

John Rogich

Two khaki-clad men with lanterns searched the bottomland along the Thornapple River looking for their missing comrade. One dragged a stretcher behind. He called out the name of his wounded comrade in a forced whisper. "Rogich!" he said. "Rogich, where are you?"

"Last I saw, he was hunkered down in the popple trees, betwixt the barn and the river," said his partner.

As they searched, their path took them nearer and nearer the dead birch stump where he'd last been seen—the hiding place from where he'd shot down Clarence.

"Rogich! For crying out loud, answer me. Where are you?"

"He's probably dead," said his partner. "We should leave before Dietz sees us and we end up in the same boat."

"No. We're here to find Rogich, alive or … otherwise. C'mon. This way." They fought their way through the underbrush, moving closer to the barn and cabin than they'd hoped they'd be.

"Here!" said one man. "Look. Blood. It goes this way. Along the river bank."

"Help me," came a weak call from the river's edge. "Over … here."

The two men soon knelt over their comrade, shot in the neck. Another slug lay deep in his hip. A third had torn off his right heel.

"Rogich," said one of his rescuers, "We figured you for dead."

"What took you so long?"

"We dared not come out before dark settled in. Too risky."

John Rogich laughed weakly. "Your courage dumbfounds me."

"Well, we're here, ain't we?"

"Just get me to a doctor before I bleed to death."

"It's awful slow going through this dang thornapple brush."

"I don't have the luxury of time. Cross the pasture. Get me to the camp. Then fetch me that doctor."

Closer and closer the two stretcher-bearers came to the barn and the Dietz home.

In the cabin, Dr. Burns tended to Clarence's wound. He applied a liberal dusting of a mixture of powdered pine tar and sulfur, followed by clean bandages. Finally, he dosed him with laudanum.

"He'll sleep now," said the doctor. "His wound is severe, but Clarence is strong and the medicine should prevent infection. Recovery is bound to take time."

"Will Clare ever hear again?" Myra asked, her voice trembling.

"His hearing may come back in a few weeks or months. Time will tell. Perhaps never. In the meantime, he needs rest. Plenty of rest."

"Oh, thank you for coming, Doctor Burns," said Hattie.

A sudden glint of light from outside shone through a window, alerting John. He grabbed his rifle and rushed out the door. "Don't leave too soon, Doc. You might have more work to do." He stood on the porch, watching the men struggle down near the river. "You, with the lantern!" he shouted, "Get off my land!"

The lantern went out. In the moonlight, John made out the shapes of two men running toward the riverbank. Seconds later, reflections in the water and the sound of splashing told him they were swimming for the other shore. As he returned inside, John chuckled at how easily he'd driven the hired thugs from his property.

"No gunfire, Mr. Dietz?" asked the doctor. "I'm relieved."

"Aw, the cowards heard my voice and scattered like rats fleeing a house afire."

"Thank the Lord," said Hattie. "I've had enough shooting for a lifetime."

John leaned his rifle behind the door. "You know? I never thought in a million years I'd fire on another man."

"No one can blame you, Mr. Dietz," said the doctor. "Every man has the right to defend home and family. The law should be on your side, not fighting against you."

"See, Mother?" said John. "Didn't I say this again and again?"

"You may have right on your side," Hattie replied, "but our son now suffers for it. And that other man who's been shot, probably suffers as well. Guns are no way to settle a dispute."

"I may be able to help," said Dr. Burns. "I was telling Myra that I have a friend, Mr. Clive Rowland, who is the editor of the *Milwaukee Journal*. I am certain he will be interested in what has transpired here. With your approval, Mr. Dietz, I'll contact Mr. Rowland and tell him what's happened."

"I think it's a capital idea, Father," said Myra.

"I agree," John replied. "Our countrymen need to know what is going on here. It's time people understood what the robber barons are doing to them as well as to me. Workers across the nation must rise up for their rights and demand a square deal."

Burns sipped from his coffee cup. "Clearly you feel this all stems from a larger problem, a nation-wide problem."

"It's no different than the coal miners who suffer at the hands of the mining corporations or the steelworkers at the hands of the mills. Or railroad workers or farmers or teamsters or dollar-a-week seamstresses. The list goes on and on."

"More coffee, Dr. Burns?" asked Myra.

"Thank you, but no. It's late. I must be on my way."

"Nonsense!" said John. "You will have supper with us and stay the night."

"That's kind of you, sir, but …"

"We insist," said Hattie.

"Yes," said Helen. "Mama and I insist."

"Alright. I will stay. That way I can check on your son's condition in the morning."

Myra filled his cup. "Then you're in for a treat, Dr. Burns. Helen and I baked blackberry pies this morning, sir. And dear Jenny Cameron left us an ice cream machine that we often put to good use. Stanley is chipping the ice as we speak."

"Oh, boy!" cried Johnny. "Pie and ice cream!"

Abandoned in thick brush along the river, Deputy John Rogich lay in agony, tormented by mosquitoes. His bleeding had stopped but the pain hadn't. Pressing his hand against the bullet wound in his neck, he raised his head to see the dim light from the oil lamps inside the Dietz cabin. Terrified at the thought of what John Dietz might do to him for shooting down his son, he turned his attention to the river. He tried to shout for help, but the night sounds absorbed his feeble cries. Determined to not die in the woods, he inched his way to the riverbank and slid into the stream. The cool water discouraged the mosquitoes and soothed the pain in his hip and neck. He pulled himself through the water, away from the Dietz land and toward the marshal's camp. Then, reaching the main channel, he lost control. The strong current washed him downstream like one of the many logs that had floated past on earlier log drives. Suddenly, the current pulled him under. Surfacing, he gasped for air before submerging again. Then, far downstream, Rogich dragged himself onto shore. The mosquitos soon found him—wet, cold, exhausted—face down in the mud.

FLED LIKE COWARDS

Wounded Man Tells How He Was Left To Die By His Companions.

Radisson, Wis., July 31.—After crawling on his hands and knees for a distance through the forest, Duyo Rogich, of Milwaukee, wounded in three places by Clarence Dietz, reached the homestead

The laudanum given Clarence by Dr. Burns assured him a good sleep.

Early the next morning, Leslie and his father knelt by his son's bed in prayer before tending to the morning chores. The sun cresting the treetops across the river sent a shaft of light into the bedroom. Clarence woke with a start, gasping as he grasped his bandaged head. A loud moan from the shock and pain brought Dr. Burns.

His mother followed, running. "Oh, Clarence," she said, placing her hands on his. "Please, you must endure."

Clarence stared at her, looking confused.

"*Endure*, Clarence," Hattie repeated.

His expression didn't change.

"Don't let it defeat you. *Endure!*"

Clarence's eyes widened with fear.

Hattie recoiled from the terror she saw in her son's eyes. *"Endure!"*

Tears welled in her son's eyes.

Myra joined them. "What is it, Mother? What's wrong?"

"*Endure*, Clarence!" Hattie screamed. "Can't you hear me?"

Dr. Burns placed a hand on Hattie's shoulder. "Give it time," he said. "I've examined his ears, His eardrums have not been damaged. Mrs. Dietz, although I cannot say when, I believe your boy will hear again."

His words reassured Hattie. She leaned forward, as if wanting to hug her son.

The doctor grasped Clarence's hand. He looked into the boy's eyes.

"Clarence," he said slowly. "You will hear again."

Clarence's expression showed he didn't understand. Dr. Burns pointed to Clarence's ear and then to his own. "You will hear again," he shouted.

Calm flooded across Clarence's face. He nodded, understanding the doctor's words. Then he put both hands to his head, feeling the bandages.

"You were shot," said Burns. He pointed to the side of his own head and jerked his hand back, mimicking a gunshot. "Shot."

"Yes, Clarence," said Hattie, pointing to her own head. "Shot."

"Someone … s-shot … me?"

His first words since falling to the mercenary's gunfire startled Hattie. Again she leaned ahead to hug him.

"When?" he asked.

"He doesn't remember," said the doctor. "It's not unusual. His memory is likely to return along with his hearing."

The children now looked on from behind. Myra took her brother's hand and smiled. "We love you, Clare. Understand? We … love … you."

Clarence nodded and smiled. He returned his hands to his bandaged head.

"Bandages," said Dr. Burns. He turned to the family. "I'll change them before I leave. Three days hence, I'll return to check on your boy. Meanwhile, he must rest. I'll leave you with a bottle of painkillers, but watch that you don't give him too many. Two pills, morning, noon, and night. It'll help him sleep. Rest is the best treatment for Clarence now."

Miles south of the Thornapple Farm, two surveyors plotting section lines stopped suddenly. "Listen," said one. "Hear that? Sounds like a cry for help."

The cry came from Deputy John Rogich, shot in the neck, hip, and heel. He'd dragged himself miles downstream along the river bottom, and now looked up at the two workers.

He tried to speak. "They … left me … to die. Help me. Please …"

Soon, the two men dragged a hastily made travois south toward Ladysmith. That evening, they delivered the nearly dead thug to the hospital.

The morning papers offered only Sheriff Gylland's version of the battle. The story shook the region.

BLOOD FLOWS AT CAMERON DAM

Ladysmith, Wis., July 27. Bloodshed at Cameron Dam, in Sawyer county, resulting from a sharp battle yesterday between the family of John Dietz and a squad of six militiamen led by Sheriff Gylland, in which Clarence Dietz and one of the militiamen were wounded, perhaps fatally, is expected to be followed by the dispatch of one or two companies of the Wisconsin national guard with orders to take Dietz dead or alive.

"The only way to take Dietz is to kill the whole family, for the women and boys shoot as good as their pa," said Sheriff Gylland, who hired the militiamen as deputies to take Dietz by force of arms. Sheriff Gylland expressed a fear, but not a definite one, that the wounded deputy may have been put to death after being left in a place of comparative safety by his companions while they hurried on to get surgical aid for him.

"I'll Shoot Anything."

"I'll shoot anything on the river hereafter," was the angry last word of Dietz yesterday. He now holds undisputed sway for the time being, even the watchers stationed near the now-famous dam having decamped in fear of death. The long-expected clash between the squatter and representatives of the state was participated in by practically the entire Dietz family.

As soon as the sheriff and militia men came in sight of the Dietz cabin, Dietz, his wife, two of his sons and one daughter came out armed with repeating rifles. After the first volley from the Dietz side, one of the militiamen fell wounded. Bullets struck him in the ankle, hip and neck. The fusillade was returned by the militiamen. After the smoke had cleared away it was seen that Clarence Dietz had fallen. Then the would-be captors of Dietz retired behind stumps and trees.

Battle Lasts an Hour.

For over an hour the battle continued. Fully 150 shots were fired by each side. Then the militiamen tramped thirty-six miles to this city for medical assistance.

Clarence Dietz, after he was wounded, was dragged by his sister to the cabin while the other son and the father remained on the field to face the sheriff and militiamen.

The Cause of the Trouble.

Dietz for a long time has held possession of the Cameron Dam on the Thornapple River, preventing the driving of several million feet of logs belonging to the Chippewa Lumber and Boom Company. The logs are rotting and the company has for some time past been endeavoring to have Dietz served with legal papers compelling him to show cause why the company should not be allowed to drive the logs.

Dietz informed the attacking party Wednesday that he had enough ammunition to last three months and intended to use it. August Ender of Eau Claire had a talk with the outlaw since the battle. Dietz told Ender that Sheriff Gylland and his party had fired the first shot and that Dietz naturally had to protect his family by returning the volley.

At Present, Everything is Quiet at Thornapple Dam.

Mr. Ender thinks that the wounds of Clarence Dietz, son of John Dietz, are fatal, his brain being exposed to view. The shot struck his forehead and glanced up, piercing his hat.

Dietz said repeatedly, pointing to the wounded boy, "Here you can see what the dirty corporation has done. But they don't get John Dietz. There is an Almighty over us who regulates these things. They would settle, I guess, but they are ashamed to at this stage of the game," he said.

"I am no desperado. Who wouldn't have shot back as I did to defend all that is near and dear to me? I don't thirst for blood or revenge as the yellow press has painted me. I want peace and was forced into this. All I ever wanted was to be left alone."

Sympathy with Dietz.

A Rice Lake dispatch says that Clarence Dietz is no worse, and that a party consisting of William Dietz, who left here yesterday, and a doctor and others will go to the Dietz farm today. At Rice Lake there was excited talk of organizing a posse to protect Dietz. Public sympathy at Rice Lake is with Dietz. A petition will be circulated there and sent to Gov. Davidson setting forth the sentiment of that section.

Governor will Order Out the Militia.

Gov. James O. Davidson himself picked the six militiamen who aided Sheriff Gylland, and it is declared that Dietz's latest flagrant defiance of the dignity and authority of the state will be punished by force of arms if necessary.

Ladysmith News-Budget, July 25, 1905

27

Stanley

Clarence spent weeks in bed. His mother and sisters changed his bandages twice daily. To ward off infection, they applied a liniment made of powdered pine tar, sulfur, and lard. Over time, he regained his hearing. A month after being shot, he could keep his balance as he walked from the bedroom to the dinner table and back. But not being able to be outside in the late summer sunshine, not able to tend to the livestock or cast a line into the pools along the river dampened his spirits.

"Clare," said Myra, hoping to cheer him up one morning, "listen to this. It's from the *Milwaukee Journal*." She sat on the edge of his bed with the paper. "'The militiamen, who wore uniforms and assisted Sheriff Gylland of Sawyer County in his raid upon Dietz without prior orders, are to be discharged from the National Guard.'"

"Discharged?" asked Clarence.

"As they should be," Myra replied. "And Gylland should be sent to prison. It says here that this was a 'breach of discipline and the commander-in-chief is sailed upon to take immediate action.'"

Myra read on. "'Six of the Milwaukee men who participated in the battle with John Dietz at the Cameron Dam last Wednesday returned home today. The seventh member of the party, John Rogich, who was wounded by Dietz and his son, is resting in the lumber camp.'"

"I thought he was in Ladysmith."

"This reporter often gets his facts wrong." She continued. "Now, listen to this! 'Of the whole Dietz family,' said the leader of the party, 'I think the daughter, Myra, is the most dangerous to a sheriff bent on making an arrest. She kept firing from the time the battle began until it was over and not once let up except to reload her rifle.'"

"You?" gasped Clarence. "You've never as much as raised a rifle to look down its sights!"

Myra laughed and then continued reading. "'She paid no attention to our shots, although of course we were as careful as possible not to shoot her. We were in danger any minute of being hit by her bullets. She is a corker and no mistake.'"

"Well, sis, they've got that right. You're a corker if ever there was one."

"Now here's the best part, Clare. It's the last line in the story." She raised the paper and read, "'If it takes a company of militia to capture the old man, it will take a *regiment of regulars* to arrest the daughter.'"

In the kitchen, Hattie listened to their laughter and then used the corner of her apron to dab tears of joy from her eyes. Clarence, her oldest son, was on the mend.

Leslie, Myra, and their father managed to get the haying done and the crops harvested by late October. As the weather turned, hunters came to camp along the river. Early one morning, they heard a shout from the front yard.

"Mr. Dietz? Mr. Dietz, are you home?"

John cracked open the door.

"Mr. Dietz, I am one of four hunters camped nearby. We're new to these woods and in need of a guide, sir. Simply put, we don't feel right heading out unprepared."

"I've no time to spare," said John.

"I've heard you know every inch of this land, sir. I'm willing to pay for your assistance."

"Just hang to the river bottom and you'll be fine."

"Please, Mr. Dietz," he begged. "If nothing else, join us for dinner today and offer some advice on our hunt."

"No, I won't do that," John replied. "But you are welcome to join us at our table, Mr. ..."

"Roese, sir. Alfred E. Roese of Osceola."

"Osceola? Are you that newspaperman?"

"A. E. Roese, Editor of the *Osceola Sun,* at your service, sir. The story of your burdens has often found its way into our paper."

"Well, why didn't you say so? Yes, I've read your commentaries. It appears you have the same disdain for the lumber trust as do I."

"It's an awful thing they've done to you and your family. Especially the shooting down of your son."

"Yes, we feared we'd lost Clarence. But the boy is strong. In spite of his head wound, he somehow pulled through."

"My, that's wonderful news. I'll be sure to post it on the front page upon my return home."

"Alfred, you and your men are welcome to join us for our noon dinner. You can meet my family and we'll set plans for your hunt. I'm sure we can help you fill your salt barrels with game."

"Oh, thank you, Mr. Dietz," said Roese. "Perhaps you can elucidate on your quest to bring a smidgeon of responsibility to the lumber syndicate, too."

"It would be my pleasure. Noon, then?"

"Noon it is."

Within a week, the hunting party hung four bucks, two does, and a bear on the buck pole. But the celebrations of the hunt came to a sudden end when eight-year-old Stanley fell ill one afternoon.

Myra placed her palm on her little brother's forehead. "Oh, dear. You're burning up," she said. "Let's get you inside." As they crossed the room, Stanley collapsed onto the rug. "Mother! Come quickly. It's Stanley. He's come down with something."

Hattie rushed from the kitchen.

Myra held the little boy's head. "He has a fever and his breathing's not right."

"Help me get him into bed," Hattie said, pulling the child to his feet.

His mother tucked him in and then looked him over. "The poor child. My, how his glands are swollen," she said. "And you're right about his breathing. It's as though Stanley is straining with each breath." She opened his mouth to check his tonsils. "Lord help us!" she gasped.

"What?" asked Myra. "What is it?"

"It has the look of … No, it can't be."

"Oh, Mother, tell me."

"It has all the signs of the scourge that took away poor little Harry eleven years ago."

"Oh, I wish Dr. Burns lived near," said Myra. "I'll ride into town …"

"No, not yet," said Hattie. "We should wait for your father to return from the woods. Meanwhile, we must let Stanley rest."

By the time the men returned from hunt, Stanley's breathing had become strained, rapid, and raspy. He struggled for each breath and trembled with chills. Myra held the oil lamp while Hattie opened his mouth. John peered at his little boy's tonsils. "Swollen," he said.

"Pa," said Leslie. "Should I go for Dr. Burns?"

"No. Stanley's a tough little monkey. He'll be better soon."

Myra set the lamp on the dresser. "Father, I've never seen him this way. Just to be safe, why not have Leslie fetch the doctor?"

"I said no, Myra. Children get sick now and then and come back from it better than before."

Stanley coughed a feeble cough. He tried again but failed.

"May I check the boy?" said Roese. "I've raised five young ones and seen most of the maladies that can afflict them."

"Oh, Alfred, please do," begged Hattie.

Myra held the oil lamp again. Stanley's mother gently opened his mouth.

"Oh, dear," said Roese. "This is not good news."

"What is it?" asked Hattie.

"Your fears were warranted, Hattie. I'm afraid Stanley has contracted black diphtheria."

"What? No! Oh, oh, no!" moaned Hattie. "Not my baby. No!"

Roese turned to John. "You'd better call for that doctor."

"My boy will pull through just fine, Alfred."

"John, that thick gray covering in his throat will soon block Stanley's windpipe. He needs to have a tube put in to keep it open."

"Or what?"

"Your boy won't be able to breathe, John. He'll suffocate."

"Father, please," begged Myra. "Send Leslie. Before it's too late."

"Aw, you're all jumping the gun. Myra, you said yourself that he was fine only a few hours ago. I'm telling all of you, Stanley is tough. He'll pull through. The best thing we can do for him right now is to stop all this poking and prodding and let the little fellow get some sleep."

"Oh, please, John," pleaded Hattie. "Let Leslie fetch the doctor."

"Mother, I said let him rest."

All but Stanley sat at the supper table that evening. No one spoke of the boy's condition, hoping John had made the right call. After their guests left for their last night in camp, Hattie slipped into the boy's room to check on her son. Her gut-wrenching wail brought the others running.

"Oh, my poor baby," she bawled. "Oh, Stanley, Stanley. Don't leave us. Don't go." She rocked his lifeless body in her arms. "John. Look what you've done. My baby. My baby. *My baby!*"

Stunned, John wrenched the child from his mother's arms and shook the limp body. "Wake up, Stanley. Wake up!" he yelled.

"Oh," wailed Hattie, "my baby's gone. My baby, my baby," she cried. "My baby's gone."

Tears streaming now, Myra held her mother, hoping her embrace might somehow comfort her. Leslie took his dead brother from his father and laid him on the bed. Standing in the doorway, Helen held baby Johnny, both in tears. Behind her, Clarence looked on. They all stared in disbelief at the limp figure of a little boy who'd been healthy and happy only hours before.

"Why did Stanley go away?" bawled Helen.

"Stanley didn't choose to leave us," said Myra. "Instead, the Lord came to take him away—to take him to a better place."

Alfred Roese's hunting party remained an extra day to help the family. By midday, they'd built a small pine coffin, adorning it with wooden toys the older boys had carved for Stanley years earlier. There'd be no time to shellac his casket. The tearstains on it would have to do.

At one o'clock, the family and the hunting party tramped up the hill that overlooked Thornapple Farm. There, Clarence and Leslie waited, their shovels leaning against a maple tree near the little boy's grave. Hattie remained home, too sick with grief to witness her child's burial.

The pallbearers rested the coffin on the forest floor and joined the others surrounding the grave in a half-circle. John opened his bible to the Book of Ecclesiastes. "There is a time for everything," he read aloud. "A time to be born and a time to die, a time to plant and a time to uproot, a time to kill and a time to heal, … a time to weep and a time to laugh, a time to mourn and a time to dance…" He closed the book. "That was our Stanley. Oh, how he loved to laugh and dance and sing. Now he's in the Lord's hands. But he will live on in our memories. Our dear little Stanley, singing and dancing and laughing in our hearts."

Helen broke into tears, burying her face in Myra's black dress. "I don't want Stanley gone," she wept.

"Please lower the casket," said John. "There's nothing more for us to say or do. Mr. Roese, if you don't mind, I'd appreciate it if you could finish up here." He turned, leading his family down the hill.

Nearing the cabin, Myra heard Helen cough. "Open up," said Myra. "I want to see your throat."

The newspapers all carried the story.

SCOURGE SEIZES DIETZ FAMILY
Diphtheria Carrying Off Famous
Defender of Cameron Dam

The famous Dietz family which, for four years stood off federal, state, and county officials and duly whipped a powerful corporation into accepting its terms, is in danger of extinction by black diphtheria. One of the Dietz children was stricken with the disease Saturday and died within two hours. A priest who had just returned from Cameron Dam says the entire family is desperately ill, but that Dietz refused to call a physician, saying it is too late.

Wood County Reporter, Dec 3, 08

But the editors never knew what the family went through. At the first sign of Helen contracting the disease, John rode into town for Doctor Burns. A day later, all but Leslie were on the way to recovery. Delirious, he hardly noticed when the doctor intubated him. By the next morning, the gray film restricting his throat had subsided.

That afternoon, Myra, still in her nightgown, knelt by Leslie's bed. "Thank you. Lord. Thank you for not taking Leslie and the others along with little Stanley. Thank you for giving them, giving *us* more time."

"Myra," called Hattie. "Get dressed. The doctor is due to return soon."

"Mother, I'm certain Doctor Burns has seen women in night gowns."

"You're well enough to wear your everyday clothes. Get dressed."

"Mrs. Dietz," said Burns, "your family is out of the woods. In fact, you've come through with flying colors. Thank God no one contracted pneumonia. You and your husband are doing well, too." He mounted his horse and turned back. "I'm dreadful sorry about Stanley, he was a firecracker, that one. But perhaps his passing had a purpose."

"And what might that be?" asked Myra. "To show life is unfair?"

"Myra, your little brother gave the rest of the family a warning call. Had he not contracted diphtheria ahead of the rest, perhaps there'd be more graves up there on that hill."

"Yes, Doctor. I suppose. But at such cost. Poor, poor little Stanley. What a shame for an innocent child to die like that."

"We all die, young lady."

Myra spun around to face him. "In our time, Doctor. In our time. Had not my father been so pigheaded, this would not have happened."

"No, Myra. You're wrong. It's a three-quarter-hour ride to my home, even at a gallop. Had Leslie summoned me, it would've been too late. I wouldn't have been able to help the child."

"I don't want to hear this!" she shouted. Looking across the yard, she saw large snowflakes drifting down. A soft blanket of snow had covered all tracks, all signs of activity.

The serene landscape calmed her. A brother had been lost, but others survived. *She* had survived. *She* still had her life. There and then, Myra vowed not to waste a single, solitary day of it.

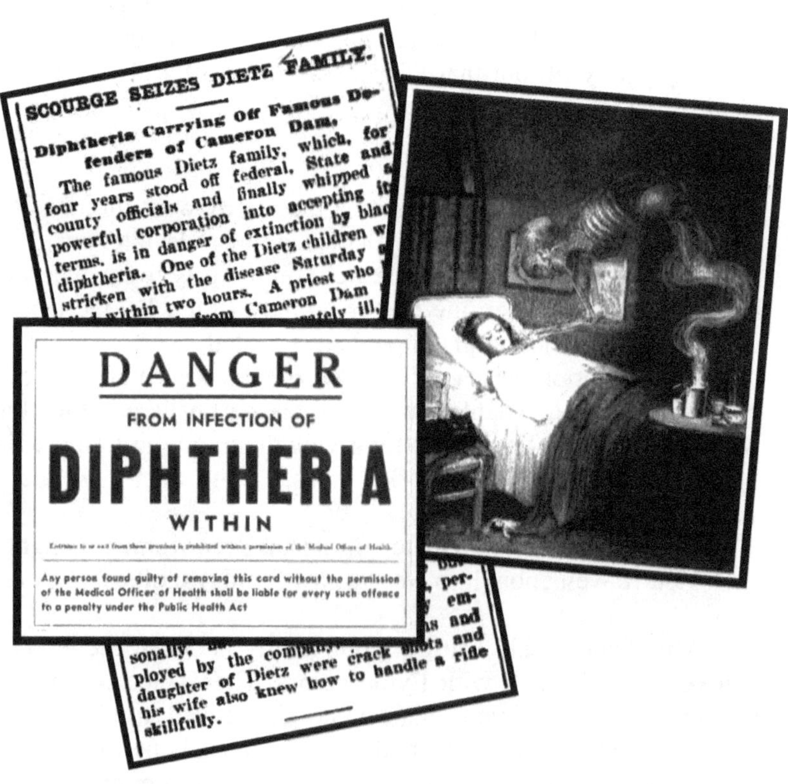

28

On Behalf of Mr. Weyerhaeuser

John rested his pen and corked the ink bottle. "Mother, I've written letters to several lumbermen, asking for bids on our timber. It's my hope that I can make a deal where they mill the logs into boards, and take a third of the lumber for their trouble. That would leave plenty here to build you a fine home."

"Oh, John, that would be wonderful."

"But first we have to make this all legal and just. William says that before we can touch that timber, it must be offered for sale to the public."

"Even though it was abandoned on *our* property?"

"Yes, even so. Will says we now own it, but the laws say we must give others a fair chance to bid on it."

"Who gets the money after it sells?"

"We do, Mother."

"So, if Chippewa Lumber and Boom Company places the winning bid, they get the logs back and we get paid for them?"

"Precisely. And wouldn't that be grand?"

"Paid enough to build a house?"

"More than enough."

"Then let's not dillydally, John. The sooner we hold the auction, the sooner we begin our new house."

Hattie, Clarence, and Myra stood on the steps of the Sawyer County Courthouse along with Schoolmaster Jeremiah C. Gates. Unbuttoning his double-breasted coat, Gates pulled an envelope from an inside pocket. He gave it to Myra who scaled the steps to the top. She turned to the handful of people gathered at the bottom of the steps and read it aloud.

"In the matter of the white pine logs stranded on the property of John and Hattie Dietz along the Thornapple River, that timber is now in its entirety up for auction to the highest bidder. Do I hear any bids?"

"How's a body supposed to get those logs of yours out of there?" shouted someone.

Hattie stepped up three steps. "That's the responsibility of the buyer," she said. "But don't worry. My husband wouldn't stand in your way."

"Them logs have been layin' for over a year now. Ain't they all et up by pine bores?"

Leslie answered. "Pa looked them over last month and said there's not much worm damage yet."

"Do I hear any bids?" Myra repeated.

"Twenty dollars," came a shout.

"One-hundred," said Hattie.

The man who bid protested. "Say, now! You can't bid on your own timber."

"Yes, she can," said Gates. "According to the state statutes, the abandoned logs must be sold at auction to the highest bidder and that the property owner shall be paid the total revenue from the auction. That's the written law. Nothing in it says the landowner cannot participate."

"Do I hear any more bids?"

"One-twenty-five," shouted Clarence, bringing a smile from his mother.

"Going once," shouted Myra.

"This don't seem right," shouted someone.

"Going twice." She paused, waiting for another bid. "Sold to Clarence Dietz for one-hundred twenty-five dollars."

"Say," shouted the man who made the first bid, "does the boy even *have* that kind of money?"

"I'll let him pay it off in time," Hattie said. "All right, children. Hop onto the buckboard. We've a long way to go."

By light of the kerosene lamp suspended above, Myra methodically read from the stacks of mail Leslie had brought from town that day. Across the table, Helen used a scissors to open envelop after envelope from supporters, admirers, and the rare critic opposing John's stand against the lumber syndicate. She placed those containing currency on one pile, those without a contribution to the family on another.

Near the fireplace, their father clipped newspaper articles for his scrapbook.

"Helen," said Myra, "be sure to write the amount on the envelope so we can send thank you notes to those who sent money."

"I am, Sis."

"And be careful with those scissors that you don't cut too deep. Last week you cut one letter clear in half."

"If you don't like the way I open them, do it yourself."

"Helen!" snapped Hattie from the kitchen. "Watch your sharp tongue."

"But she's always telling me what to do." She turned to her sister. "You're not the boss of me, Myra."

"Now, Helen," Myra replied, "you have a simple task. Do it right."

Helen slapped her scissors onto the table.

Her father looked up from his newspapers. "Helen Dietz! Behave yourself and mind your big sister."

Myra waved a bill in the air. "Look, everyone, another five-dollar note! That makes three so far tonight," she said, "and over a thousand dollars since Clarence got shot. *Everybody* seems to be on our side these days. Here," she said, holding a letter, "listen to this press clipping they included." She held the article nearer the lamp. "'My opinion of the Dietz case is that Mr. Dietz is right in defending himself and his home. If he surrendered, he wouldn't get a fair trial, as the lumber company has more money and money talks. I think everyone should help Mr. Dietz fight for his freedom.'"

"My goodness," said Hattie.

"And here's a *Milwaukee Journal* clipping," said John. "'I say that Governor Davidson should go to Sawyer County and give John Dietz immunity and make the logging company pay what is justly due him. This is the sentiment of ninety-five per cent of the people in northern Wisconsin. The people of the State of Wisconsin ought to give John Dietz about three terms in the United States Senate. I think he would be a great man to help curb corporations. He is only doing what every honest man ought to give him credit for and what he has been driven to do.'"

Myra read another. "'Had Governor Davidson sent troops to defend Dietz against such outrageous treatment, he would have shown himself more of a man. I think when Governor Davidson calls people outlaws and criminals he had better lay his false names where they justly belong. I hope if they molest Dietz any more, his ammunition will hold out and he will make good aim.'"

"Oh, dear!" said Hattie. "Let's hope it never comes to that."

"Fear not, Mother," said John. "The lawmen lack the courage to show their faces. And with public sentiment against them, they won't risk the humiliation of being chased off like scared rabbits again."

"I hope you're right, dear. Oh, how I hope you're right."

Myra slid another letter from an envelope. "Father, here's a letter for you. It's from a Mr. Moses."

"Moses?" asked Helen. "Like in the bible?"

"Not *that* Moses, Sis," Myra replied. "He's been dead and gone for ages now."

John studied the letter. "Well, halleluiah! Mother, children, listen to this. Mr. Moses says the Chippewa Lumber and Boom Company wants to send him here to negotiate. He says outright that they are ready to come to terms. Can you imagine that?"

"It's because of the newspapers," said Myra. "Perhaps the timber tycoons are embarrassed to see so many newspapermen taking our side, agreeing that your rights have been disregarded."

Her father leaned back in his chair, struck a match, and lit his pipe. He took a long draw and grinned. "Princess," he said, "I want you to write back to Mr. Moses."

"Me?"

"Yes. I want you to say your father has little time for strangers these days, but if he so desires, he can come for a visit. Mention that he must be alone and unarmed and come by way of the west road. And within a week's time of receipt of your letter."

"But, why me? Why don't you write him?"

John drew on his pipe. "To keep him in his place. We don't want to look as though we're too eager."

"Okay. I'll write the letter tonight. Leslie can get it to the post office tomorrow."

"Not tomorrow," he replied, going back to his newspaper. "Too soon. Let's let him dangle. Make him wait a spell."

Outside, the noise of boots crossing the porch floor made them turn.

"Must be the boys," said Hattie, "all done with chores."

Clarence and Leslie, entering the house, hung their hats and barn coats on the pegs near the door.

"Boots off," said Hattie. "And go wash up."

"Pa," said Clarence, "I think Meggie might be on her last leg."

"Seems her age is creeping up on her," said Leslie.

"I know just how she feels," said Hattie, bringing a quizzical look from Helen.

"How would you know that, Mama?"

"Oh, let's say I feel it in my bones."

Clarence dried his hands and then sat at the table with the others. "Meggie isn't eating much these days," he said. "And her breathing doesn't seem quite right."

"Well," said John, "keep an eye on her for now. We'll see how she does."

"Is Meggie going to die?" asked Helen. "Like Stanley did?"

"Don't fret over it," said Clarence. "Every creature has its time. To everything there is a season, remember?"

"I don't want Meggie to die," said Helen. "She's my pal."

"Look," said Myra. "Another five-dollar note! And listen to this. 'We don't think for one minute that John Dietz is an *outlaw* as Governor Davidson has called him. Sham prosecutions amount to persecutions.'"

"Who is it from?" asked her father.

"Well, that's just it. You see, it is signed by Sherburn M. Becker."

"Who the blazes is that?" asked Clarence.

"Only the Mayor of Milwaukee!"

"No foolin'?"

John looked at the letter. "Yep. Sherburn Becker, the boy mayor of Milwaukee. Now, don't that beat all!"

Two weeks later, W. E. Moses, a fellow member of the Masonic Temple, pulled up a chair at the table. Helen poured coffee and left the coffee pot on the table next to a plate of molasses cookies. Abe and Quincy lay near the fireplace, eyes locked on the visitor.

"Brother Dietz," said Moses, "as I mentioned in my letter, I'm prepared to make an offer that will finally put an end to all this folderol."

"I'd hardly call it folderol, Brother Moses. I'm standing tall for my constitutional rights and the rights of all Americans to challenge those business moguls, those despicable tycoons, who think common folks can be stepped on at every turn."

"Well, nevertheless, I am here to help you."

"And, what do you, a company man, plan get out of this?"

"Me, sir? You misunderstand. I am here to help."

"You didn't answer my question."

"If we can come to terms, I will get the contract to haul the balance of the company's pine out of here. Oh, I won't get much, mind you, but it's good, honest work. Now, please, let's get down to business."

"Spoken like a company man."

"Yes. All right. First, let's discuss the logs. By your estimation, you have a quarter-million board feet of Chippewa Lumber and Boom Company logs stranded on your land. Is that right?"

"Yes and no. The number is right, but the company doesn't own those logs. My wife does. Fair and legal. My intention is to have them sawn into boards this summer."

"That's all well and good, but those logs were cut by the company and came from company land. At the going price of seven-dollars-per-thousand, they have a value of one-thousand, seven-hundred and fifty dollars. Thus, you've already gained that amount, seventeen-fifty." Moses pulled a sheet of paper from his briefcase. "Let's put that in column one, the amount you've already received from the company."

"The company did not give those logs to me. The good Lord did. The company could have bid on them during the auction. They did not. Scratch that from your list, Brother Moses.

"But, Brother Dietz ..."

"The company can purchase them from me at the bargain price of two thousand dollars, if he wants."

Moses scratched the first figure from his list. "Let's move on."

"Yes, please do," said John.

"In the matter of your claim for wages paid for watching the Price Dam. In column one, I'll place the seventy-two dollars paid for thirty-six days."

"Scratch that, too, Brother Moses. I worked for that money and I was paid. Don't try to make the figures look as though they reflect compensation related to our present disagreement."

"All right, all right," said Moses. "Though I think you're missing Mr. Weyerhaeuser's intention. He merely wants to help you recognize his benevolence toward you and your family."

"Benevolence? Try telling that to Clarence and he'll box your ears."

"Now, in the matter of your claim for ..."

"Let me help you with your list," John said, lighting his pipe. "First, there's ninety-six dollars in crop damage."

"Sir?"

"Ninety-six dollars. Write it down."

"I'm not aware of ..."

"Then you've neglected to do your homework. Read my first letter to Horace Chichester, one of your many bosses."

"I have no boss, Brother Dietz."

"So you say. Next there's my back pay for 845 days working at the Price Dam. Put $1,717 on your paper. Subtotal is $1,813. Write it down, Brother Moses." John drew on his pipe. "Next is my claim for ten cents per thousand for logs sluiced across my wife's dam without her consent for four years. I originally asked for seven-thousand. But since then, your boss has his newspaper cronies claiming I want fifteen to twenty. So, place twenty-thousand in your column."

"But, sir ..."

"Go ahead. It's a nice round number. Write it down. This is your idea, not mine."

"All right. But I can tell you right now that ..."

"Your boss won't pay that amount?"

"I told you, Brother Dietz. I have no boss."

"So, Brother Moses, what now?"

Moses looked at the numbers. "I'll tell you right now that I am not authorized to pay you twenty-thousand. Perhaps we can look at the other figures."

"Let's do," said John, pulling on his pipe.

"John, er, may I call you John?"

John nodded.

Moses took an envelope from his briefcase.

Abe growled.

John pulled his pistol and laid it on the table. "If that's another warrant or a court order, you're taking your life into your own hands."

"No, sir," said Moses. "It's cash." He removed a thick stack of bills from the envelope and placed it on the table across from the pistol. "It's yours today if we can come to terms."

"What terms?"

"If you'll drop all claims other than the seventeen-hundred for back pay, I'll pay you right now."

"That's it? That's your offer?"

"That and I'll see to it all indictments, all warrants, all court actions against you and your family are dropped."

"I don't care about them. They've never been properly served nor enforced. You may as well guarantee that you will melt the snow in the spring."

Moses picked up the money. Taking his time, he slid it back into the envelope. "I was so hoping we could come to terms."

"Your terms, Brother Moses. That's not negotiating. It's temptation. If you think you can persuade me to give up my rights by brandishing a stack of greenbacks, you're a fool."

Moses pulled the money from the envelope again. "You'd turn up your nose at seventeen-hundred dollars?" He waved the money in the air, Abe and Quincy following it with their eyes.

"You've caught the attention of our dogs," said John. "As for me, I'm not impressed." He pointed to a wooden apple crate stacked full of envelopes. "See that box? It represents over two-thousand dollars in contributions to my cause—contributions from good folks who want to see people like your boss put in his place. Now, if I were to sell out to him for the meager sum you offer, how could I ever face any of them?"

Moses thumbed through his stack of bills. "A bird in hand, John. If we don't come to terms today, I must return this cash and deliver the sour news."

"Fifteen-thousand," said John. "In greenbacks."

"Preposterous. That's nearly ten-fold of what I can offer."

"But a drop in the bucket for your boss. So take it to him."

"He'll laugh me right out of his office."

"Will he? You and I both know he's risking a hundred-thousand in profits by turning me down. Meanwhile, his pine remains stranded. Have you seen it? Have you? The bark's all peeled off by the heat. The pine bores are already after it. They'll have it chewed so full of holes that no carpenter will accept it. A total loss to your boss. And to you, Brother Moses. But *no* loss to me. Don't you see? In spite of all the money that your boss may have, *I John F. Dietz, hold the upper hand.* Tell him that, Brother Moses. Run back to your boss. Tell him John Dietz is not like some child tempted by a penny's worth of licorice when the whole candy store's at stake."

"It will do no good. He's as stubborn as you, Brother Dietz."

John reached down and rapped his pipe on the hearth, clearing the tobacco ash. "In which case, he will lose a small fortune and you won't be hauling any of those logs out there."

Moses stood, waving the stack of bills again. "Dammit, Dietz! You've got some spine." He threw the seventeen-hundred onto the table next to the pistol. "Here! Take it. This satisfies your back pay. It's all I can do for you today. I'll speak with Mr. Weyerhaeuser. I'll ask for more. If he doesn't throw me out on my ear, I'll be back."

"So be it," said John, returning his Luger to its holster. "Let me know when the old skinflint is ready to come to his senses."

29
"Dietz Wins!"

"Father!" said Myra in the middle of the night. "You must come see this!"

Her father cast aside the curtain covering his bedroom doorway. A single kerosene lamp lit the kitchen table. "What on earth are you doing up at this hour?" he said.

"I couldn't sleep," replied Myra. "My mind's been abuzz, thinking about these newspapers Leslie brought from Ladysmith late last night."

"Go back to bed. You need your sleep. We both do."

"Dietz wins!" she replied.

"What?"

DIETZ FIGHT OVER

Says Dietz Will Build Mill and Cut up Logs.

LADYSMITH, Wis., June 16.—W. W. Dietz of Rice Lake, brother of John Dietz, thinks the fight at Cameron dam is over. The logging companies have spent more than $100,000 trying to move a quarter million dollars' worth of logs from the Cameron dam pond and the last of a half dozen squads of deputies sent there has left with the statement that nothing but a criminal warrant will do the business. The logging company at first involved tried to get a criminal warrant and, failing, transferred their claim to the logs to an interstate concern in order to get into the United States courts, but here again a criminal warrant was refused. Feeling that at one time was very favorable to the logging concerns has turned into sympathy for Dietz.

It is now now reported that Dietz purposes putting in a sawmill and cutting up enough of the 20,000,000 feet of pine now held to cover his claims against the logging companies.
—Milwaukee Journal.

"Look at this headline, Father." She shoved the paper in front of him. He stared at the headline and snatched it from her hands.

"Well, now, look at that. *Dietz wins.*" He read the first paragraph aloud. "On June tenth, one W. E. Moses made his appearance on Thornapple Farm, claiming to be an agent for F. Weyerhaeuser. He paid $1,717.00 in back wages owed to John F. Dietz. Dietz is the same man who is called the defender of Cameron Dam by some, and an outlaw by others. Dietz accepted the money as a goodwill gesture. He will now allow the Chippewa Lumber and Boom Company to harvest logs stranded along the river."

"You won, Father," said Myra. "The whole nation will soon know. Look." She handed him the *Minneapolis Tribune.* "Look. It's the same story. And here's another!"

"Bah. It matters little."

"Father! This is a red-letter day. How can you say that?"

"Until I'm paid the eight thousand I'm owed according to law for logs sluiced over our dam, the lumber syndicate prevails." He took a dipper of water from the pail and drank it down.

"For four long years I have been the target of conspiracy, blackmail, and bullets of the land pirates and timber wolves. If such a state of affairs is allowed to continue, the stars and stripes should be hung at half-mast to mourn the death of our nation, for the grasping tentacles of the corporation has liberty by the throat."*

"Goodness, Father."

"I'm owed over eight-thousand. I'll not yield until I'm paid."

"And what of your family? We've been subjected to the same dangers, the same perils as you. My word! Clare was shot in the head! And we all suffered the scorn of the press until then. The sheriff's men and the marshals and God knows how many company mercenaries have been watching us likes ravens waiting to eat the robin's chicks when she's a moment away. Father! What about us?"

"I know it's not been easy, Princess. Especially for you. You've come of age. You need to spread your wings, as do your brothers. And this … this … *clash* I have with the company stands in the way."

"It needn't be that way, Father. Read the headline again. *Dietz wins!* This is your chance to end this stalemate, to save face, to claim victory." Myra studied the article.

"What the dickens are you two doing up at this hour?" said Hattie as she pushed aside the bedroom curtain.

"Rising to the rooster's cock-a-doodle-do, Mother. And speaking of barnyard birds, take a *gander* at this!" He held the front page of the paper before her.

"Halleluiah!" she yawned.

"Father seems to have made a splash," said Myra. "It's in many of the papers."

"I imagine the mail will come like a flood, now," said Hattie. "Though the money won't."

"The money's not important," John replied. "The very idea of having our compatriots see how I've bested the syndicate is the prize." He held up the *Minneapolis Tribune* front page again. "Dietz wins," he said. "Oh, what I'd given to see the look on the old rascal's face when he saw this. And to think that my victory was paid for with *company* money. My stars, this *is* a red-letter day!"

Myra looked up from the article. "What happens now, Father?"

"We go on with our normal life, Princess. Rise early, tend to the animals, put up another winter's worth of firewood, weed the garden, make hay, and enjoy life here on Thornapple Farm. In the meantime, I've heard from a fellow from Northfield, Minnesota, who might be willing to mill our logs. If so, by spring we'll have enough lumber to start your house, Mother."

*From a letter to the *Osceola Sun* by John Dietz. Posted December 23, 1907.

"Oh, dear," she sighed.

"What's wrong?" asked Myra.

"It's been so long since life has been normal around here that I don't know where I'll start."

Myra laughed. "If I know you, you'll start the same way as always."

"And, what way is that?"

"With a breakfast of hens' eggs, hot cakes, jam, and sausage."

Every morning that winter, as John and the boys tended to chores, they could hear the sound of W. E. Moses's crew removing logs from the far side of the river. The timber had been stranded there when the dam was blown. The Phoenix steam hauler that the company provided could pull eight loaded sleighs across the ice roads to the landing on the Flambeau River.

In March, John and his sons set up a portable sawmill near the Cameron Dam. Then they watched their own pine turn from logs into lumber. Slowly but steadily, stacks of white pine boards filled the pasture until they totaled twenty-five, each twelve-feet high, drying in the sun.

Then came October. As the leaves began to fall, the work came to an end. The whine of the saw no longer sliced through the river bottom air. Silence replaced the continuous chugging of the steam-powered saw.

"Papa," said Helen, late one December evening. "Someone is here."

John put down his bible, rose from his chair, and answered the door. "Brother Moses!" he said. "Come in. Can I get you a cup of coffee?"

"Anything stronger in the house?" asked Moses, pulling off his coat.

"If you mean liquor, you won't find a drop on Thornapple Farm. It's the scourge of the working man, a menace unto life itself."

"You won't draw that Luger of yours if I disagree, will you?"

"To each his own, my friend. But I've seen good men go from triumph to tragedy all because of evil spirits thrust upon the masses by the liquor industry. My word, they make it easy for a man to stay drunk these days. Temptation on every street corner."

"But wouldn't you agree that one must know his limits, John?"

"True, but liquor is like a sneak thief in the alleyway, luring the unsuspecting man or woman into the dark, muddling the mind before stealing all it can prior to casting the poor soul into the gutter."

"Well, John, that's fine gobbledygook for the liquor abolitionists. But as for me, I enjoy a strong drink from time to time. It helps me relax.

John patted his bible. "This helps one to relax, too, my friend. So what brings you to Thornapple Farm today?"

"I've been sent here by a Masonic brother of ours, William Irvine, overseer of the Chippewa Lumber and Boom Company. Know him?"

John pulled out his pipe. "Enough to know I can't trust him."

"I disagree. However, he asked me to tell you that the company is interested in rebuilding Cameron Dam."

"Rebuilding? Whatever for? There's not enough pine left upstream to make it worthwhile."

"Brother Irvine's landlookers think otherwise. And the swamps around here make it awful hard to haul logs cross-country."

"Are you here to ask if I'll allow the dam to be rebuilt? Even though the company *still* owes me ten-thousand dollars?" John opened a can of Tuxedo tobacco. He stuffed a pinch into his pipe. "Excuse my poor manners," he said, pushing the can forward. "Tobacco?"

"Oh, dear me, no," said Moses. "I never touch it. Hard on the lungs, you know."

John struck a match and lit his pipe. "So? What about my rightful comeuppance?"

"The company wants to settle, John."

"What?"

"They want to buy you out."

"Well, halleluiah!" John drew on his pipe, sending a curl of smoke drifting upward. "Let me guess. They want to offer me a pittance."

"A pittance? I hardly think so. Brother Irvine has authorized me to make a generous offer."

"I've already gone one round with Irvine. And won, mind you."

"Yes, he told me. But this is another offer. A *better* offer." Moses pulled his chair closer to the table and leaned forward. "What would you say to starting over?"

Puzzled, John raised his left eyebrow and waited for more.

"I can put you and your family on a fine farm in Manitoba, right in the heart of the Red River Valley. Three hundred acres of good soil. Two of the three-hundred acres are already under till. A stream runs right down the middle. There's a house, a barn, calving pens, chicken coop, implements, and, what's more, no mortgage. And here's the best part. The whole place can be yours free and clear, and no neighbors up there will be aware of the trouble you've had with the law."

"At what cost to me?"

"Just sign Thornapple Farm over to the Chippewa Lumber and Boom Company and the whole shebang is yours."

"What of the money owed me for sluicing of logs over my dam?"

"You can't be serious, Brother Dietz."

John drew on his pipe and blew a smoke ring toward the ceiling. "This farm you describe might be worth several hundred dollars. Who knows? Maybe even a thousand. But I'm owed at least ten. Some of the newspapers say I'm owed twenty!"

"Now, don't be too hasty in your decision. This offer is a way for you and your family to break free from this entire lopsided affair, this circus of events that has both the company and you scrapping like wolves over a kill. My word, John! You've even been branded an outlaw."

"Others call me a hero."

"Some say a lunatic."

"Others, strong and steadfast."

"Only a fool would pass this by."

"A fool? Or a man capable of seeing a ruse?"

"You mustn't turn this down. Not until you've seen the farm."

John drew on his pipe and tapped his bible. "I'm not inclined to succumb to a serpent's temptation. No, Brother Moses, I shan't bite into your venomous apple."

"Please, Brother Dietz. Think it over. Discuss it with Hattie, with your children. Listen, I've set up camp beyond the river. Join me midday tomorrow for dinner. Bring the family. We can talk more about this."

John considered his words as he shook the spent ashes from his pipe onto the hearth. "I know what you're up to," he said.

"Up to?"

"You come here clad in sheep's' clothing, but hiding the fangs of a wolf. You invite us to leave our home under the guise of offering a meal. And all the while, your spies are watching my home from the riverbank, waiting for their chance to move in."

"Spies? What on earth are you talking about?"

"I've seen them. Perhaps your plan is to lure us away and then burn us out while you serve us pork belly and potatoes."

"But, John …"

"I'll not fall for your ploy. Nor will I sell my birthright, trade my pride for some far-off farm that may not even exist. Moreover, I will not be a traitor to all those who consider me a champion. Frederick Weyerhaeuser be damned! He owes me ten thousand. Do you have it? Do you, Brother Moses?"

Moses placed his briefcase on the chair between them and snapped open each latch. "John," he said, "the last time we spoke, you insisted on ten thousand to settle."

"Yes. In greenbacks. Go on."

"I have it right here, Brother. All ten thousand, a fortune by any sensible man's estimation. It's all yours, yours in addition to that farmland in Manitoba." Moses pulled a thick stack of bills from a bank envelope and placed it on the table. "Yours merely for signing a statement that you no longer hold the Chippewa Lumber and Boom Company responsible for further claims. Yours for agreeing to turn Thornapple Farm and the Cameron Dam over to the company. It's all yours, Brother Dietz."

John stared at the money.

"Yours for good."

"Good for whom?" he asked.

"What?"

"Good for me? Good for my wife? My children? Good for those who believe in me? Or … good for the company? No, Brother Moses. I need no more time to consider your offer. The answer is no. Plain and simple."

30

The Boycott

That evening, W. E. Moses left disappointed. He'd tried to achieve the company's objective to remove Dietz, but failed. He couldn't help his new friend, John Dietz, extract himself from the controversy surrounding the Thornapple Farm. His effort was for naught. W. E. Moses would not try again.

A week later, John and the boys loaded the buckboard and set off for town over a fresh blanket of snow. The first of a half-dozen stops they planned to make was the general store where they would deliver two dressed and skinned steers that stretched out in the bed of the wagon.

John jumped from the wagon and opened the back door of the store. "Hello, Calvin," he called. "I brought that beef we spoke of last month."

Calvin Olson, met the Dietz men in the alley.

"I have two fine steers for you, Cal. Skun, dressed out, and ready to be butchered. Aren't they beauts?"

"Yep," Calvin replied. "Fine looking beef, John. But I can't take them."

"Cal, we had a bargain."

"That's all ka-put, now. I've been given the word by the lumber company that I'm not to do business with you no more. I'm awful sorry, John."

"The company? What do they have to say about it? It's your store, Cal. You don't have to pay them no mind. Now help me unload this beef."

"Like I said, I'm sorry, John. But I can't do it, see? I can't afford to lose the company's business. They have over a hundred lumberjacks who need food and supplies. I've been told to make my choice. It's them or you, John. I got no say in it. I'm sorry."

"All right. I'll just have to find someone else to butcher them."

"I doubt if you will, at least not here in Winter. And don't bother going to Hayward. The word is out. Ain't nobody in these parts who will deal with you no more. You might try Fifield or maybe Park Falls."

"Well, that's fine kettle of soup! All right. I'll just pick up my dry goods and go."

"Not here you won't."

"You mean to say ..."

"Like I said, try Park Falls or Fifield. Or maybe Ladysmith. So long, John. And good luck."

Whether the call had been made by Red Mulligan, foreman of Camp Four, or men from the Chippewa Lumber and Boom Company, or the North Wisconsin Lumber Company, the Dietz family was victim of a boycott.

The Dietz men spent most of the next two weeks butchering their steers. They wrapped many roasts and steaks in oiled paper, allowing the meat to freeze. More meat filled the salt barrels stored in the root cellar. Hundreds of pounds went to neighbors. Much of the beef would hang in the smokehouse for the next month. In spite of these efforts, over a ton of marketable beef went to their dumpsite where crows, ravens, and eagles would feast on it for months.

Uncle Will came for a visit on Christmas Day. He knocked twice and entered, greeted by the aroma of a sirloin roast in the oven and bread made fresh earlier that morning. In the corner stood a tree adorned with strings of popcorn and cranberries. Popcorn balls hung suspended from sewing thread. Atop the tree stood a miniature angel, looking down as if there to protect all those before her.

"Clarence, Leslie, Myra?" said William, "I dragged a toboggan from the train. It's outside and heavy with Christmas gifts. Unload it for me, if you'd be so kind."

Leslie dashed outside.

"Good Lord, Lester!" shouted Hattie. "Use your noggin, young man. Put on your hat and coat. I'll not go through another bout of sickness."

Leslie came back in as Clarence and Myra stepped out. Soon the toboggan was empty and gifts from Uncle Will lay beneath the tree.

"Clarence," his mother said, "go load up your Uncle Will's toboggan with roasts and steaks."

"Now, Hattie," said William, "there's no need for that."

"Au contraire, Uncle," Myra replied, watching to see his reaction to her French, "there's *every* need. We have a surplus of meat due to the boycott, and you have a family to feed."

"William," said John, "it's our pleasure to send a load of beef back with you. And there's more where that came from. You need only to bring your empty toboggan when you visit."

William placed a stack of mail on the table. "I heard about the boycott. Word around town has it that the company is out to do you in for good this time, John. I came today because I'm not one to let the company dampen your family's Christmas spirit."

"If the company thinks they can starve us out, they've got another think coming," John said.

"You'll find that several of the packages under the tree are from friends. They come from supporters who want to help."

"Like this one," said Leslie," handing a heavy box to his father. "It's from Mr. Roese of the *Osceola Sun*."

John hefted the package and then peeled away the brown paper wrapper. "My word!" said John. "It's a case of rifle cartridges! Five-hundred rounds. Alfred must think trouble's heading our way."

"Oh, dear," said Hattie. "Pray to God he's wrong."

"Here, Helen," said William, handing her a gift. "This one's for you. From your cousins. And if you look, you'll find a gift for baby Johnny. Clarence, Leslie, there are pocket knives waiting for you."

"Four blades?" asked Clarence.

"Yes, sir. Arrived last week from Monkey Wards. Just wait till you see them."

William pulled another box from under the tree. "Myra, here's something for you. I think you'll like this." He handed her the present. "I found it at the music store just yesterday. In Rice Lake."

"Oh, thank you, Uncle. How I loved snooping around in that store when we lived there." Myra tore away the wrapper and opened the package, revealing a set of records. "Gramophone recordings," she shouted, rushing to the Victrola. "I can't wait to play them." She cranked up the mainspring, placed the top record on the turntable, and lowered the needle. "Listen, everyone." A lovely German version of *Silent Night* filled the room. "Oh, Uncle Will, thank you," she said. "What a *perfect* gift for the season."

John set three more logs in the fireplace and then turned to his brother. "This notion that the lumber syndicate has, that they can end their troubles by boycotting the Dietz family, is absurd."

"I agree," said William. "In fact, I've already made plans to have provisions brought here by sleigh in the event you run low."

Myra stood near the Victrola, reading the labels on the other records. "It's merely one more failed effort on the part of the company to punish Father," she said. "Instead, they've caused our friends to create their own version of an underground railroad. Honestly! Will the company never tire of this?" She cranked up the mainspring on the record player again.

"Wash up, children," said Hattie. "Time to sit. Supper's almost ready." She opened the oven, removing a large roaster. Placing it on top of the stove, she removed the cover, exposing a large, steaming beef roast surrounded with potatoes, carrots, and onions. The room filled with the delicious aroma of a country Christmas supper.

Beaming with pride, Hattie asked, "Who's going to say grace?"

31

A Fine Kettle of Soup!

Hattie peered through the window at the far-off river as her husband came through the back door. "It's nice to see the snow melting again," he said. "Won't be long and we'll be planting."

"I see the lawmen are back, John," she sighed. "There've been two spies across the river watching with field glasses all morning." She poured a bucket of cream into the butter churn. "Myra? Helen?" she called. "Come help make butter."

John looked out the window. "They're just burning up the public's tax dollars," he said. He placed a bucket of drinking water from the spring on the counter and dropped in the dipper. "We mean no harm to them or them to us."

"I don't like them there."

"Mother, there's no reason for worry."

"John, you still have a price on your head."

John laughed. "I'm certain that reward money has long been spent by the courthouse gang. I'm no longer a prize."

"Or so you think."

Myra and her sister came from the schoolroom. Helen took the first turn at the butter churn, rhythmically pumping the handle up and down slowly. At the sink, Myra dunked the tin dipper into the water pail and sipped.

"How are your studies going?" Hattie asked.

Helen looked up. "I wish Mr. Gates would come back."

Myra slipped the dipper into the bucket again. "We are keeping up, Mother. It's not like having a real teacher, but we can get along until the school board provides another."

"Is Mr. Gates *ever* coming back, Mama?" Helen asked. "He left all his books and teacher things. Surely he wants them."

Myra took a turn with the butter churn. "Helen, the school board hasn't paid him for a coon's age. Can you blame him for leaving?"

"Nor have they paid your father for your teacher's room and board or the upkeep of the schoolroom," said Hattie.

"Oh, they will pay me," said John. "Sooner or later."

A half-hour later, with a pound and a-half of butter in a bowl on the table, Myra and Helen set aside the buttermilk and rinsed out the churn.

Hattie added a palmful of salt to the butter. She stared out the window as she mixed it in with a wooden spoon. "Lord, I don't like seeing men over there staring at our home through spyglasses. What the dickens do they hope to see?"

"I'll chase the cowards off," said John, levering a cartridge into the chamber of the rifle by the front door.

"John, please don't," begged Hattie.

Ignoring her request, John stepped onto the porch, pulled the hammer back, and fired into the air. Across the river, the lawmen vanished into the woods. "Run, you fools!" he shouted. He returned to the living room, laughing.

"Mother," said Myra, snitching a taste of the butter with her finger, "Helen and I will be in the schoolroom if you need us. We have our history lessons and arithmetic to finish by suppertime."

"Take your time," Hattie replied. "I'm making us a fine kettle of soup, but it will be a while until it's ready." She added chopped rutabaga and carrots to the steaming kettle. "Supper can wait until you finish."

John stared out the window. "Mother, it's a disgrace that those lawmen over there can get paid day after day for sitting on their rumps."

"That money could be better used elsewhere," she said as she scraped a platter of browned stew meat into her soup. "For education, perhaps?" She stirred the simmering mixture and then sipped from the spoon. "All it needs now is salt, pepper, and a touch of flour to thicken it up a smidge."

Lured by the aroma of the vegetable beef soup, the girls returned to the kitchen. Myra took another drink from the dipper and handed it to Helen. "I'm going to sit for a spell," she said, slumping into her father's chair. "I'm not feeling my best."

"Oh, dear," said Hattie, stirring the soup. "Are you coming down with something?"

"Just a bellyache. I'm sure it's nothing."

"Should I fix a glass of my tonic to settle your stomach?"

"Oh, please do." Myra leaned her head back. Eyes closed, she winced from pain.

"Here, Mama," said Helen, pouring a dipperful of water into a glass."

Hattie added a teaspoon of baking soda and stirred the mixture. "Drink, Myra," she said. "This will help."

Myra drank half and paused.

"Finish it up," said Hattie. "You'll feel better soon."

Myra drank the rest, handing the glass to Helen. She leaned back in the chair again and closed her eyes.

Hattie rinsed the glass and returned it to the cupboard. "Perhaps you should lie down."

"I'll be fine soon. I'm already feeling better."

Hattie returned to the kitchen to stir the soup again.

Helen heard talking on the porch. She rushed to the window to see Leslie, Clarence, and Father pointing across the pasture. Suddenly, the boys jumped from the porch and trotted toward the barn. John entered the cabin, hanging his hat and coat near the door. "Something's amiss, Mother."

"Oh, dear. What now?"

"Clarence found two of our sheep in the pasture."

"So?"

"Both were dead."

Myra's eyelids fluttered but didn't open. "Oh, no," she whispered, "our poor little sheep."

"Shot?" Hattie asked, looking up from her work.

"No. Some sort of … ailment. Can't tell for sure." He reached for a book, *The Practical Stock Doctor,* and turned to the section on livestock disease. "Clarence says some of our cows seem out of sorts, too."

Myra moaned, her hands clutching her abdomen.

"Something wrong with Myra?" John asked.

"She has a tummy ache," said Helen.

"I made her a tonic," said Hattie, stirring the soup again. She blew on the wooden spoon before tasting it.

"How is it, Mama?" Helen asked.

"Delicious. It'll be ready soon, sweetie. Help me set the table."

Myra stood slowly, still clutching her abdomen. "I'll be in my bedroom," she groaned. "Wake me for supper."

Hattie and Helen set the table. John placed another log on the fire and sat back in his chair with his copy of *The Practical Stock Doctor,* paging through diseases common on farms. As he read, Leslie opened the door.

"Pa, we found three more dead sheep down by the river."

"Three more? What in blazes is going on?"

"Blackie is one of 'em."

"Blackie?" blurted Helen. "She's dead?"

"'Fraid so," Leslie replied.

Helen burst into tears. "Not my little Blackie! Not Blackie!" Hattie rushed to embrace her daughter.

"Same as the others?" asked John.

"Far as we can tell, Pa. I'm going back to look for more sheep. Clare's checking the Herefords now."

"Leslie," said Hattie, "do try to be back soon. I've a big kettle of soup on the stove. Tell Clarence."

A muffled moan came from the girls' bedroom. Helen, in tears, left to check on Myra.

Leslie crossed the room, dipped a spoon into the soup, blew on it a moment, and tasted. "Mmm. Delicious, Ma." Seconds later, he left by the back door.

Hattie closed the door behind him. She turned to her husband, still flipping pages. "Have you found anything?"

"Not yet."

They looked up to see Clarence cross before the windows, lugging something heavy. He dropped the object onto the porch with a thud and then burst through the door. "Pa," he exclaimed. "Come see this!"

John followed his son outside. On the porch sat a salt lick, stark-white except for a bright blue stain on top. He stared at it a moment and rushed back inside to his book. "Copper sulfate?" he wondered aloud, turning to his wife. "Lord help us, Hattie! Our animals have been poisoned!" He looked to his son. "Clare, go round up every one of our salt licks. The company is trying to kill our livestock. Trying to poison the poor creatures!"

"Mama," cried Helen from the girls' bedroom. "Myra wants you."

"God in Heavens!" Hattie screamed. "The water! John! They've poisoned our cistern!" She rushed to the stove, grabbed the soup kettle with her potholders, and threw kettle and all out the back door. "Oh, dear!" she cried, running to her bedroom, "Myra!"

John dashed to the kitchen, cursing as he hauled the bucket outside. "Hattie, they've gone too far this time." He grabbed his livestock book and opened to the sections on poisons. "Copper sulfate!" he shouted. "By God, that's it. The murderous cowards have poisoned us. Tried again to kill us!" He read on. "Quick! We need a mix of linseed oil, laundry soap, and eggs. One part each. And milk. Enough milk to bring it to about a gallon. It says here that this antidote will help wash the poison out. Oh, please, Lord!" he cried. "Let this revelation not come too late for my poor princess!" He turned to Clarence. "Saddle the buckskin. We need Doc Burns."

Six days later, after three visits from Dr. Burns, Myra was back on her feet.

That morning, the doctor sat at the table sipping a cup of coffee—made with river water. "Mrs. Dietz, you caught this just in time," he said. "Another dose or two of sodium bicarbonate, combined with that copper sulfate, and we might not have been able to …"

"I don't want to hear this," said Hattie. "Not now. I've too much on my mind."

"I understand, Mrs. Dietz. You're family's been through hell."

Hattie shuddered. "It's not merely what we've been through, Doctor. It's what lies ahead. My husband's temperament has been hardened more than ever. Seems every night, like a miser counting his coins, I find him counting the number of rifle cartridges he has stored up. But instead of money, John is counting …" She raised her apron to wipe her tears.

"What, Mrs. Dietz? What is John counting?"

"Deaths, Dr. Burns. Deaths."

32

Old Paul

In time, the large animals affected by the poison recovered by drinking only river water. John sold the sheep that survived the poisoning. Eventually the copper sulfate in the cistern was purged by fresh spring water. The efforts to poison the family and livestock at Thornapple Farm served only one purpose—it affected them with a new awareness of the lumber trust's determination to drive them from the farm by *any* means. As diabolical as the attack seemed, the company was far from finished.

Within weeks, sunshine and warm weather transformed the Thornapple River bottomland to the rich greens of spring. The Dietz farm sparkled in the sunshine. In the south pasture, the cows devoured the grasses now shooting skyward. In the barnyard, hens and chicks pecked at bugs, grasses, and seeds, and old Paul grazed out in the pasture with Suzybell, the replacement workhorse for their dear Meggie. Long after her passing, songs of joy sung by Myra and the children flowed across the farm fields. Livestock confined to the barn over the winter, now meandered around the pasture like tourists on holiday.

Then, one morning, as Leslie headed to the barn to begin chores, he saw Paul asleep near the barn. Leslie whistled. Paul raised his head and lowered it to the ground again. Leslie came closer. Something seemed wrong.

"Paul? Paul!"

The huge, black draft horse didn't move.

Leslie quickened his pace, whistling again. "Paul!" he shouted.

The horse lifted his head again.

Closer, now, Leslie saw it.

Blood.

Blood on Paul's neck.

Blood on the grass underneath.

He rushed over and knelt, seeing a wound.

He stroked Paul's forehead.

"What happened, fella? Did you run into the fence?" Leslie placed his hand on the puncture wound on Paul's neck. Wet with blood, his fingers probed the wound.

Leslie jumped to his feet and raced to the cabin.

Inside, the family heard Leslie's shouts. "Pa! Come quick! Paul's been stabbed!"

John knelt next to Paul, stroking his forehead as Leslie had done earlier. The entire family stood there, silently waiting for the head of the family to speak.

Holding back tears, Clarence asked, "Must we put him down, Pa?"

"I don't know, Clare. Depends on how he does through the morning." John stood. "Leslie, go fetch the kit. We need to clean the wound, apply liniment, and bandage it if we hope to stop the bleeding. Run, now. Hear?"

"Right, Pa," shouted Leslie, already on his way to the cabin.

"Father, who could have done such a thing?" sobbed Myra.

"Someone who doesn't know a fiddly fig about horses."

"What makes you say that?" asked Clarence.

"If he knew what he was doing, he'd have sliced through the jugular. Or stabbed into the lungs. If so, old Paul would be gone by now. No, this villain didn't know a fig about horses."

"John," said Hattie, "you know very well who did this."

Myra turned. "Who, Mother?"

"Those so-called lawmen across the river. Sworn to keep the peace. Instead, they prey upon defenseless animals. Keep the peace, indeed!"

"Sent by Red Mulligan, I'd wager," added Clarence.

"I can't watch this anymore," said Hattie. Taking Johnny by the hand, she hurried back toward the house.

"Father," said Myra, stroking Paul's forehead, "how could a human being do such a thing to a kind, gentle animal like our Paul?"

"There are cruel men in this world, Princess. Men who will stoop low. They'll do *anything* to damage a foe, even strike down a dear sweet horse like old Paul."

"But think of it," she said. "Paul probably just stood there while this villain strolled up, stroked Paul's forehead like I'm doing now and then heartlessly plunged a dagger into his neck. Knowing Paul, he probably just stood there and let the villain do his evil deed, and then watched him walk away. Old, trusting Paul."

Leslie rushed up with the family medical kit. "Here, Pa," he said, out of breath.

"Turpentine, Son."

"Here you go."

The others watched John pour it onto the wound. Paul blinked, but didn't raise his head from the bloodied ground.

"Now your mother's Carbolic liniment."

Myra unscrewed the lid from the jar. "Here, Father."

Using three fingers, John scooped out half-a-handful of ointment. "Clare, I need you to pull a hair from Paul's tail for the stitches. Myra, find a big needle."

"Yes, Father." Myra pulled a curved needle from the kit, wiped it and the horsehair with turpentine, and then threaded the needle. "Here," she said, handing it to her father.

They watched as John placed five sutures in the gaping knife wound, tying each as he did.

"Is Paul going to heaven," asked Helen.

"Not yet, sweetheart," said Myra. "Maybe someday, but not yet."

John looked up. "Let's pray to the good Lord for his help. Paul is one of his creatures—a far better creature than the despicable ne'er-do-well who stabbed him. Perhaps one day the Lord will have something to say to the villain who did this. But for now, we all pray."

The children and their father lowered their heads and stood surrounding their faithful friend lying in the sunshine.

"Father?"

John looked up at Myra.

"Are you planning …"

"Yes?"

"I mean … Mulligan? Will you hold him accountable for this?"

"What you really ask, Myra, is whether or not I will seek revenge on Mulligan. You wish to know whether or not I will attempt to inflict the same punishment on him? Well, Princess, I can't say I've not already considered it. But I think it's best to take no action right now. Going after Mulligan would only result in more hatred, more threats, more fear flying from one side of the river to the other. God willing, old Paul will recover. If so, we will put this behind us. On the other hand, if Paul dies, I'll need a new draft horse. And that expense will be on the company— tallied up on top of what they already owe. Meanwhile, let's give dear old Paul a rest. Leslie, keep a bucket of water close by to quench the poor fellow's thirst. And cover him with blankets. Let him rest in the sunshine until he's better or ..."

"Or gone to a better place?" asked Leslie.

"Is there such a thing, Father?" asked Myra. "A place better for our animal friends than Thornapple Farm?"

"Only if you believe, child. With all your heart."

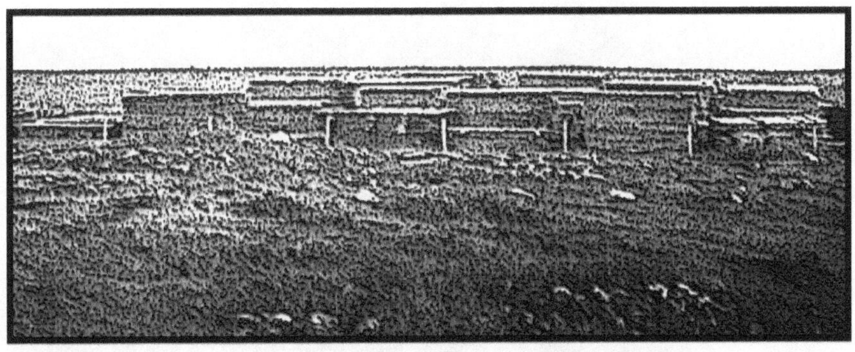

Committee Formed To Aid Deitz Family

(By United Press Leased Wire.)

MILWAUKEE, Oct. 24.—Still wering bandages over the wounds they received a... ...ds of deputies in the s... his cabin at C... ago, the defen... rived here to... for the defen... mother and... charged with... uty Sheriff Oscar Harp. Harp was shot during the fighting around the Dietz cabin.

The appeal of the Dietz children met with instant response ...defense committee ...multane... ...he news ...lumber ...with ...ble, had ...on dam.

DEPUTIES MOVE ON DIETZ'S DEFENSES

Brother of Defiant Settler Appeals to La Follette—Dietz May Resort to Dynamite.

33

Election Day, 1910

"Clarence! C'mon!" shouted his father. "We're wasting daylight."

A derby hat in his hand and his coat unbuttoned, Clarence came running from the privy. His long legs quickly carried him across the yard. In a moment he was aboard the wagon with his father and brother.

"Pa," said Leslie, "I still don't see why we have to wear our Sunday outfits on a weekday just for a run to town."

"Because it's Election Day, my boy, as special a day as they come. It's our opportunity to cast our votes and help mold our government. Most of the men in the county will turn out today. And, by God, the Dietz men will be right there with them." He grabbed the reins. "Giddy up," he shouted. The pair of buckskins jumped to a start and then trotted across the yard. As they passed, their two draft horses, Suzybell and old Paul looked their way. The buckskins splashed through the shallow stream and crossed onto the road leading to Winter.

"Pa?" said Leslie, "aren't you worried that Sheriff Madden might be in town? Seems he could set a snare for you easy as pie."

John laughed. "Madden? He knows better. Four sheriffs and a pack of United States marshals have tried to haul me in. Every last one of them left with their tails between their legs."

"But there are still warrants out for you, right, Pa?" asked Clarence. "And a reward?"

"True, Son. But ever since I settled with the company for my back pay and let Mr. Moses and Chippewa Lumber haul out their logs, there's been no talk of any more legal action against me. My sources tell me they've dropped the charges. It's their way of offering an olive branch, hoping for peace along the Thornapple."

"What about the royalty money owed you? They ran millions of board feet across your dam without your say-so."

"You're right. They still owe us for that. I'd be willing to settle for eight-thousand dollars. But between you boys and me, I doubt I'll ever see a penny of it. Meanwhile, things have quieted down a lot. I've not had a lawman cross my path for four years now, although we did have to fight off that cowardly poisoning of our cistern."

"And the stabbing of old Paul, Pa," said Leslie. "I think we better keep an eye out."

"I have friends around here, boys. Folks who would let me know if trouble's headed our way. The few lawmen who dare show their face near here know they'd have a hornets' nest on their hands, should they try anything."

"But there's still that five-hundred dollar price on your head," said Clarence. "Don't you worry about that?"

John put his hand on his holster. "That's why I carry this Luger."

Dressed in their best, the three Dietz men suffered the rocky buckboard ride into Winter to find the village crowded with buggies, wagons, horses, and men who'd come to town to celebrate Election Day. With the failed boycott against the family now lifted, Leslie and Clarence purchased supplies from the feed mill before filling Hattie's list of dry goods from the mercantile. From there they walked to the Town Hall where they met their father and cast their ballots. Finally, the Dietz men ordered a dinner of fried pork and baked potatoes in the dining room of Dick and Mary Phelan's Hotel Winter. After, while John paid for their meal, the boys stepped outside onto the boardwalk to find two men engaged in a heated quarrel.

"Look," said Clarence, pointing at a fat man wearing wire-rimmed glasses and a top hat. "Isn't that Charlie O'Hare, the head of the school board?"

"I believe you're right, Clare."

Clarence, three inches taller than either of the arguing men, butted in. "Say, Mr. O'Hare. I'd like a word with you."

Surprised, O'Hare turned. Squinting at Clarence through finger-smudged glasses, he asked, "Who the blazes are you, sonny?"

"Clarence Dietz. From Thornapple Farm."

"Oh, yes. One of the outlaws."

"What? Outlaws! No sir. We proudly defend our home."

"Or so you say. Well, what is it? What do you want?"

"I want to know why *your* school board is no longer paying for schooling my little brothers and sisters."

"Go away," griped O'Hare. "I've no time for this, sonny."

"Now, just a dang minute, Charlie."

"Say now, young man! What gives you the right to speak to me like that?"

"What gives me the right? Listen, O'Hare, I have the same right to demand an education for my little brothers and sisters as any other American voter."

A crowd began to surround them.

"Clarence, your family has had more than your share of benefit from this town. Your outlaw pa won't receive one more red cent from me."

"What's that, Charlie?" said John from the hotel doorway. "Would you mind saying that to my face?"

O'Hare stepped back. "Dietz, I've no quarrel with you. However, I've decided against funding your school any more. It's not fair to the children in town."

"So those of us who make our living outside of town must fend for ourselves? Hire our own schoolteachers? O'Hare, you're no different than those other fat-headed bandits that run this county. You're only concerned about kowtowing to the dag-blasted lumber syndicate."

"Just a minute, Dietz," said a man from behind. "I don't like your tone."

John turned. "Well, if it isn't Bert Horel."

"That's right, Dietz."

"Butt out, Bert. This is between me and O'Hare." He turned back.

"Yeah? Well, now you're talking to me," said Horel, grabbing John by the shoulder.

John shrugged him off. Staring at O'Hare again, he said, "Listen, Charlie, if my children don't get their rightful schooling, I'll see to it you won't survive."

"What?"

"The next school board election, you fool!"

"Dietz!" shouted Horel, "I've had it with you!"

"Pa! Lookout!" yelled Clarence as Horel's huge, clenched fist came down on the back of his father's head, knocking him off the boardwalk and into the street.

Stunned, John looked up to see Bert Horel descending on him. Horel struck John again and again before John could roll out from underneath.

Clarence dove onto Horel.

John tried to come to his feet.

Leslie reached to help his father.

O'Hare pushed him aside, then pulled Clarence off.

Leslie shoved O'Hare up against a street lamp, knocking his wire-rim glasses and top hat into the dirt.

Horel punched John again, shouting, "Joe! Dan!" to his men. "Hold him for me. Hold Dietz!"

Horel's workers each grabbed an arm. They hoisted John to his feet as Horel wheeled back for a haymaker.

John twisted and pulled, forcing his right hand free from Joe Buckwheat's grip.

"I said hold him, Joe!"

Joe Buckwheat clamped his arms around John in a bear hug.

John fumbled for his Luger. Unable to raise it, he aimed from the hip, flipped off the safety, and pulled the trigger.

The sharp crack of the pistol startled everyone and stopped the fight, sending all but John and his sons back several steps.

Horel fell back, holding his neck. He came to his feet and staggered down the alley.

Hearing the shot, Mrs. Phelan looked out the front door of the Winter Hotel as John stepped onto the boardwalk, his Luger still smoking.

"Mary, I just shot one of your tavern regulars. He's headed down the alley behind the livery and might need a doctor." John turned back to the street. "Leslie, Clarence,, climb aboard the wagon. We best be on our way."

Although clearly done in self-defense, the September 6, 1910, shooting of Bert Horel on Winter's dusty Main Street strained the tenuous truce between the Sawyer County authorities and the Dietz family. Now the undying support of nearly everyone who lived in the region changed. No longer did people see John Dietz as a man defending his family and farm. He'd come to town armed and showed that he had no reservations about using his pistol against another man.

Within hours, news reached the county seat by way of the only telephone in town, recently installed in the Winter Post Office. The news of Bert Horel being shot by John Dietz renewed Harry Shue's desire to see John brought to justice. The logs, the dam, the issues that made the county officials and the lumber syndicate push to have John arrested four, five, and six years earlier were gone. Now, the Courthouse Gang wanted him to pay for the embarrassment he'd caused them. Shue sent Sheriff Madden to Winter. Madden returned with Joe Buckwheat, Winter's Town Chairman, who swore out a complaint, charging Dietz with attempted murder. And County Board Chairman, Harry Shue, dusted off the offer made one year earlier—the offer of a one-thousand-dollar reward for John F. Dietz—dead or alive.

SHOOTS AT DEITZ

FRIENDS OF HOREL, WOUNDED IN POLITICAL QUARREL, EVIDENTLY SEEK REVENGE.

PREPARING FOR A SEIGE

Nervy German Lays In More Ammunition and Supplies and Will Fight to the Last Ditch.

Hayward. — Another attempt was made to kill John F. Deitz at Cameron Dam. A shot was fired at him from ambush while he was en route from the cabin to the barn about 5:30 a. m. The bullet whistled by his head and buried itself in a log store house directly in line and some fifty feet beyond. Smokeless powder was used by the would-be-slayer and Dietz and his two sons, Clarence and Leslie were unable to definitely locate his hiding place.

Evidently the assailant crept down along an ambush to the road during the night, secreted himself in low brush and awaited the coming of daylight when he knew Deitz would come within range of his rifle while at work about the stable.

Te Deitz family is positive this attempt at murder was made by the son of Horel, who seeks revenge for the shooting of his father last Tuesday.

Ladysmith News-Budget

34
Floyd Gibbons
October 1, 1910

A young reporter for the *Minneapolis Tribune* stood on the far edge of the footbridge across from Thornapple Farm. He waved his tan skimmer overhead, hoping to get the attention of those in the cabin beyond. Behind stretched a ten-mile walk back to Winter, now crowded with other newspapermen. Like him, each one hoped to get a new angle on a story six years in the making.

"Hello?" shouted the reporter. "Mr. Dietz, are you there?" He listened for a reply. Instead, he heard a young woman singing.

"East Side, West Side, all around the town. The tots sang, 'ring-around-rosie, London Bridge is falling down.'"

Her clear, angelic voice carried across the meadow.

"Boys and girls together, me and Jimmy O'Rourke."

The reporter leaned forward.

"Tripped the light fantastic on the sidewalks of New York."

There, ahead, he saw the dark-haired young woman with the sweet voice. She carried two pails of water toward the cabin.

"Can I help you with those?" he asked.

Myra turned with a jerk, splashing water onto her white apron and button shoes. "Father!" she shrieked. "Father!" she yelled again. "Someone's here! Father!" She turned back to the young man. "Who in blazes are you?"

"Floyd Gibbons," he replied. "From the *Minneapolis Tribune*. You must be Miss Dietz. I've read your columns."

"Yes. I am." She nodded toward the cabin. "And *he* is my father!"

The screen door sprang open. Rifle in hand, John bounded off the porch. As he rushed toward them, Clarence, also armed, stepped out. Then Leslie, who scanned the river bottom with binoculars.

"And those must be your brothers," said Gibbons.

John raised his rifle. "Myra," he shouted. "Get back!"

"I mean no harm, Mr. Dietz," said Gibbons, raising his hands. "I'm from the *Trib*. I'm here to get your side of the story."

"How do I know you're not some spy sent here by the lumber trust?"

Myra set her pails on the ground. "He is who he says, Father. I recognize him from his photo in the newspaper. Mr. Gibbon's articles have been quite sympathetic all along."

Gibbons handed his satchel to Myra and picked up the water pails. "I'm terribly sorry I startled you."

Myra looked down at her water-soaked shoes. "Oh, no real harm done, Mr. Gibbons."

157

"Please, miss," he said with a smile, "call me Floyd. All my friends do."

Within minutes, Gibbons was scribbling notes, listening to the man beside him on the front porch. John, still within reach of his Winchester, rocked slowly to his daughter's songs, coming from inside the cabin.

"This sure is a beautiful spot, Mr. Dietz. Is the farm and the Cameron Dam are owned entirely by you?"

"I'm proud to say that I paid it off by trapping beaver and otter."

"Along with money paid you by the lumber company?"

"Bah! To this day I've seen only a fraction of what they owe me. The scoundrels refuse to pay me my rightful comeuppance."

"Mr. Dietz, if you're owed money, why not take them to court?"

"Oh, I dassn't go before a judge."

"Why, sir?"

"Because the lumber syndicate controls everything. They own most of the land, most of the lumber camps, the railroads, the county board, the sheriff, *and* the judge. Heck, they run the whole shebang. You see, Mr. Gibbons, Hayward is a company town. No, I wouldn't stand a ghost of a chance in court."

"What else can you do, Mr. Dietz?"

"I'll wait them out. The situation has changed, Mr. Gibbons. Now *I'm* the one holding the cards. The company won't float a log past Thornapple Farm until I am paid every last red cent I have coming!" John pointed to the notepad. "Tell your readers that I have every right to claim what's lawfully coming to me. That's all I ask. And those signs I posted mean what they say. No trespassing. I vow I will shoot any company man or hired hooligan who sets foot on my property. And the lumber company knows it. They have but two choices—pay up or lose more timber."

"Can you do that?" Gibbons asked. "Hold their property ransom?"

"Ransom? I am merely asking to be paid what's owed me. You see, the Wisconsin Charter of 1874 gives owners of dams that were built for log drives the right to assess ten cents per each one thousand board feet of timber that passes through."

"That means they owe you ..."

"I figure eight thousand for the pine."

"Eight thousand?"

"Plus the ninety-six dollars for crop damage, let's not forget. Write that down in your notes, Mister Gibbons. Eight-thousand, ninety-six dollars. That's what I'm rightfully owed by those rapscallions."

"Gracious sakes!"

"Oh, they can afford it. Keep in mind, Gibbons, that Frederick Weyerhaeuser has an interest in most of the mills from here to St. Louis. It's what made him rich. Why, even President Roosevelt scolded him."

"Yes, I read that in the paper. Roosevelt said Weyerhaeuser's idea of developing the country is to cut every stick of timber off and leave it a barren desert."

"Precisely,"

"Some say he may someday be wealthier than Rockefeller."

"So, now you see how easy it would have been for the company to pay what they owed me for crop damage and my work at the Price Dam in the first place. Frankly, I'd never have put up a fuss about what's owed me for the pine upstream if they'd paid me my rightful comeuppance."

"Now you are embroiled in an eight-thousand-dollar stand-off."

"Oh, but now, the shoe is on the other foot. You see, *I* control the dam. And I'll not let one of the company's logs float downstream until I've been paid. Look, Mr. Gibbons, it's my right to claim that which I am legally entitled to. Put that in your notes. Tell your readers it's my *right* to claim what's owed to me, and *right* always wins out over *might*."

"I will tell them. Now, what's behind this talk of you shooting a man last Election Day?"

"Self-defense," said John. "Be sure to write that down, too. Self-defense. I was being held down by two men so a third could suffer his blows upon me. I fought back the only way I could."

"Some say you tried to kill him."

John laughed. "Had I wanted Bert Horel dead, I would've shot twice. No, I was only trying to protect myself and my boys from the wrath of three company thugs."

"I assume you're aware that the county board has placed a thousand-dollar reward on your head for ignoring the warrants they've sworn out for your arrest?"

"I have two things to say about that. First, there's not a man in Sawyer County with enough gumption to come here, look me in the eye, and try to take me in. Second, don't believe for one tick of the clock that this county board can come up with money like that. No, Mr. Gibbons, if there's a pot of gold to be had for my scalp, it surely comes straight from the treasury of the Chippewa Lumber and Boom Company."

"Pa?" came a shout from the barn. "Are we still going to town?"

John turned back to his guest. "Saturday is when we go in for our mail, Mr. Gibbons." Turning toward the barn, he shouted to Clarence, "This young fellow came all the way from Minneapolis. I think it's best if I stay behind and talk with him. You and Leslie can go without me."

"Can Myra come along?"

"That's up to your ma."

Clarence rushed inside to find Myra giving a haircut to seven-year-old Johnny. "Myra," said Clarence, "Pa says you can go to town with us today." He turned to his mother. "If that's all right with you, Ma."

"Hmm?" said Hattie. "Oh, I suppose,"

"Oh, dear," said Myra, "I'd love to go, Clare, but I've so much to tend to."

"Nonsense," said Hattie "It's not often you get a chance to go to town. Today is the first of October, a beautiful fall day. Perfect for a ride through the woods. I'll finish up here. You go get ready."

"I'd better not."

"Young lady, you are going with your brothers and that's all there is to it."

"Are you sure? There's still sewing to be done and …"

"It will wait. This fine fall sunshine won't. Go get ready. You've earned an afternoon of fun." Hattie turned to her son. "Clarence, I've a list of items for you to get at the dry goods store. Take three dollars out from the egg money jar. You can spend the change on ice creams for the three of you."

"Gee, thanks, Ma!"

Minutes later, Leslie walked the pair of buckskins pulling the buckboard from the barn. Clarence climbed aboard, taking the reins. Leslie hopped on next. He reached down to help Myra, dressed in a snug, black brilliantine suit and white blouse. She took her place on the springboard seat, squeezing in between her brothers.

"My, don't you look snazzy," said Clarence. "Hoping to find a beau in town today?"

"One never can tell, Mr. Nosey."

John called to his children. "Now, don't you go talking to folks about our family matters. Just get the mail, pick up your ma's goods and get on back home. Should anybody ask about the goings on with me and Weyerhaeuser, you tell 'em I said it's nobody's business but mine."

Myra turned back. "Yes, Father. Goodbye, Mr. Gibbons ... err ... Floyd."

"And see to it you're home by suppertime. Mr. Gibbons will be sharing our table and staying the night."

"You bet, Pa," said Leslie. "We'll be back before sundown."

Myra waved as Clarence snapped the reins, shouting, "Giddy up!"

Gibbons watched as the horses trotted away. "That daughter of yours is quite a looker."

"And smart as a whip-snap."

"You let them go to town alone? After all the threats made against you? After shooting that fellow last month?"

"Folks around here know me, Mr. Gibbons. No one would *dare* touch my children. No one."

35

Bushwhacked!

The afternoon ride down the winding, ten-mile country road to the tiny village of Winter was delightful. The leaves had turned brilliant reds and golds. The air felt crisp and clean. As they rode, Myra, Leslie, and Clarence sang every song they knew at the top of their lungs, a Dietz tradition while traveling. Myra's clear, strong voice carried far into the surrounding woods and down the road. Rounding a bend, a family of raccoons skittered off the trail. A half-mile later, a covey of partridge flushed in front of the team, causing the buckskins to rear up. Every turn in the road brought more surprises, laughter, and fun. Until ...

A gunshot from the woods shattered the air. Then another. Myra jerked back as the bullet tore through her midriff.

Clarence reeled when a slug smashed through his arm.

Then another blast. And another. Then, a volley of gunshots, each bullet sending splinters flying from the wagon.

Writhing with pain, Myra fell below the buckboard's seat.

Clarence, bleeding, held fast to the reins.

Both horses reared up when a black-faced gunman jumped from the woods aiming at the Dietz children.

Leslie sprang from the wagon onto the road and dashed into the woods. Seven more gunshots sent bullets screaming past him. Crawling on hands and knees, he hid behind a windfall, waiting to see what would happen next and listening to his sister, moaning from pain, calling for help.

"Hands up, Clarence!" shouted one of the black-faced thugs.

"One got away," shouted another.

"Get after him, you fool!" screamed a third man as he emerged from hiding. "Check these two for guns."

"We're unarmed," said Clarence. "And keep your filthy hands off my sister. Anybody can see she's got no place to hide a gun in that outfit."

Myra looked up at the man. "I ... I know you. I brought our eggs to your house. I've helped your wife with your children. No charcoal grease paint can hide you, Fred Thorbahn."

"Raise your hands, the both of you," he shouted.

"I'm hurt," Myra groaned. "Please! I need a doctor."

"Roy! Go find the boy who ran off," shouted the third gunman. "We can't let him escape."

"The hell you say! What if he's got a pistol? I could get shot."

The third thug looked at Clarence, "Does your brother got a gun?"

Neither Clarence nor Myra answered.

"I asked you a question!" shouted the assailant, aiming his rifle at Clarence. "Does Lester got a gun?"

"He's got one of Pa's Lugers. And he knows how to use it, Sheriff."
Madden fell silent.

"Yeah, I figured it was you," said Clarence, bleeding and trying to control the buckskins. "You're behind this. Big tough Sheriff Madden shooting the children of a man who is too much for you."

"Shut your mouth!" snapped Madden. "Where's your pa? He's the one we want, not you."

"Home," Clarence answered. "And you cowards are in for it when he hears you shot me and my sister."

Madden squirmed. "You're both under arrest for helping that outlaw father of yours." He holstered his revolver.

"Show me your warrant, Sheriff."

"What?"

"We did nothing wrong," said Clarence. "Not one dag-blasted thing! My Uncle Will taught me enough about the law to know you can't arrest us without a warrant. Show it to me!"

"Help me," Myra moaned. "Get me a doctor. Please!"

"Aw, them are only flesh wounds," said Madden. "You'll heal up in time."

"I'm bleeding!" cried Myra. "*Please Sheriff!*"

"Fred! Look!" shouted one of the ambushers, pointing down the road. "It's the other boy!"

Clarence looked up to see Leslie wave from far up the hill and then turn and run toward the farm. Thorbahn raised his pistol and fired, squeezing off shot after shot.

"Hold your fire, you fool," ordered the sheriff. "He's far out of range."

"Pa won't let us down, Sheriff," said Clarence, clutching his bleeding arm with one hand and the reins with the other. "If I was you, I'd hightail it into Winter and get Doc Burns to tend to my sister."

"You don't run this outfit, boy. I do." He motioned to his two partners. "Quick!" he said. "Get aboard. We gotta get back to Winter."

Madden took the reins. "Hyah! Giddy up!" The Dietz team bolted, galloping toward town.

Myra felt every rock and rut as the wagon raced down the road. Meanwhile, Leslie crossed the river to Thornapple Farm. He burst into the cabin. Between breaths, he told of the ambush. John jumped from his chair and reached for his Winchester.

"You can't go, John," said Gibbons. "You'll be shot down before you ever reach town."

"I'll go," said Hattie, in tears. "I must tend to my children."

"No," said Gibbons. "Mrs. Dietz, you stay here with your young ones. I'll go to town. I'll make sure Myra and Clarence are safe and see to it they get the care they need. Nobody would dare stop a newspaperman from helping an injured youngster."

Hattie looked at her husband and then turned to their guest. "Thank you so much, Mr. Gibbons. Godspeed."

"Gibbons," added John.

"Yes, sir?"

"Watch your back trail."

Myra, her hands manacled behind her blood-soaked suit, stretched out face-down on the wagon bed. She groaned with every bump and stone the wheels struck.

"Watch the road behind," ordered Madden. "If you see *anyone*, open fire."

"You won't see Pa," said Clarence. "Not until it's too late."

Madden snapped the reins. "Hyah! Hyah!"

As soon as they reached town, the sheriff ordered deputies Fred Thorbahn and Roy Van Alstine to seat their handcuffed prisoners in the depot waiting room. While they guarded Myra and Clarence, Madden shut down every saloon and store in town and deputized every able-bodied man willing to take up a gun. Soon, a dozen tense men with deer rifles and shotguns spread out, hoping to protect the town from an angry father they felt sure would come to avenge the shooting of his children.

An hour later, Dr. Burns arrived by train to find Myra and Clarence in the depot, both bleeding. He placed a tourniquet on Clarence's arm as Sheriff Madden walked in.

"Get these handcuffs off the girl," Burns ordered.

"She's my prisoner. They stay."

"No, Sheriff. She's *my* patient and in jeopardy of dying. I must treat her. Remove the handcuffs. That's an order. Now!"

Madden unlocked the cuffs. "There," he huffed. "Satisfied, Doc?"

Burns leaned Myra toward him, inspecting her back. "I need to get her to the Winter Hotel where I can remove her blouse and inspect the wound."

"No," Madden insisted. "I can't risk it. Dietz is probably out there right now, plotting a way to rescue them. I'm taking the both of them to Hayward. They can recover in the county jail."

"Sheriff," said Burns, "Myra might not survive. Look at her. The poor girl's been shot through the abdomen. She's lost a lot of blood. There's no telling how long she will last. It's bad enough you've gunned down two youngsters. Unless you want this young woman's death on your hands, Myra stays here under my care, and *without* shackles!"

Madden considered the doctor's words. "All right. She stays." He turned to Thorbahn. "Make sure she's under guard at all times. I don't want her escaping."

"What?" shouted Thorbahn. "You mean to say you're leaving town? Leaving me and Roy here to face Dietz?"

Dr. Burns laughed. "Looks to me like you *lawmen* bit off more than you can chew."

Madden glared at him.

"She's quite a prize for you, isn't she, Sheriff? A young woman shot through the abdomen, wondering if she will live through the night. Quite a prize, all right."

"Another wisecrack out of you, Burns, and I'll throw *you* in the hoosegow with them." He turned to his deputy. "Fred, I need to board the train with the boy. You help Doc Burns get the girl to the hotel."

That night, Deputy Fred Thorbahn sat near a second floor Winter Hotel window several feet from his unconscious captive. His nervous glances alternated between Myra and the dusty street below.

Hours later, a second physician arrived. Thorbahn cautiously opened the hotel room door. "She's been out cold ever since we got here, Doc."

Dr. Grafton removed the blanket to find the bed soaked with blood. Myra winced when he pushed the bandage aside and then covered her again. "Let's hope the bleeding stops," he said. He placed a bottle of heroine tablets on the dresser. "I will tell Mrs. Phelan to give her one or two of these pills if she has pain. I will stop back in the morning. If she makes it through the night, we'll see if we can get her to a hospital."

"If she makes it?" blurted Thorbahn. "Doc, she's *gotta* make it!"
"It's not up to me, Fred. If that was your bullet that did this damage, you better pray to God that she not die. It's up to Him, now."

36

Sunday, October 2, 1910

Floyd Gibbons arrived after dark. Two men with rifles stopped him on the outskirts of the village. They stood watch as a third deputy searched him.

"Who are you?" asked one of the deputies.

"Floyd Gibbons. Reporter for the *Minneapolis Star*."

"You came in on the road from Thornapple Farm. That's the Dietz place."

"How bad are his children hurt?" asked Gibbons.

"What business is it of yours?"

"I'm working on a story. Tell me about their wounds."

"They're a bunch of outlaws."

"Only in the eyes of the lumber company."

"They all belong behind bars."

"My readers don't agree, sir."

"Where's Dietz?" asked the first deputy.

"Last I saw, he was at the farm. But he could be almost anywhere by now. Maybe behind one of those trees, looking down his sights at you right now."

Shifting uncomfortably, both men looked around.

"Let's take him to jail," said one. "Thorbahn can deal with him."

"Are you placing me under arrest?" asked Gibbons. "A newspaperman just out doing his job? How will that look in the papers? How will that look to a judge when I file a court claim against you?"

"What? Oh, no. You're not under arrest, Gibbons. But you're coming with us, anyway."

"Look. I'm neither on his side nor yours. I'm a reporter. I have a story to write. Now tell me, how bad are the Dietz children hurt?"

"The boy got his arm shot, but he'll be all right. He's on his way to Hayward with the sheriff. The girl, well, she's worse off."

"What do you mean?"

"She's up in the hotel. Shot through the belly. Doc Burns said she might not make it."

"Some other doc is tending to her," said the other deputy.

"I need to talk to Burns," said Gibbons. "Right away." He reached for his notepad. "Here, write down your names. I'll see to it both of you are mentioned in the paper. Daring citizens who are willing to put their lives on the line to protect their town. How's that sound?"

"It was Fred who shot the girl," said one of deputies, printing his name. "They figure Roy Van Alstine fired the bullet that hit Clarence in the arm."

"Why did they shoot?" asked Gibbons, taking notes. "Did the Dietz children do anything wrong?

"Why'd they shoot? Well, because the Dietz wagon come down the road, that's why."

"But so did I. And nobody shot at me."

"Well, maybe you're lucky it was them that got shot and not you."

Later, in the hotel lobby, Gibbons interviewed Doctor Guy Grafton, the second physician to see Myra that evening. In order to file his story for the morning edition of the *Trib,* Gibbons crossed the street to the post office in search of the only telephone in town. Gibbons knew his article about two of the Dietz children gunned down by a county sheriff and his pals would be nationwide news. And *he* had the scoop.

As Gibbons approached the post office, he noticed telephone poles in the alley behind the building. He knocked on the front door. A man cracked it open.

"Can't you read?" he asked, pointing to the sign in the window. "We're closed."

"Sir, I need to use your telephone. It's urgent," Gibbons explained. "I'm a reporter with the *Minneapolis Tribune.* There's been a shooting and I need to call my story in to my editor so it makes the Sunday paper."

"Who got shot this time?"

"The Dietz girl and her older brother. Ambushed along the road by the Sheriff."

"All right," said the postmaster, opening the door wider. "Get in here and make your dang telephone call. But it will cost you a sawbuck. In advance."

Gibbons handed the man a ten-dollar bill and filed his story by wire. Leaving the post office, he spotted two more reporters comparing notes across the street. Gibbons glanced back at the telephone wire behind the post office. He slipped down the alley and pulled a jackknife from his hip pocket. Gibbons' coverage of the shooting of Myra and Clarence Dietz would be the only report of the ambush that would go nationwide the next day.*

*Floyd Gibbons got the scoop on the ambush of the Dietz children. But his boss, the editor of the *Minneapolis Daily Tribune,* didn't approve of Gibbons' cutting the Winter Post Office telephone wire and fired Gibbons. Hearing this, another newspaper hired Gibbons. The aggressive, suave, no-holds-barred newsman's on-the-scene coverage of of Poncho Villa's raids and countless battles during World War I for the *Chicago Tribune* cost him an eye but earned him the reputation as one of America's finest journalists.

Myra woke around noon, Sunday, October 2, 1910. Her eyes focused on a man sitting in a chair with a shotgun across his lap. As she gazed around the room, she saw a woman and another man, both standing. "Uncle Will?" she breathed."

William Dietz stepped closer. "I came as soon as I heard, Myra."

"How is Clarence?"

"He's okay. Doc Burns says his arm will heal. So will you, in time."

"In time for a judge to send you both to prison," said Thorbahn.

The woman stepped closer to him. "Now you listen here, Fred Thorbahn. It's bad enough you sit there staring at this poor girl. You've no right to say anything. Not one single word." The woman came closer to Myra and her uncle. "Are you in pain, Myra?"

"Mrs. Phelan?"

"Yes, dear. Are you in pain?"

Myra moved her shoulders. "My … my back hurts. And I can't feel my legs."

"Oh, dear. Dr. Burns said this might happen."

"She had it coming," said Thorbahn.

William Dietz turned. "That's enough out of you, deputy!"

"Fred," said Mrs. Phelan, "it's plain to see that this young woman is no risk to anyone. She doesn't need you glaring at her and making snide remarks. If you're so intent on guarding her, you'll have to do it from the hallway."

"Says who?"

"Me, that's who. I own this hotel, and as of this minute you are trespassing. Now get out!"

"Or what?" said Thorbahn, defiantly.

William took three steps toward him. "You heard the lady. Move!"

Thorbahn rose, staring at William who stood before him, hands on his hips.

"Thorbahn, don't be a fool. Just take your chair and that shotgun of yours and sit in the hall like Mary said."

The deputy shrugged his shoulders. "All right. You win," he grunted. "This time."

Mary Phelan opened a small bottle of pills. "Here, Myra, Doc Grafton said these will help."

Myra swallowed the pill with a sip of water. "Where's my father?"

"John and Hattie are still at the farm," said William. "I'll head out there soon and let them know we talked."

"Don't let my father come to town, Uncle Will. It's too dangerous."

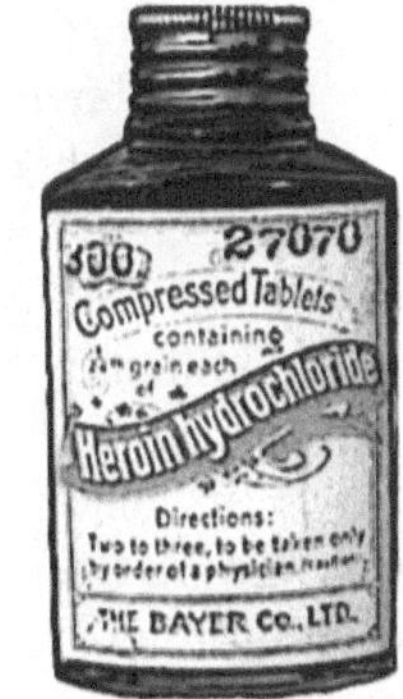

"You poor girl," said Mary. "Getting shot like that. And for no good reason at all. Shame on that spineless sheriff and those cowardly deputies."

A tap on the door told them the doctor had returned.

"Oh, you're awake," Burns said. "Good. Good." He placed his palm on her forehead. "No fever. That's good, too."

"I can't feel my legs. Will I ever walk again? Doctor, am I …?"

"I think the bullet grazed your spine as it passed through, Myra. It caused some swelling that is putting pressure on your spinal nerve. When the swelling goes down, the feeling in your legs should return."

"Oh, dear, what a relief," said Mary.

"Uncle Will, tell Father and Mother they needn't worry.

"Yes, I'll tell them, Myra."

"Young lady," said Burns, "you can rest here for now. However, if there's no improvement, I'll need to move you to a hospital so that wound of yours can be probed."

"Probed?" asked William.

"By a surgeon, Will. To learn what damage has been done, reduce the chance of complications, see if there are bone fragments near the spinal cord, that kind of thing." He turned toward the bed. "I need to change your bandage, Myra. Then you should rest. If you haven't improved by tomorrow, we'll get you to a hospital."

William took his niece's hand. "Be strong, Myra. I'll go now. I'll let your parents know you are on your way to a full recovery."

"Uncle Will?"

William looked into his niece's eyes.

"Please, don't let my father do anything rash. You know how he is."

"I'll do what I can."

In Hayward, the jailor slid Clarence's breakfast under the cell door. Clarence picked up the tin plate using his good arm. "Is there any coffee?" he asked.

"Not for outlaws," replied the man in the next cell.

"Outlaws?"

"These lawmen believe all you Dietzes belong in prison."

"Is he right?" Clarence asked the jailor. "Have we all been painted with the same brush?"

"Look, sonny. I just do what I'm told."

"Painted by Sheriff Madden? By Harry Shue?"

The jailor didn't reply.

"For Pete's sake, you should know better. Look," said Clarence, revealing a deep scar on his head. "I got shot down by some mercenary in militia uniform. I nearly died! Now I've been shot again. And not once have I done anything against the law. Not once! Madden, that crooked boss of yours, ambushed us yesterday. Him and two more cowards hid in the woods and shot us down as we rode by. My sister was gut shot and might die. And neither one of us ever did *anything* to deserve this."

"I'm sorry, son. Like I said, I only work here. You'll get your chance to explain all this to the judge. He'll sort things out. Meanwhile, I'll get you that cup of coffee."

One floor above, drinking from the same coffeepot as the prisoners, Sheriff Mike Madden sat across from Harry Shue, Chairman of the Sawyer County Board.

Shue's hand shook as he sipped from his cup. "What in God's name were you thinking, Mike? Shooting down two youngsters? Do you realize how that makes us look in the eyes of the public? How it makes *me* look?"

"It didn't go as I figured, Harry. John Dietz was supposed to be on that wagon, not the girl. If it was Dietz who we shot yesterday, you'd be whistling a different tune."

"But it wasn't Dietz!" yelled Shue. "How in blazes could you be so reckless? So *foolish* as to shoot the girl? Now what do I do?"

"Calm down, Harry," said Madden, sipping from his cup. "All you need to do is remind folks that John Dietz is a desperate criminal. A threat to society. An outlaw who needs to be thrown in prison. Heck, you've already convinced half the town of that."

"Half isn't enough, Sheriff. As soon as today's newspapers come out, the public outcry will drown out everything I've said about Dietz. Instead of the villain we've painted him to be, Dietz will become the *hero* of Cameron Dam."

"He's still facing warrants for his arrest. An outlaw."

"Don't be a fool, Mike. Not one of those warrants or court complaints will mean more than a hill of beans once folks hear what you did to the Dietz children. Why, in two weeks, the whole gol-dang Dietz family will be known nationwide as victimized, persecuted heroes, champions of the downtrodden. And it's all your fault."

"Say! Don't you go putting this on me, Harry Shue. We *both* know that the company is behind this—hook, line, and sinker. You could've ended your little scheme to bring Dietz in years ago, and it wouldn't have hurt you or me or this town one single iota. But you didn't, Harry. No, you wanted to lick the boots of the lumbermen. Get a pat on the back from William Irvine. Maybe get a case of whiskey from Edward Hines. I don't know. But don't you *dare* go putting this on me!"

Glaring at the sheriff, Shue pitched his half-full coffee cup against the wall. "*You* ambushed those young people, Madden. You!"

"What's done is done."

"Now what? What, Sheriff?"

"Okay, Harry, you are right when it comes to public sentiment. It will skyrocket once word of this gets out. And when it does, there will be no way to convince the public that Dietz should be arrested. We have to act fast. Get this over with. Let me put together my own squad, a posse big enough to overwhelm even John Dietz. Then I'll bring him in, one way or another. But it has to be soon."

"You think you can find enough men? Men brave enough to go up against Dietz?"

"If you promise me another fifteen hundred and I'll round up forty or fifty deputies, more than enough to do the job."

"Fifteen hundred? Are you daft?"

"Do you want Dietz or not?"

"There's already a thousand dollar reward out there, Mike. Isn't that enough?"

LADYSMITH NEWS-BUDGET

WAR ON CHILDREN

SHERIFF MADDEN HIDES IN AMBUSH AND DISTINGUISHES HIMSELF.

DIETZ COMING TO TOWN

Defender of Cameron Dam Laughs at Terrible Village's Plans.—Small Army Defends Town Against the Desperate Man.

Winter. — Two children of John Deitz are under arrest, the boy Clarence, with a slight wound in his arm, and the daughter, Myra, in a critical condition, with a bullet thru her abdomen.

Sheriff Madden decided Saturday evening to make an effort to stop public criticism of his failure to get Deitz, and posted an ambuscade along the road to Winter, expecting Deitz to come for his mail. Instead of Deitz, three of his children, unarmed were the victims, and when they laughed at Madden's commands to hold up their hands, the sheriff and his posse opened fire at fifteen feet and after a rain of bullets the girl and one boy fell, while the younger boy escaped through the woods to their house.

"If you want a posse, you'll have to pay each man a daily wage. I'll need another fifteen hundred."

"When?"

"Within a week."

"All right, Mike. You've got it. But this time, *I want Dietz*. I want him in handcuffs. I want him in a jail cell. Or, better yet, Greenwood Cemetery. Now, get on with it!"

37

St. Joseph's Hospital

Dr. Burns stopped at the hotel early Monday morning to check on Myra. Fred Thorbahn was fast asleep at his post outside her door. Burns walked right in.

Myra, eyes glazed and open, stared at the ceiling.

"How are you feeling?" asked Burns.

Myra didn't answer.

"Myra?

She didn't respond.

"Wake up, Myra!" Burns shouted, shaking her. "Wake up!" Burns rushed out. "Mrs. Phelan!" he yelled.

Mary Phelan came running from the kitchen. She looked up to the second story balcony.

"It's Myra," he said. "I need your help."

Burns rushed back to Myra's side. Mary Phelan joined him.

"Myra," he shouted, shaking her again. "Myra!"

Myra finally turned her head toward him, her eyes unfocused.

Burns grabbed the half-empty pill bottle from the dresser. "It's these pills that Doctor Grafton gave her," he said. "She's had too many."

"What can we do?" asked Mrs. Phelan.

"First, no more pills." He stuffed the bottle into his coat pocket. "Mary, I've got to get this poor girl to a hospital. I need you to find four strong men. Tell them there's a stretcher behind the door to my office. They should fetch it and then help me move Myra to the railway station. There's a train due in soon. There's no time to lose."

Mary Phelan ran down the steps. Within minutes, four men steadied the stretcher next to Myra's bed.

Groggy, Myra mouthed. "What …? What are you …?"

"We have to get you to the depot, Myra," said Burns. "Then to a hospital."

"Wait just a dang minute," said Thorbahn, standing in the doorway. "She's my prisoner. Who said you could move her?"

"And *my* patient! I am in charge, here."

"The hell you say!"

"Get out of my way, Fred."

Mary Phelan shoved Thorbahn aside. "Doc Burns is about to save the life of the girl you shot. Are you just going to stand there? Or help?"

"Well, all right," said Thorbahn. "But I won't let you take her down Main Street. It's too risky. Dietz might try something."

"Nonsense," said Burns. "This is his daughter. He wouldn't do anything to risk Myra's safety."

"I won't allow it," Thorbahn insisted. "Take her out the back way and down the alley."

"Past the horse barns?" Mary asked. "What of the manure?"

"It's the alley or nothing," said Thorbahn. "Take your pick."

Four men carried a stretcher bearing a delirious Myra Dietz down the alley. They gagged from the stench of the ankle-deep horse manure shoveled each morning from the stalls. Doc Burns climbed into the baggage car, reached down, and lifted as the men raised the stretcher. Myra moaned as they slid her across the floor of the car. Two of the men climbed in behind, taking their seat against the wall. Mrya winced with pain when the train pulled out.

"Say, Doc," said one of the guards. "Where we headed?"

"Ashland," he replied.

"What? Say, I thought Hayward was …"

"Hayward's surgeon isn't the man for the job," Burns said.

"I don't like the sound of this," said the other guard.

"Oh, for Pete's sake, look at her," said Burns. "The poor girl's dying. Do you really think she's going to make a break for it?"

St. Paul Pioneer Press
October, 1910

SHERIFF MADDEN'S BLUNDER

The reports from Winter, Wisc., indicate that Sheriff Madden and his deputies have made a mess of what was already a bad job. John Dietz was sought on a warrant for shooting a man and wounding him. But Dietz had defied arrest. Known to be a desperate man, the sheriff wisely took precautions to avoid getting hurt or having any of his deputies injured. But the shooting of his children Saturday morning was without the shadow of an excuse, nothing short of an outrage. The two victims and the three officers agree, according to the reports, that the order from the sheriff to halt was followed almost immediately by a volley from the sheriff's anxious posse, wounding one of the boys and his sister. Why the shooting was done we can't now imagine, unless the sheriff or some of his men lost their heads and saw in this young girl and her tame brothers riding so peacefully down the road as a raid on the town. It requires no sympathy with John Dietz in his defiance of the law to see what a terrible blunder the sheriff has committed, and how Dietz may be expected to make more serious trouble in retaliation for this shooting of his peaceful children.

The train rolled out of the yard beginning a long painful trip to the Ashland Depot. Myra was admitted to St. Joseph's Hospital that afternoon. She would remain there for sixty-two days and through three surgeries on her spine and kidneys, damaged by the bullet fired by Fred Thorbahn, a storekeeper so recently deputized by the Sheriff of Sawyer County, Mike Madden.

Red Mulligan rounded up his Camp Four lumberjacks. They crowded into the mess hall to hear what he had to say.

"Pipe down!" he shouted, to get their attention. "The company wants to rebuild the dam. They plan to start first thing next spring."

"What's that got to do with us, Red?" asked a man in the back.

"There's still the problem of John and Hattie Dietz owning the land," Mulligan replied.

"Why the heck doesn't Weyerhaeuser just buy the dang farm?" asked a third man. "Is he short on pocket change this week?"

A wave of laughter rolled through the room.

"Say Red," a man hollered, "why don't *you* borrow him the money?"

"All right. All right. Now listen up. Mr. Irvine tried to buy Dietz out. He won't sell. Not for a king's ransom."

"That don't explain why you called us here, Red."

"You all know Dietz tried to kill a man in town on Election Day."

"Dietz shot Bert Horel in self-defense, Red. Everybody knows that."

"Self-defense or not, there's another arrest warrant out for Dietz," said Mulligan.

"How many warrants does that make, Red?"

"All right. That's enough! Men, Sheriff Madden needs our help."

A tall, bearded man in the middle of the mess hall stood. "Mulligan, you're barking up the wrong dang tree. Firstly, I don't agree that John Dietz has done anything but try to protect his family. Second, I know for a fact that he's a crack shot with that Winchester of his, as are his boys. Now, I don't mind risking my life in the woods cutting timber, but that's my limit. I'm not about to take a bullet for the gol-dang lumber trust, Red. No sir. Count me out!"

"And another thing," shouted the next man, "the sheriff had two of the Dietz children, a boy and a girl, shot last Saturday—ambushed while on their way to town to get the mail. Yesterday, I heard they got the girl laid out on a hospital bed up in Ashland, waitin' to die. Mulligan, I'll have no part of what you and Sheriff Madden are plannin' next for the Dietz family."

"Well, fine," said Mulligan. "That's up to you, Frank. So, what about the rest of you men?"

Oscar Harp, a short, stocky fellow with a handlebar moustache, stood. "Red, you ain't spelled out just what it is that you want from us."

"Chippewa Lumber will pay you men ten dollars each if you'll sign on as a deputy and take up a rifle against Dietz. Ten dollars. More than you make in a week! Raise your hand right now if I can count on you." Mulligan watched as hands slowly rose. He counted twenty-nine.

"Say, Red. When does all of this take place?"

"Soon, Oscar," Mulligan replied. "Sooner than you think."

38

The Governor Writes

On October 4, 1910, Sheriff Madden sat before the fire in the marshals' camp, surrounded by a squad of forty men. Forty rifles leaned against the trees surrounding them. The camp cook set platters of roast beef, boiled potatoes, and molasses cookies on crude, makeshift tables.

"All right, men," said Madden. "Dig in. But keep in mind that you're not just here to fill your bellies. The object is to bring in John Dietz and his outlaw family. But if you expect to draw pay for this from the county treasury, I'll have to deputize you. So each of you put down your spoon for now and raise your right hand. I'm about to make Sawyer County deputies out of the lot of you."

A tall, brawny deputy approached. "Sheriff," he said, interrupting, "there's a fellow by the footbridge who wants to cross over to Thornapple Farm. Says his name is William, brother to John Dietz."

"I know William Dietz. He's a good man and means no harm. Let him cross."

"But, sheriff, he has seen that we have a posse."

"That won't be news to John Dietz. His field glasses have already told him as much. As I said, let William Dietz cross. Who knows? He might even talk some sense into his brother before this whole episode explodes into a calamity."

Four hundred miles south, a large crate left the Chicago stockyards in a boxcar, hidden between thirty-six barrels of beef packed in salt, bound for northern Wisconsin's lumber camps. By daybreak the car had crossed into Wisconsin. By noon it was switched to another train at Marshfield and headed for Park Falls. Before the Wisconsin Central train left the Park Falls freight station, the crate sat on the loading dock next to four barrels of beef.

A man in a wool overcoat and woodsman's boots handed the stationmaster a ten-dollar bill before loading the crate and the barrels onto his wagon. The stationmaster slipped the bill into his pocket as he watched the driver ride off. By nightfall the cargo reached Camp Four.

"Any trouble?" asked Red Mulligan.

"Why would there be trouble?" replied the driver.

"Oh, yes. You're right. No trouble."

"What do you want done with it?"

"We'll transfer him to my wagon. It's behind the cook shanty."

"Where's my money?"

Mulligan handed him three twenty-dollar bills.

"I could use a hand. Two of these barrels of salted beef are for Camp Four. You have men who can take them off my hands?"

"Yes. But we need to move the crate off your wagon first."

Both men struggled to slide the crate from one wagon to the next. When finished, Mulligan said, "Wait here. I'll get the help you need to roll those meat barrels into the cook shanty."

"Say," said the driver, "It's none of my business, but ..."

Mulligan slipped him another twenty. "You're right. It's none of your business, pal. Keep a tight lip."

Life on Thornapple Farm went on in spite of Myra, critically wounded and confined to an Ashland hospital bed, and Clarence held without charges in the Sawyer County Jail. Hattie, now four months pregnant, counted on help from thirteen-year-old Helen. Together they did what they could to stay ahead of the household chores and care for Johnny. Meanwhile, Leslie and his father tended to the farm chores. Crops had to be harvested and stored for winter. Corn, carrots, turnips, and onions didn't take long, but digging potatoes and rutabagas became burdensome for just two men.

Three days after the shooting of his children, John sat on a milk stool in the barn as Leslie led another cow into a stanchion.

"I saw more men across the river, Pa," he said.

"Carrying rifles?"

"Yep."

"How many?"

"I'd say about ten men. They were taking turns staring at me through field glasses."

"As long as they stay there and we stay here, things are fine."

Leslie grabbed a second milk stool and a bucket. "What if they don't? What if they mount an attack?"

"The law says a man has a right to defend his castle, and that's what we'll do, Leslie."

"I don't want to shoot anybody."

"Nor do I. But sometimes we have to do things we don't like in order to protect ourselves."

"Pa, I think you should turn yourself in."

"What?"

"Get Uncle Will to plead your case in front of Judge Parish. You saw what Mr. Gibbons wrote in the paper. Everybody now knows that Harry Shue's Courthouse Gang is in league with the lumber syndicate and that Madden is out for blood. If ever there was a time when folks thought you a hero, it is right now. I say turn yourself in. It's the best time. You've said it many times, Pa. Strike while the iron is hot."

"Parish would like nothing more than to toss me in jail and throw away the key."

"He would be a fool to put you, a *hero*, in jail. He'd never get elected again."

"Sounds like you've been putting some thought into this, Leslie. That's good."

"Huh?"

"A man needs to think things through." John moved his stool to the next cow. "But I've been mulling things over, too. With winter coming on, your mother with child, your sister laid up, and Clarence in jail, what choice do I have but to stay here, tend the farm, and stand my ground?"

"I … I don't follow you, Pa."

"I can't risk having Shue set the odds against me. The Courthouse Gang would like nothing better than to land me in jail for who-knows-how-long, maybe long enough for them to finagle a way to get hold of our land. No, right now, I must stay here to make sure we are set for winter. My duty is to provide for our family and watch over Thornapple Farm." John dumped his full bucket into a milk can and moved his stool to the next stanchion.

"And besides," he added, "the company wants that dam rebuilt. I can't give in now. No, Leslie, I'll stand my ground no matter what."

"But Pa, those men are carrying rifles. Is it worth the gamble?"

"Gamble? Hmm. That's the key word, isn't it? In life, it seems that everything always comes down to risk versus reward."

"I don't get your gist," said Leslie, moving to the next stanchion.

"Hardly a day goes by when we don't take some risk, large or small, hoping for a reward. Your ma puts a cake in the oven, hoping it doesn't fall when she takes it out. It's a minor risk for a tasty reward. You and Clarence planted five acres of squash and pumpkins last June, hoping there'd not be a drought or some kind of a blight. Your risk paid off and now we have a full root cellar to show for it. You see, Leslie, life is a gamble. Always has been. Always will be. Risk versus reward."

"What about you, Pa? What's your reward? What reward is worth having all our lives hanging on tenterhooks? Each of us worried about getting attacked? Shot to pieces? Is it so you can show the world that you beat the lumber syndicate? Is that *your* reward, Pa? Besting Frederick Weyerhaeuser? Besting the king of the lumber tycoons?"

"My reward? Look, when this all started, I only wanted what was owed me. But now I have an obligation to thousands upon thousands of folks who've stood up behind me. Those people want the lumber syndicate put in its place just as much as I do. Maybe even more."

Leslie dumped his bucket into another milk can and returned. "All right. So that's the reward. Beating the lumber trust. So, what about the risk? You've told reporters that you will fight to the death, that the only way they'll get you off Thornapple Farm is feet-first. So far, Myra's been shot and Clarence shot twice. Both came close to dying. You've been shot at and so have I. So, tell me, Pa, is what you are doing *really* worth that much risk?"

Leslie spun to the right. "Shh. Someone's coming." He grabbed his deer rifle and silently stepped toward the open barn door.

John pulled his Luger from its holster, aiming toward the door. He clicked off the safety.

Leslie raised his Winchester and inched back the hammer. Trembling, he waited—and waited—then gasped—as Helen came in. Exhaling in relief, he and lowered the rifle, easing the hammer down. Leslie glared at his father. "Is it really worth the risk, Pa?"

John turned away.

"Papa," said Helen, "Uncle William is here. He brought the mail."

"Did he mention your sister?"

"Yes."

"Is Myra … is she all right?"

"Uncle Will said she is being well cared for."

"Leslie, finish up here and then get these milk cans onto the wagon. Maybe your uncle can find someone to buy the milk in Ladysmith." He emptied his bucket into the milk can. "I'll be in the cabin. Join us when you can."

"Okay, Pa. But, please. Think about it."

"About what?"

"What you're gambling with. And if what you're doing is worth this much risk."

William Dietz sat at the table watching Hattie sort through an enormous stack of mail. Johnny played on the rug with wooden toys carved by Clarence and Leslie for Stanley, now handed down to him. Helen brought two cups of tea from the kitchen as her father walked in.

"William!" said John. "Good to see you."

"Can I get you a cup of tea, Papa?" asked Helen.

"Yes, Princess," he replied. "One lump." He turned to his brother. "What news of Myra do you bring?"

"I visited her yesterday. She is in St. Joseph's hospital, comfortable, and in good hands. The nuns tend to her night and day. I spoke with Doctor Dodd, her surgeon. He said she lost a lot of blood but has no infection. He thinks she will pull through in time."

"Thank Heaven the Lord is looking out for us," said Hattie, opening another letter.

"Mother," said John, "had the Lord been looking out for us, our daughter would not have been shot down in the first place."

William continued. "She has her own room. John, you'll be pleased to hear it is plumb filled with flowers sent from wide and far by your supporters."

"Is she in pain?" asked Hattie.

"The doctor and his nurses keep her comfortable." William sipped from his cup. "Helen," he said, "Myra wanted me to tell you something."

"Me?"

"She said to tell you that you can read her magazines if you want."

"Her *Harper's*?"

"That's what she said."

Helen searched through the pile of mail on the table and ran into her room with a magazine.

"It's amazing how today's children grow up so fast," said William.

Hattie picked up another letter. "John, have you ever seen so many letters?"

"How is Clarence?" he asked.

"The good news is that bullet missed the bone. Doc Grafton says his arm will heal up just fine."

"Has Clare been charged with a crime?"

"Not yet. Sheriff Madden told me your son will be held until the district attorney makes up his mind."

John slammed his fist on the table, rattling the teacups in their saucers. "There! See? What have I been saying all along? They do as they please in utter disregard of the law. Clarence committed no crime whatsoever. And those tyrants have the nerve to call *me* an outlaw?"

"I'll have Clare out on bail soon," said William. "A boy like yours, always on the go, doesn't do well sitting in a jail cell day in and day out."

"We can pay his bond, Will," said Hattie, placing another dollar bill on her stack. "We've tucked away plenty."

"Good, good. I'll get him out soon."

"Not if Harry Shue has anything to say about it," said John as he pawed through the mail. "Will, there are lawmen across the river again."

"Yes. I saw them," he replied. "More than before."

"How many?"

"Does it matter?"

"How many, William?"

"I counted about thirty. Thirty … that I could see."

"Militia?"

"No. Sheriff's deputies. I think most are friends of Bert Horel."

"Say, now!" said John, holding a letter. "It's from James Davidson."

"The governor?" said Hattie. "My stars!"

John sliced it open with his knife. "Hmm," he grunted.

"Well, what does he say?" asked Hattie.

"He wonders if my concern is that I will not receive a fair trial."

"He's worried," said Will. "I saw in the *Milwaukee Journal*, that Davidson has received thousands of letters supporting you. Sheriff Madden attack on your children, especially Myra, has created a public outcry this state has never before seen."

"Thousands of letters?" asked Hattie.

"Nothing like that has ever happened in Wisconsin," said Will.

John continued reading. "Listen to this. *'As governor of the state, actuated by a desire to prevent further bloodshed, I send Attorney General Gilbert and O. G. Munson, my personal secretary to represent me and full, personal protection and a fair trial and council to defend you.'"**

John lowered the letter. "Did you hear that? The governor wants his attorney general to serve as my lawyer. My word! He must be under some terrific public pressure."

"I've heard there are posses of men coming," said Will. "Coming to *defend* you. One from Milwaukee and another from St. Paul."

"Coming to defend me? Now there's a turnabout for you. Wait until Davidson hears about this."

"Oh, you can bet the governor knows."

John read more. *"'If you still refuse to peaceably submit to the orderly process of the law, the responsibility of any bloodshed and loss of life must rest upon you alone. I am very truly yours, J. O. Davidson.'"**

"What nerve! I have every right to protect my home and family." John grunted in disgust. "So, Davidson says he is sending his personal secretary and the attorney general."

"Now, *that* is news," said William. He pulled his watch from his pocket. "John, Hattie, I need to be on my way if I'm going to catch the train to Ladysmith."

"Leslie can take you over to the railroad grade and help hoist the milk cans aboard," said John, still holding the Governor's letter. He looked at the date. "My word, Mother! They'll be here today!"

"Oh, my," said Hattie looking around. "I'll need to fix a nice meal and put on my Sunday dress."

"Nonsense," said John. "No need to put on airs. Let them see us as we are, besieged and harassed and struggling to get our crops harvested before winter sets in."

"Pa!" shouted Leslie from the porch. "There's a buggy crossing the river. Two men wearing citified duds."

"I suppose that's them," said William, stepping outside. "Leslie, keep that Winchester out of sight. These men are on your pa's side."

*Direct quotes from a 1910 letter to John Dietz from Governor James O. Davidson.

39

A Snap of My Fingers

As William and Leslie rode off, Wisconsin's Attorney General, Frank Gilbert, took a seat at the table across from John. Next to him sat Oliver Goldsmith Munson, Governor Davidson's personal secretary. Munson stared at a wide set of deer antlers hanging on the wall.

"Mr. Dietz, I don't know that I've ever seen such a rack of deer horns. Did you shoot that buck?"

John turned, looking at the antlers. "Three years ago. Across the river."

"You don't find deer like that where we live," said Goldsmith.

"Come here next month," said Hattie. "John will guide you. You're welcome to sleep in the schoolroom."

"Schoolroom?" Gilbert wondered aloud.

John laughed. "Might just as well. The county no longer provides a teacher for our children."

"No teacher?" said Munson. "Absurd!"

"Oh, no," said Hattie. "Not for the *Dietz* family. Heaven forbid!"

Munson pointed at the antlers. "Mr. Dietz, would you help me bag a buck like that?"

"Gentlemen, you're both welcome to join our hunt later this month. Just say the word. But, there's still the matter of those lawmen over there."

"Oh, yes," said Munson. "Mr. Gilbert and I can settle that today."

"And resolve this nonsense about your children having no teacher," said Gilbert. "With your approval of course."

John pointed to a wooden apple crate in the corner. Bundles of envelopes, tightly tied with string, packed the box. "See those letters?" he asked. "They came from people who say I am right to demand fair treatment from the lumber syndicate. People who also urge me to defend my family by fending off government-paid intruders."

"You gentlemen are excepted, of course," said Hattie. She turned to Helen, now sitting on the hearth with Johnny. Both of their dogs lay at her feet. "Helen, please bring these gentlemen some lemonade."

"And cookies?" Helen asked.

"Yes, Princess," said John. "A plate of cookies and lemonade for our guests." He pointed at the crate of letters. "Mr. Munson, *thousands* wrote to us after our son Clarence was shot down two years ago."

"It's a wonder the poor boy didn't die," said Hattie, shaking her head. "Land sakes, it was an awful wound. Oh, but *now* you should see the number of letters coming," she said. "And, goodness gracious, what they say!"

"Governor Davidson has been getting mail, too," said Munson, staring at the antlers again. "Over ten thousand letters, I'm told."

"Ten thousand?" gasped Hattie. "My stars!"

"Perhaps he should stop referring to me as an outlaw," said John.

"I assure you, he no longer uses that term," said Munson.

"He hopes we'll achieve a peaceable solution," Gilbert added.

"You saw the lawmen across the river," said John. "Did they look like they desire a peaceable solution, Mr. Gilbert?"

"We saw them," said Gilbert. "But keep in mind that my office gives me the power to order the sheriff to stand aside, to call this off. A snap of my fingers and this entire affair would end on the spot."

"And then what?" asked John. "They lock me up and my wife struggles to keep the farm from going broke?"

"Oh my, no," said Munson. "Mr. Dietz, I have the Governor's pledge that you will be safely transported to the courthouse where all charges against you but one will be dropped."

"But one?"

"You must answer to the wounding of Bert Horel last month."

"My husband only shot in self-defense," said Hattie.

"Oh, I believe you, Mrs. Dietz," said Gilbert, "And I will personally serve as your husband's defense attorney."

John raised an eyebrow. "You? The Attorney General of Wisconsin? You would defend me? Go up against District Attorney Davis?"

"Yes."

"But you, sir, are a prosecutor, are you not?"

"Under normal conditions, yes. But as Oliver said, Governor Davidson wants this over and done with. So, yes, I will defend you in court. And I know the ropes, Mr. Dietz, the tricks of the trade, if you will. I will get you the most lenient sentence possible, probably probation, if even that. It's more likely that I can't have the case against you dropped completely."

"This is a rare opportunity," said Munson, sipping his lemonade.

"All other charges will be dropped?"

"A snap of my fingers, Mr. Dietz," said Gilbert.

"You have our solemn promise," added Munson, his eyes fixed on the antlers again. "My word, that *is* a nice rack!"

"Well?" said Gilbert. "What say you, Mr. Dietz? Do we have a bargain? Do I win the honor of defending the hero of Cameron Dam in court?"

John sat quietly, considering the Attorney General's offer.

"Mr. Dietz?" Gilbert repeated.

"Oh, I think ... not."

"What? But, why?"

"Your offer sounds good, gentlemen," John began. "But ... perhaps too good."

"Sir?"

"Mr. Gilbert, you know as well as I do that Governor Davidson, like all politicians, depends upon a bevy of industrial tycoons to get him elected. And to keep that plush office of his, he needs to do favors for his rich friends from time to time."

"But, Mr. Dietz …"

"And you both know Frederick Weyerhaeuser is by far the wealthiest man in the Upper Midwest. And money, gentlemen, translates into influence. Therefore, although your offer might be made in total sincerity on your part, your boss and the county officials and those lawmen across the river might not be operating by the same rules as you."

"But, sir …"

"Now, suppose I surrendered myself to you. What would you do if a dozen men with guns then accosted you and abducted me from your custody? Why, look at you, armed only with gold-handled walking sticks."

"But, Mr. Dietz …" said Gilbert.

"Why, in *a snap of your fingers*, Mr. Gilbert, those men could have me hanging from some oak limb."

"Mr. Dietz …" said Munson.

"And should that happen, in *a snap of your fingers*, the governor would have the whole thing swept under the rug. Would he not?"

Neither Munson nor Gilbert answered.

"I thought so," said John. "Gentlemen, if you wish to succeed in your mission, then come back within one week's time with a statement signed by Governor Davidson agreeing to have all charges forever dropped. Not just for me, mind you, but for my entire family, including our poor daughter, Myra, who lies in a hospital bed, incapacitated yet under arrest, only because she happened to be the person shot down by the sheriff and his men."

"But, Mr. Dietz …"

"Look. I was offered ten thousand dollars and a farm somewhere in Manitoba by the lumber syndicate. I turned them down. Let William Irvine know I will accept twelve thousand dollars in greenbacks and bring me that statement from the governor and I'll surrender to you on the spot."

"We've no authority over the lumber company," said Gilbert. "You'll have to negotiate with them yourself."

"And I want a teacher sent here for my children."

Gilbert shook his head. "Please, Mr. Dietz. We came here to help, but you must be reasonable."

"You are passing up a rare opportunity," said Munson.

John stood. He stepped over to the fireplace and lifted the antlers that hung above the mantel, and turned around. "Mr. Munson," he said, "these are for you."

"What?"

"A farewell gift."

Munson and Gilbert returned to Winter in silence, dumbfounded by their offer being refused. Behind the seat lay a handsome rack of antlers, given by a skeptical man that many knew to be a hero, but his boss, the Governor of Wisconsin, had termed the Outlaw of Cameron Dam, again and again.

Attorney General Gilbert and Oliver Munson met with Sawyer County District Attorney J. C. Davis and Sheriff Mike Madden that afternoon. They sat facing each other in the lobby of the Hotel Winter. Deputy Thorbahn eavesdropped from the hotel bar.

"It's hopeless," said Munson. "Dietz is asking for more than we are authorized to offer."

"The problem, Mr. Davis," Gilbert added, "is that he can't trust you or your sheriff. Dietz pledged again that he would rather die fighting for his rights than subject himself to what he believes would be a predisposed, prejudiced court case."

"Sheriff, it's now up to you," said Davis. "You have forty men ready and waiting. Men who know how to handle a deer rifle."

"Hold on, now," said Munson. "The governor doesn't want this to escalate. We have to find a way to get Dietz to surrender."

Davis huffed. "I want action, not words."

"I'll attack tomorrow," said Madden. "We'll storm Thornapple Farm at dawn."

"No!" said Gilbert. "Someone's sure to die out there. We've been on the farm. That log cabin of theirs is banked with soil. The land around it had been cleared. No deputy could approach within two-hundred yards without being exposed.

"I agree," added Munson. "From what we've learned, John Dietz is a crack shot. It would be a blood bath."

"Sheriff, do your duty," ordered Davis. "Bring in Dietz one way or another."

"I say no!" countered Gilbert. "This is not a war. I'll not let you send a band of bloodthirsty thugs across that field like they're charging up San Juan Hill."

"Are you siding with Dietz?" asked Davis. "A menace to society? A desperado?"

"He's a back country farmer who's been denied his rights," Gilbert replied. "*Cheated* by the lumber trust."

"Yet, a wanted man," said Davis. "For six years he has evaded arrest on warrants ranging from assault to attempted murder. Even the Governor calls him an outlaw."

Gilbert slammed his fist on the arm of the chair. "That, sir, is because Davidson trusted the reports *you* sent to him about this disgraceful … charade … this mockery. This *abuse* of your office!"

Munson stopped Gilbert from saying more. "Look, gentlemen, the governor does not want a gunfight at Thornapple Farm. We came here seeking a peaceful solution. Sheriff, my suggestion is that you dismiss your army of deputies and let *us* resolve this matter. I am certain that Mr. Gilbert and I can convince Dietz to surrender to us. All we need is time."

"There *is* no time," said Madden. "Every day we wait is another day for word to spread that John Dietz is some kind of hero. Have you not seen all the newspapermen here? Have you not read their articles? Why, they compare him to Nathan Hale, to John Brown, even to Robin Hood! No, Mr. Munson. We can't afford to wait for Dietz to become a hero in the eyes of the entire nation. We attack tomorrow."

"I'll not allow it," said Gilbert. "There will be *no* such attack."

Davis laughed. "You're not in Madison now. I make the decisions, here."

"Listen, Davis," snapped Gilbert. He pointed a finger at Madden. "If your sheriff orders one man to fire one shot at Thornapple Farm without provocation, I'll have you both thrown into prison for attempted murder. Do you hear me?"

A young boy entered the lobby. "Telegram for Mister Oliver Munson."

Munson waved and fished a nickel from his pocket. "Here, boy," he said, giving him the tip. Munson read the telegram, then handed it to Gilbert, saying, "I have the solution. Earlier, I sent word of our dilemma to the governor. He contacted William Irvine of the Chippewa Lumber and Boom Company. Irvine has agreed to offer twelve thousand for the right to rebuild the Cameron Dam and resolve Dietz's claims for good. And he agrees to let the family stay on the farm."

"And the warrants?" asked Madden. "I got a fistful of them, each waiting to be served on that outlaw."

"Gentlemen," said Gilbert, "We are peacekeepers, all four of us. And that is precisely what we are going to do—keep the peace. If John Dietz accepts this offer, I will drop every charge against him."

Davis read the telegram. "Except the attempted murder of Burt Horel," he said. "Dietz *will* stand trial for that crime."

"No, Mister Davis, he won't," replied Gilbert. "You stood to lose that case anyway. It's clear that Dietz shot in self-defense."

"But …"

"That does it for now," said Gilbert. "First thing tomorrow, Mr. Munson and I will return to the farm and share the good news with the family. They'll be thrilled to learn their troubles with the Chippewa Lumber and Boom Company and Sawyer County are over and done."

"Mark my words," said Madden, "this fight will *never* be done, not until that outlaw is either in prison or a grave. And that goes for his two sons, his daughter, and his wife, as well. And maybe William Dietz, too."

"Madden," snapped Gilbert, "one more statement like that and I'll see to it you're removed from office and never serve again. Never!"

Satisfied they'd found a peaceful solution, Munson and Gilbert left.

Madden motioned to Thorbahn, in the bar. "You get all that, Fred?"

Thorbahn joined them. "Every word."

Madden leaned closer to the district attorney. "If those city slickers think this is over, they've got another think coming. They're going out to parlay with Dietz in the morning." He turned to Thorbahn. "Fred, you and I are going out there, too. And while they're inside keeping Dietz busy, our men will slip across the river and set up for an attack."

"What if Dietz accepts their offer?" asked Davis.

"It'll be too late. As soon as those two politicians step out onto the front porch with Dietz, I'll have him in handcuffs. Heck, I'll have the whole family in cuffs. Dietz won't know what hit him. He's sure to blame Munson and Gilbert for hoodwinking him, plotting against him, see? Those newspapermen will have a field day blaming the governor and his two highbrow henchmen. It's perfect!"

"And we'll be seen as merely doing our jobs," said Davis with a grin. "All right, Sheriff. Do your duty."

Madden and Thorbahn left by the back door. In the alley, Thorbahn quietly asked, "Mike, about that thousand-dollar reward …"

"Fred, not only is there a thousand-dollar prize for nabbing Dietz, but only a handful of people know about it. Help me get that SOB and I'll see to it you get the reward … although it would be considerate of you to … show your *appreciation*, if you get my drift."

"You can count on me, Mike."

"Oh, I am, Fred. I am."

Ladysmith News-Budget

The sketch shows how the deputies surrounded and drew in upon the home of the Wisconsin outlaw. The home is marked by a cross, while the arrow at the right indicates the Cameron Dam, the point in dispute.

40

The Siege of Thornapple Farm

An eerie fog hugged the river bottom as the first glow of morning light awakened Thornapple Farm on October 8, 1910.

While Hattie sliced a slab of bacon for breakfast, Helen hoisted the Stars and Stripes on the flagpole that towered over the schoolroom. Brought by Mr. Gates four years earlier, the flag hung limp in the damp, morning air. Helen walked to the privy and then the henhouse where she collected an apronful of eggs before returning to the cabin.

Across the river, Deputy Fred Thorbahn divided his men into teams. He told some to take positions in the woods across the river west of the farm. Others, he said, would cross the Thornapple River and secure themselves by the huge pine stumps lumberjacks had left years earlier. A third flank would cover the Dietz buildings from the south. All were told to be in position by 8 o'clock sharp, but not to fire unless fired upon or until hearing orders from him or Madden.

Father James Pilon, the only priest in the region, waited in the marshals' camp along with Doctors Burns and Grafton. They prayed their services wouldn't be needed. With them, a horde of newspapermen and several spectators looked forward to witnessing newsworthy action. They waited, listening to the crowing of the rooster perched atop the Thornapple Farm henhouse.

As his men left to take up their posts, Thorbahn tramped through the woods to the Camp Four mess hall where Red Mulligan and his group of volunteers from the Chippewa Lumber and Boom Company waited.

"All right," Mulligan shouted over the racket of twenty-nine men at breakfast. "The time has come for you men to do your part. Over on the sidetrack, you will find your rifles waiting on a flatcar. Each man is to take two boxes of bullets. That's forty rounds apiece."

"Sheriff Madden put me in charge," said Thorbahn. "You men will hike south along the river, then cross at the shallows. From there, you will go north and take up positions among the stumps to the east of the farm. No man here is to fire even one shot until you hear a volley of gunfire from my deputies stationed west of the river. Is that understood?"

"But Fred," came a shout from the back, "doesn't that mean we will be firing toward your men? And them toward us?"

"You'll be a good quarter mile from the house and barn," Thorbahn replied. "So will my other deputies. I shouldn't think you need worry about any crossfire as much as you should John Dietz getting you in his sights. He's a crack shot and so are his wife and children. I figure he will hole up in his cabin. It's made up from stout logs. And they've banked three feet of dirt all around it, so it's like Fort Sumter."

"If it's like a fort, why don't you use a field cannon?"

"The governor won't allow it. That's politics for you. Instead, train your rifles on the cabin. If you can get a bullet through a window or through the chinking between two logs, you might put a quick end to it."

"I don't know about this, Fred," said another man. "It sounds a whole lot more dangerous than what Mulligan told us last week. And what if I shot one of the children? What then?"

"Look, Elmer," said Mulligan, "there's a job to be done—an outlaw to be taken down. You will be one of seventy-three men who've been deputized to do the job. The company is counting on you. The Governor is counting on you. And, by God, the county is paying you ten dollars for your help. Last week each one of you pledged to join us. If, since then, any man here has turned yellow, say so now by raising your hand." Thirty men looked around the room in silence.

"All right," said Thorbahn. "Your rifles are waiting on the flatcar."

Hidden by the mist and carrying a milk pail, Leslie crossed the yard to the barn at half-past-seven. A short time later he returned with enough warm milk for breakfast.

Madden checked his pocket watch. He turned to Thorbahn. "It's seven-thirty. Are your men in position?"

"Most are," Thorbahn replied. "The rest will be soon. This fog might be a problem. If we can't see Dietz when he surrenders to those two government men, this could get complicated."

"Let's hope it lifts in time," said Madden. "If not, we might be in for a long day. All right. You better take your post, Fred."

"Where will you be, Sheriff?"

"I'll coordinate things from here."

"Here? In the camp?"

"I'll keep the reporters at bay. I don't want them getting too close."

"You're scared," said Thorbahn. "You think Dietz might get you in his sights. Admit it."

"Look. These days it makes no sense for a general to lead the attack. Besides, it's no concern of yours. I'll be here, that's all." Madden looked at his watch again. "Get to your post, Fred. It's going on eight o'clock. Gilbert and Munson are due anytime now."

As Thorbahn walked off, a faint melody drifted across the river. He turned around. "Listen," he said. "It sounds like ..."

"Yes," Madden replied. "I heard it yesterday, too. Father Pilon tells me that every morning the Dietz family worships and sings hymns as Hattie plays their organ. It seems strange."

"Strange, Sheriff?" Thorbahn asked, checking his rifle.

"Strange that it has all come to this. Over seventy lawmen, armed to the teeth, prepared to take the lives of folks who worship the same God."

Thorbahn spit. "Not all of us," he said, plugging cartridges into his rifle. He stepped back into the fog. "God or no God, I'll get Dietz."

The music drifting from the cabin filled the fog-veiled valley. John's deep voice and Hattie's soprano carried far. Tears came to the eyes of men who understood that they might soon send a bullet through the heart of one of their neighbors. Some removed their hats and bowed their heads. One deputy stood, unloaded his rifle, and left for home.

After breakfast, Leslie walked through the fog to tend to his milking chores, unaware of the horde of armed men now surrounding Thornapple Farm. Quincy, their water spaniel, followed close behind.

"Hello!" came a faint call, stopping Leslie on the path. "Mr. Dietz?"

Staying low, Leslie moved toward the river. He saw movement near the footbridge. He drew closer. There, Oliver Munson waved a white handkerchief. Beside him stood Wisconsin Attorney General Gilbert.

"May we come across?" shouted Munson.

Leslie hesitated, then motioned, signaling them to approach.

Inside, Hattie poured coffee. "I'd thought we'd seen the last of you fellows," she said.

"Oh no, Mrs. Dietz," said Munson. "Governor Davidson is not one to simply give up."

John laughed. "Mother," he said, "they say the difference between politicians and wood ticks is that the politicians hang on longer."

"Fine woodland humor, Mr. Dietz," said Munson with an awkward smile. "But I assure you, we don't bite."

Helen brought two more plates.

"On the contrary," said Gilbert. "Mr. Munson here has good news for you."

Munson sipped his coffee. "Good news indeed. I telegraphed Governor Davidson. He, in turn, pulled some strings down in Madison."

"Pulled some strings?"

"Mr. Dietz, the governor got you the whole shebang, lock, stock, and barrel, signed, sealed, and delivered."

"Come again?"

Gilbert leaned forward. "Mr. Dietz, *all* charges are now dropped, including the case involving Bert Horel."

"I wasn't concerned about that," said John.

"Oh, but there's more," said Munson. "The governor contacted William Irvine. He now agrees to pay you twelve thousand dollars to settle all disputes. Furthermore, you can stay here on Thornapple Farm in peace, no more threats, no more worries for you or your family."

"My stars!" said Hattie from the kitchen. She handed the spatula to Helen and joined her husband.

Munson handed John a paper. "I have it in writing."

John read the single-page offer.

"Well, Mr. Dietz?" said Munson.

"I'm not sure."

Hattie gasped. "John! This is our chance to return to a normal life! You must agree!"

"Mr. Dietz," said Gilbert, "your followers, coast-to-coast, will celebrate your victory over the lumber syndicate. Don't you see? This is the brass ring! You, John F. Dietz, have prevailed! You won!"

"Won?" said John. "Perhaps. But what might be lost?"

Hattie lowered her head into cupped hands. "Oh, John, no," she muttered.

"My supporters won't understand," John began. "They'll think my only goal all along was to profit from this—to make money. No different from the greed that drives the lumber trust."

"But Mr. Dietz," said Munson.

"John, please," begged Hattie.

"Mother, I can't accept this."

Gilbert shook his head. "Jesus, Oliver. What else can we do? Must we guarantee this man passage through the Gates of Heaven?"

"What about Myra?" asked Hattie. "What about the other children? Their lives? Their futures?"

"Gentlemen," said John, "You've made your offer. I appreciate your effort. However, my decision is to wait this out. I now know what the governor is willing to do. I only need to hear that Frederick Weyerhaeuser will offer better working conditions and more pay to the men in the woods, on the rivers, and in the sawmills. Should he choose to continue to thumb his nose at the common man, then on behalf of all working stiffs, I shall thumb mine at him."

"Oh, John," said Hattie. "Please?"

"Mother, that's enough. My mind's made up."

"Mr. Dietz, please be reasonable," Munson pleaded. "Sheriff Madden desires nothing more than to attack your home full-force."

"The government can only kill me once, Mr. Munson. And I don't know of any nobler way of losing my life than in defense of my home and family. Should I become known as the John Brown of the north woods, then so be it."

"Think of your children. Don't put them in harm's way."

"Gentlemen," said John, "I will not succumb! I've said it before and the sheriff knows it well. I have a right to protect my home and family. Tell Sheriff Madden, tell them *all*, that any man who sets foot on my land is taking his life into his own hands."

"We won't be able to stop them," said Gilbert.

"Let them come. Tell Madden that if I leave Thornapple Farm, it will be feet first, but I won't be alone."

"All right," said Munson. "Have it your way. We've tried our utmost."

"Mr. Dietz," said Gilbert, "for safety's sake, let us take your wife and children with us."

"I'll not hear of it," he replied. "The children stay. You'll not force any of us off our property."

Helen served the bacon and eggs.

"Enjoy your breakfast, gentlemen," John said.

Hearing sudden thumping of boots on the porch, they all turned. Leslie rushed inside.

"Pa!" he said. "Somebody's out there."

John rushed to the window.

Leslie pointed across the field through the slowly lifting fog. "I'm sure I saw men near the lumber stacks," he said. "And I heard voices down by the river."

John turned to Munson and Gilbert. "Turncoats!" He rushed to the mantel and pulled his pistol from its holster. "You planned this!"

"What? No! We ..."

John raised his Luger. "You came under a white flag to keep me busy while your men moved in for attack!"

"No, Mr. Dietz," said Munson. "I can assure you that ..."

"Liars! Oh, but your ploy failed. Go! Get out of here. Gather up your cowardly accomplices and be gone! And you tell them all either stay off my land or expect to be shot."

"But Mr. Dietz ..."

"Get out! Get out before I fill you both full of lead!"

Gilbert and Munson grabbed their hats and rushed to the door. "We came in good faith," said Munson. "We had no idea ..."

"Go!" bellowed John. "Before I shoot!"

The family watched the two government men vanish into the fog.

"What now, Pa?" asked Leslie.

"Same as usual," he replied. "As soon as those lawmen know we're onto them, they'll all turn tail and run. Meanwhile, let's have our eggs before they get cold."

Disappointment showed in Hattie's eyes. "I thought it was over," she muttered.

"Be patient, Mother," he replied. "Perseverance always wins out."

Pushing her chair back, she left for the bedroom, trying to hide her tears.

Helen cleared the table and poured her father a second cup of coffee.

"I better stay here with Mother awhile, Princess," he said. "Can you help your brother with the milking?"

"Yes, Papa," she replied, pulling on her coat. Seconds later, she and Leslie sprinted to the barn with Abe, their shepherd, leading the way.

In the marshal's camp on the far side of the river, the two government officials conferred with the Sheriff.

"No, Mr. Munson!" shouted Madden. "I will *not* call it off! It's now or never!"

"Sheriff," said Gilbert, "this is madness. To move in on him now will only bring bloodshed."

"What will be will be. No more waiting. We take him today while we have the men. Tomorrow might be too late."

"The governor will be disappointed, Sheriff."

"Look, Munson. My job is to enforce. Yours is to shine the governor's boots. I'll do my job. You do yours. If the governor had any real interest, he'd be here. Now if either of you possess a lick of good sense, you'll strike out for the railroad grade and flag down the next southbound."

Two-hundred yards away, Fred Thorbahn stared into the fog with his binoculars. "Look!" he said to another deputy. He pointed toward figures running across the barnyard. "That's him! That's Dietz! Shoot!"

The deputy raised his rifle. "I … I can't tell."

"Well, who else could it be?"

"Maybe the wife, Fred. Or the little girl."

"Open fire! That's an order!"

"I'm not shooting at no youngster, Thorbahn."

Another veil of fog masked the yard. "Dang it! You had him in your sights."

"You could have taken the shot, Thorbahn. Why didn't you?"

Thorbahn didn't reply.

"You won't fire on the Dietz familiy, but you expect the rest of us to? Is that it? Well, no sir. That's not for me. I'm done with this. *Done!*" He walked off, leaving Thorbahn alone.

As the sun rose over the trees to the east of the farm, the fog slowly lifted. Leslie, done with his morning chores, left Helen in the barn to tend to the horses. Two deputies, hiding near the riverbank, watched him walk toward the cabin, Quincy, their spaniel, trotting by his side.

"Stop or I'll shoot!" screamed one of the deputies. "You're under arrest!"

Surprised, Leslie stopped and turned toward the river.

"Hands up, boy," bellowed the deputy, some fifty yards away. "You're under arrest."

Leslie bolted toward the cabin, running at his fastest with Quincy alongside.

The deputy fired, his bullet striking the ground behind the boy. Another deputy, hearing the shot and seeing Leslie on the run, fired a second, stray bullet.

Leslie bounded across the yard as more men opened fire. A dozen bullets struck the ground before and behind him, sending tufts of sod into the air.

"I ain't never seen *nobody* run like that," said a man levering another round into his rifle. "Look at him. He's faster than nobody's business."

Hearing gunfire, John looked out the window to see his son and Quincy coming on the run. Leslie bounded up onto the porch as his father opened the door. Leslie dove through just before the door slammed shut. Quincy, outside, sat looking up at the door.

"I'll show them," said the deputy, bearing down on his rifle sights.

Quincy yelped as the .30-30 round smashed through his gut. He jumped from the porch and took four bounds before collapsing. Three gasps later, the water spaniel lay dead in the yard within sight of a dozen deputies and the family.

"Are you hit, son?" asked John.

"No," Leslie gasped.

"Mama!" screamed Johnny. "Why'd they have to go and shoot Quincy?"

Leslie pointed toward the barn. "Helen's out there! She must be scared out of her wits. What'll we do?"

Hattie opened the door. "Helen!" she screamed. "Are you all right?"

A bullet hit the door frame, throwing splinters into the room. Startled, Hattie stepped back, tripped, and fell onto the porch.

"Mother!" shouted Leslie. He grabbed her ankle and yanked her across the threshold into the cabin.

John slammed the door shut. He looked out the window. "My God!" he shouted. "It's Helen. She's coming on the run! Open the door! Quick! Quick!"

Thirteen-year-old Helen raced across the yard with Abe. No lawman fired. She flew past Quincy and jumped onto the porch. Abe followed her into the cabin. Leslie slammed the door again. Two more shots echoed down the river bottom.

John hugged his daughter, tears streaming down his face. "Thank God you're all right, Princess," he sobbed. "Oh, thank God."

Hattie stood. She wrapped her arms around them, hugging both. "Oh, John, what have you done?"

Leslie looked out the window. "There must be a dozen of them this time, Pa. What are we going to do?"

A bullet shattered the window glass.

"Get away from there," he ordered. He grabbed two rifles. Handing one to his son, he said, "Leslie, it's up to you to guard your ma and the little ones." He turned to Hattie, "Mother, I can't have them shooting at you and the children. I'm heading for the barn to draw their fire. They won't shoot at you if they know I'm in the barn."

"John, no!" Hattie screamed. "You'll be shot!"

"Don't argue with me, Mother," he shouted. "This has to be." He turned to Leslie. "The second I go out that door, I want you to open fire on them. Shoot all nine rounds as fast as you can. That'll keep their heads down until I reach the barn. Then you shut and bar this door and don't open it for anyone but me." He turned to his wife again. "Mother, you and the children hide behind the cook stove. If you stay low, no bullet will find you."

"John, don't leave us."

"It's the only way," he replied. "We've been through this before. That small handful of deputies will scatter as soon as I send a few bullets their way. This will all be over in a few minutes. Just like when Clarence got shot four years back."

"Oh, I hope you're right, John," Hattie cried. "Please, *please* come back safe."

"Safe?" said John. "It's the fools out there who need to worry about safety. God is on our side, Mother. Always has been. Always will be."

John dashed down the path to the barn. Leslie followed orders, firing round after round into the fog-shrouded thornapple trees lining the river. No one returned fire, giving his father clear passage to the barn where he'd earlier secured two more rifles, a double-barrel shotgun, and a dozen boxes of ammunition. John pitched his Winchester and three boxes of shells up into the hayloft and climbed the steps.

A bullet tore through a cedar shake twenty feet from him. Another hit closer, but not near enough to concern him. Using his gun barrel, John loosened a shingle and peeked beyond the barnyard at the river below. The rising sun had burned off most of the fog that cloaked the farm only minutes ago. Now, against a hazy blue sky, bright, blood-red thornapple berries painted the bushes all down the valley. But the serene beauty of the landscape soon turned ugly as John made out figures concealed on the far side of the river. He forced the shingle aside and raised his field glasses, counting more and more riflemen, dozens of them, all out of range. He realized then, they were waiting for the order to attack. He thought of his family, frightened beyond words, hiding behind the thick walls of their home. And of his oldest son, wounded in the arm, sitting in the county jail. And of his daughter, suffering in a far-away hospital after being shot by Fred Thorbahn a week before.

Meanwhile, sixty miles north in an Ashland hospital bed, Myra slumbered. Against the wishes of the hospital staff, a deputy from Sawyer County earned his four-dollar-a-day wage by standing guard to prevent the severely wounded young woman from escaping. Myra rested, her mind numb from heroine, unaware that the siege of Thornapple Farm, a battle her father felt sure would never take place, had begun.

41

The John Brown of the North Woods

Shortly after nine o'clock, Sheriff Madden got word of the botched attempt to arrest Leslie Dietz.

"What?" he shouted at the messenger. "You mean to say they shot at the boy?"

"I think Thorbahn shot first, Sheriff. Fog was thick. He missed by a mile."

"That fool!" Madden slammed his fist onto the table. "I told him ..."

"Then some other fellas took some potshots. Killed one of the family's dogs. The rest of us figured that was our signal so we opened fire. I don't think it did much good."

"My orders were to not shoot unless Dietz fired first!"

"Well, Sheriff, that's between you and Fred Thorbahn."

"That buffoon!" Madden shouted toward the ceiling. He turned to the messenger. "What's going on now? I hear a lot of shooting. Is Dietz returning fire? Is *anyone* shooting back?"

"I think somebody in the cabin fired out the front door. We couldn't tell for sure due to all the fog."

"Front door? Good. That gives me full authority to defend my men by returning fire."

"Won't do much good."

"What?"

"Seems a waste of bullets shooting into those logs, Sheriff. And all that dirt piled around the cabin? Why, it protects anybody inside smart enough to stay low to the floor."

"What a gol-dang muddled up mess!" griped Madden. "Look. You go tell Thorbahn that my orders are to move in. Rush the place. Put an end to this ... this ..."

"Mistake, Sheriff?"

"Get back to your post! And tell Thorbahn my orders are to attack. At once!"

"Yes, sir. I'll let him know."

In the barn, John pried up several more shingles. Through his binoculars he spotted four deputies near the river, approaching on hands and knees. He slid the barrel of his rifle through the opening, took careful aim, and squeezed the trigger.

The first bullet fired from the barn that morning sent a message. He watched as all four men jumped to their feet and fled back to the safety of the riverbank.

Suddenly, a dozen or more bullets crashed through the barn roof, zipping past John. He dove across the loft and ran to the other end of the barn as more bullets snapped through the shingles near his former position. Prying another aside, he looked south toward the dam to see a man lying on the ground with a rifle pointed his way. John aimed two feet in front of him. His bullet struck the ground, blasting dirt into the man's face. John laughed as the man scrambled away on his belly until out of sight.

"Fools," he said. "You won't get me. I'll drive you off one by one."

In the cabin, Hattie and the children huddled in the corner behind the cast iron cook stove. They listened to bullets striking their home, each solid thud followed by a distant rifle report. "Stay low, children," she said in a calming tone. "Your father will send these bullies on their way soon. You'll see. They'll all be gone. Papa will be back and we'll all sit down for our midday dinner like nothing ever happened."

"What about Quincy?" Johnny asked. "He can't be with us like nothing ever happened. He's dead."

"Quincy isn't dead, Johnny," said Helen. "Remember what Myra said? Quincy is over on the other side of the rainbow, running and playing and having fun with all his animal friends." Tears streamed down Helen's cheeks. "Quincy is with Meggie and Blackie and the other sheep."

"And Stanley?" asked Johnny.

"Yes," said Helen. "Stanley's there with them too, singing songs and happy as can be."

A bullet crashed through a window, sending shards of shattered glass onto the children and their mother. Helen screamed. Hattie held her tight.

"Mama," sobbed Johnny, "I don't want to go to the other side of the rainbow."

"We're not going anywhere, Johnny. Not for a long, long time."

Fred Thorbahn and three others crawled on their bellies from the river toward the lumber piles on the west edge of the farm. The stacked boards, drying in the October sunshine, provided good cover. It seemed to be the only part of the battleground that John could not reach with a bullet. Sporadic rifle fire could be heard from the men to the west along the river and southeast in the woods. Nearing their new position, the four deputies spread out among the tall stacks of pine lumber.

Thorbahn stayed tight to the ground. Knowing Dietz was out of earshot, he peered through his field glasses and shouted orders to his men. "Bill!"

"Yeah?"

"Sneak forward a ways. Up that knoll. Try to get a bead on the front door."

"Right," came Bill's muffled reply.

"Otto!"

"What?"

"You move around to the side of that lumber pile. See if you can get a clear shot into the cabin through the north window."

"Right, boss," came a reply.

The fourth lawman, Norman Thayer, lying prone next to Thorbahn, wondered out loud. "He might not be in the cabin, Fred."

"What?" said Thorbahn. "What do you mean?"

"Bob Dunster and Ernie Wiley thought someone shot from the barn loft. Tom Ackley said so, too."

"I was told he was in the cabin." Thorbahn replied. "That's our target, Norman. The cabin."

A half-dozen bullets slammed into the pine above Thorbahn, followed by rifle reports southeast of the cabin.

"Dammit!" yelled Thorbahn. "Those shots are coming from our own men!"

Another bullet struck closer.

"Move back!" shouted Thorbahn. "Move back!"

Four more shots tore up the ground in front of Bill Bonk. He jumped to his feet and ran for the riverbank screaming "Holy Mary Mother of God! Don't shoot. Don't shoot!" He dove into the thornapple trees, his hat, coat, and skin torn by the sharp thorns. A dozen shots followed, the bullets ricocheting off branches above.

"What the hell are you doing?" screamed Thorbahn across the pasture. "He's one of us! Hold your fire!"

Another volley of shots rattled down the river valley, fired by the deputized lumberjacks to the west.

"They can't hear you, Fred," said Norman. "We better pull back."

"Madden's orders are to advance."

"Madden can go to blazes. He's too yellow to be at the front. And I'm not about to die over this. You can stay if you want, Fred. I'm taking cover beyond the riverbank."

Thorbahn watched Thayer crawl off. He turned to his right. "Otto?" he shouted.

"Yeah, Fred?"

"Can you get a bullet through the window from there?"

"I think so."

"Go ahead. Send a few rounds inside. I'll cover the door in case somebody comes out." Another bullet struck the pine above Thorbahn. "Cripes sake!" he muttered, "What kind of a fix did I get myself into?" He listened as Otto Tainter fired three times. Suddenly a volley of shots came from the lumberjacks across the pasture. Bullets snapped into the boards above, sending pine splinters flying. "Otto?" shouted Thorbahn. "You all right?" Otto didn't answer. "Otto!" he screamed. "Otto!"

"I'm back here," Otto replied from behind.

Thorbahn looked back. Otto was crawling toward the river. "Dang it! Get back here. That's an order."

"What?" Otto replied. "Can't hear a word you're saying. See you around, Fred."

From his hayloft vantage point, John could scan all directions through spyholes he'd made by moving shingles aside. Looking southeast, he saw the lumberjacks hiding behind stumps, darting up, firing a shot at the cabin, and dropping down to safety again.

To the south, he watched as a handful of men peeked from behind the remains of Cameron Dam, not firing.

To the west along the river, men occasionally moved from one position to the next. Now and then one would pop up over the riverbank, fire a shot at the cabin, some three-hundred yards away and vanish behind the bank again.

Trading the Winchester for his double-barrel twelve-gauge shotgun, John took aim at the lumberjacks, knowing the birdshot in the shells would do no harm, other than send a message that he could pick them off at any time with his deer rifle. He slid the barrel out through the shingles, aimed high, drew back both hammers, and pulled both triggers. The recoil from both barrels firing simultaneously set him back into the haystack. A thousand tiny lead pellets clattered into the leaves surrounding the deputized woodsmen.

John came to his feet. He looked through his binoculars and laughed as dozens of men retreated into the woods far beyond range of their rifles. "Fools!" he said. Ejecting two spent shells, he crossed to the west side of the loft. After plugging two more shotgun shells into their chambers, he fired more birdshot, this time at the men hiding along the river.

Bullets pinged and popped through the barn roof. John dropped the shotgun and ran to the other end of the loft. Grabbing his deer rifle, he slid the barrel out a knothole, looking for a target. There, beyond the river, nearly five-hundred yards off, he saw a man sitting on a stump, watching from his safe vantage point. Knowing there was no breeze to affect his shot, John considered the distance, raised his rifle's rear tang sight, adjusted it for five-hundred yards, aimed, and squeezed the trigger.

Bill Bonk jumped when the .30-30 bullet smacked into the stump next to him, five feet away. He ran through the thornapples, again screaming, "Holy Mary Mother of God!"

Grinning, John changed positions. His binoculars scanned the lumber piles to the north. There, almost

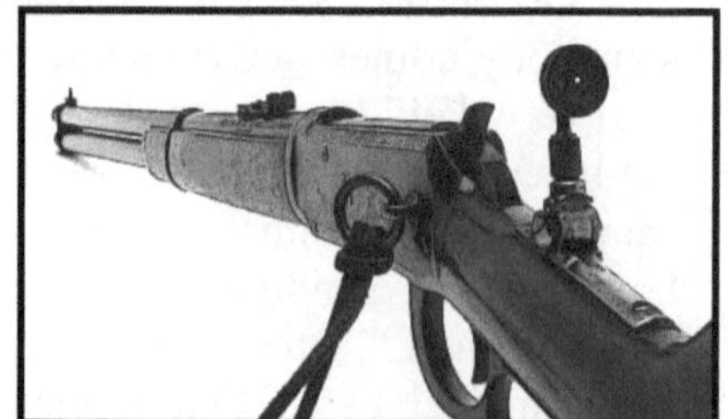

hidden from view, lay a lone lawman lying tight to the ground, field glasses hiding his face. John locked his gaze on this man, waiting for him to lower his binoculars.

As John watched, another bullet snapped through the barn wall and out the other side of the roof. "There'll be some repairs that need tending once this is over with," he supposed out loud. He watched as the man near the lumber piles lowered his binoculars. "Fred Thorbahn!" he said. "You miserable pole cat! You shot my daughter! You shot my son! You tried your best to bushwhack me! By God, now it's *my* turn."

John lowered his field glasses and raised his Winchester. He slid the barrel through the opening and aligned the rear and front sight—seven inches above Thorbahn's head. Seven inches. Enough to allow for the drop of the 150-grain, .30-30 bullet as it spanned the two-hundred yard distance between his rifle and his target. At 2,300 feet per second, the bullet would be there in an instant. Thorbahn would die before he heard the crack of the rifle. There was no wind to drift the bullet left or right. No trees or brush in the way. Nothing stopping him now. John pulled the hammer back. The sunlight lit his target perfectly. And then, in a momentary lull between gunfire from other lawmen, John felt his index finger on the trigger. He inhaled deeply, exhaled half the breath, focused a final time, and … paused.

Tears came to his eyes. Staring across his sights at the man who'd tried to ambush him, to kill him, who'd nearly killed his daughter, John did not have the heart to pull the trigger. He lowered the hammer and pulled in his rifle just as another bullet snapped through the barn roof above him.

"Dammit!" he shouted to no one there. He slid the barrel back out, aimed, and fired, striking a board a foot away from Thorbahn.

Thorbahn scrambled from his vantage point to the lumber pile on his left. Then, hoping to get a clear shot at the living room window of the Dietz cabin, he moved again. Another bullet, from another direction, snapped into the lumber pile above. Thorbahn crawled back behind the stacks. When he knew he was out of sight of the farm, he scrambled to his feet and ran for the safety of the riverbank.

Within minutes, Mike Madden knew of the failure. Within minutes, another order came from the sheriff for a full-on, frontal attack. Within minutes, a dozen more deputies quit the siege on Thornapple Farm. They left on foot, no pay in their pocket, but alive to tell their tales.

His field glasses up, John watched as men left. "It's about time," he said. "Now, if I can spot more of you fools, I'll send you your walking papers, too." He scanned the riverbank once more and the woods to the southeast. He focused again on the lumber piles. Suddenly, a bullet cracked through the wall behind, burying deep into a beam overhead.

John moved to the east wall and scanned the woods beyond to see a rifleman lying prone under an oak. Focusing his binoculars, he noticed a dead limb fifteen feet above. A squeeze of the Winchester's trigger brought the branch down onto the man, who jumped up and ran back into the woods. Behind him, three more lumberjacks followed. "That's right, boys. Run for it!" John said. "Take to the woods with the rest of the lumber company cowards. The sooner you all leave, the sooner we can get back to our chores."

By noon, almost a quarter of the sheriff's men had deserted. But Madden's siege of Thornapple Farm wasn't over. Though nearly twenty deputies had abandoned their posts, over fifty remained, hidden behind trees, shielded from view by the riverbank, or secreted behind the rolling knolls of the pasture.

Concealed by pine stumps in the pasture, two deputies conversed.

"Flannigan," whispered one.

"What?"

"See that flagpole next to the cabin?"

"What about it?"

"Two bits says I can take down that flag before you can."

"You're on, Jake."

Flannigan, lying out of sight of the barn, set his sights on the top of the flagpole. The crack of his rifle split the air and echoed down the river valley, but his aim was off.

Jake Walters took his turn. He fired and missed.

Flannigan bungled his second shot.

Walters did too.

Flannigan and Walters each shot three more rounds. Finally one of Flannigan's bullets clipped the rope holding the flag atop the pole.

By now, everyone within view of the farm wondered what these two deputies were shooting at. Then, when the flag fluttered to the ground, a cheer went up. Flannigan cheered because he'd won the two-bit bet. The others cheered, thinking the falling flag signaled the surrender of the Dietz family. Within seconds, all rifles lowered and the serenity of a sunny October day returned to the Thornapple River valley. Deputies, north, south, east, and west, stood and stretched, relieved that the battle had ended.

"Stay down!" shouted Thorbahn. "Take cover and remain at your posts! Pass the word."

"Get down," screamed a deputy to the west. "And stay put!"

"Get down," echoed someone near the dam.

Not knowing what had happened, no lawman fired. "Is it over, Boss?" yelled one of the lumberjacks.

"No," shouted Thorbahn. "Not until John Dietz is in handcuffs or dead. Stay at your dang post."

Inside the Dietz home, Hattie scooted across the kitchen floor. Bread from the breadbox, a jar of apple butter, and a pitcher of milk left from breakfast would satisfy her children's appetites for now. Staying low, she returned to the children, still hiding on the floor behind the cook stove.

"When is Papa coming back?" cried Johnny.

"Don't fret, precious," Hattie replied, holding him tight. "Your papa will be here anytime now."

"But what if he's on the other side of the rainbow already?"

Hattie tried to answer but no words came to her. She hugged Johnny tighter as another slug cracked through the chinking between logs.

Hattie, Leslie, Helen, and Johnny Dietz huddled closer together, wishing it would end.

The Detroit Times

ALL THAT NOW REMAINS OF CAMERON DAM, WHERE DEITZ DEFIED POSSES FOR SEVEN YEARS

All that remains of Cameron dam on Thornapple creek, object of the long war on Deitz, is shown in the upper picture, one-half utterly blown away by dynamite at night, the other now crumbling in the creek. Below is the lonely Deitz cabin, a log stronghold maintained against repeated attacks of scores of hired mercenaries and deputy sheriffs.

in the head and John Rogich, one of the deputies was shot through the neck, the hip and the ankle.

The first brush with the sharpshooting Deitzes gave the Milwaukee men all the fighting they wanted. They put Rogich on a crude litter and fled. An hour or two later, when they were in the heart of the deep woods between Cameron dam and Winter, one of the deputies, imagining that he heard someone pursuing, cried, "Look out! Deitz!" The bearers dropped the litter and scattered, beating it through the woods for dear life.

Two days later Rogich more dead than alive was found accidentally by timber cruisers. He finally recovered.

42

Hold Your Fire!

"John Dietz," shouted Thorbahn, hiding behind a rock pile in the pasture. Facing the barn, he shouted again. "John, you're surrounded. Give up now. Save your family. Save yourself."

John looked through a knothole in the wall, making out a half dozen men, some of them neighbors, secluded along the river. He knew more hid behind the huge pine stumps in the pasture and watched from the marsh near the dam. Others in the woods to the west waited for Thorbahn's signal to commence firing. John reloaded his rifles, wondering what might come next. Another call made him raise his field glasses.

"Deputy Thorbahn," shouted a tall, robed man standing on the footbridge.

John's binoculars focused on Father Pilon, the priest from Winter.

"Stay back, Father!" shouted Thorbahn. "Dietz says he'll shoot anybody entering his farm."

"Come now!" shouted the priest. "I know John far better than you. He is not a killer." Father Pilon started across the bridge. When halfway across, he yelled, "John, this has gone far enough."

John moved to the closed hayloft door. He lifted the bar and held it open a few inches. "It's up to the sheriff to call this madness off, not me," he shouted back.

"I can guarantee you and your family safe passage to the courthouse in Hayward where this can all be sorted out."

"Sorry, Father," John replied, opening the door an inch wider. "I can't go to Hayward. Cold weather's coming. Too many chores need tending. Tell Madden to pull out and leave us be."

"I have word from your daughter," shouted the priest, walking closer to the barn.

"From Myra? How is she?"

"The doctors say she is coming along well. I plan to visit her soon. Will you come with me?"

John opened the loft door another inch. "Oh, but that I could, Father," he replied. Then, as he held the door part way open with his left hand, a shot sounded from the pasture. The bullet struck the corner of the door and smashed through the frame, striking him in the hand. He reeled and fell onto the loft floor, blood rushing from the wound.

"Haymow door!" screamed Thorbahn. "Open fire! Shoot! Shoot!"

John rolled away from the loft door as a volley of bullets slammed into beams overhead. Keeping low, he crept to the other end of the loft, leaving a trail of blood. More slugs snapped through the walls from each side as John drew near the hayloft steps.

"Give up, Dietz," bellowed Thorbahn.

Bullets zipped and zinged through the loft. Despite the pain in his hand, he crawled down the top two steps. Then, dazed and light-headed, he slipped, falling onto his back. Staring up from the barn floor, he watched as more slugs sent splinters flying overhead. From outside, he heard more shouting.

"Aim for the haymow door," yelled Thorbahn. "Shoot! Shoot!"

Flat on his back, John pulled his handkerchief from his hip pocket and wrapped his wounded left hand. He rolled over, rose to his knees, and stood. Dizzy from the fall, he staggered to the barn door.

More shouts came from outside. "Haymow door," Thorbahn repeated. "Fire at the haymow door!"

John slowly opened the barn door wide enough to slip through. Realizing his opportunity, he looked left and right before staggering to the cabin. As he stumbled onto the porch, two bullets struck the wall ahead of him. He pounded on the door. "It's Pa! Open up!" he bellowed.

Inside, Helen cried, "Did you hear something?"

"Only gunfire," said Hattie.

Helen dashed across the floor and removed the bar from the door. A moment later, her father lay safe on the living room floor. Staying low, Hattie placed a tourniquet around her husband's arm and bandaged the wound on his swollen hand.

Outside, Thorbahn's attention turned to the cabin. Hundreds of bullets from Madden's possemen pounded into the home from all directions. Some found their way through broken windows or between

logs. They snapped and crashed into objects in the room, shattering dishes, breaking the oil lamps, and ricocheting off the fireplace. One bullet blasted through the chinking between two logs and into the Dietz family portrait, shattering the glass.

"Leslie," said his father, "hand me a rifle."

"No, John," said Hattie. "No more! You've been hurt. You need a doctor. It's time you surrender."

John looked at the blood-soaked bandage and then his family, cowering on the floor near the kitchen range.

"Yes, Mother," he breathed. "The time has come to yield."

"And how the heck do we go about doing that?" asked Leslie. "Those men out there are just itching for a target, any Dietz to shoot at!"

"Here," said Hattie, untying her apron. "I'll use this."

"No, Ma," said Leslie. "The instant you step out there, white flag or no white flag, they'll cut you down!"

Helen looked at her brothers and mother as they hunched low to the floor. She stared at her father and his blood-soaked bandage. Suddenly she sprang to her feet, tore the apron from her mother's hands, and dashed out the door onto the porch.

"Don't shoot!" screamed Father Pilon from the meadow. "It's the little girl! Don't shoot!"

"Hold your fire!" ordered Thorbahn from the riverbank.

Father Pilon ran across the pasture, climbed through the rail fence and scooped Helen into his arms. He lifted her and hugged her. "It's all right, child," he said, turning toward the house. "John? Hattie?" he called, "it's safe, now. You can come out."

Hattie breathed a sigh of relief. "We can trust the Father. Come, John. Come with me."

John peered through the shattered window and then stepped outside, arm-in-arm with Hattie. Leslie followed, leading Johnny by the hand.

Thorbahn approached, a pistol in one hand, handcuffs in the other.

"No need for those handcuffs," said John, holding his bloody left hand high. "You have my word. I surrender."

Thorbahn snatched John's right hand, snapped on the cuffs, and attached the other shackle to Roy Van Alstine's left. "John Dietz, you're under arrest for murder," he said.

"Murder? That's preposterous!"

"Yes, murder! One of my men is dead and you shot him," Thorbahn replied. "He was only doing his duty, helping the sheriff bring you to justice and you killed him."

"John," gasped Hattie, "Did you shoot a man today?"

"It's a bald-faced lie, Mother" said John. "I have *never* shot to kill another person. Fred, who is this dead deputy?"

"Oscar Harp. And he's stretched out in the back of a Camp Four wagon—with *your* bullet in him, Dietz."

"Impossible!"

"Save it for the judge, Dietz. The court will decide your fate. I hope you get life in prison for all the crimes you've committed against our society."

"Our society?" John asked. "Or the lumber syndicate's society?"

Sheriff Madden left the marshal's camp and joined the arresting deputies. Three horse-drawn wagons were readied. John, Hattie, and Leslie, all under arrest, rode in the back of one wagon. Helen and Johnny rode with Father Pilon in the back of the second. Fred Thorbahn, Red Mulligan, and a corpse covered with a tan tarp occupied the third.

With the Village of Winter abuzz, the family and their captors boarded the train to Hayward, arriving nearly an hour later. News of their capture preceded their arrival. Citizens turned out to see the family being hauled from the railroad depot to the county jail in the back of a horse-drawn buckboard. Some bellowed insults and foul language, convinced they were a family of outlaws. But for every disparager, three cheered for John F. Dietz, the heroic defender of Cameron Dam and champion of the rights of the common worker.

Frederick
Weyerhaeuser

As the wagon ambled past the Sawyer County Bank, John stared at a group of men in business suits who watched them pass. One man in particular looked familiar. John thought he'd seen his photo somewhere. The elderly, bearded man smiled and tipped his hat, perhaps in contempt or maybe out of respect for John F. Dietz, the bold man who so valiantly defended Thornapple Farm and his rights.

Sawyer County Record.

VOLUME VII   HAYWARD, WISCONSIN, THURSDAY EVENING, OCTOBER 13, 1910.   NUMBER 47

Sheriff Madden Gets the Deitz Outlaws

A DEPUTY KILLED DEITZ WOUNDED HOUSE IS RIDDLED

Terrors of Town of Winter Give Up When Less Than Twenty Determined Men Make Sieve of Their Home

AN EIGHT HOURS BATTLE

Miraculous Escape of the Family Under a Scathing Rifle Fire that Began with High Aim and Ended Low

CHARGED WITH MURDER OF OSCAR HARP

On Sunday afternoon Drs. Grafton and Burns obtained for Dist. Atty. Davis the bullet which killed Oscar Harp. It is a 30-30 steel tipped rifle ball and was found, slightly flattened, just below the thigh joint in the leg, having passed into the mouth and down through the lungs.

Dist. Atty. Davis motored to Winter Sunday afternoon and the inquest was held there early Monday morning by residents of the town of Winter, res Iting in a verdict that

The above likeness of John F. Deitz and his second son, Leslie, was obtained by the Record Sunday morning ...

SOUTHERN SAWYER COUNTY IN MOURNING

Special to The Record

RADISSON, Wis., Oct. 11.—Radisson is today in deepest sorrow over the death of Mrs. Cat Whited, one of our most dearly beloved and truly Christian women. Mrs. Whited died at three o'clock Monday morning, Oct. 10, from blood poisoning which started from a slight eruption on the forehead. She was taken sick Saturday evening and Sunday was not able to leave the bed.

The funeral occurred from the home today, Rev. C. J. McConnell conducting the services, and was very largely attended. The remains were shipped to Rochester, Minn., for burial, the husband and son, Clarence accompanying them.

The deceased was born at ...

CLARENCE LET OUT ON BAIL SET AT $2,000

Hearing Again Continued on Wednesday to Monday, Nov. 7, by Mutual Agreement to Prepare for the Examination

IS IN CHARGE OF H. VOIGT

Bill Deitz and Voigt Sign as Equal Bondsmen---Two Youngest In Care of Maternal Grandparents at Rice Lake

Posing for the newspapermen are (L to R) Deputies Roy Van Alstine and Fred Thorbahn, Sheriff Mike Madden, and District Attorney, J. C. Davis. Note that Van Alstine and Thorbahn each carry a pair of Luger pistols.

LIBERTY FOR BOY

BROTHER OF JOHN DEITZ IS WORKING FOR CLARENCE'S RELEASE.

IS A BAILABLE CRIME

Mob Violence Feared When Famil[y] Comes Into Court.—Cases Postponed to Oct. 19.

Hayward.—At least one mem[ber] of the Deitz family will be at li[ber]ty and in a position to lend aid t[o] parents and brothers and sister, i[n] plans and intentions of William [,] a brother of John F. Deitz, ma[y mater]ize. Bail in any amount to $3,00[0] be placed for Clarence Deitz w[ho] appear before J. F. Riordan of [munic]ipal court on two warrants, one [charg]ing him with assault with i[ntent to] kill Bert Horel and the oth[er with] assault with intent to kill Joh[n ——] and John Heft in September, [Horel] was one of the latter two [who] fractured Clarence's skull wi[th a gun] and injured one eye so bad[ly ...]

SURROUND DIETZ'S HOME WITH TROOPS

PROBABLE OUTCOME OF CONFERENCE BETWEEN GOVERNOR AND SHERIFF.

BLOODSHED IS LOOKED FOR

WISCONSIN PEOPLE EXPECT ANOTHER BATTLE AT CAMERON DAM.

Madison, Wis., Aug. 1.—It is probable that several companies of the Wisconsin state militia will be called out to repress John F. Dietz, in Sawyer county, and bring Dietz into court to answer to the criminal charge of assault with intent to murder.

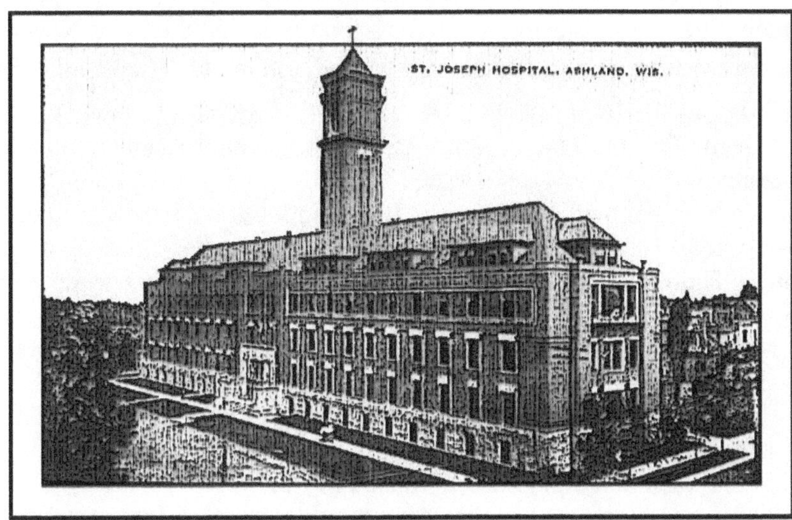

43
St. Joe's

The halls of St. Joseph Hospital were quiet that evening. Myra sat in a chair near the window overlooking the harbor lights when a nurse entered, followed by a tall mustached man carrying two satchels.

"Myra, you have a visitor," said the nurse. "Do you feel up to it?"

"Uncle Will?" Myra cried. "Oh, dear, thank you for coming."

William Dietz set the satchels in the corner. "I see you're coming along."

"They could neither kill me with poison nor with bullets. Perhaps it's the Dietz blood in me."

"No doubt you heard about the trouble today."

"Yes. I've been on pins and needles ever since I heard of more shooting at the farm. Please tell me everyone is all right, Uncle Will. Oh, please!"

"Rest easy, Myra." William drew closer to his niece. "Everyone is safe. Your father has a bandaged hand after taking a bullet. He will recover. No injuries befell anyone else in the family. John, Hattie, and Leslie were taken to the county jail. They'll be charged tomorrow, I'm sure. I've already talked to Judge Parish. I am confident that I will have Leslie and Hattie out on bail and back home by the end of the day. Clarence, too. As for your father, well, that's a different matter."

"Because he shot Bert Horel last month?"

"No. There's more to it than that. Seems one of the lawmen got shot today, a fellow by the name of Harp."

"Oscar Harp? His wife came to visit me after the shooting. Strange woman. She just sat staring at me for a long time and then left. Never said a word. Her husband suffered a wound, today? Will he be all right?"

"Myra, I'm afraid not. You see, he's dead."

"Dead? Oh, no, Uncle Will. Oh, that poor, poor woman. What will happen now?"

"Your father will be charged. But I doubt John fired the shot that killed Oscar Harp. It was more likely a stray bullet fired by another deputy. The county coroner is looking into it now, trying to determine precisely what happened."

Myra lowered her head into her hands. "I'm so sorry it came to this," she sighed.

"It may take some doing, but I should have your father out on bail before too long."

"What of Johnny and Helen?" asked Myra.

"They're being cared for by Mrs. Phelan at the Hotel Winter."

"Oh, she is such a dear to help us. Especially now."

"Yes, Mary Phelan has a good heart." William lifted one of the satchels, placing it on the bed. "Myra, I brought your gramophone. I thought it might help you pass the time." He placed the record player on the dresser near Myra's bed.

"Oh, thank you, Uncle Will."

"It's the least I could do to help you now," he said, adjusting the cone.

"And the recordings? Did you bring …?"

"Most of them. Some were broken during today's turmoil." He placed a record on the turntable and turned the crank. "But you'll soon have plenty of money to buy more."

"I will?"

"Oh, yes. Myra, there were newspapermen from all corners, clamoring to cover today's events. Every paper in the country will carry the story. Why, the whole nation will be up in arms over today's attack. With the expense of a trial looming ahead, folks will donate plenty. The money your family received after Clarence was shot was a mere drop in the bucket compared to what will come now."

William flipped a lever. Soon *Bill Baily Won't You Please Come Home* filled the room and flowed down the hospital hallway. For the next hour, William shared news of the day's events played his niece's records.

"I must go now," he said. "But I'll soon be in touch."

"Oh, please give them my love," she said, holding back her tears.

"Of course, Myra."

"And thank you, Uncle Will—from the bottom of my heart."

44
St. Paul Union Depot

The 5:15 from Hayward pulled into the St. Paul Union Depot four minutes early. Among the passengers who disembarked was a short, stocky fellow with a handlebar moustache. He looked left and right as if worried. With a tight grip on his valise, he hurried across the lobby to a ticket window.

"Yes?" said the clerk.

"Denver," he said, glancing over his shoulder. He turned back. "One way. Pullman car."

"Twenty-two dollars and fifty cents, sir."

"Here you go," said the traveler as he slid the fare to the clerk.

"Very well." The clerk dipped his pen in the inkwell and began writing out the ticket. "Name?"

"What?"

"I need your name, sir. For the ticket?"

"Oh. Oscar Harp ... err ... yes ... Harper. Oscar Harper. From ... Stillwater."

"The clerk slid the ticket to the traveler. "Here you are, Mr. Harper. Enjoy your trip."

"Oh, I will, young man. I'm sure of it." He smiled as he walked away. "Dead sure."

— The End —

This Dietz family portrait was taken two weeks prior to Myra and her brothers being ambushed. Left to right are Myra, Helen, Hattie, John and Johnny, Leslie, and Clarence.

Afterword

Author's note: The following excerpts are taken directly from the 204-page memoir of Myra Dietz, written two decades after her father's arrest and six years after his death. We pick up her story shortly after she had been shot. Bleeding internally, she was transported in a baggage car from Winter, Wisconsin, to the Ashland freight yard. From there, she was taken to the hospital in an ambulance, Myra's first motorcar ride.

"Dr. J. M. Dodd, head physician of St. Joseph's hospital [was] waiting for me, for I was rushed into the operating room after a short examination. When the bandages were removed, I heard Dr. Dodd say: 'The traitors! This girl has had no medical attention—just some little antiseptic gauzes!' Then for the first time I learned how badly I had been shot. According to Dr. Dodd's report, the bullet entered my body at the left side at the waist line just over the hip bone, passing through the left kidney and lower bowels and through the spinal region, coming out one quarter of an inch to the right of the spine, shattering the vertebra.

"The worry and anxiety at our farm home over my condition must have been intense, from the story my mother tells of those days. They saw no one from that Saturday when we were shot to the following Wednesday. Then two men [Munson and Gilbert] appeared across the river and crossed to our farm over the footbridge. When they reached the house they told my father they were representing Governor Davidson, and had come to take my father out with them.

"'I would like to go with you, if you are from the governor,' said my father. 'But my children have been shot down in cold blood and taken away from home. When officers stoop low enough to do that, I don't know what their next move will be. How can I trust you and go out myself, or take my family with me, when you have nothing to show us your good intentions!'

"The men agreed with him that it would be an unwise thing, and departed, telling him they would go to Winter and wire the governor for the proper credentials. Instead of doing that they went out and reported that my father had refused to accompany them and therefore deserved no sympathy. Immediately a posse of twenty lumberjacks and thrill-loving young men of Winter, led by Thorbahn and Van Alstine, were sworn in and plans were made to capture my family—dead or alive!"

The Siege

"My brother Leslie and sister, Helen, then 12 years of age, went out in the field early Saturday morning to drive the cows in to be milked. A volley of bullets were fired at them, one bullet passing through Leslie's trousers leg near the calf of his leg. The cows were excited and jumped to their feet and began to run and the frightened children ran back to the house. That seemed to be the signal for general firing from every

"

direction. The firing became so bad that my father said he would go to the barn and perhaps draw the fire there and save the lives of my mother and the children. He took his hat, coat and gun, and walked rapidly to the barn. Not a single shot was fired at him as he made the trip. And, once he was inside the barn, the firing at the home continued as strong as before, with an additional bombardment of the barn.

"[Five hours later] a bullet hit the palm of his hand. Suffering from pain, he ran back to the house with bullets peppering his pathway. Mother and the children had miraculously escaped injury, but our little brown spaniel lay dying in the yard. The bullets were still pouring into the home and my mother and father decided that some desperate action must be taken. Surely there was someone who would help us if a white flag were waved. But who? If either my father or mother appeared they would be shot down instantly. Mother said: 'Let Helen go!'

"No sooner were the words out than little Helen seized the towel and ran into the yard, waving it above her head. Instantly the firing ceased! The posse came in from every direction and entered the house ... led by Sheriff Madden, Thorbahn, and Van Alstine, the three men who had shot me just a week before. They seized my father and said: 'You killed a man! You killed Harp when you shot him from the barn!'

"My father was placed in a cell in the county jail. Mother, Leslie and the children were kept in the home of the sheriff until it was decided what disposition should be made of them."

The Trial

"The trial opened May 1st, 1911 at Hayward. Charged with the murder of Oscar Harp, Father felt confident that he would be proved innocent and in a few days, be a free man. He knew he had not killed Harp—that his only crime lay protecting the rights of himself and his family ... that *right* was stronger than *might!*

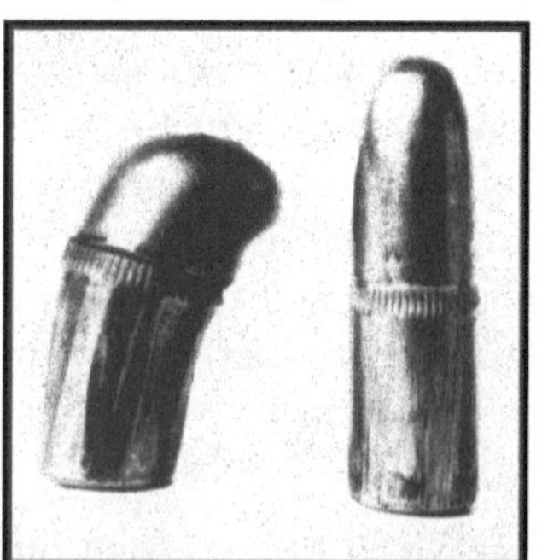

"Captain Kane was called in on all questions pertaining to bullets in murder trials all over the country for his keen, unbiased testimony. No one in the courtroom had any idea what his testimony would be! To the great surprise of everyone his findings were all in my father's favor.

"[Captain Kane] testified that the bullet could not have been shot from my father's gun—the bullet was too heavy for thirty-thirty ammunition. Second: The creasings on the bullet given him by the District Attorney did not correspond, to the creasings of my father's gun bore, nor to the creasings on other bullets he fired from my father's gun in tests made at the farm.

"Third: In his trip to the farm, he had not found a single point from which my father could have seen a man crawling toward the lumber piles, as the topography of the land hid the lumber piles from the barn. Captain Kane testified that if it had ever entered the body of a man it had done so after it had struck a rock and had glanced sharply to one side or the other.

"Father Pilon had told the press that the men were in ambush all around our clearing and had been cross firing from every direction throughout the day. The firing was so rapid and unsupervised that it was great wonder many of the posse were not injured by their companions according to the statements of Father Pilon and others who were present during the siege. They also repeated many times that not a shot was fired from the house, to their knowledge.

"Captain Kane's testimony came as a distinct shock to the state, and immediately after he left the stand he was ousted by the attorneys for the state and told to go back to Milwaukee on the next train.

"The strangest part of the whole affair was the complete absence of any murdered man's body on the farm at the time the shooting was alleged to have taken place. The records of Sawyer County contained no burial certificate and no record of a coroner's inquest over a dead body. But despite the overwhelming evidence in my father's favor, he was sent to prison for life! Then the fight began to get him pardoned or released!"

MR. AND MRS. JOHN F. DIETZ

JOHN DIETZ IS FOUND GUILTY OF MURDER IN FIRST DEGREE

Jury Holds Mrs. Dietz and Son, Leslie, Innocent of the Killing of Deputy Oscar Harp.

GETS LIFE SENTENCE; NEW TRIAL IS DENIED

Long-Waged War in Sawyer County Comes Again to a Stirring Climax---Dietz Will Appeal Case.

Public Appearances

"Clarence, Leslie and I [spoke] in theatres in Minnesota all the winter of 1911, with frequent expeditions to the northern part of Michigan. There was such a demand for us that we had to split up and each of the boys played in different localities. I wasn't strong enough to travel alone, so I took turns with the boys, traveling first with Clarence in the towns where he was speaking, and then with Leslie. I was the chief attraction and the boys would scrap over which could have me! We had a set of pictures accumulated from various photographers ... made into stereopticon slides and these were thrown on the screen. Then I would give my little talk about being shot. It seemed that my shooting was the thing the public cared most about! The theatre managers asked us to stress that point, and we were willing to oblige. There we would put up a little booth and get signers to petitions to be sent to the Governor asking for my father's pardon. We wrote to the governor asking for a hearing, which was granted. The whole family attended the hearing with our lawyers. It was held in the big executive office and the governor sat beside the big table and heard our plea. A few days later we were overjoyed to find that Father's sentence was reduced from life to twenty years. At least that was a start! Now we could work for his full pardon."

"The Dietz Battle of Cameron Dam"

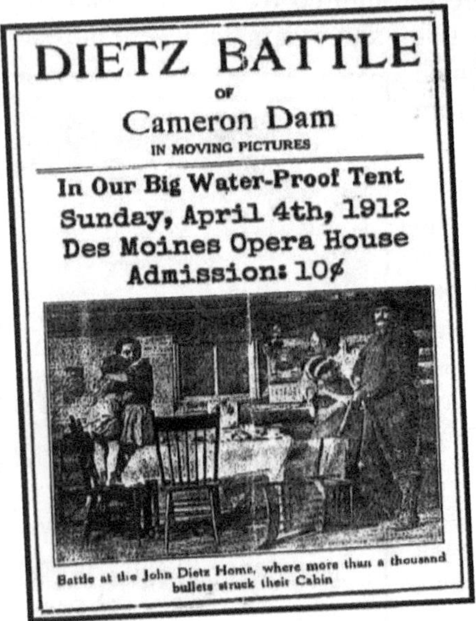

"In June, 1913, we made arrangements with the Advance Motion Picture Company to make a motion picture of our lives, using our farm at Cameron Dam as the location. In July, my mother, the boys, the children, and I with a group of twenty actors and a camera man returned to Cameron Dam and made a moving picture of the feud and the final battle. It was the first time I had seen the farm since that day three years before when I had dressed in my new brilliantine suit and started to town for the mail with my brothers! What a lot had happened since that day!

"Competent actors took the roles of my father and mother. My brother John took the part of my sister, Helen. My brothers, Clarence and Leslie, played their own parts and I played my own. We drove our team over the road to the exact spot where the men with blackened faces shot us from ambush. The actual making of the picture was a pleasant experience—not the gruesome time we had anticipated.

"The moving picture was finished by October of that year, and the autumn of 1913 found us with something far more interesting than our old slides as we went about the theatres. Moving pictures were not so common as they are now, and ours was a three-reel feature picture of great importance. We paid $5,000 for its production, but we took in many times that amount with it.

"In 1921 we wrote to Governor Blaine, who had just been elected, requesting another hearing. He replied that if we would give him the evidence in the proper form he would give us a hearing, after which he would make his decision. A week later Governor Blaine called at midnight telling me to take my mother to Waupun to bring my father home! There was no sleep that night in the Dietz home."

Finally, Freedom and Exoneration

"It was pouring rain the next morning, but that didn't keep us from Waupun. We were there by nine o'clock. The Governor had sent the necessary papers for me to give to the Warden, and everything was in readiness for my father's departure. He was well-dressed in a good gray suit, black shoes, good hat, and new overcoat, all furnished by the prison. The warden and my father shook hands and laughed and talked like two old friends parting at a summer resort.

"It was a happy family reunion we had that night in Milwaukee—many friends came in to see my father and it was a happy day indeed. We appreciated Governor Blaine's kindness in choosing that day to pardon him—it was just ten years to the day from the time my father entered the prison—and somehow, being pardoned on that day took away the sting of that terrible day when he was sentenced.

"But the long imprisonment had seriously affected my father's health. He had been a model prisoner, with many privileges but he felt that his whole trouble had been brought about through no wrong doing of his own, and it made the years at confinement even more tedious. He lived just three years after his release from prison. During that time he visited Rice Lake frequently, but never again did he go to Cameron Dam. He was buried at Rice Lake, in the family burial ground.

"This ends the story of that staunch farmer, who so firmly fought for his rights—and my brothers and myself, whose early days were lived in a manner vastly different from the usual youngsters due to my father's stern, unyielding disposition. He lived a righteous life, according to his ideals. He was strong and fearless. He made but one mistake—and that was in his claim that right is always stronger than might. He found in the last thirteen years of his life that might is the stronger."

Myra Dietz
February, 1929

Images from some of the 4" X 4" glass stereopticon slides used during Myra's 1911 - 1913 fundraising presentations.

Above left: Winter depot.
Above: John and children.
Left: A deputy guards the road to the farm.
Below: Camp 4.

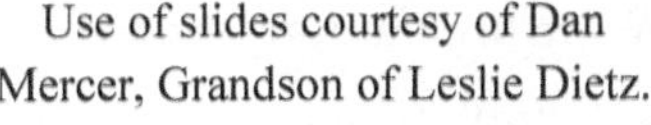

Use of slides courtesy of Dan Mercer, Grandson of Leslie Dietz.

DARK—A CAMPFIRE COMPANION

56 very scary short stories & delightfully frightening poems. Spine-tingling tales of ghosts, dragons, ne'er-do-wells, and monsters—each waiting to raise goose bumps. Every story is morbidly illustrated by long-dead master artists of the macabre. Chilling, yet wonderful fireside reading. A "must-have" for every cabin bookshelf and home library.

THE MOOSE & WILBUR P. DILBY
Plus 36 Fairly True Tales from Up North.

Thirty-seven short stories straight from the heart & the heart of the north. All fairly true, more or less. Some are sad, some shocking, most are hilarious. Small town tales of baseball, fishing and hunting, tavern tales, jokesters, murderers, gangsters, and flimflam men. Lost treasure, lumberjacks, and legends of the north. Includes several short stories based on the Chief Namakagon trilogy tales. **Features *two* 1st place award-winning stories.**

SAVING OUR LAKES & STREAMS:
101 Practical Things You Can Do Today

A handbook for all who enjoy our surface waters. Simple tips, ideas, and articles from award-winning conservationist and author, James Brakken. Foreword by Dan Small, host of "OUTDOOR WISCONSIN." 200-pages, 101 tips, 75 articles, 75 photos. **Deep discounts at BadgerValley.com**. All ages. Great for fundraisers. Ships free. If you care for our lakes and streams, you will love this book! Profits help support efforts to protect Wisconsin's waters!

Give the gift of a good read!

BadgerValley.com offers secure ordering. The Wisconsin sales tax is pre-paid and USA & APO shipping is still free!

BADGER VALLEY PUBLISHING
45255 East Cable Lake Road
Cable, Wisconsin 54821
715-798-3163
treasureofnamakagon@gmail.com

ALIAS RAY OLSON:
The Complete Story Behind the
1939 Chequamegon Forest Manhunt

A true-life crime thriller. An exposé based on press reports, court documents, & personal interviews. A fugitive wanted for a double homicide in Hayward leads a posse of over 200 deputies & FBI agents on **Wisconsin's largest manhunt.** Now, after 8 decades, learn the ***TRUTH*** behind **Northwest Wisconsin's *CRIME OF THE CENTURY*!** An eye-opening, fact-based novel. Brakken's exposé is thrilling historical fiction at its best. 280 pages. Illustrated.

James Brakken's ANNOTATED EARLY LIFE
AMONG THE INDIANS, the 1892
Memoir of Benjamin G. Armstrong

Tales of Indian wars, animal encounters, treaty problems, Indian lore, & more. Penned by Ben Armstrong, an 1850s trader & trusted friend of the Ojibwe people who writes of his fascinating encounters. Includes: Tales of Chief Buffalo; Indian councils with Presidents Fillmore & Lincoln; Lost silver mines; Fur trade troubles; Indian laws & customs; Sioux & Ojibwe wars; The Battle of the Brule, & more. Illustrated. All ages. 222 pages.

BILLYBOY, THE CORNER BAR BEAR
Plus 36 Fairly True Tales from Up North.

Thirty-seven *more* short stories straight from the heart & the heart of the north. Some are sad, some shocking, most are hilarious. But, like the tales in *Moose,* all 37 of these are fairly true, more or less. Includes 6 Corner Bar yarns, 5 "gangster" tales, several Warden Snook Wilson yarns, and many more stories from the good old days. A must for your "up north" bookshelf and a great gift for all ages. 206 pages.

INFAMOUS: The Crimes of John Henry Seadlund

Brakken's latest true-crime novel, delves into the life of an Iron Range lad who, in desperation, turned to crime and quickly became the FBI's 1937 Public Enemy #1. Seadlund's worst crime attracted J. Edgar Hoover to Spooner in 1938 to view the scene of the crime. Based closely on 1938 newspaper reports, FBI files, and court documents. Includes 7 bonus short stories. Illustrated. 230 pages.

Some of James Brakken's Awards

2nd PLACE: AMAZON BREAKTHROUGH NOVEL AWARDS,
out of 10,000 novels entered worldwide in 2013!

1st PLACE: Wisconsin Writers Assn JADE RING competition. 2015

1st PLACE: LAKE SUPERIOR WRITERS AWARD: 2013, 2014, 2016

Critical reviews of James Brakken's 12 books and more than 140 short stories and poems:

"Wonderfully written .... Compelling" "A good piece of writing with suspense and action ..." **Jerry Apps, award-winning Wisconsin author.**

"Weaving mystery into history, James Brakken's writing vivifies the tumultuous nature of 19th-century life in the legendary north woods."
Michael Perry, NYT bestselling Wisconsin author

"A fascinating tale ... "Rip-roaring action ..." "So well-written." "Difficult to put down; a great read." **Publisher's Weekly Magazine**

"The writing style of this piece is its greatest strength." "The flow of the words is like an old fashioned song." **Amazon Books**

"It's the dialog and characters that drive The Treasure of Namakagon, a book that, ... in the 1950s, would likely be sitting at or near the top of the best seller's lists. It appears as if author James A. Brakken is determined to make a go of this series, and ... he's made at least one fan of this reader."
22nd Writer's Digest Book Awards Judge

"Wisconsin history buffs will find this book a treasure in itself. An exciting adventure for all ages." **Waldo Asp, AARP Chairman**

"Open with caution. You won't want to put this one down."
LaMoine MacLaughlin, President, Wisconsin Writers Assn

"I thoroughly enjoyed it!" **Larry Meiller, Wisconsin Public Radio**

"Saving Our Lakes & Streams should be required reading for all state, county, and town officials, for those who plan a career in natural resources, and for everyone who treasures water recreation."
Dan Small, Public TV's Outdoor Wisconsin

"James Brakken has captured all of the current science, technology, and leadership necessary to preserve our lakes and streams."
Mary Platner, Founder & Past-president of Wisconsin Lakes

About the Author

Bayfield County author, James Brakken, began writing in college when "Muskie Madness," his story of a fishing trip with his father, appeared in *Boy's Life Magazine* in 1974. More articles followed in *Sports Afield, Outdoor Life, Field & Stream, School Arts,* and other publications.

His first novel, *The Treasure of Namakagon (2012),* features a boy in an 1883 northern Wisconsin lumber camp and Chief Namakagon's legendary lost silver mine. The suspicious 1886 death of Namakagon and the 1846 disappearance of a Sault Ste. Marie murder fugitive led to two more novels, *Tor Loken & the Death of Chief Namakagon* (2013) and *The Secret Life of Chief Namakagon* (2014), where Brakken solved a 168-year-old cold case when he proved Chief Namakagon was actually John Falcon Tanner, the adventurer and war hero who'd vanished in 1846. Brakken's *Annotated Early Life Among the Indians* (2016) documents the existence of Chief Namakagon's silver mine and offers many great 1800s Lake Superior tales.

Treasure won 2nd place out of 10,000 worldwide entries in the 2013 Amazon Breakthrough Novel Awards. Brakken also received the 2013, 2014, and 2016 Lake Superior Writers Award and the coveted Wisconsin Writers Association Jade Ring for his collection, *The Moose and Wilbur P. Dilby plus 36 Fairly True Tales from Up North* (2015).

Brakken earned statewide recognition for conservation as reflected in his *Saving Our Lakes & Streams: 101 Practical Things You Can Do Today* (2016). Brakken offers discounts of this book to conservation clubs and lake associations. *Alias Ray Olson* (2017) is a true-crime thriller that exposes the truth behind the June 1939 homicides in Sawyer County and Wisconsin's largest-ever manhunt. It's a close look at the *perceived* guilt of a man convicted in the press and hunted by hundreds. Brakken's *INFAMOUS (2019)* is another true-life, north woods crime novel from the 1930s. It chronicles John Henry Seadlund's rise to Public Enemy #1 in only 4 years. *DARK: A Campfire Companion* (2012) is an illustrated collection of 56 of the author's delightfully frightening short stories and poems. It's ideal for dark and stormy nights or for reading under the blankets by flashlight.

45 Fairly True Tales from the Old Corner Bar offers hilarious tales of life way back when. It's a must-read for anyone who's ever been "up north."

Brakken's most recent fact-based novel, *Thornapple Girl,(2020)* chronicles the life of Myra Dietz, a young woman caught up in her father's 1910 struggle against lumber barons who denied him of his earnings. It is accompanied by the long overdue publishing of Myra's lost 1929 memoir.

Of Brakken's writing, *Publisher's Weekly Magazine* and *Amazon Books* said, "Difficult to put down. ... A great read," and "the flow of words is like an old fashioned song." James Brakken illustrates most of his stories. All are intended for adults but great for younger readers as well. Find them at BadgerValley.com, where shipping to USA and APO addresses is free.